Making
it New

CLARK BLAISE

MAVIS GALLANT

HUGH HOOD

NORMAN LEVINE

JOHN METCALF

ALICE MUNRO

LEON ROOKE

Making it New

Contemporary Canadian Stories

Edited by
John Metcalf

with photographs by Sam Tata

ⓝ Methuen

Toronto New York London Sydney Auckland

Making it New

Canadian Cataloguing in Publication Data
Main entry under title:
Making it new

ISBN 0-458-95520-5 (bound).—ISBN 0-458-95470-5 (pbk.)

1. Short stories, Canadian (English).* I. Metcalf,
John, 1938-

PS8321.M34   C813'.0108   C82-094415-7
PR9197.32.M34

Printed and bound in Canada
1 2 3 4 5   82   87 86 85 84 83

Contents

Acknowledgements

-"A North American Education" from *A North American Education* by Clark Blaise. Copyright © 1973 Clark Blaise. Reprinted by permission of Doubleday and Company, Inc.
-"How I Became a Jew" from *Tribal Justice* by Clark Blaise. Copyright © 1968 Clark, Irwin and Company, Ltd. Reprinted by permission of Doubleday and Company, Inc.
-Essay: "On Ending Stories" Copyright © 1982 Clark Blaise.
-"Baum, Gabriel, 1935-( )" and "His Mother" from *From the Fifteenth District* by Mavis Gallant. Copyright © 1979 Mavis Gallant. Reproduced by permission of Mavis Gallant, Random House, and Johnathan Cape.
-Essay: "What Is Style?" Copyright © 1982 Mavis Gallant.
-"Breaking Off" from *None Genuine Without This Signature* by Hugh Hood. Copyright © 1980 Hugh Hood. Reproduced by permission of E.C.W. Press.
-"The Small Birds" by Hugh Hood. Copyright © 1982 Hugh Hood.
-Essay: "Floating Southwards" Copyright © 1982 Hugh Hood.
-"A Small Piece of Blue" from *One Way Ticket* (Secker and Warburg) 1961, and in *I Don't Want to Know Anyone Too Well,* Macmillan, 1971. Re-issued (Deneaux) 1982 in paperback. It is the title story of a selection of stories published by Claassen, 1971 in West Germany in a translation by Annemarie and Heinrich Böll. Copyright © Norman Levine 1961, 1971. Reproduced by permission of Norman Levine.
-"We All Begin in a Little Magazine" was commissioned by the CBC for the radio series *Anthology* and was first published in *Encounter.* It was collected in *Thin Ice* (Deneaux, 1979; and Wildwood, 1980). Copyright © 1979 Norman Levine. Reproduced by permission of Norman Levine.
-Essay: "Afterword" Copyright © 1982 Norman Levine.
-"Gentle As Flowers Make the Stones" from *The Teeth of My Father* was first published in *Queen's Quarterly.* Copyright © 1975 John Metcalf. Reproduced by permission of E.C.W. Press.
-"Single Gents Only" was first published in *The Malahat Review.* Copyright © 1982 John Metcalf.
-Essay: "Building Castles" Copyright © 1982 John Metcalf.
-"Royal Beatings" and "Who Do You Think You Are?" from *Who Do You Think You Are?* published in Canada by Macmillan of Canada, and published in the U.K. and the U.S.A. as *The Beggar Maid: Stories of Flo and Rose.* "Royal Beatings" was first published in *The New Yorker.* Copyright © 1978 Alice Munro. Reproduced by permission of Alice Munro, Knopf, and Allen Lane.
-Essay: "What Is Real?" Copyright © 1982 Alice Munro.
-"Winter Is Lovely, Isn't Summer Hell" and "The Problem Shop" from *Death Suite* by Leon Rooke. "The Problem Shop" was first published in *Canadian Fiction Magazine.* Copyright © 1981, 1982 Leon Rooke. Reproduced by permission of E.C.W. Press.
-Essay: "Voices" Copyright © 1982 Leon Rooke.
-A quotation in "Single Gents Only" from Kenneth Grahame, *The Wind in the Willows* (New York: Charles Scribners Sons, 1908). Reproduced with the permission of Charles Scribners Sons.

Introduction

Gathered in this volume are fourteen stories by seven of Canada's most interesting and exciting fiction writers. Each has written novels, but with the exception of perhaps Hugh Hood—whose extraordinary series of novels in "The New Age" set him apart—each writer's real achievement to date has been in the short story, in its modernist form and at its best. These stories represent that most complex, subtle and poetic of prose fictional forms, consistently demanding the reader's full participation in "the fine art of reading." The modern or lyrical short story is much more metaphoric than either the novel or the epical or syllogistic short story— the story of traditional plot. Ranging structurally from the ironically epiphanic (Metcalf's "Gentle As Flowers Make the Stones") through the emblematically ironic (Levine's "A Small Piece of Blue") to the disturbingly open-ended (Gallant's "His Mother"), all of the stories here are thoroughly modern or poetic in their use of such techniques as indirection or implication, ellipsis, understatement, distillation and telescoping.

These stories are poetic, too, in their focus on internal conditions, moods, feelings. They offer to the reader, through the subtlety and complexity of their linguistic and metaphoric patterns, a brief but intense insight into life at its most fundamental psychological level—although our interest is not necessarily directed to character as such. In these subtle stories, the words become points of departure for the actual story that we, the reader, create with an imaginative response; for although it is not plot development either to which our interest is necessarily directed— there is no plot in any conventional sense, for example, in "Single Gents Only"—these stories, through their conciseness and intensity, ask us to fill out their narrative or dramatic frames by acts of inference and imagination. All these writers are thus masters of the suggestively concrete detail. Consider, for instance, the way in which Alice Munro's "Royal Beatings" circles around the controlling metaphors of ceremony and perverse dramatic ritual, both compulsive and dream-like; or the various ways in which the notions of breaking off and breaking down function metaphorically in Hood's "Breaking Off." In their synecdochal structures and metaphoric texture of details, these stories move imagistically and associationally as poems do.

Because these writers are texture workers, there is a strong sense in which their stories straddle the line between treating language and story as referential, pointing to and contingent for meaning upon some reality ("life") beyond the linguistic artifact, on the one hand, and treating language and story as a self-referential, contextual linguistic world, on the other. These stories are images or metaphors of realities, but they are also realities in themselves; and, as in poetry, any descriptions of the fictional external reality in a story that we receive work less as precise, detailed descriptions of particular objects than correlatively as metaphors—sometimes evocatively, more often subtlely—conveying the attitudes and feelings of a perceiving consciousness, usually the central character. This desire to control perception so precisely—reflected in voice as a unifying device in someone like Rooke, Blaise, or Gallant— accounts in part, I think, for the exclusive use of either a first-person point of view (Blaise's and Levine's stories, and both are at their best in first person) or a limited third-person point of view (the stories of Metcalf, Gallant, Hood, Munro and Rooke) in which the sensibility is first-person perception but which allows the writer the possibility of detachment and rhetorical flexibility. In short, one should read these fourteen stories as closely, as carefully, as one would a good lyric poem.

Even though Canadian literature is still in its adolescence, if not infancy, the literary explosiveness of roughly the past decade and a half in Canada has nevertheless produced a recognizable and relatively large body of worthwhile Canadian work. The writers presented here are indeed part of that explosion, but most if not all of them have not been accorded the full critical attention and respect that they deserve, either inside or outside academe. This is primarily because, I believe, they have not been exclusively concerned with either a Canadian content or so-called

Canadian themes, such as vexed questions of national identity, survival, isolation or a garrison-wilderness motif—none of which, either in a conceptual or imagistic form, is unique or indigenous to Canadian literature anyway.

When one studies *Canadian* literature, however, one is studying the literature written in Canada or by Canadians in a nationalist context and not simply as literature *per se*. In such a context, it sometimes happens that a writer who has less artistic merit may turn out to be more important in a social or historical sense; he may speak more directly to Canadians about matters of concern to them as Canadians than the more talented writer who addresses them merely as human beings. Thus Hugh MacLennan, for example, may be exalted at the expense of, say, Hugh Hood; Margaret Laurence at the expense of Mavis Gallant or Alice Munro; W. P. Kinsella at the expense of Leon Rooke or Norman Levine; or W. D. Valgardson at the expense of John Metcalf or Clark Blaise. This sort of tension between social or historical—and, in a broad sense, cultural—significance and artistic merit exists, of course, whenever literature is viewed in a nationalist context, but that tension is exacerbated, intensified, when one is dealing with an emergent or nascent literature such as Canada's. I suspect this observation might apply to many, if not all, Commonwealth literatures.

Another reason that these writers have not received the recognition they deserve lies in the ubiquitous prejudice that the short story as a literary form is inferior to the novel, that it is merely an apprenticeship for writing novels. Thus Robertson Davies, the author of seven fairly well-received novels, or Margaret Atwood, the well-known author of five novels, will appear on the curriculum before, say, Mavis Gallant, the author of five books of short stories and only two novels. (Speaking of Mavis Gallant reminds me of a telling remark of Clark Blaise's: ". . . what, pray tell, is the difference between a Mavis Gallant story when she's working at her richest and fullest and most polyphonic and someone else's novel? It's just that the novel becomes smaller and thinner than her story.") Even in terms of so-called aesthetic or literary values, however— let alone in terms of moral, social, or historical values—such comparative judgements seem to me to be completely unjustified. The short story should be judged on its own terms for what it is. But if one does wish to indulge in comparative judgements, perhaps one should remember Faulkner's remark about the novelist as failed poet: "Maybe every novelist wants to write poetry first, finds he can't, and then tries the short story, which is the most demanding form after poetry. And, failing at that, only then does he take up novel writing." The simple fact of the matter is that, as Clark Blaise has said, the novel should be at least as rich as the short story but that most novels are not.

Even if they wished to do so, there is no formal tradition of short story writing in Canadian literature on which these seven writers can draw. Of necessity, if not desire or intelligence, then, they all write out of various phases of the great European and American traditions of the short story and fiction in general. Behind Metcalf, for example, is Mansfield, Joyce, Hemingway, Waugh, Cary and Amis; behind Blaise is Flaubert, Proust, Mann and Malamud; behind Munro is Flannery O'Connor and Eudora Welty; behind Hood is Dante, Spenser, Dickens and Proust; and behind all of them are Turgenev and Chekhov. And it is in the context of these great writers that the seven we have here should be viewed. What we should finally remember, however, is that because in Canada we are living not after the archetypes of our literary traditions, as George Woodcock has said, but beside them, these writers themselves are in the very significant process of forging a Canadian tradition of short story writing. The rich stories you have before you are literary history in the making.

BARRY CAMERON

BARRY CAMERON, a professor of English at the University of New Brunswick, where he teaches Canadian and Renaissance literature, has published numerous reviews and articles on a wide range of contemporary Canadian writers in addition to articles and reviews on contemporary American poetry and on Chaucer, Donne and Shakespeare. He edited the journal *Studies in Canadian Literature* from 1976 to 1979 and has been the book review editor of *The Fiddlehead* since 1976. With Michael Dixon, he co-edited an important collection of critical essays in 1977 called *Minus Canadian: Penultimate Essays on Literature*.

Clark Blaise

CLARK BLAISE was born in Fargo, North Dakota, in 1940 to Canadian parents and is married to the Indian novelist Bharati Mukherjee. He taught English at Concordia University in Montreal and at York University in Toronto. He is presently teaching at the University of Iowa and completing work on two new books.

Other Works

A North American Education, (1973) Stories
Tribal Justice, (1974) Stories
Days and Nights in Calcutta (with Bharati Mukherjee), (1977) Autobiographical Travel Book
Lunar Attractions, (1979) Novel

A North American Education

Eleven years after the death of Napoleon, in the presidency of Andrew Jackson, my grandfather, Boniface Thibidault, was born. For most of his life he was a *journalier,* a day labourer, with a few years off for wars and buccaneering. Then at the age of fifty, a father and widower, he left Paris and came alone to the New World and settled in Sorel, a few miles down river from Montreal. He worked in the shipyards for a year or two then married his young housekeeper, an eighteen-year-old named Lise Beaudette. Lise, my grandmother, had that resigned look of a Quebec girl marked early for a nursing order if marriage couldn't catch her, by accident, first. In twenty years she bore fifteen children, eight of them boys, five of whom survived. The final child, a son, was named Jean-Louis and given at birth to the Church. As was the custom with the last boy, he was sent to the monastery as soon as he could walk, and remained with the Brothers for a dozen years, taking his meals and instructions as an apprentice.

It would have been fitting if Boniface Thibidault, then nearly eighty, had earned a fortune in Sorel—but he didn't. Or if a son had survived to pass on his stories—but none were listening. Or if Boniface himself had written something—but he was illiterate. Boniface was cut out for something different. One spring morning in 1912, the man who had seen two child brides through menopause stood in the mud outside his cottage and defied Sorel's first horseless carriage to churn its way through the April muck to his door, and if by the Grace of God it did, to try going on while he, an old man, pushed it back downhill. Money was evenly divided on the man and the driver, whom Boniface also defamed for good measure. The driver was later acquitted of manslaughter in Sorel's first fatality and it was never ascertained if Boniface died of the bumping, the strain, or perhaps the shock of meeting his match. Jean-Louis wasn't there. He left the church a year later by walking out and never looking back. He was my father.

The death of Boniface was in keeping with the life, yet I think of my grandfather as someone special, a character from a well-packed novel who enters once and is never fully forgotten. I think of Flaubert's *Sentimental Education* and the porters who littered the decks of the *Ville-de-Montereau* on the morning of September 15, 1840, when young Frédéric Moreau was about to sail. My grandfather was already eight in 1840, a good age for cabin boys. But while Frédéric was about to meet Arnoux and his grand passion, Boniface was content to pocket a tip and beat it, out of the novel and back into his demimonde.

I have seen one picture of my grandfather, taken on a ferry between Quebec and Levis in 1895. He looks strangely like Sigmund Freud: bearded, straw-hatted, buttoned against the river breezes. It must have been a cold day—the vapour from the nearby horses steams in the background. As a young man he must have been, briefly, extraordinary. I think of him as a face in a Gold Rush shot, the one face that seems both incidental and immortal guarding a claim or watering a horse, the face that seems lifted from the crowd, from history, the face that could be dynastic.

And my father, Jean-Louis Thibidault, who became Gene and T. B. Doe—he too stands out in pictures. A handsome man, a contemporary man (and yet not even a man of this century. His original half-brothers back in France would now be 120 years old; he would be, by now, just seventy); a salesman and businessman. I still have many pictures, those my mother gave me. The earliest is of a strong handsome man with very short legs. He is lounging on an old canvas chaise under a maple tree, long before aluminum furniture, long before I was born. A scene north of Montreal, just after they were married. It is an impressive picture, but for the legs, which barely reach the grass. Later he would grow into his shortness, would learn the vanities of the short and never again stretch out casually, like the tall. In another picture I am standing with him on a Florida beach. I am five, he is forty-two. I am already the man I was destined to be; he is still the youth he always was. My mother must have taken the shot—I can tell, for I occupy the centre—and it is one of those embarrassing shots parents often take. I am in my wet transparent underpants and I've just been swimming at Daytona Beach. It is 1946, our first morning in Florida. It isn't a vacation; we've arrived to start again, in the sun. The war is over, the border is open, the old black Packard is parked behind us. I had wanted to swim but had no trunks; my father took me down in my underwear. But in the picture my face is worried, my cupped hands are reaching down to cover myself, but I was late or the picture early—it seems instead that I am pointing to it, a fleshy little spot on my transparent pants. On the back of the picture my father had written:

Thibidault et fils,
Daytona, avr/46

We'd left Montreal four days before, with snow still grey in the tenements' shadow, the trees black and budless over the dingy winter street. Our destination was a town named Hartley where my father had a friend from Montreal who'd started a lawn furniture factory. My father was to become a travelling salesman for Laverdure's Lawn Laddies, and I was to begin my life as a salesman's son. As reader of back issues, as a collector of cancelled stamps (the inkier the better), as student and teacher of languages.

Thibidault et fils; Thibidault and son. After a week in Hartley I developed worms. My feet bled from itching and scratching. The worms were visible; I could prick them with pins. My mother took me to a clinic where the doctor sprayed my foot with a liquid freeze. Going on, the ice was pleasant, for Florida feet are always hot. Out on the bench I scraped my initials in the frost of my foot. It seemed right to me (before the pain of the thaw began); I was from Up North, the freezing was a friendly gesture for a Florida doctor. My mother held my foot between her hands and told me stories of her childhood, ice-skating for miles on the Battleford River in Saskatchewan, then riding home under fur rugs in a horse-drawn sleigh. Though she was the same age as my father, she was the eldest of six—somewhere between them was a missing generation. The next morning the itching was worse and half a dozen new worms radiated from the ball of my foot. My mother then consulted her old *Canadian Doctor's Home Companion*—my grandfather Blankenship had been a doctor, active for years in curling circles, Anglican missions, and crackpot Toryism—and learned that footworms, etc., were unknown in Canada but sometimes afflicted Canadian travellers in Tropical Regions. Common to all hot climes, the book went on, due to poor sanitation and the unspeakable habits of the non-white peoples, even in the Gulf Coast and Indian Territories of our southern neighbour. No known cure, but lack of attention can be fatal.

My mother called in a neighbour, our first contact with the slovenly woman who lived downstairs. She came up with a bottle of carbolic acid and another of alcohol, and poured the acid over the worms and told me to yell when it got too hot. Then with alcohol she wiped it off. The next morning my foot had peeled and the worms were gone. And I thought, inspecting my peeled, brown foot, that in some small way I had become less northern, less hateful to the kids around me though I still sounded strange and they shouted after me, "Yankee, Yankee!"

My father was already browned and already spoke with a passable southern accent. When he wasn't on the road with Lawn Laddies he walked around barefoot or in shower clogs. But he never got worms, and he was embarrassed that I had.

Thibidault and son: he was a fisherman and I always fished at his side. Fished for what? I wonder now—he was too short and vain a man to really be a fisherman. He dressed too well, couldn't swim, despised the taste of fish, shunned the cold, the heat, the bugs, the rain. And yet we fished every Sunday, wherever we lived. Canada, Florida, the Middle West, heedless as deer of crossing borders. The tackle box (oily childhood smell) creaked at our feet. The fir-lined shores and pink granite beaches of Ontario gleamed behind us. Every cast became a fresh hope, a trout or *doré* or even a muskie. But we never caught a muskie or a trout, just the snake-like fork-boned pike that we let go by cutting the line when the plug was swallowed deep. And in Florida, with my father in his Harry Truman shirts and sharkskin pants, the warm bait-well sloshing with half-dead shiners, we waited for bass and channel cat in Okeechobee, Kissimmee and a dozen other bug-beclouded lakes. Gar fish, those tropical pike, drifted by the boat. Gators churned in a narrow channel and dragonflies lit on my cane pole tip. And as I grew older and we came back North (but not all the way), I remember our Sundays in Cincinnati, standing shoulder-to-shoulder with a few hundred others around a clay-banked tub lit with arc-lamps. Scummy pay-lakes with a hot dog stand behind, a vision of hell for a Canadian or a Floridian, but we paid and we fished and we never caught a thing. Ten hours every Sunday from Memorial Day to Labour Day, an unquestioning ritual that would see me dress in my fishing khakis, race out early and buy the Sunday paper before we left (so I could check the baseball averages—what a normal kid I might have been!), then pack the tacklebox and portable radio (for the Cincinnati doubleheader) in the trunk. Then I would get my father up. He'd have his coffee and a few cigarettes then shout, "Mildred, Frankie and I are going fishing!" She would be upstairs reading or sewing. We were still living in a duplex; a few months later my parents were to start their furniture store and we would never fish again. We walked out, my father and I, nodding to the neighbours (a few kids, younger than I, asked if they could go, a few young fathers would squint and ask, "Not again, Gene?"); and silently we drove, and later, silently, we fished.

Then came a Sunday just before Labour Day when I was thirteen and we didn't go fishing. I was dressed for it and the car was packed as usual, but my father drove to the County Fair instead. Not the Hamilton County Fair in Cincinnati—we drove across the river into Boone County, Kentucky, where things were once again southern and shoddy.

I had known from the books and articles my mother was leaving in the bathroom that I was supposed to be learning about sex. I'd read the books and figured out the anatomy for myself; I wondered only how to ask a girl for it and what to do once I got there. Sex was something like dancing, I supposed, too intricate and spontaneous for a boy like me. And so we toured the Fair Grounds that morning, saying nothing, reviewing the prize sows and heifers, watching a stock-car race and a miniature rodeo. I could tell from my father's breathing, his coughing, his attempt to put his arm around my shoulder, that this was the day he was going to talk to me about sex, the facts of life, and the thought embarrassed him as much as it did me. I wanted to tell him to never mind; I didn't need it, it was something that selfish people did to one another.

He led me to a remote tent far off the fairway. There was a long male line outside, men with a few boys my age, joking loudly and smelling bad. My father looked away, silent. So this is the place, I thought, where I'm going to see it, going to learn something good and dirty, something they couldn't put on those Britannica Films and show in school. The sign over the entrance said only: *Princess Hi-Yalla. Shows Continuously.*

There was a smell, over the heat, over the hundred men straining for a place, over the fumes of pigsties and stockyards. It was the smell of furtiveness, rural slaughter and unquenchable famine. The smell of boy's rooms in the high school. The smell of sex on the hoof. The "Princess" on the runway wore not a stitch, and she was already lathered like a racehorse from her continuous dance. There was no avoiding the bright pink lower lips that she'd painted; no avoiding the shrinking, smiling, puckering, wrinkled labia. "Kiss, baby?" she called out, and the men went wild. The lips smacked us softly. The Princess was more a dowager, and more black than brown or yellow. She bent forward to watch herself, like a ventriloquist with a dummy. I couldn't turn away as my father had; it seemed less offensive to watch her wide flat breasts instead, and to think of her as another native from the *National Geographic.* She asked a guard for a slice of gum, then held it over the first row. "Who gwina wet it up fo' baby?" And a farmer licked both sides while his friends made appreciative noises, then handed it back. The Princess inserted it slowly, as though it hurt, spreading her legs like the bow-legged rodeo clown I'd seen a few minutes earlier. Her lower mouth chewed, her abdomen heaved, and she doubled forward to watch the progress. "Blow a bubble!" the farmer called, his friends screamed with laughter. But a row of boys in overalls, my age, stared at the woman and didn't smile. Nothing would amaze them—they were waiting for a bubble. Then she cupped her hand underneath and gum came slithering out. "Who wants this?" she called, holding it high, and men were whistling and throwing other things on the stage: key rings, handkerchiefs, cigarettes. She threw the gum toward us—I remember ducking as it came my way, but someone caught it. "Now then," she said, and her voice was as loud as a gospel singer's, "baby's fixin' to have herself a cig'rette." She walked to the edge of the stage (I could see her moist footprints in the dust), her toes curled over the side. "Which of you men out there is givin' baby a cig'rette?" Another farmer standing behind his fat adolescent son threw up two cigarettes. The boy, I remember, was in overalls and had the cretinous look of fat boys in overalls: big, sweating, red-cheeked, with eyes like calves' in a roping event. By the time I looked back on stage, the Princess had inserted the cigarette and had thrust baby out over the runway and was asking for matches. She held the match herself. And the cigarette glowed, smoke came out, an ash formed . . .

I heard moaning, long low moans, and I felt the eyes of a dozen farmers leap to the boy in overalls. He was jumping and whimpering and the men were laughing as he tried to dig into his sealed-up pants. Forgetting the buttons at his shoulders, he was holding his crotch as though it burned. He was running in place, moaning, then screaming, "Daddy!" and I forgot about the Princess. Men cleared a circle around him and began clapping and chanting, "Whip it out!" and the boy was crying, "Daddy, I cain't hold it back no more!"

My father grabbed me then by the elbow, and said, "Well, have you seen enough?" The farm boy had collapsed on the dirt floor, and was twitching on his back as though a live wire were passed through his body. A navy-blue stain that I thought was blood was spreading between his legs. I thought he'd managed to pull his penis off. My father led me out and he was mad at me for something—it was *me* who had brought him there, and his duties as my father—and just as we stepped from the tent I yelled, "Wait—it's happening to me too." I wanted to cry with embarrassment for I hadn't felt any urgency before entering the tent. It seemed like a sudden, irresistible need to urinate, something I couldn't hold back. But worse than water; something was ripping at my crotch. My light-coloured fishing khakis would turn brown in water, and the dark stain was already forming.

"Jesus Christ—are you *sick?* That was an old woman—how could *she* ... how could *you* ..." He jerked me forward by the elbow. "Jesus God," he muttered, pulling me along down the fairway, then letting me go and walking so fast I had to run, both hands trying to cup the mess I had made. Thousands of people passed me, smiling, laughing. "I don't know about you," my father said. *"I think there's something wrong with you,"* and it was the worse thing my father could say about me. We were in the car. I was crying in the back seat. "Don't tell me someone didn't see you—didn't you think of that? Or what if a customer saw *me*—but you didn't think of that either, did you? Here I take you to something I thought you'd like, something any *normal* boy would like, and—"

I'd been afraid to talk. The wetness was drying, a stain remained. "You know Murray Lieberman?" my father asked a few minutes later.

"The salesman?"

"He has a kid your age and so we were talking—"

"Never mind." I said.

"Well, what in the name of God is wrong with two fathers getting together, eh? It was supposed to *show* you what it's like, about women, I mean. It's better than any drawing, isn't it? You want books all the time? You want to *read* about it, or do you want to see it? At least now you *know*, so go ahead and read. Tell your mother we were fishing today, O.K.? And *that*—that was a Coke you spilled, all right?"

And no other talk, man-to-man, or father-to-son, had ever taken place.

I think back to Boniface Thibidault—how would he, how *did* he, show his sons what to do and where to do it? He was a Frenchman, not a North American; he learned it in Paris, not in a monastery as my father had. And I am, partially at least, a Frenchman too. My father should have taken me to a *cocotte*, to his own mistress perhaps, for the initiation, *la déniasement*. And I, in my own love-making, would have forever honoured him. But this is North America and my father, despite everything, was in his silence a Quebec Catholic of the nineteenth century. Sex, despite my dreams of something better, something nobler, still smells of the circus tent, of something raw and murderous. Other kinds of sex, the adjusted, contented, fulfilling sex of school and manual, seems insubstantial, willfully ignorant of the depths.

At thirteen I was oldest of eighty kids on the block, a thankless distinction, and my parents at fifty had a good twenty years on the next oldest, who, it happened, shared our duplex.

There lived on that street, and I was beginning to notice in that summer before the sideshow at the county fair, several girl brides and one or two maturely youthful wives. The brides, under twenty and with their first or second youngsters, were a sloppy crew who patrolled the street in cut-away shorts and bra-less elasticized halters that had to be pulled up every few steps. They set their hair so tightly in pin curlers that the effect, at a distance, was of the mange. Barefoot they pushed their baby strollers, thighs sloshing as they walked, or sat on porch furniture reading movie magazines and holding tinted plastic baby bottles between their knees. Though they sat in the sun all day they never tanned. They were spreading week by week while their husbands, hard athletic gas-pumpers, played touch football on the street every Sunday.

But there were others; in particular the wife next door, our two floors being mirror images of the other, everything back-to-back but otherwise identical. What was their name? She was a fair woman, about thirty, with hair only lightly bleached and the kind of figure that one first judges slightly too plump until something voluptuous in her, or you, makes you look again and you see that she is merely extraordinary; a full woman who had once been a lanky girl. She had three children, two of them girls who favoured the husband, but I can't quite place his name or face. Her name was Annette.

She was French. That had been a point of discussion once. Born in Maine, she would often chat with my father in what French she remembered while her husband played football or read inside. By that time I had forgotten most of my French. And now I remember the husband. His name was Lance—Lance!—and he was dark, square-shouldered, with a severe crewcut that sliced across an ample bald spot. He travelled a lot; I recall him sitting in a lawn chair on summer evenings, reading the paper and drinking a beer till the mosquitoes drove him in.

And that left Annette alone, and Annette had no friends on the block. She gave the impression, justified, of far outdistancing the neighbourhood girls. Perhaps she frightened them, being older and by comparison, a goddess. She would sit on a lawn chair in the front yard, on those male-less afternoons of toddling children and cranky mothers and was so stunning in a modest sundress that I would stay inside and peek at her through a hole I had cut in the curtains. Delivery trucks, forced to creep through the litter of kids and abandoned toys, lingered longer than they had to, just to look. At thirteen I could stare for hours, unconscious of peeping, unaware, really, of what I wanted or expected to see. It was almost like fishing, with patience and anticipation keeping me rooted.

My parents were at the new property, cleaning it up for a grand opening. I was given three or four dollars a day for food and I'd spend fifty or sixty cents of it on meaty and starchy grease down at the shopping centre. I was getting fat. Every few days I carried a bulging pocketful of wadded bills down to the bank and cashed them for a ten or twenty. And the bills would accumulate in my wallet. I was too young to open an account without my parents' finding out; the question was how to spend it. After a couple of weeks I'd go downtown and spend astounding sums, for a child, on stamps.

While I was in the shopping centre I began stealing magazines from the drugstore. The scandal mags, the Hollywood parties, the early *Playboy* and its imitators—I stole because I was too good to be seen buying them. I placed them between the pages of the *Sporting News*, which I also read cover-to-cover, then dropped a wadded five-dollar bill in the newspaper honour box, raced home, and feasted. Never one for risks, I burned the residue or threw them out in a neighbour's garbage can, my conscience clear for a month's more stealing and secret reading. There was never a time in my life when sex had been so palpable; when the very sight of any girl vaguely developed or any woman up to forty and still in trim could make my breath come short, make my crotch tingle under my baggy pants. In the supermarket, when young mothers dipped low to pick a carton of Cokes from the bottom shelf, I dipped with them. When the counter girl at the drugstore plunged her dipper in the ice cream tub, I hung over the counter to catch a glimpse of her lacy bra; when the neighbour women hung out their clothes, I would take the stairs two at a time to watch from above. When those young wives hooked their thumbs under the knitted elastic halters and gave an upward tug, I let out a little whimper. How close it was to madness; how many other fat thirteen- and fourteen-year-olds with a drop more violence, provocation, self-pity or whatever, would plunge a knife sixty times into those bellies, just to run their fingers inside the shorts and peel the halter back, allowing the breasts to ooze aside? And especially living next to Annette whose figure made flimsy styles seem indecent and modest dresses maddening. Her body possessed the clothes too greedily, sucked the material to her flesh. She was the woman, I now realize, that Dostoyevski and Kazantzakis and even Faulkner knew; a Grushenka or the young village widow, a dormant body that kindled violence.

The duplexes were mirror images with only the staircases and bathrooms adjoining. In the summer with Annette at home, her children out playing or taking a nap, her husband away, or just at work, she took many baths. From wherever I sat in our duplex watching television or reading my magazines, I could hear the drop of the drain plug in her bathroom, the splash of water rushing in, the quick expansion of the hot water pipes.

I could imagine the rest, exquisitely. First testing the water with her finger, then drying the finger on her shorts and then letting them drop. Testing the water again before unhooking the bra in a careless sweep and with another swipe, peeling off her panties. The thought of Annette naked, a foot away, made the walls seem paper-thin, made the tiles grow warm. Ear against the tiles I could hear the waves she made as she settled back, the squeaking of her heels on the bottom of the tub as she straightened her legs, the wringing of a face cloth, plunk of soap as it dropped. The scene was as vivid, with my eyes closed and my hot ear on the warm tile, as murders on old radio shows. I thought of the childhood comic character who could shrink himself with magic sand; how for me that had always translated itself into watching the Hollywood starlets from their bathroom heating registers. But Annette was better or at least as good, and so available. If only there were a way, a shaft for midgets. It wasn't right to house strangers so intimately without providing a way to spy. I looked down to the tile floor—a crack? Something a bobby pin could be twisted in, just a modest, modest opening? And I saw the pipes under the sink, two slim swannecks, one for hot, one for cold, that cut jaggedly through the tile wall—they had to connect! Then on my hands and knees I scraped away the plaster that held the chromium collar around the pipe. As I had hoped, the hole was a good quarter-inch wider than the pipes and all that blocked a straight-on view of the other bathroom were the collars on Annette's pipes. It would be nothing to punch my way through, slide the rings down, and lie on the tile floor in the comfort of my own bathroom and watch it all; Annette bathing! Ring level was below the tub, but given the distance the angle might correct itself. But detection would be unbearable; if caught I'd commit suicide. She was already out of the bath (but there'll be other days, I thought). She took ten-minute baths (how much more could a man bear?), the water was draining and now she was running the lavatory faucet which seemed just over my head. How long before she took another bath? It would seem, now that I had a plan, as long as the wait between issues of my favourite magazines.

I rested on the floor under the sink until Annette left her bathroom. Then I walked down to the shopping centre and had a Coke to steady myself. I bought a nailfile. When I got back Annette was sitting in her yard, wearing a striped housedress and looking, as usual, fresh from a bath. I said hello and she smiled very kindly. Then I turned my door handle and cried, "Oh, no!"

"What is it, Frankie?" she asked, getting up from her chair.

"I left my key inside."

"Shall I call your father?"

"No," I said, "I think I can get in through the window. But could I use your bathroom first?"

"Of course."

I checked upstairs for kids. Then I locked myself inside and with the new file, scraped away the plaster and pulled one collar down. Careful as always, aware that I would make a good murderer or a good detective, I cleaned up the plaster crumbs. I'd forgotten to leave our own bathroom light on, but it seemed that I could see all the way through. Time would tell. *Take a bath,* I willed her, as I flushed the toilet. It reminded me of fishing as a child, trying to influence the fish to bite. It's very hot, sticky, just right for a nice cool bath . . . My own flesh was stippled, I shivered as I stepped outside and saw her again. She'd soon be *mine*—something to do for the rest of the summer! My throat was so tense I couldn't even thank her. I climbed inside through the living-room window that I had left open.

I took the stairs two at a time, stretched myself out under the sink to admire the job. I'd forgotten to leave *her* light on, but I thought I could see the white of her tub in the darkened bathroom, and even an empty tub was enough to sustain me.

How obvious was the pipe and collar? It suddenly seemed blatant, that she would enter the bathroom, undress, sit in the tub, turn to the wall, and scream. Do a peeper's eyes shine too brightly? In school I'd often been able to stare a kid into turning around—it was now an unwanted gift.

You're getting warm again, Annette. Very very hot. You want another bath. You're getting up from the chair, coming inside, up the stairs . . . I kept on for hours till it was dark. I heard the kids taking baths and saw nothing. The white of the bathtub was another skin of plaster, no telling how thick. I'd been cheated.

Another day. There had to be another link—I had faith that the builders of duplexes were men who provided, out of guilt, certain amenities. Fans were in the ceiling. Windows opened on the opposite sides, the heating ducts were useless without a metal drill. Only the medicine cabinets were left. They had to be back-to-back. I opened ours, found the four corner screws, undid them, took out the medicines quietly (even my old Florida carbolic acid), then eased the chest from its plaster nest. It worked. I was facing the metal backing of Annette's medicine chest. The fit was tight and I could never take a chance of tampering with hers—what if I gave it a nudge when Lance was shaving and the whole thing came crashing down, revealing me leaning over my sink in the hole where our medicine chest had been?

The used-razor slot. A little slot in the middle. I popped the paper coating with the nailfile. I darkened our own bathroom. If Annette opened her chest, I'd see her. But would she open it with her clothes off? Was she tall enough to make it count? How many hours would I have to stand there, stretched over the sink, waiting, and could I, every day, put the chest back up and take it down without some loud disaster. What if my father came home to shave, unexpectedly?

I waited all afternoon and all evening and when eight o'clock came I ended the vigil and put the chest back up. With a desire so urgent, there *had* to be a way of penetrating an inch and a half of tile and plaster. When she was in her bath I felt I could have devoured the walls between us. Anything *heard* so clearly had to yield to vision—that was another natural law—just as anything dreamt had to become real, eventually.

I became a baby-sitter; the oldest kid on the block, quiet and responsible. I watched television in nearly every duplex on the street, ignored the whimpers, filled bottles, and my pockets bulged with more unneeded cash. I poked around the young parents' bedrooms and medicine cabinets, only half-repelled by the clutter and unfamiliar odours, the stickiness, the greyness of young married life in a Midwest suburb. I found boxes of prophylactics in top drawers and learned to put one on and to walk around with it on until the lubrication stuck to my underwear. Sex books and nudist magazines showing pubic hair were stuffed in nightstands, and in one or two homes I found piles of home-made snaps of the young wife when she'd been slim and high school young, sitting naked in the sun, in a woods somewhere. She'd been posed in dozens of ways, legs wide apart, fingers on her pubic hair, tongue curled between her teeth. Others of her, and of a neighbour woman, on the same living-room sofa that I was sitting on: fatter now, her breasts resting on a roll of fat around her middle, her thighs shadowed where the skin had grown soft. *This is the girl I see every day,* pushing that carriage, looking like a fat girl at a high school hang-out. Those bigger girls in my school, in bright blue sweaters, earrings, black curly hair, bad skin, black corduroy jackets, smoking. They became like this; they *are* like this.

These were the weeks in August, when my mother was leaving the articles around. Soon my father would take me to the county fair. There were no answers to the questions I asked, holding those snapshots, looking again (by daylight) at the wife (in ragged shorts and elastic halter) who had consented to the pictures. They were like murder victims, the photos were like police shots in the scandal magazines, the women looked like mistresses of bandits. There was no place in the world for the life I wanted, for the pure woman I would someday, somehow, marry.

I baby-sat for Annette and Lance, then for Annette alone, and I worked again on the lavatory scheme, the used-razor slot, and discovered the slight dificiencies in the architecture that had thrown my calculations off. I could see from their bathroom into ours much better than I could ever see into theirs. Annette kept a neat house and life with her, even I could appreciate, must have been a joy of lust and efficiency, in surroundings as clean and attractive as a *Playboy* studio.

One evening she came over when my parents were working, to ask me to baby-sit for a couple of hours. Lance wasn't in. Her children were never a problem and though it was a week night and school had begun, I agreed. She left me a slice of Lance's birthday cake, and begged me to go to sleep in case she was late.

An hour later, after some reading, I used her bathroom, innocently. If only I lived here, with Annette over there! I opened her medicine chest to learn some more about her: a few interesting pills "for pain," Tampax Super (naturally, I thought), gauze and adhesive, something for piles (for him, I hoped). And then I heard a noise from our bathroom; I heard our light snap on. My parents must have come home early.

I knew from a cough that it wasn't my mother. The Thibidault medicine chest was opened. I peered through the razor slot and saw young fingers among our bottles, blond hair and a tanned forehead: Annette. She picked out a jar, then closed the door. I fell to the floor and put my eye against the pipes. Bare golden legs. Then our light went out.

I looked into our bathroom for the next few seconds then ran to Annette's front bedroom where the youngest girl slept, and pressed over her crib to look out the window. She was just stepping out and walking slowly to the station wagon of Thibidault Furniture, which had been parked. She got in the far side and the car immediately, silently, backed away, with just its parking lights on . . .

And that was all. For some reason, perhaps the shame of my complicity, I never asked my father why he had come home or why Annette had been in our bathroom. I didn't have to—I'd gotten a glimpse of Annette, which was all I could handle anyway. I didn't understand the rest. *Thibidault et fils,* fishing again.

Jean-Louis Thibidault, twice-divorced, is dead; buried in Venice, Florida. Bridge of Sighs Cemetery. I even asked his widow if I could have him removed to Sorel, Quebec. She didn't mind, but the *prêtre-vicaire* of my father's old parish turned me down. When my father was born, Venice, Florida, was five miles offshore and fifty feet underwater. The thought of him buried there tortures my soul.

There was another Sunday in Florida. A hurricane was a hundred miles offshore and due to strike Fort Lauderdale within the next six hours. We drove from our house down Las Olas to the beach (Fort Lauderdale was still an inland city then), and parked half a mile away, safe from the paint-blasting sand. We could hear the breakers under the shriek of the wind, shaking the wooden bridge we walked on. Then we watched them crash, brown with weeds and suspended sand. And we could see them miles offshore, rolling in forty feet high and flashing their foam like icebergs. A few men in swimming suits and woollen sweaters were standing in the crater pools, pulling out the deep-sea fish that had been stunned by the trip and waves. Other fish littered the beach, their bellies blasted by the change in pressure. My mother's face was raw and her glasses webbed with salt. She went back to the car on her own. My father and I sat on the bench for another hour and I could see behind his crusty sunglasses. His eyes were moist and dancing, his hair stiff and matted. We sat on the bench until we were soaked and the municipal guards rounded us up. Then they barricaded the boulevards and we went back to the car, the best day of fishing we'd ever had, and we walked hand in hand for the last time, talking excitedly, dodging coconuts, power lines, and shattered glass, feeling brave and united in the face of the storm. My father and me. What a day it was, what a once-in-a-lifetime day it was.

How I Became a Jew

Cincinnati, September 1950

"I don't suppose you've attended classes with the coloured before, have you, Gerald?" the principal inquired. He was a jockey-sized man whose dark face collapsed around a greying mustache. His name was DiCiccio.

"No, sir."

"You'll find quite a number in your classes here—" he gestured to the kids on the playground, and the Negroes among them seemed to multiply before my eyes. "My advice is not to expect any trouble and they won't give you any."

"We don't expect none from them," my mother said with great reserve, the emphasis falling slightly on the last word.

DiCiccio's eyes wandered over us, calculating but discreet. He was taking in my porkiness, my brushed blond hair, white shirt and new gabardines. And my Georgia accent.

"My boy is no troublemaker."

"I can see that, Mrs. Gordon."

"But I'm here to tell you—just let me hear of any trouble and I'm going straight off to the po-lice."

And now DiCiccio's smile assessed her, as though to say *are you finished?* "That wouldn't be in Gerald's best interest, Mrs. Gordon. We have no serious discipline problems in the elementary school but even if we did, Mrs. Gordon, outside authorities are never the answer. Your boy has to live with them. Police are never a solution." He pronounced the word "pleece" and I wanted to laugh. "Even in the Junior High," he said, jerking his thumb in the direction of the black, prisonlike structure beyond the playground. "There are problems there." His voice was still far-off and I was smiling.

DiCiccio's elementary school was new: bright, low and long, with greenboards and yellow chalk, aluminum frames and blond, unblemished desks. My old school in Georgia, near Moultrie, had had a room for each grade up through the sixth. Here in Cincinnati the sixth grade itself had ten sections.

"And Gerald, *please* don't call me 'sir.' Don't call anyone that," the principal said with sudden urgency. "That's just asking for it. The kids might think you're trying to flatter the teacher or something."

"Well, I swan—" my mother began. "He learned respect for his elders and nobody is taking that respect away. Never."

"Look—" and now the principal leaned forward, growing smaller as he approached the desk, "I know how Southern schools work. I know 'sir' and 'ma'am.' I know they must have beaten it into you. But I'm trying to be honest, Mrs. Gordon. Your son has a lot of things going against him and I'm trying to help. This intelligence of his can only hurt him unless he learns how to use it. He's white—enough said. And I assume Gordon isn't a Jewish name, is it? Which brings up another thing, Mrs. Gordon. Take a look at those kids out there, the white ones. They look like little old men, don't they? Those are *Jews,* Gerald, and they're as different from the others as you are from the coloured. They were born in Europe and they're living here with their grandparents—don't ask me why, it's a long story. Let's just say they're a little hard to play with. A little hard to like, O.K.?" Then he settled back and caught his breath.

"They're the Israelites!" I whispered, as though the Bible had come to life. Then I was led to class.

But the sixth grade was not a home for long; not for the spelling champ and fastest reader in Colquitt County, Georgia. They gave me tests, sent me to a university psychologist who tested my memory and gave me some codes to crack. Then I was advanced.

Seventh grade was in the old building: Leonard Sachs Junior High. A greenish statue of Abraham Lincoln stood behind black iron bars, pointing a finger to the drugstore across the street. The outside steps were pitted and sagging. The hallways were tawny above the khaki lockers, and clusters of dull yellow globes were bracketed to the walls, like torches in the catacombs. By instinct I preferred the used to the new, sticky wood to cold steel, and I would have felt comfortable on that first walk down the hall to my new class, but for the stench of furtive, unventilated cigarette smoke. The secretary led me past rooms with open doors; all the teachers were men. Many were shouting while the classes turned to whistle at the ringing *tap-tap* of the secretary's heels. Then she stopped in front of a closed door and rapped. The noise inside partially abated and finally a tall bald man with furry ears opened the door.

"This is Gerald Gordon, Mr. Terleski. He's a transfer from Georgia and they've skipped him up from sixth."

"They have, eh?" A few students near the door laughed. They were already pointing at me. "George, you said?"

"Gerald Gordon *from* Georgia," said the secretary.

"Georgia Gordon!" a Negro boy shouted. "Georgia Gordon. Sweet Georgia Gordon."

Terleski didn't turn. He took the folder from the girl and told me to find a seat. But the front boys in each row linked arms and wouldn't let me through. I walked to the window row and laid my books on the ledge. The door closed. Terleski sat at his desk and opened my file but didn't look up.

"Sweet Georgia," crooned the smallish, fair-skinned Negro nearest me. He brushed my notebook to the floor. I bent over and got a judo chop on the inside of my knees.

"Sweet Georgia, you get off the floor, hear?" A very fat, coal-black girl in a pink sweater was helping herself to paper from my three-ring binder. "Mr. Tee, Sweet Georgia taking a nap," she called.

He grumbled. I stood up. My white shirt and baggy gabardines were brown with dust.

"This boy is *not* named Sweet Georgia. He *is* named Gerald Gordon," said Terleski with welcome authority. "And I guess he's some kind of genius. They figured out he was too smart for the sixth grade. They gave him tests at the university and—listen to this—Gerald Gordon is a borderline genius."

A few whistled. Terleski looked up. "Isn't that *nice* for Gerald Gordon? What can we do to make you happy, Mr. Gordon?"

"Nothing, sir," I answered.

"Not a thing? Not an itsy-bitsy thing, sir?"

I shook my head, lowered it.

"Might we expect you to at least look at the rest of us? We wouldn't want to presume, but—"

"Sweet Georgia crying, Mr. Tee," giggled Pink Sweater.

"And he all dirty," added the frontseater. "How come you all dirty, Sweet Georgia-man?" Pink Sweater was awarding my paper to all her friends.

"Come to the desk, Mr. Gordon."

I shuffled forward, holding my books over the dust smears.

"Face your classmates, sir. Look at them. Do you see any borderline types out there? Any friends?"

I sniffled loudly. My throat ached. There were some whites, half a dozen or so grinning in the middle of the room. I looked for girls and saw two white ones. Deep in the rear sat some enormous Negroes, their boots looming in the aisle. They looked at the ceiling and didn't even bother to whisper as they talked. They wore pastel T-shirts with cigarette packs twisted in the shoulder. And—God!—I thought, they had mustaches. Terleski repeated his question, and for the first time in my life I knew that whatever answer I gave would be wrong.

"*Mr. Gordon's reading comprehension is equal to the average college freshman.* Oh, Mr. Gordon, just *average?* Surely there must be some mistake."

I started crying, tried to hold it back, couldn't, and bawled. I remembered the rows of gold stars beside my name back in Colquitt County, Georgia, and the times I had helped the teacher by grading my fellow students.

A few others picked up my crying: high-pitched blubbering from all corners. Terleski stood, scratched his ear, then screamed: "Shut up!" A rumbling monotone persisted from the Negro rear. Terleski handed me his handkerchief and said, "Wipe your face." Then he said to the class: "I'm going to let our borderline genius himself continue. Read this, sir, just like an average college freshman." He passed me my file.

I put it down and knuckled my eyes violently. They watched me hungrily, laughing at everything. Terleski poked my ribs with the corner of the file. "Read!"

I caught my breath with a long, loud shudder.

"*Gerald Gordon certainly possesses the necessary intellectual equipment to handle work on a seventh grade level, and long consultations with the boy indicate a commensurate emotional maturity. No problem anticipated in adjusting to a new environment.*"

"Beautiful," Terleski announced. "Beautiful. He's in the room five minutes and he's crying like a baby. Spends his first three minutes on the floor getting dirty, needs a hanky from the teacher to wipe his nose, and he has the whole class laughing at him and calling him names. Beautiful. That's what I call real maturity. Is that all the report says, sir?"

"Yes, sir."

"You're lying, Mr. Gordon. That's not very mature. Tell the class what else it says."

"I don't want to, sir."

"You don't want to. *I* want you to. *Read!*"

"It says: *'I doubt only the ability of the Cincinnati Public Schools to supply a worthy teacher.'*"

"*Well*—that's what we wanted to hear, Mr. Gordon. Do you doubt it?"

"No, sir."

"Am I worthy enough to teach you?"

"Yes, sir."

"What do I teach?"

"I don't know, sir."

"What have you learned already?"

"Nothing yet, sir."

"What's the capital of the Virgin Islands?"

"Charlotte Amalie," I said.

That surprised him, but he didn't show it for long. "Then I can't teach you a thing, can I, Mr. Gordon? You must know everything there is to know. You must have all your merit badges. So it looks like we're going to waste each other's time, doesn't it? Tell the class where Van Diemen's Land is."

"That's the old name for Tasmania, sir. Australia, capital is Hobart."

"If it's Australia that would make the capital Canberra, wouldn't it, Mr. Gordon?"

"For the whole country, yes, sir."

"So there's still something for you to learn, isn't there, Mr. Gordon?"

The kids in the front started to boo. "Make room for him back there," the teacher said, pointing to the middle. "And *now,* maybe the rest of you can tell me the states that border on Ohio. Does *anything* border on Ohio?"

No one answered while I waved my hand. I cared desperately that my classmates learn where Ohio was. And finally, ignoring me, Mr. Terleski told them.

Recess: on the sticky pavement in sight of Lincoln's statue. The windows of the first two floors were screened and softball was the sport. The white kids in the gym class wore institutional shorts; the other half—the Negroes—kept their jeans and T-shirts since they weren't allowed in the dressing room. I was still in my dusty new clothes. We all clustered around the gym teacher, who wore a Cincinnati Redlegs cap. He appointed two captains, both white. "Keep track of the score, fellas. And tell me after how you do at the plate individually." He blew his whistle and scampered off to supervise a basketball game around the corner.

The captains were Arno Kolko and Wilfrid Skurow, both fat and pale, with heavy eyebrows and thick hair climbing down their necks and up from their shirts. Hair like that—I couldn't believe it. I was twelve, and had been too ashamed to undress in the locker room. These must be Jews, I told myself. The other whites were shorter than the captains. They wore glasses and had bristly hair. Many of them shaved. Their arms were pale and veined. I moved towards them.

"Where *you* going, boy?" came a high-pitched but adult voice behind me. I turned and faced a six-foot Negro who was biting an unlit cigarette. He had a mustache and, up high on his yellow biceps, a flag tattoo. "Ain't nobody picked you?"

"No," I hesitated, not knowing if they were agreeing or answering.

"Then stay where you're at. Hey—y'all want him?"

Skurow snickered. I had been accustomed to being a low-priority pick back in ball-playing Colquitt County, Georgia. I started to walk away.

"Come back here, boy. Squirrel picking you."

"But you're not a captain."

"Somebody *say* I ain't a captain?" The other Negroes had fanned out under small clouds of blue smoke and started basketball games on the painted courts. "That leaves me and you," said Squirrel. "We standing them."

"I want to be with them," I protested.

"We don't want you," said one of the Jews.

The kid who said it was holding the bat cross-handed as he took some practice swings. I had at least played a bit of softball back in Colquitt County, Georgia. The kids in my old neighbourhood had built a diamond near a housing development after a bulldozer operator had cleared the lot for us during his lunch hour. Some of the carpenters had given us timber scrap for a fence and *twice*—I remember the feeling precisely to this day—I had lofted fly balls tightly down the line and over the fence. No question, my superiority to the Arno Kolkos of this world.

"We get first ups," said Squirrel. "All *you* gotta do, boy, is get yourself on base and then move your ass fast enough to get home on anything I hit. And if I don't hit a home run, you gotta bring me home next."

"Easy," said I.

First three times up, it worked. I got on and Squirrel blasted on one hop to the farthest corner of the playground. But he ran the bases in a flash, five or six strides between the bases, and I was getting numb in the knees from staying ahead even with a two-base lead. Finally, I popped up for an out. Then Squirrel laid down a bunt and made it to third on some loose play. I popped out again and had to take his place on third, anticipating a stroll home on his next home run. But he bunted again, directly at Skurow the pitcher, who beat me home for a force-out to end the inning.

"Oh, you're a great one, Sweet Georgia," Squirrel snarled from a position at deep short. He was still biting his unlit cigarette. "You're a plenty heavy hitter, man. Where you learn to hit like that?"

"Georgia," I said, slightly embarrassed for my state.

"Georgia? *Joe-ja?*" He lit his cigarette and tossed me the ball. "Then I guess you're the worst baseball player in the whole state, Sweet Georgia. I *thought* you was different."

"From what?"

"From them." He pointed to our opponents. They were talking to themselves in a different language. I felt the power of a home-run swing lighten my arms, but it was too late.

"I play here," said Squirrel. "Pitch them slow then run to first. Ain't none of them can beat my peg or get it by me."

A kid named Izzie, first up, bounced to me and I tagged him. Then a scrawny kid lifted a goodly fly to left—the kind I had hit for doubles—but Squirrel was waiting for it. Then Wilfrid Skurow lumbered up: the most menacing kid I'd ever seen. Hair in swirls on his neck and throat, sprouting wildly from his chest and shoulders. Sideburns, but getting bald. Glasses so thick his eyeballs looked screwed in. But no form. He lunged a chopper to Squirrel, who scooped it and waited for me to cover first. Skurow was halfway down the line, then quit. Squirrel stood straight, tossed his cigarette away, reared back, and fired the ball with everything he had. I heard it leave his hand, then didn't move till it struck my hand and deflected to my skull, over the left eye. I was knocked backwards, and couldn't get up. Skurow circled the bases; Squirrel sat at third and laughed. Then the Jews walked off together and I could feel my forehead tightening into a lump. I tried to stand, but instead grew dizzy and suddenly remembered Colquitt County. I sat alone until the bells rang and the grounds were empty.

Every Saturday near Moultrie, I had gone to the movies. In the balcony they let the coloured kids in just for Saturday. Old ones came Wednesday night for Jim Crow melodramas with coloured actors. But we came especially equipped for those Saturday mornings when the coloured kids sat in the dark up in the balcony, making noise whenever we did. We waited for too much noise, or a popcorn box that might be dropped on us. Then we reached into our pockets and pulled out our broken yo-yos. We always kept our broken ones around. Half a yo-yo is great for sailing since it curves and doesn't lose speed. And it's very hard. So we stood, aimed for the projection beam, and fired the yo-yos upstairs. They loomed on the screen like bats, filled the air like bombs. Some hit metal, others the floor, but some struck home judging from the yelps of the coloured kids and their howling. Minutes later the lights went on upstairs and we heard the ushers ordering them out.

A second bell rang.

"That burr-head nigger son-of-a-bitch," I cried. "That goddamn nigger." I picked myself up and ran inside.

I was late for geometry but my transfer card excused me. When I opened the door two Negro girls dashed out pursued by two boys about twice my size. One of the girls was Pink Sweater, who ducked inside a girls' room. The boys waited outside. The windows in the geometry room were open, and a few boys were sailing paper planes over the street and sidewalk. The teacher was addressing himself to a small group of students who sat in a semicircle around his desk. He was thin and red-cheeked with a stiff pelt of curly hair.

"I say, do come in, won't you? That's a nasty lump you've got there. Has it been seen to?"

"Sir?"

"Over your eye. Surely you're aware of it. It's really quite unsightly."

"I'm supposed to give you this—" I presented the slip for his signing.

"Gerald Gordon, is it? Spiro here."

"Where?"

"Here—I'm Spiro. Geoffrey Spiro, on exchange. And you?"

"Me what?"

"Where are you from?"

"Colquitt County, Georgia."

He smiled as though he knew the place well and liked it. "That's South, aye? Ex-cellent. Let us say for tomorrow you'll prepare a talk on Georgia—brief topical remarks, race, standard of living, labour unrest and what not. Hit the high points, won't you, old man? Now then, class"—he raised his voice only slightly, not enough to disturb the coloured boys making *ack-ack* sounds at pedestrians below—"I should like to introduce to you Mr. Gerald Gordon. You have your choice, sir, of joining these students in the front and earning an 'A' grade, or going back there and getting a 'B', provided of course you don't leave the room."

"I guess I'll stay up here, sir," I said.

"Ex-cellent. Your fellow students, then, from left to right are: Mr. Lefkowitz, Miss Annaliese Graff, Miss Marlene Leopold, Mr. Willie Goldberg, Mr. Irwin Roth, and Mr. Harry Frazier. In the back, Mr. Morris Gordon (no relative, I trust), Miss Etta Bluestone, Mr. Orville Goldberg (he's Willie's twin), and Mr. Henry Moore. Please be seated."

Henry Moore was coloured, as were the Goldberg twins, Orville and Wilbur. The girls, Annaliese, Marlene, and Etta, were pretty and astonishingly mature, as ripe in their way as Wilfrid Skurow in his. Harry Frazier was a straw-haired athletic sort, eating a sandwich. The lone chair was next to Henry Moore, who was fat and smiled and had no mustache or tattoo. I took the geometry book from my scuffed, zippered notebook.

"The truth is," Mr. Spiro began, "that both Neville Chamberlain and Mr. Roosevelt were fascist, and quite in sympathy with Hitler's anticommunist ends, if they quibbled on his means. His evil was mere overzealousness. Public opinion in the so-called democracies could never have mustered against *any* anticommunist, whatever his program—short of invasion, of course. *Klar?*" He stopped in order to fish out a book of matches for Annaliese, who was tapping a cigarette on her desk.

"*Stimmt?*" he asked, and the class nodded. Harry Frazier wadded his waxed paper and threw it back to one of his classmates by the window, shouting, "Russian MIG!" I paged through the text, looking for diagrams. No one else had a book out and my activity seemed to annoy them.

"So in conclusion, Hitler was merely the tool of a larger fascist conspiracy, encouraged by England and the United States. What *is* it, Gerald?"

"Sir—what are we talking about?" I was getting a headache, and the egg on my brow seemed ready to burst. The inner semicircle stared back at me, except for Harry Frazier.

"Sh!" whispered Morris Gordon.

"At *shul* they don't teach it like that," said Irwin Roth, who had a bald spot from where I sat. "In *shul* they say it happened because God was punishing us for falling away. He was testing us. They don't say nothing from the English and the Americans. They don't even say nothing from the Germans."

"Because we didn't learn our letters good," said Morris Gordon. The matches were passed from the girls to all the boys who needed them.

"*What* happened?" I whispered to Henry Moore, who was smiling and nodding as though he knew.

"Them *Jews*, man. Ain't it great?"

"Then the rabbi is handing you the same bloody bullshit they've been handing out since I went to *shul*—ever since the bloody Diaspora," Spiro said. "God, how I detest it."

"What's *shul*, Henry? What's the Diaspora?"

"Look," Spiro continued, now a little more calmly, "there's only one place in the world where they're building socialism, really honestly *building* it"—his hands formed a rigid rectangle over the desk—"and that's Israel. I've seen children your age who've never handled money. I've played football on turf that was desert a year before. The desert blooms, and the children sing and dance and shoot—yes, shoot—superbly They're all brothers and sisters, and they belong equally to every parent in the *kibbutz*. They'd die for one another. No fighting, no name-calling, no sickness. They're big, straight and strong and tall, and handsome, like the Israelites. I've seen it for myself. Why any Jew would come to America is beyond me, unless he wants to be spat on and corrupted."

"*Gott,* if the rabbi knew what goes on here," said Roth, slapping his forehead.

"What's a rabbi, Henry? *Tell me what a rabbi is!*"

"What*ever* is your problem, Gerald?" Spiro cut in.

"Sir—I've lost the place. I just skipped the sixth grade and maybe that's where we learned it all. I don't understand what you-all are saying."

"I must say I speak a rather good English," said Spiro. The class laughed. "Perhaps you'd be happier with the others by the window. All that *rat-tat-tat* seems like jolly good fun, quite a lift, I imagine. It's all perfectly straightforward here. It's *your* country we're talking about, after all. Not mine. Not theirs."

"It's not the same thing up North," I said.

"No, I daresay . . . look, why don't you toddle down to the nurse's office and get something for your head? That's a good lad, and you show up tomorrow if you're feeling better and tell us all about Georgia. Then I'll explain the things you don't know. You just think over what I've said, O.K.?"

I was feeling dizzy—the bump, the smoke—my head throbbed, and my new school clothes were filthy. I brushed myself hard and went into the boys' room to comb my hair, but two large Negroes sitting on the window ledge, stripped to their shorts and smoking cigars, chased me out.

Downstairs, the nurse bawled me out for coming in dirty, then put an ice pack over my eye.

"Can I go home?" I asked.

The nurse was old and fat, and wore hexagonal Ben Franklin glasses. After half an hour she put an adhesive patch on and since only twenty minutes were left, she let me go.

I stopped for a coke at the drugstore across from Lincoln's statue. Surprising, I thought, the number of school kids already out, smoking and having cokes. I waited in the drugstore until the sidewalk was jammed with the legitimately dismissed, afraid that some truant officer might question my early release. I panicked as I passed the cigar counter on my way out, for Mr. Terleski was buying cigarettes and a paper. I was embarrassed for him, catching him smoking, but he saw me, smiled, and walked over.

"Hello, son," he said, "what happened to the head?"

"Nothing," I said, "sir."

"About this morning—I want you to know there was nothing personal in anything I said. Do you believe me?"

"Yes, sir."

"If I didn't do it in *my* way first, they'd do it in their way and it wouldn't be pretty. And Gerald—don't raise your hand again, O.K.?"

"All right," I said. "Good-by."

"*Very* good," said Mr. Terleski. "Nothing else? No sir?"

"I don't think so," I said.

The street to our apartment was lined with shops: tailors with dirty windows, cigar stores piled with magazines, some reading rooms where bearded old men were talking, and a tiny branch of a supermarket chain. Everywhere there were school kids: Jews, I could tell from their heads. Two blocks away, just a few feet before our apartment block, about a dozen kids turned into the dingy yard of the synagogue. An old man shut the gates in a hurry just as I stopped to look in, and another old man opened the main door to let them inside. The tall spiked fence was painted a glossy black. I could see the kids grabbing black silk caps from a cardboard box, then going downstairs. The old gatekeeper, a man with bad breath and puffy skin, ordered me to go.

At home, my mother was preparing dinner for a guest and she was in no mood to question how I got the bump on the head. The guest was Grady, also from Moultrie, a whip-thin red-faced man in his forties who had been the first of my father's friends to go North. He had convinced my father. His wife and kids were back in Georgia selling their house, so he was eating Georgia food with us till she came back. Grady was the man we had to thank, my father always said.

"Me and the missus is moving again soon's she gets back," he announced at dinner. "Had enough of it here."

"Back to Georgia?" my father asked.

"Naw, Billy, out of Cincinnati. Gonna find me a place somewheres in Kentucky. Come in to work every day and go back at night and live like a white man. A man can forget he's white in Cincinnati."

"Ain't that the truth," said my mother.

"How many niggers you got in your room at school, Jerry?" Grady asked me.

"That depends on the class," I said. "In geometry there aren't any hardly."

"See?" said Grady. "You know five years ago there wasn't hardly no more than ten per cent in that school? Now it's sixty and still going up. By the time your'n gets through he's gonna be the onliest white boy in the school."

"He'll be gone before *that*," my father promised. "I been thinking of moving to Kentucky myself."

"Really?" said my mother.

"I ain't even been to a baseball game since they got that nigger," Grady boasted, "and I ain't ever going. I used to love it."

"You're telling me," said my father.

"If they just paid me half in Georgia what they paid me here, I'd be on the first train back," said Grady. "Sometimes I reckon it's the devil himself just tempting me."

"I heard of kids today that live real good and don't even see any money," I said. "Learned it in school."

"That where you learned to stand in front of a softball bat?" my mother retorted, and my parents laughed. Grady coughed.

"And let me tell you," he began, "them kids that goes to them mixed schools gets plenty loony ideas. That thing he just said sounded comminist to me. Yes, sir, that was a Comminist Party member told him that. I don't think no kid of mine could get away with a lie like that in my house. No, sir, they got to learn the truth sometime, and after they do, the rest is lies."

Then Father slapped the fork from my hands. "Get back to your room," he shouted. "You don't get no more dinner till I see your homework done!" He stood behind me, with his hand digging into my shoulder. "Now say good night to Grady."

"Good night," I mumbled.

"Good night *what?*" my mother demanded. "Good night, *what?*"

"Sir," I cried, "sir, sir, sir! Good night, sir!" the last word almost screamed from the hall in front of my bedroom. I slammed the door and fell on the bed in the darkened room. Outside, I could hear the threats and my mother's apologies. "Don't hit him too hard, Billy, he done got that knot on the head already." But no one came.

They started talking of Georgia, and they forgot the hours. I thought of my first school day up North—then planned the second, the third—and I thought of Leonard Sachs Junior High, Squirrel, and the Jews. The Moultrie my parents and Grady were talking about seemed less real, then finally, terrifying. I pictured myself in the darkened balcony under a rain of yo-yos, thrown by a crowd of Squirrels.

I concentrated on the place I wanted to live. There was an enormous baseball stadium where I could hit home runs down the line; Annaliese Graff was in the stands and Mr. Terleski was a coach. We wore little black caps, even Squirrel, and there were black bars outside the park where old men were turning people away. Grady was refused, and Spiro and millions of others, even my parents—though I begged their admission. *No, stimmt?* We were building socialism and we had no parents and we did a lot of singing and dancing (even Henry Moore, even the chocolatey Goldberg twins, Orville and Wilbur) and Annaliese Graff without her cigarettes asked me the capitals of obscure countries. "Israel," I said aloud, letting it buzz; "Israel," and it replaced Mozambique as my favourite word; *Israel, Israel, Israel,* and the dread of the days to come lifted, the days I would learn once and for all if Israel could be really real.

On Ending Stories

Stories begin mysteriously, but end deliberately. A writer can't really *will* a story to open, but in the act of writing, the appropriate ending (event, tone, revelation, effect) will probably suggest itself. Most endings arise in the act of writing (a few stories "arrive" so fully formed that the ending is as mysterious as the opening; the writer is rarely so fortunate), and they all share a single purpose: to give a final emphasis to a particular aspect of the story. Literally, it's the writer's last word on the subject: he'd better choose those words carefully. The opening anticipates the conflict. The ending immortalizes the resolution.

There are only two kinds of endings: those that lead you back into the story, and those that lead you—gently, or violently—away. I associate the first kind of ending with de Maupassant and Chekhov, and with modernists who adapted those stories for their own purposes— Hemingway, Joyce, James. Of authors who lead away from the story, who wish to emphasize the artifice of the story, or wish to address the reader directly, I associate dozens of our contemporaries. Impatience with art is as old as faith in art; the choice of ending is the battlefield for those particular feelings.

You are aware of stories that end with a let-down. "That's it? It's over?" you ask yourself. There's a Hemingway story (there are many Hemingway stories like it) that ends, "Bill selected a sandwich from the lunch basket and walked over to have a look at the rods." That's an ending? Norman Levine can fade out in the same way. It's subversive, of course, a subversion of the expected neatness of closure, the gathering up of narrative and thematic threads, the welling-up of music, the frozen gesture that summarizes *the whole meaning of the story* . . . . We realize that the short story initially paid its debts to theatre, or to fable; audiences expected a big pay-off at the end. When it didn't happen, it was revolution, it was art. Chekhov subverted the expectation dramatically: his vision of a static, purposeless society required the destruction of climax and resolution; the lack of an expected ending makes us feel the lack of resolution, vitality, movement. It preserves tension. You can read that last paragraph, then go back in a circular fashion to the first sentence, and *it almost makes sense.* Joyce adapted the Russian vision to the Irish reality, seeing in that paralysis and indecision an opening to unconscious inhibitions. The so-called "epiphanies" that end his stories are merely the revelation of the subconscious exerting mastery over the blighted, conscious lives. Joyce's stories end when the buried life is suddenly manifest. In their separate ways, James and Hemingway and a number of other modernists and their followers have done the same: sunk the ending deep in the story's texture, forced the reader to dig up the whole story in order to resolve its tensions. The author is not overtly helping the reader: the story *is* its ending.

I think of these endings as the most disturbing. They hit a glancing blow at the reader, but generally ignore him. By approximating the most casual of voices, they manage (in the hands of masters) to sound most urgent. By ignoring us, they speak to us directly. What remains unresolved and undisclosed becomes inviting and forbidding. They offer us no way out of their bland circularity; thus, they linger with us. For me, they are the saddest stories. (Certainly a mastery of that kind of openness, and that kind of "dropped" ending, accounts for the remarkable power of the American author Ray Carver—a very contemporary Hemingway-like voice.)

Endings that lead us away from the story can do so gently or abruptly. The most traditional kind of ending is the one that serves as a prose equivalent to the theatrical last scene, the rising of music and receding of the camera, as lights go out, one-by-one, and characters fade off together in a figurative sunset. Such endings announce a faith in continuity, order, harmony—no matter what particular horrors may have been investigated in the story. They are sophisticated and traditional ways of updating the old "happily ever after" ending so familiar from the fables. Even if the endings are thematically "sad," they are formally (or cosmically) "happy"; they lead us away from the specific exemplum (the story) to a generalized harmony. They are religious in form, if not in content.

How can you detect such an ending? Well, they *sound* like endings.

From Eudora Welty we get, "Outside the redbirds were flying and criss-crossing, the sun was in all the bottles on the prisoned trees, and the young peach was shining in the middle of them with the bursting light of spring. . . ." From Margaret Laurence's first collection, "The sea spray was bitter and salt, but to them it was warm, too. They watched on the sand their exaggerated shadows, one squat and bulbous, the other bone-slight and clumsily elongated, pigeon and crane. The shadows walked with hands entwined like children who walk through the dark." Again, from Laurence's second volume of stories, "It seemed to me now that in some unconscious and totally unrecognised way, Piquette might have been the only one, after all, who had heard the crying of the loons."

Such endings strike me as reassuring, reconciling. A writer with a disturbing, alienated vision probably would not employ such an ending (and, indeed, individual authors hold a number of endings in their repertory; as I said earlier, it all depends on the desired effect from any particular story). These endings, however, are "safe," and they grow out of essentially recollective experiences; they are mellow, and they are the kinds of endings that self-conscious writers have instinctively subverted.

There are other endings to be discussed: they are violent, or playful; metafictional or accusatory. In some stories, I think of the image of a trap-door—Cheever does this well—in which the last paragraph is so *utterly* at odds with the material that has come before that an entirely new, last-minute interpretation is forced onto the whole story. (Why not? Anything that works is legitimate.) Cheever himself seems particularly fond of the ending to "The Country Husband" (he even mentions it in the foreword to his *Collected Stories*). It goes like this:

> "Here, pussy, here, poor pussy!" But the cat gives her a skeptical look and stumbles away in its skirts. The last to come is Jupiter. He prances through the tomato vines, holding in his generous mouth the remains of an evening slipper. Then it is dark; it is a night where kings in golden suits ride elephants over the mountains.

A rhetorical flourish, then—the opposite of the stoical close of Hemingway and friends. An impulsive reaching out; the tension between the dreamer and the fouled dreamland is always present in Cheever (it has its terse side, too; the ending of "O Youth and Beauty!" reads, "The pistol went off and Louise got him in mid-air. She shot him dead."); Cheever's endings never slide off the page, and if they close with the music welling up, it's a full symphonic number.

I must confess to my own fondness for this kind of close—as though the full possibility of the story did not occur to the author (or to me, since I often use it) until the last minute. In both the stories selected for this anthology, I used variants of this ending, choosing to close the nightmare of a Cincinnati school-day with questions about the promised land, and rounding off the tale of generational conflict, sexual discovery, disillusionment (all that stuff that won't let go of me) with a deliberately skewered vision taken from a different time and place, emphasizing the titanic force of connectedness, on the one occasion it had indisputably happened. (As Hemingway said in a different close, "it was a good thing to have in reserve." And as he said in another one, one that also won't let me go, "Seems like when they get started they don't leave a guy nothing.")

There are other endings: the interrogative, ending with an accusing question that throws the whole story up in the air, but aiming it for the reader's heart. There are Judgemental endings, such as Flannery O'Connor's: "The tide of darkness seemed to sweep him back to her, postponing from moment to moment his entry into the world of guilt and sorrow."

All I would leave a good reader with is the injunction to look at endings as urgent, final communications. They are the cords we have bitten (sometimes only raggedly chewed) in the act of giving birth.

Mavis Gallant

MAVIS GALLANT was born in Montreal, Quebec, in 1922. She
worked for a short time as a journalist in Montreal but in 1950
decided to live and work in Paris, where she has remained ever
since. Her stories are usually first published in the *New Yorker*.

Other Works

The Other Paris, (1956) Stories
Green Water, Green Sky, (1959) Novel
My Heart is Broken, (1964) Stories
A Fairly Good Time, (1970) Novel
The Affair of Gabrielle Russier, (1971) Non-fiction
The Pegnitz Junction, (1973) Stories
The End of the World, (1974) Stories
From the Fifteenth District, (1979) Stories
Home Truths, (1981) Stories

Baum, Gabriel, 1935-(   )

Uncle August

At the start of the nineteen-sixties Gabriel Baum's only surviving relative, his Uncle August, turned up in Paris. There was nothing accidental about this; the International Red Cross, responding to an appeal for search made on Gabriel's behalf many years before, had finally found Gabriel in Montparnasse and his uncle in the Argentine. Gabriel thought of his uncle as "the other Baum," because there were just the two of them. Unlike Gabriel's father and mother, Uncle August had got out of Europe in plenty of time. He owned garages in Rosario and Santa Fe and commercial real estate in Buenos Aires. He was as different from Gabriel as a tree is from the drawing of one; nevertheless Gabriel saw in him something of the old bachelor he too might become.

Gabriel was now twenty-five; he had recently been discharged from the French army after twenty months in Algeria. Notice of his uncle's arrival reached him at the theatre seating two hundred persons where he had a part in a play about J. K. Huysmans. The play explained Huysmans' progress from sullen naturalism to mystical Christianity. Gabriel had to say, "But Joris Karl has written words of penetrating psychology," and four or five other things.

The two Baums dined at the Bristol, where Gabriel's uncle was staying. His uncle ordered for both, because Gabriel was taking too long to decide. Uncle August spoke German and Spanish and the pale scrupulous French and English that used to be heard at spas and in the public rooms of large, airy hotels. His clothes were old-fashioned British; watch and luggage were Swiss. His manners were German, prewar— pre-1914, that is. To Gabriel, his uncle seemed to conceal an obsolete social mystery; but a few Central Europeans, still living, would have placed him easily as a tight, unyielding remainder of the European shipwreck.

The old man observed Gabriel closely, watching to see how his orphaned nephew had been brought up, whether he broke his bread or cut it, with what degree of confidence he approached his asparagus. He was certainly pleased to have discovered a younger Baum and may even have seen Gabriel as part of God's subtle design, bringing a surrogate son to lighten his old age, one to whom he could leave Baum garages; on the other hand it was clear that he did not want just any Baum calling him "Uncle."

"I have a name," he said to Gabriel. "I have a respected name to protect. I owe it to my late father." He meant his own name: August Ernest Baum, b. Potsdam 1899-( ).

After dinner they sat for a long time drinking brandy in the hushed dining room. His uncle was paying for everything.

He said, "But were your parents ever married, finally? Because we were never told he had actually *married* her."

Gabriel at that time seemed to himself enduringly healthy and calm. His hair, which was dark and abundant, fell in locks on a surprisingly serene forehead. He suffered from only two complaints, which he had never mentioned. The first had to do with his breathing, which did not proceed automatically, like other people's. Sometimes, feeling strange and ill, he would realize that heart and lungs were suspended on a stopped, held breath. Nothing disastrous had come of this. His second complaint was that he seemed to be haunted, or inhabited, by a child—a small, invisible version of himself, a Gabriel whose mauled pride he was called on to salve, whose claims against life he was forced to meet with whatever thin means time provided, whose scores he had rashly promised to settle before realizing that debt and payment never interlock. His uncle's amazing question and the remark that followed it awoke the wild child, who began to hammer on Gabriel's heart.

He fixed his attention on a bottle—one of the dark bottles whose labels bear facsimiles of gold medals earned at exhibitions no one has ever heard of, in cities whose names have been swept off the map: Breslau 1884, Dantzig 1897, St. Petersburg 1901.

"The only time I ever saw her, they certainly were not married," his uncle resumed. "It was during the very hot autumn of nineteen-thirty. He had left the university announcing that he would earn his living writing satirical poetry. My father sent me to Berlin to see what was going on. *She* was going on. Her dress had short sleeves. She wore no stockings. She had a clockwork bear she kept winding up and sending round the table. She was hopelessly young. 'Have you thought about the consequences?' I asked him. 'No degree. Low-grade employment all your life. Your father's door forever closed to you. And what about *her?* Is she an heiress? Will her father adopt you?' She was said to be taking singing lessons," he added, as if there were something wrong with that.

"Shut him up," ordered the younger Gabriel, but Gabriel was struggling for breath.

"I have lost everything and everyone but I still have a name," said his uncle. "I have a name to protect and defend. There is always the trace of a marriage certificate somewhere. Even when the registry office was bombed. Even when the papers had to be left behind. How old were you the last time you saw them?"

"Eight," said Gabriel, now in control.

"Were they together?"

"Oh, yes."

"Did they have time to say goodbye?"

"They left me with a neighbour. The neighbour said they'd be back."

"Where was this?"

"Marseilles. We were supposed to be from Alsace, but their French sounded wrong. People noticed I wasn't going to school. Someone reported them."

"Sounded wrong!" said his uncle. "Everything must have sounded wrong from the minute he left the university. It is a terrible story," he said, after a moment. "No worse than most, but terrible all the same. Why, why did he wait until the last minute? And once he had got to Marseilles what prevented him from getting on a boat?"

"He was a man of action," said Gabriel.

If his uncle wanted another Baum, he did not want a frivolous one. He said, "He was much younger than I was. I never saw him after nineteen-thirty. He went his own way. After the war I had the family traced. Everybody was dead—camps, suicide, old age. In his case, no one knew what had happened. He disappeared. Of course, it took place in a foreign country. Only the Germans kept accurate records. I wish you knew something about the marriage. I know that my late father would not have wanted a bastard in the family."

Uncle August visited Nice, Lugano, and Venice, which he found greatly changed, then he returned to South America. He sent long letters to Gabriel several times a year, undeterred by the fact that he seldom received an answer. He urged his nephew to take a strong, positive line with his life and above all to get out of Paris, which had never amounted to more than an émigré way station. Its moral climate invited apathy and rot.

Gabriel read his uncle's letters in La Méduse, a *bar-tabac* close to the old Montparnasse railway station. Actors and extras for television were often recruited there; no one remembered how or why this arrangement had come about. Gabriel usually sat with his back to the window, at a table to the right of the door facing the bar. He drank draught beer or coffee and looked at magazines other customers had left behind. Glancing up from one of his uncle's letters, he saw the misted window in the mirror behind the bar. In a polluted winter fog neon glowed warmly—the lights of home.

His uncle wrote that he had liquidated his holdings at a loss and was thinking of settling in South Africa. He must have changed his mind, for a subsequent letter described him retired and living near a golf course, looked after by the housekeeper he had often told Gabriel about—his first mention of any such person. A heart attack made it tiring for him to write. The housekeeper sent news. Gabriel, who did not know Spanish, tried to get the drift. She signed "Anna Meléndes," then "Anna Baum."

Gabriel was playing a Brecht season in a suburban cultural centre when word came that his uncle had died. *The Caucasian Chalk Circle* and *Mother Courage* alternated for an audience of schoolchildren and factory workers brought in by the busload, apparently against their will. Gabriel thought of Uncle August, his obstinacy and his pride, and truly mourned him. His uncle had left him an envelope he did not bother to open, being fairly certain it did not contain a cheque.

No Baum memorial existed, and so he invented one. Upon its marble surface he inscribed:

> Various Baums: Gone
> Father: 1909-1943 (probably)
> Mother: 1912-1943 (probably)
> Uncle: 1899-1977
> Gabriel B.: 1935-( )

Beneath the last name he drew a line, meaning to say this was the end. He saw, however, that the line, far from ending the Baum question, created a new difficulty: it left the onlooker feeling that these dates and names were factors awaiting a solution. He needed to add the dead to the living, or subtract the living from the dead—to come to some conclusion.

He thought of writing a zero, but the various Baums plus four others did not add up to nothing. His uncle by dying had not diminished the total number of Baums but had somehow increased it. Gabriel, with his feet on the finish line and with uncounted Baums behind him, was a variable quantity: for some years he had been the last of the Baums, then there had been two of them. Now he was unique again.

Someone else would have to work it out, he decided—someone unknown to him, perhaps unborn. In the meantime he had the memorial in his head, where it could not be lost or stolen.

Gabriel's Liselotte

Soon after Gabriel's uncle's visit, a generation of extremely pretty German girls suddenly blossomed in Paris. There would be just that one flowering—that one bright growth. They came because their fathers were dead or exiled under unremarkable names. Some of them were attracted to Gabriel—Gabriel as he was, with the dark locks, the serene brow—and he was drawn in turn, as to a blurred reflection, a face half-recalled.

Gabriel at that time still imagined that everyone's life must be about the same, something like a half-worked crossword puzzle. He was always on the lookout for definitions and new solutions. When he moved close to other people, however, he saw that their lives were not puzzles but problems set in code, no two of which ever matched.

The pretty girls went home, finally, whistled back by solemn young men with solemn jobs. They had two children apiece, were probably rinsing the grey out of their hair now. (Gabriel cut his own as short as possible as it grew scarce.) He remembered Freya, who had thrown herself in the Seine over a married man, but who could swim, and Barbara, whose abortion two or three of them had felt bound to pay for, and Marie, who had gone to Alsace and had nearly been crowned Miss Upper Rhine before they found out she was a foreigner. Gabriel's memory dodging behind one name after the other brought him face-to-face with his Liselotte. Daughter of a dead man and a whore of a mother (which seemed to be a standard biography then), embarked on the au-pair adventure, pursuing spiritual cleanness through culture, she could be seen afternoons in Parc Monceau reading books of verse whose close print and shoddy bindings seemed to assure a cultural warranty. There was something meek about the curve of her neck. She had heard once that if one were arrested and held without trial it was an aid to sanity to have an anthology of poems in one's head. Poor Liselotte, whose aid to sanity never got beyond "Le ciel est, par-dessus le toit, Si bleu, si calme!," held the book flat on her knees, following the words with her finger.

"Who would want to arrest you?" Gabriel asked.

"You never know."

Well, that was true. Thinking there might be a better career for her he gave her lines to try. She practised, "Is it tonight that you DIE?" "Is it TONIGHT that YOU die?" Gabriel counted six, seven, eight shades of green around the place in Parc Monceau, where she sat asking this. He used to take the No. 84 bus to see her—he who never went out of Montparnasse unless he had to, who had never bothered to learn about bus routes or the names of streets. For the sake of Liselotte he crossed the Seine with prim, gloved women, with old men wearing slivers of ribbon to mark this or that war. Liselotte, now seeking improvement by way of love, made him speak French to her. She heard, memorized, and recited back to him without flaw his life's story. He had promised the child-Gabriel he would never marry a German, but it was not that simple; in an odd way she did not seem German *enough*.

She had learned her lines for nothing. The director he introduced her to also thought she did not look German. She was one of the brown-eyed Catholic girls from around Speyer. She prayed for Gabriel, but his life after the prayers was the same as before. She had a catch in her voice, almost a stammer; she tried to ask Gabriel if he wanted to marry her, but the word caught. He said to himself that she might not enjoy being Liselotte Baum after having been Liselotte Pfligge. Her stepfather, Wilhelm Pfligge—of Swiss origin, she said—had tried to rape her; still, she had his name. Gabriel thought that if the custom of name-changing had been reversed and he had been required, through marriage, to become Gabriel Pfligge, he might have done so without cringing, or at least with tact. Perhaps he would have been expected to call Wilhelm Pfligge "Papa." He saw Papa Pfligge with a mustache, strangely mottled ears, sporty shoes, a springy walk, speaking with his lips to Gabriel's ear: "We both love Liselotte so much, eh?"

While Gabriel continued to develop this, giving Papa Pfligge increasingly preposterous things to say, Liselotte gave up on love and culture and the au-pair adventure and went home. He accompanied her to the Gare de l'Est and lifted her two cases to the overhead rack. Then he got down and stood on the grey platform and watched her being borne away. The train was blurred, as if he were looking at it through Liselotte's tears.

For a time her letters were like the trail of a child going ever deeper into the woods. He could not decide whether or not to follow; while he was still deciding, and not deciding, the trail stopped and the path became overgrown behind her.

The Interview

Until he could no longer write letters, Gabriel's uncle nagged him with useless advice. Most of it was about money. Owing to Gabriel's inability to produce his father's marriage certificate (in fact, he never tried), his uncle could not in all conscience leave him Baum possessions. It was up to Gabriel, therefore, to look after his own future. He begged Gabriel to find a job with some large, benevolent international firm. It would give him the assurance of money coming in, would encourage French social-security bureaucrats to take an interest in him, and would put him in the way of receiving an annuity at the age of sixty-five.

"Sixty-five is your next step," his uncle warned, for Gabriel's thirtieth birthday.

He counselled Gabriel to lay claim to those revenues known as "German money," but Gabriel's parents had vanished without trace; there was no way of proving they had not taken ship for Tahiti. And it would not have been in Gabriel's power to equate banknotes to a child's despair. His uncle fell back on the Algerian war. Surely Gabriel was entitled to a pension? No, he was not. War had never been declared. What Gabriel had engaged in was a long tactical exercise for which there was no compensation except experience.

The Algerian-pension affair rankled with Gabriel. He had to fill out employment forms that demanded assurance that he had "fulfilled his military obligations." Sometimes it was taken for granted he had been rejected out of hand. There was no rational basis for this; he supposed it must be because of "Profession: Actor." After his return he continued to take an interest in the war. He was like someone who has played twenty minutes of a match and has to know the outcome. As far as he could make out, it had ended in a draw. The excitement died down, and then no one knew what to put in the magazines and political weeklies any more. Some journalists tried to interest Gabriel in Brittany, where there was an artichoke glut; others hinted that the new ecumenicity beginning to seep out of Rome was really an attack on French institutions. Gabriel doubted this. Looking for news about his pension, he learned about the Western European consumer society and the moral wounds that were being inflicted on France through full employment. Between jobs, he read articles about people who said they had been made unhappy by paper napkins and washing machines.

Most of the customers in La Méduse were waiting for a television call. The rest were refugees, poets' widows, and foreign students looking for work to supplement their scholarships. Up at the bar, where drinks were cheaper, were clustered the second-generation émigré actors Gabriel thought of as bachelor orphans. Unlike Gabriel, they had been everywhere—to Brazil, where they could not understand the language, and to New York, where they complained about the climate, and to Israel, where they were disappointed with the food. Now they were in Paris, where they disliked the police.

Sometimes Dieter Pohl shared Gabriel's table. He was a Bavarian Gabriel's age—thirty—who played in films about the Occupation. Dieter had begun as a private, had been promoted to lieutenant, and expected to become a captain soon. He had two good facial expressions, one for victory and one for defeat. Advancing, he gazed keenly upwards, as if following a hawk to the vanishing point. Sometimes he pressed binoculars to his eyes. Defeat found him staring at his boots. He could also be glimpsed marching off into captivity with a bandage around his head. The captivity scene took place in the last episode. Gabriel, enrolled as a victim, had generally been disposed of in the first. His rapid disappearance was supposed to establish the tone of the period for audiences too young to recall it.

It was around this time, when French editorial alarm about the morally destructive aspect of Western prosperity was at its most feverish, that a man calling himself Briseglace wandered into the bar and began asking all the aliens and strangers there if they were glad to be poor. He said that he was a journalist, that his wife had left him for a psychiatrist, and that his girlfriend took tickets in a cinema farther along the street. He said that the Montparnasse railway station was to be torn down and a dark tower built in its place; no one believed him. He wore a tie made of some yellow Oriental stuff. His clothes looked as if they had been stitched by nuns on a convent sewing machine. Gabriel and his generation had gone into black—black pullovers, black leather jackets, soft black boots. Their haircuts still spoke of military service and colonial wars. Briseglace's straggling, greyish locks, his shapeless and shabby and oddly feminine-looking overcoat, his stained fingers and cheap cigarettes, his pessimism and his boldness and his belief in the moral advantages of penury all came straight from the Latin Quarter of the nineteen-forties. He was the Occupation; he was the Liberation, too. The films that Dieter and Gabriel played in grew like common weeds from the heart of whatever young man he once had been. Gabriel's only feeling, seeing him, was disgust at what it meant to grow old.

The dark garments worn in La Méduse gave the place the appearance of a camp full of armed militia into which Briseglace, outdated civilian, had stumbled without cause. Actually, the leather jackets covered only perpetual worry. Some people thought Briseglace was with the CIA, others saw a KGB agent with terrifying credentials. The orphans were certain he was an inspector sent to see if their residence permits were forgeries. But his questions led only to one tame conclusion, which he begged them to ratify: it was that being poor they were free, and being free they were happy.

Released from immediate danger, a few of the aliens sat and stood straighter, looked nonchalant or offended, depending on how profound their first terrors had been. Dieter declared himself happy in a profession that had brought him moral satisfaction and material comfort, and that provided the general public with notions of history. Some of those at the bar identified themselves as tourists, briefly in Paris, staying at comfortable hotels. Someone mentioned the high prices that had to be paid for soccer stars. Another recalled that on the subject of personal riches Christ had been ambiguous yet reassuring. Briseglace wrote everything down. When he paid for his coffee he asked for the cheque, which he had to turn in for expenses. Gabriel, who had decided to have nothing to do with him, turned the pages of *Paris-Match*.

Six weeks later Gabriel emerged in the pages of a left-wing weekly as "Gabriel B., spokesman for the flotsam of Western Europe."

"His first language was German," Gabriel read. "Lacking the rudder of political motivation, his aimless wanderings have cast him up in Montparnasse, in the sad fragrance of coffee machines. Do you think he eats in the Jewish quarter, at Jo Goldenberg's, at La Rose d'Or? Never. You will find Gabriel B. gnawing veal cutlets at the Wienerwald, devouring potato dumplings at the Tannhaüser. For Gabriel B. this bizarre nourishment constitutes a primal memory, from infancy to age twelve." "Seven," Gabriel scrupulously corrected, but it was too late, the thing was in print. "This handsome Prince of Bohemia has reached the fatal age of thirty. What can he do? Where can he go? Conscience-money from the wealthy German republic keeps him in cigarettes. A holdover from bad times, he slips through the good times without seeing them. The Western European consumer society is not so much an economic condition as a state of mind."

Gabriel read the part about the Prince of Bohemia two or three times. He wondered where the Wienerwald was. In the picture accompanying the article was Dieter Pohl, with his eyes inked over so that he could not be identified and use the identification as an excuse for suing the magazine.

There was no explaining it; Dieter was sure he had not sat for a portrait; Gabriel was positive he had not opened his mouth. He thought of posting the article to Uncle August, but his uncle would take it to be a piece of downright nonsense, like the clockwork bear. Dieter bought half a dozen copies of the magazine for his relatives in Bavaria; it was the first time that a picture of him had ever been published anywhere.

Gabriel's escape from annihilation in two real wars (even though one had been called something else) had left him with reverence for unknown forces. Perhaps Briseglace had been sent to nudge him in some new direction. Perhaps the man would turn up again, confessing he had never been a journalist and had been feigning not in order to harm Gabriel but to ensure his ultimate safety.

Nothing of the kind ever happened, of course. Briseglace was never seen again in La Méduse. The only reaction to the interview came from a cousin of Dieter's called Helga. She did not read French easily and had understood some of it to mean that Dieter was not eating enough. She sent him a quantity of very good gingerbread in a tin box and begged him, not for the first time, to pack his things and come home and let a woman look after his life.

Unsettling Rumours

As he grew older and balder, stouter, and more reflective, Gabriel found himself at odds with the few bachelors he still saw in Montparnasse. They tended to cast back to the nineteen-sixties as the springtime of life, though none of them had been all that young. Probably because they had outlived their parents and were without children, they had no way of measuring time. To Gabriel the decade now seemed to have been like a south wind making everyone fretful and jumpy. The colder their prospects, the steadier his friends had become. They slept well, cashed their unemployment cheques without grumbling, strolled along the boulevards through a surf of fallen leaves, and discarded calls to revolution, stood in peaceful queues in front of those cinemas that still charged no more than eleven francs. Inside, the seats and carpets were mouldering slowly. Half the line shuffling up to the ticket office was probably out of work. His friends preferred films in which women presented no obstacles and created no problems and were shown either naked or in evening dress.

Much of Gabriel's waking time was now spent like this, too—not idly, but immersed in the present moment.

Soon after the Yom Kippur War, a notice had been posted in La Méduse: "Owing to the economic situation no one may sit for more than thirty minutes over a single order." The management had no legal means of enforcing this; still the notice hung there, a symptom of a new harshness, the sourness engendered by the decline.

"That sign was the end of life as we knew it in the sixties," said Dieter Pohl. He was a colonel now, and as fussy as a monarch at a review about a badge misplaced or a button undone. Gabriel had no equivalent staircase to climb; who ever has heard of a victim's being promoted? Still, he had acquired a variety of victim experiences. Gabriel had been shot, stoned, drowned, suffocated, and marked off for hanging; had been insulted and betrayed; had been shoved aboard trains and dragged out of them; had been flung from the back of a truck with such accidental violence that he had broken his collarbone. His demise, seen by millions of people, some eating their dinner, was still needed in order to give a push to the old dishonourable plot—told ever more simply now, like a fable—while Dieter's fate was still part of its moral.

On this repeated game of death and consequences Dieter's seniority depended. He told Gabriel that the French would be bored with entertainment based on the Occupation by about 1982; by that time he would have been made a general at least once, and would have saved up enough money to buy a business of some kind in his native town.

He often spoke as if the parting were imminent, though he was still only a colonel: "Our biographies are not the same, and you are a real actor, who took lessons, and a real soldier, who fought in a real war. But look at the result—we ended up in the same place, doing the same work, sitting at the same table. Years and years without a disagreement. It is a male situation. Women would never be capable of such a thing."

Gabriel supposed Dieter to mean that women, inclined by nature to quick offence and unending grudges, were not gifted for loyal friendship. Perhaps it was true, but it seemed incomplete. Even the most solitary of the women he could observe—the poets' widows, for instance, with their crocheted berets, their mysterious shopping bags, their fat, waddling dogs—did not cluster together like anxious pigeons on the pretext of friendship. Each one came in alone and sat by herself, reading whatever fascinating stuff she could root out of the shopping bag, staring at strangers with ever-fresh interest, sometimes making comments about them aloud.

A woman can always get some practical use from a torn-up life, Gabriel decided. She likes mending and patching it, making sure the edges are straight. She spreads the last shred out and takes its measure: "What can I do with this remnant? How long does it need to last?" A man puts on his life ready-made. If it doesn't fit, he will try to exchange it for another. Only a fool of a man will try to adjust the sleeves or move the buttons; he doesn't know how.

Some of the older customers were now prey to unsettling rumours. La Méduse was said to have been sold by its owner, a dour Breton with very small eyes. It would soon be converted to a dry-cleaner's establishment, as part of the smartening-up of Montparnasse. The chairs, the glasses, the thick, greyish cups and saucers, the zinc-covered bar, the neon tubes on the ceiling—sociological artifacts—had been purchased at roaring prices for a museum in Stockholm. It seemed farfetched to

Gabriel but not impossible; the Montparnasse station had been torn down, and a dark ugly tower had been put in its place. He remembered how Briseglace had predicted this.

Gabriel had noticed lately that he was not seeing Paris as it was but the way it had stayed in his mind; he still saw butchers and grocers and pastry shops, when in reality they had become garages and banks. There was a new smell in the air now, metallic and hot. He was changing too. Hunger was drawn to his attention by a feeling of sadness and loss. He breathed without effort. The child-Gabriel had grown still. Occupation films had fallen off a little, but Gabriel had more resources than Dieter. He wore a checked cap and sang the "Internationale"; he was one of a committee bringing bad news to Seneca. He had a summer season playing Flavius in *Julius Caesar,* and another playing Aston in *The Caretaker* and the zoo director in *The Bedbug.* These festivals were staged in working-class suburbs the inhabitants of which had left for the Côte d'Azur. During one of those summers La Méduse changed hands, shut for three months, and opened with rows of booths, automobile seats made of imitation leather, orange glass lampshades, and British First World War recruiting posters plastered on the walls. The notice about not sitting for more than thirty minutes had vanished, replaced by an announcement that ice cream and hamburgers could be obtained. Washrooms and telephones were one flight up instead of in the basement; there was someone on hand to receive tips and take messages. At each table was a bill of fare four pages long and a postcard advertising the café, which customers could send to their friends if they wanted to. The card showed a Medusa jellyfish with long eyelashes and a ribbon on its head, smiling out of a tiny screen. Beneath this one could read:

PUB LA MÉDUSE
THE OLDEST AND MOST CELEBRATED
MEETING-PLACE FOR TELEVISION
STARS IN PARIS

Gabriel tried a number of booths before finding one that suited him. Between the automobile seat and a radiator was a space where he could keep magazines. The draught beer was of somewhat lower quality than before. The main difference between the old place and the new one was its smell. For a time he could not identify it. It turned out to be the reek of a chicory drink, the colour of boot polish, invented to fight inflation. The addition of sugar made it nauseating, and it was twice as expensive as coffee had ever been.

The Surrender

Dieter heard that a thirteen-hour television project about the Occupation was to be launched in the spring; he had seen the outline.

He said, "For the moment they just need a few people to be deported and to jump off the train."

Some old-timers heard Dieter say, "They want to deport the Poles," and some heard, "They are rounding up the foreign-born Socialists," and others swore he had asked for twelve Jews to be run over by a locomotive.

Dieter wore a new civilian winter costume, a light-brown fur-lined winter coat and a Russian cap. He ate roasted chestnuts, which he peeled with his fingernails. They were in a cornucopia made of half a page of *Le Quotidien de Paris*. In the old Méduse eating out of newspaper would have meant instant expulsion. Dieter spread the paper on Gabriel's table, sat down, and told him about the film. It would begin with a group of Resistance fighters who were being deported jumping out of a train. Their group would include a coal miner, an anti-Semitic aristocrat, a Communist militant, a peasant with a droll Provençal accent, a long-faced Protestant intellectual, and a priest in doubt about his vocation. Three Jews will be discovered to have jumped or fallen with them: one aged rabbi, one black-market operator, and one anything.

The one anything will be me, Gabriel decided, helping himself to chestnuts. He saw, without Dieter's needing to describe them, the glaring lights, the dogs straining at their leads, the guards running and blowing whistles, the stalled train, a rainstorm, perhaps.

The aristo will be against taking the extra three men along, Dieter said, but the priest will intercede for them. The miner, or perhaps the black-market man, will stay behind to act as decoy for the dogs while the others all get in a rowboat and make for the maquis. The peasant will turn out to be a British intelligence agent named Scott. The Protestant will fall out of the rowboat; the priest will drown trying to save him; the Communist . . .

"We know all that," Gabriel interrupted. "Who's there at the end?"

The aristo, said Dieter. The aristo and the aged rabbi will survive twelve episodes and make their way together back to Paris for the Liberation. There they will discover Dieter and his men holed up in the Palais du Luxembourg, standing fast against the local Resistance and a few policemen. The rabbi will die next to the Medici fountain, in the arms of the aristo.

Gabriel thought this did not bode well for the future, but Dieter reassured him: the aristo will now be a changed man. He will storm the Palais and be seen at the end writing "MY FRIENDS REMEMBERED" on the wall while Dieter and the others file by with their hands up.

"What about the one anything?" said Gabriel. "How long does he last?"

"Dear friend and old comrade," said Dieter, "don't take offence at this. Ten years ago you would have been the first man chosen. But now you are at the wrong age. Who cares what happens to a man of forty-three? You aren't old enough or young enough to make anyone cry. The fact is—forgive me for saying so—but you are the wrong age to play a Jew. A uniform has no age," he added, because he was also forty-three. "And no one is expected to cry at the end, but just to be thoughtful and satisfied."

While Gabriel sat mulling this over, Dieter told him about the helmets the Germans were going to wear. Some were heavy metal, museum pieces; they gave their wearers headaches and left red marks on the brow. A certain number of light plastic helmets would be distributed, but only to officers. The higher one's rank, the lighter the helmet. What Dieter was getting around to was this: he wondered if Gabriel might not care to bridge this stage of his Occupation career by becoming a surrendering officer, seen in the last episode instead of vanishing after the first. He would be a colonel in the Wehrmacht (humane, idealistic, opposed to extreme measures) while Dieter would have to be the S.S. one (not so good). He and Dieter would both have weightless helmets and comfortable, well-cut uniforms.

Gabriel supposed that Dieter was right, in a way. Certainly, he was at a bad age for dangerous antics. It was time for younger men to take their turn at jumping off moving vehicles, diving into ice-cold streams, and dodging blank shot; nor had he reached that time of life when he could die blessing and inspiring those the script had chosen to survive him. As an officer, doomed to defeat, he would at least be sure of his rank and his role and of being in one piece at the end.

Two weeks later Dieter announced to the old-timers that the whole first scene had been changed; there would now be a mass escape from a convoy of lorries, with dozens of men gunned down on the spot. The original cast was reduced, with the Protestant, the Communist, and the miner eliminated completely. This new position caused some argument and recrimination, in which Gabriel did not take part. All he had to wait for now was the right helmet and good weather.

The usual working delays occurred, so that it was not until May that the last of the Baums tried on his new uniform. Dieter adjusted the shoulders of the tunic and set the plastic helmet at a jaunty angle. Gabriel looked at himself. He removed the helmet and put it back on straight. Dieter spoke encouragingly; he seemed to think that Gabriel was troubled about seeming too stout, too bald, too old for his rank.

"There is nothing like a uniform for revealing a man's real age to him," said Dieter. "But from a distance everyone in uniform looks the same."

Gabriel in his new uniform seemed not just to be looking at himself in a glass but actually to be walking through it. He moved through a liquid mirror, back and forth. With each crossing his breath came a little shorter.

Dieter said generously, "A lot of soldiers went bald prematurely because the helmets rubbed their hair."

The surrender was again delayed, this time on account of bad weather. One sodden afternoon, after hanging about in the Luxembourg Gardens for hours, Dieter and Gabriel borrowed capes from a couple of actors who were playing policemen and, their uniforms concealed, went to a post office so that Dieter could make a phone call. His cousin, Helga, destined by both their families to be his bride, had waited a long time; just when it was beginning to look as if she had waited too long for anything, a widower proposed. She was being married the next day. Dieter had to call and explain why he could not be at the wedding; he was held up waiting for the surrender.

Helga talked to Dieter without drawing breath. He listened for a while then handed the receiver to Gabriel. Helga continued telling Dieter, or Gabriel, that her husband-to-be had a grandchild who could play the accordion. The child was to perform at the wedding party. The accordion was almost as large as the little girl, and twice as heavy.

"You ought to see her fingers on the keyboard," Helga yelled. "They fly—fast, fast."

Gabriel gave the telephone to Dieter, who assumed a look of blank concentration. When he had heard enough he beckoned to Gabriel. Gabriel pressed the receiver to his ear and learned that Helga was worried. She had dreamed that she was married and that her husband would not make room for her in his apartment. When she wanted to try the washing machine, he was already washing his own clothes. "What do you think of the dream?" she said to Gabriel. "Can you hear me? I still love you." Gabriel placed the receiver softly on a shelf under the telephone and waved Dieter in so that he could say goodbye.

They came out of the post office to a drenching rain. Dieter wondered what shape their uniforms would be in by the time they surrendered. Gabriel argued that after the siege of the Palais du Luxembourg the original uniforms must have shown wear. Dieter answered that it was not up to him or Gabriel to decide such things.

Rain fell for another fortnight, but, at last, on a cool shining June day, they were able to surrender. During one of the long periods of inextricable confusion, Dieter and Gabriel walked as far as the Delacroix monument and sat on its rim. Dieter was disappointed in his men. There were no real Germans among them, but Yugoslavs, Turks, North Africans, Portuguese, and some unemployed French. The Resistance forces were not much better, he said. There had been complaints. Gabriel had to agree that they were a bedraggled-looking lot. Dieter recalled how in the sixties there used to be real Frenchmen, real Germans, authentic Jews. The Jews had played deportation the way they had seen it in films, and the Germans had surrendered according to film tradition, too, but there had been this difference: they had at least been doing something their parents had done before them. They had not only the folklore of movies to guide them but—in many cases—first-hand accounts. Now, even if one could assemble a true cast of players, they would be trying to imitate their grandfathers. They were at one remove too many. There was no assurance that a real German, a real Frenchman would be any more plausible now than a Turk.

Dieter sighed, and glanced up at the houses on the other side of the street edging the park. "It wouldn't be bad to live up there," he said. "At the top, with one of those long terraces. They grow real trees on them—poplars, birches."

"What would it cost?"

"Around a hundred and fifty million francs," said Dieter. "Without the furniture."

"Anyone can have a place like that with money," said Gabriel. "The interesting thing would be to live up there without it."

"How?"

Gabriel took off his helmet and looked deeply inside it. He said, "I don't know."

Dieter showed him the snapshots of his cousin's wedding. Helga and the groom wore rimless spectacles. In one picture they cut a cake together; in another they tried to drink out of the same champagne glass. Eyeglasses very like theirs, reduced in size, were worn by a plain little girl. On her head was a wreath of daisies. She was dressed in a long, stiff yellow gown. Gabriel could see just the hem of the dress and the small shoes, and her bashful anxious face and slightly crossed eyes. Her wrists were encircled by daisies, too. Most of her person was behind an accordion. The accordion seemed to be falling apart; she had all she could do to keep it together.

"My cousin's husband's granddaughter," said Dieter. He read Helga's letter: " 'She can play anything—fast, fast. Her fingers simply fly over the keyboard.' "

Gabriel examined every detail of the picture. The child was dazzled and alarmed, and the accordion was far too heavy. "What is her name?" he said.

Dieter read more of the letter and said, "Erna."

"Erna," Colonel Baum repeated. He looked again at the button of a face, the flower bracelets, the feet with the heels together—they must have told her to stand that way. He gave the snapshot back without saying anything.

A crowd had collected in the meantime, drawn by the lights and the equipment and the sight of the soldiers in German uniform. Some asked if they might be photographed with them; this often happened when a film of that kind was made in the streets.

An elderly couple edged up to the two officers. The woman said, in German, in a low voice, "What are you doing here?"

"Waiting to surrender," said Dieter.

"I can see that, but what are you *doing?*"

"I don't know," said Dieter. "I've been sitting on the edge of this monument for thirty-five years. I'm still waiting for orders."

The man tried to give them cigarettes, but neither colonel smoked. The couple took pictures of each other standing between Dieter and Gabriel, and went away.

Why is it, said Gabriel to himself, that when I was playing a wretched, desperate victim no one ever asked to have his picture taken with me? The question troubled him, seeming to proceed from the younger Gabriel, who had been absent for some time now. He hoped his unruly tenant was not on his way back, screaming for a child's version of justice, for an impossible world.

Some of the men put their helmets upside-down on the ground and tried to make the visitors pay for taking their pictures. Dieter was disturbed by this. "Of course, you were a real soldier," he said to Gabriel unhappily. "All this must seem inferior." They sat without saying anything for a time and then Dieter began to talk about ecology. Because of ecology, there was a demand in Bavaria for fresh bread made of authentic flour, salt, water, and yeast. Because of unemployment, there were people willing to return to the old, forgotten trades, at which one earned practically nothing and had to work all night. The fact was that he had finally saved up enough money and had bought a bakery in his native town. He was through with the war, the Occupation, the Liberation, and captivity. He was going home.

This caused the most extraordinary view in Gabriel's view of the park. All the greens in it became one dull colour, as if thunderous clouds had gathered low in the sky.

"You will always be welcome," said Dieter. "Your room will be ready, a bed made up, flowers in a vase. I intend to marry someone in the village—someone young."

Gabriel said, "If you have four or five children, how can you keep a spare room?"

Still, it was an attractive thought. The greens emerged again, fresh and bright. He saw the room that could be his. Imagine being wakened in a clean room by birds singing and the smell of freshly baked bread. Flowers in a vase—Gabriel hardly knew one from the other, only the caged flowers of parks. He saw, in a linen press, sheets strewn with lavender. His clothes hung up or folded. His breakfast on a white tablecloth, under a lime tree. A basket of warm bread, another of boiled eggs. Dieter's wife putting her hand on the white coffee pot to see if it was still hot enough for Gabriel. A jug of milk, another of cream. Dieter's obedient children drinking from mugs, their chins on the rim of the table. Yes, and the younger Gabriel, revived and outraged and jealous, thrashing around in his heart, saying, "Think about empty rooms, letters left behind, cold railway stations washed down with disinfectant, dark glaciers of time." And, then, Gabriel knew nothing about the country. He could not see himself actually *in* it. He had never been to the country except to jump out of trains. It was only in films that he had seen mist lifting or paths lost in ferns.

They surrendered all the rest of the afternoon. The aristo wrote "MY FRIENDS REMEMBERED" on the wall while Dieter and Gabriel led some Turks and Yugoslavs and some unemployed Frenchmen into captivity. The aristo did not even bother to turn around and look. Gabriel was breathing at a good rhythm—not too shallow, not too fast. An infinity of surrenders had preceded this one, in colour and in black-and-white, with music and without. A long trail of application forms and employment questionnaires had led Gabriel here: "Baum, Gabriel, b. 1935, Germany, nat. French, mil. serv. obl. fulf." (Actually, for some years now his date of birth had rendered the assurance about military service unnecessary.) Country words ran meanwhile in Gabriel's head. He thought, Dense thickets, lizards and snakes, a thrush's egg, a bee, lichen, wild berries, dark thorny leaves, pale mushrooms. Each word carried its own fragrance.

At the end of the day Dieter's face was white and tired and perfectly blank. He might have been listening to Helga. The aristo came over, smoking a cigarette. About twenty-three years before this, he and Gabriel had performed before a jury in a one-act play of Jules Renard's. The aristo had received an honourable mention, Gabriel a first. The aristo hadn't recognized Gabriel until now because of the uniform. He said, "What's the matter with him?"

Dieter sat slumped in an iron chair belonging to the park administration, staring at his boots. He jerked his head up and looked around, crying, "Why? Where?" and something else Gabriel didn't catch.

Gabriel hoped Dieter was not going to snap now, with the bakery and the flowers and the children in sight. "Well, well, old friend!" said

Dieter, clutching Gabriel and trying to get to his feet. "Save your strength! Don't take things to heart! You'll dance at my wedding!"

"Exhaustion," said the aristo.

Gabriel and Dieter slowly made their way to the street, where Volkswagen buses full of actors were waiting. The actors made signs meaning to tell them to hurry up; they were all tired and impatient and anxious to change into their own clothes and get home. Dieter leaned on his old friend. Every few steps he stopped to talk excitedly, as people put to a great strain will do, all in a rush, like the long babbling of dreams.

"You'll have to walk faster," said Gabriel, beginning to feel irritated. "The buses won't wait forever, and we can be arrested for wearing these uniforms without a reason."

"There's a very good reason," said Dieter, but he seemed all at once to recover.

That night at La Méduse Dieter drew the plan of the bakery and the large apartment above it, with an X marking Gabriel's room. He said that Gabriel would spend his summers and holidays there, and would teach Dieter's children to pronounce French correctly. The light shining out of the orange glass lampshade made the drawing seem attractive and warm. It turned out that Dieter hadn't actually bought the bakery but had made a down payment and was negotiating for a bank loan.

The proprietor of La Méduse now came over to their table, accompanied by a young couple—younger than Dieter and Gabriel, that is—to whom he had just sold the place. He introduced them, saying, "My oldest customers. You know their faces, of course. Television."

The new owners shook hands with Gabriel and Dieter, assuring them that they did not intend to tamper with the atmosphere of the old place; not for anything in the world would they touch the recruiting posters or the automobile seats.

After they had gone Dieter seemed to lose interest in his drawing; he folded it in half, then in half again, and finally put his glass down on it. "They are a pair of crooks, you know," he said. "They had to get out of Bastia because they had swindled so many people they were afraid of being murdered. Apparently they're going to turn La Méduse into a front for the Corsican Mafia." Having said this, Dieter gave a great sigh and fell silent. Seeing that he had given up talking about the bakery and Gabriel's room, Gabriel drew a magazine out from behind the radiator and began to read. Dieter let him go on reading for quite a while before he sighed again. Gabriel did not look up. Dieter unfolded the drawing and smoothed it flat. He examined it, made a change or two with a pencil, and said something indistinct.

Gabriel said, "What?" without raising his head. Dieter answered, "My father lived to be ninety."

His Mother

His mother had come of age in a war and then seemed to live a long greyness like a spun-out November. "Are you all right?" she used to ask him at breakfast. What she really meant was: Ask me how I am, but she was his mother and so he would not. He leaned two fists against his temples and read a book about photography, waiting for her to cut bread and put it on a plate for him. He seldom looked up, never truly saw her—a stately, careless widow with unbrushed red hair, wearing an old fur coat over her nightgown; her last dressing gown had been worn to ribbons and she said she had no money for another. It seemed that nothing could stop her from telling him how she felt or from pestering him with questions. She muttered and smoked and drank such a lot of strong coffee that it made her bilious, and then she would moan, "God, God, my liver! My poor head!" In those days in Budapest you had to know the black market to find the sort of coffee she drank, and of course she would not have any but the finest smuggled Virginia cigarettes. "Quality," she said to him—or to his profile, rather. "Remember after I have died that quality was important to me. I held out for the best."

She had known what it was to take excellence for granted. That was the difference between them. Out of her youth she could not recall a door slammed or a voice raised except in laughter. People had floated like golden dust; whole streets of people buoyed up by optimism, a feeling for life.

He sat reading, waiting for her to serve him. He was a stone out of a stony generation. Talking to him was like lifting a stone out of water. He never resisted, but if you let go for even a second he sank and came to rest on a dark sea floor. More than one of her soft-tempered lovers had tried to make a friend of him, but they had always given up, as they did with everything. How could she give up? She loved him. She felt shamed because it had not been in her to control armies, history, his stony watery world. From the moment he appeared in the kitchen doorway, passive, vacant, starting to live again only because this was morning, she began all over: "Don't you feel well?" "Are you all right?" "Why can't you smile?"—though the loudest sentence was in silence: Ask me how I am.

After he left Budapest (got his first passport, flew to Glasgow with a soccer team, never came back) she became another sort of person, an émigré's mother. She shed the last of her unimportant lovers and with the money her son was soon able to send she bought a white blouse, combs that would pin her hair away from her face, and a blue kimono. She remembered long, tender conversations they had had together, and she got up early in the morning to see if a letter had come from him and then to write one of her own describing everything she thought and did. His letters to his mother said, Tell me about your headaches, are you still drinking too strong coffee, tell me the weather, the names of streets, if you still bake poppy-seed cakes.

She had never been any sort of a cook, but it seemed to her that, yes, she had baked for him, perhaps in the early years together, which she looked back upon as golden, and lighter than thistledown.

On Saturday afternoons she put on a hat and soft grey gloves and went to the Vörösmarty Café. It had once had a French name, Gerbeaud, and the circle of émigrés' mothers who met to exchange news and pictures of grandchildren still called it that. "Gerbeaud" was a sign of caste and the mark of a generation, too. Like herself, the women wore hats and sometimes scarves of fur, and each carried a stuffed handbag she would not have left behind on a tabletop for even a second. Their sons' letters looked overstamped, like those he sent her now. She had not been so certain of her rank before, or felt so quietly sure, so well thought of. A social order prevailed, as it does everywhere. The aristocrats were those whose children had never left Europe; the poorest of the poor were not likely ever to see their sons again, for they had gone to Chile and South Africa. Switzerland was superior to California. A city earned more points than a town. There was no mistaking her precedence here; she was a grand duchess. If Glasgow was unfamiliar, the very sound of it somehow rang with merit. She always had a new letter to show, which was another symbol of one's station, and they were warm messages, concerned about her health, praising her remembered skill with pies and cakes. Some mothers were condemned to a lowly status only because their children forgot to write. Others had to be satisfied with notes from foreign daughters-in-law, which were often sent from table to table before an adequate reading could be obtained. Here again she was in demand, for she read three foreign languages, which suggested a background of governesses and careful schools. She might have left it at that, but her trump credentials were in plain sight. These were the gifts he bestowed—the scarves and pastel sweaters, the earrings and gloves.

What she could not do was bring the émigré ritual to its final celebration; it required a passport, a plane ticket, and a visit to the absent son. She would never deliver into his hands the three immutable presents, which were family jewellery, family photographs, and a cake. Any mother travelling to within even a few miles of another woman's son was commissioned to take all three. The cake was a bother to carry, for the traveller usually had one of her own, but who could say no? They all knew the cake's true value. Look at the way her own son claimed his share of nourishment from a mother whose cooking had always been a joke.

No one had ever been close to Scotland, and if she had not applied for her own passport or looked up flight schedules it was for a good reason: her son had never suggested she come. And yet, denied even the bliss of sewing a garnet clip into a brassière to be smuggled to an unknown daughter-in-law, she still knew she was blessed. Other women were dismissed, forgotten. More than one had confided, "My son might as well be dead." She did not think of him as dead—how could she?—but as a coin that had dropped unheard, had rolled crazily, lay still. She knew the name of his car, of his street, she had seen pictures of them, but what did she know?

After he disappeared, as soon as she had made certain he was safe and alive, she rented his room to a student, who stayed with her for three years in conditions of some discomfort, for she had refused, at first, to remove anything belonging to her son. His books were sacred. His records were not to be played. The records had been quite valuable at one time; they were early American rock slipped in by way of Vienna and sold at a murderous rate of exchange. These collected dust now, like his albums of pictures—like the tenant student's things too, for although she pinned her hair up with combs and wore a spotless blouse, she was still no better a housekeeper. Her tenant studied forestry. He was a bumpkin, and somewhat afraid of her. She could never have mistaken him for a son. He crept in and out and brought her flowers. One day she played a record for him, to which he listened with deference rather than interest, and she remembered herself, at eighteen, hearing with the same anxious boredom a warped scene from "Die Walküre," both singers now long dead. Having a student in the flat did not make her feel she was in touch with her son, or even with his generation. His room changed meanwhile; even its smell was no longer the same. She began to wonder what his voice had been like. She could see him, she dreamed of him often, but her dreams and memories were like films with the sound track removed.

The bumpkin departed, and she took in his place a future art historian—the regime produced these in awesome numbers now—who gave way, in turn, to the neurasthenic widow of a poet. The poet's widow was taken over in time by her children, and replaced by a couple of young librarians. And then came two persons not quite chosen by herself. She could have refused them, but thought it wiser not to. They were an old man and his pregnant granddaughter. They seemed to be brokenly poor; the granddaughter almost to the end of her term worked long hours in a plasma laboratory. And yet they appeared endowed with dark, important connections: no sooner were they installed than she was granted a telephone, which her tenants never used without asking, and only for laconic messages—the grandfather to state that his granddaughter was not yet at home, or the girl to take down the day and hour of a meeting somewhere. After the granddaughter had her baby they became four in a flat that had barely been comfortable for two. She cleared out the last of her son's records and his remaining books (the rest had long ago been sold or stolen), and she tried to establish a set of rules. For one, she made it a point to remain in the kitchen when her tenants took their meals. This was her home; it was not strictly a shared and still less a communal Russian apartment. But she could go only so far: it was at Gerbeaud's that she ranked as a grand duchess. These people reckoned differently, and on their terms she was, if not at the foot of the ladder, then dangerously to one side of it; she had an émigré son, she received gifts and money from abroad, and she led in terms of the common good a parasitic existence. They were careful, even polite, but they were installed. She was inhabited by them, as by an illness one must learn to endure.

It was around this time—when her careless, undusted, but somehow pure rooms became a slum, festooned with washing, reeking of boiling milk, where she was seldom alone or quiet—that she began to drift away from an idea she had held about her age and time. Where, exactly, was the youth she recalled as happy? What had been its shape, its colour? All that golden dust had not belonged to her—it had been part of her mother. It was her mother who had floated like thistledown, smiled, lived with three servants on call, stood with a false charming gaucherie, an arm behind her, an elbow grasped. That simulated awkwardness took suppleness and training; it required something her generation had not been granted, which was time. Her mother had let her coat fall on the floor because coats were replaceable then, not only because there had been someone to pick it up. She had carried a little curling iron in her handbag. When she quarrelled with her husband, she went to the station and climbed into a train marked "Budapest-Vienna-Rome," and her husband had thought it no more than amusing to have to fetch her back. Slowly, as "eighteen" came to mean an age much younger than her son's, as he grew older in Scotland, married, had a child, began slipping English words into his letters, went on about fictitious apple or poppy-seed cakes, she parted without pain from a soft, troubled memory, from an old grey film about porters wheeling steamer trunks, white fur wraps, bunches of violets, champagne. It was gone: it had never been. She and her son were both mistaken, and yet they had never been closer. Now that she had the telephone, he called her on Easter Sunday, and on Christmas Eve, and on her birthday. His wife had spoken to her in English:

"It's snowing here. Is it snowing in Budapest?"

"It quite often snows."

"I hope we can meet soon."

"That would be pleasant."

His wife's parents sent her Christmas greetings with stern biblical messages, as if they judged her, by way of her son, to be frivolous, without a proper God. At least they knew now that she spoke correct English; on the other hand, perhaps they were simple souls unable to imagine that anything but English could ever be.

They were not out of touch; nor did he neglect her. No one could say that he had. He had never missed a monthly transfer of money, he was faithful about sending his overstamped letters and the coloured snapshots of his wife, his child, their Christmas tree, and his wife's parents side by side upon a modern-looking sofa. One unposed picture had him up a ladder pasting sheets of plastic tiles on a kitchen wall. She could not understand the meaning of this photograph, in which he wore jeans and a sweater that might have been knitted by an untalented child. His hair had grown long, it straggled in brown mouse-tails over the collar of the lamentable pullover. He stood in profile, so that she could see just half of a new and abundant mustache. Also—and this might have been owing to the way he stood, because he had to sway to hold his balance—he looked as if he might have become, well, a trifle stout. This was a picture she never showed anyone at Vörösmarty Place, though she examined it often, by several kinds of light. What did it mean, what was its secret expression? She looked for the invisible ink that might describe her son as a husband and father. He was twenty-eight, he had a mustache, he worked in his own home as a common labourer.

She said to herself, I never let him lift a finger. I waited on him from the time he opened his eyes.

In response to the ladder picture she employed a photographer, a former schoolfriend of her son's, to take a fiercely lighted portrait of her sitting on her divan-bed with a volume of Impressionist reproductions opened on her lap. She wore a string of garnets and turned her head proudly, without gaping or grinning. From the background wall she had removed a picture of clouds taken by her son, then a talented amateur, and hung in its stead a framed parchment that proved her mother's family had been ennobled. Actually a whole town had been ennobled at a stroke, but the parchment was legal and real. Normally it would not have been in her to display the skin of the dog, as these things were named, but perhaps her son's wife, looking at the new proud picture of his mother, might inquire, "What is that, there on the wall?"

She wrote him almost every morning—she had for years, now. At night her thoughts were morbid, unchecked, and she might have been likely to tell about her dreams or to describe the insignificant sadness of a lifetime, or to recall the mornings when he had eaten breakfast in silence, when talking to him had been like lifting a stone. Her letters held none of those things. She wrote wearing her blue, clean, now elderly kimono, sitting at the end of her kitchen table, while her tenants ate and quarrelled endlessly.

She had a long back-slanting hand she had once been told was the hand of a liar. Upside down the letter looked like a shower of rain. It was strange, mysterious, she wrote, to be here in the kitchen with the winter sun on the sparkling window (it was grimy, in fact; but she was seeing quite another window as she wrote) and the tenant granddaughter, whose name was Ilona, home late on a weekday. Ilona and the baby and the grandfather were all three going to a funeral this morning. It seemed a joyous sort of excursion because someone was fetching them by car; that in itself was an indication of their sombre connections. It explained, in shorthand, why she had not squarely refused to take them in. She wrote that the neighbours' radios could be heard faintly like the sounds of life breaking into a fever, and about Ilona preparing a boiled egg for the baby, drawing a face on the shell to make it interesting, and the baby opening his mouth, patting the table in a broken rhythm, patting crumbs with a spread-out hand. Here in the old kitchen she shared a wintry, secret, morning life with strangers.

Grandfather wore a hearing aid, but he had taken it apart, and it lay now on the table like parts of a doll's skull. Wearing it at breakfast kept him from enjoying his food. Spectacles bothered him, too. He made a noise eating, because he could not hear himself; nor did he see the mess around his cup and plate.

"Worse than an infant!" his granddaughter cried. She had a cross-looking little Tartar face. She tore squares of newspaper, one to go on the floor, another for underneath his plate. He scattered sugar and pipe ash and crusts and the pieces of his hearing aid. At the same time he was trying to attend to a crossword puzzle, which he looked at with a magnifying glass. But he still would not put his spectacles on, because they interfered with his food. Being deaf, he travelled alone in his memories and sometimes came out with just anything. His mind plodded back and forth. Looking up from the puzzle he said loudly, "My granddaughter has a diploma. Indeed she has. She worked in a hospital. Yes, she did. Some people think too much of themselves when they have a diploma. They begin to speak pure Hungarian. They try to speak like educated people. Not Ilona! You will never hear one word of good Hungarian from *her*."

His granddaughter had just untied a towel she used as a bib for the child. She grimaced and buried her Tartar's grimace in the towel. Only her brown hair was seen, and her shaking shoulders. She might have been laughing. Her grandfather wore a benign and rather a foolish smile until she looked up and screamed, "I hate you." She reminded him of all that she had done to make him happy. She described the last place they'd lived in, the water gurgling in the pipes, the smell of bedbugs. She had found this splendid apartment; she was paying their rent. His little pension scarcely covered the coffee he drank. "You thought your son was too good for my mother," she said. "You made her miserable, too."

The old man could not hear any of this. His shaking freckled hands had been assembling the hearing aid. He adjusted it in time to hear Ilona say, "It is hard to be given lessons in correct speech by someone who eats like a pig."

He sighed and said only, "Children," as one might sound resigned to any natural enemy.

The émigré's mother, their landlady, had stopped writing. She looked up, not at them, but of course they believed they could be seen. They began to talk about their past family history, as they did when they became tense and excited, and it all went into the letter. Ilona had lost her father, her mother, and her little sister in a road accident when, with Grandfather, they had been on their way to a funeral in the suburbs in a bus.

Funerals seemed to be the only outing they ever enjoyed. The old man listened to Ilona telling it again, but presently he got up and left them, as if the death of his son allowed him no relief even so many years later. When he came back he had his hat and coat on. For some reason, he had misunderstood and thought they had to leave at once for the new excursion. He took his landlady's hand and pumped it up and down, saying, "From the bottom of my heart . . . ," though all he was leading up to was "Goodbye." He did not let her hand go until he inadvertently brought it down hard on a thick cup.

"He has always embarrassed us in public," said Ilona, clearing away. "What could we do? He was my father's father."

That other time, said the old man—calmed now, sitting down in his overcoat—the day of the *fatal* funeral, there had been time to spare, out in a suburb, where they had to change from one bus to another. They had walked once around a frozen duckpond. He had been amazed, the old man remembered, at how many people were free on a working weekday. His son carried one of the children; little Ilona walked.

"Of course I walked! I was twelve!" she screamed from the sink.

He had been afraid that Ilona would never learn to speak, because her mother said everything for her. When Ilona pointed with her woolly fist, her mother crooned, "Skaters." Or else she announced, "You are cold," and pulled a scarf up over Ilona's apple cheeks.

"That was my sister," Ilona said. "I was twelve."

"Now, a governess might have made the child speak, say words correctly," said the old man. "Mothers are helpless. They can only say yes, yes, and try to repeat what the child seems to be thinking."

"He has always embarrassed us," Ilona said. "My mother hated going anywhere in his company."

Once around the duckpond, and then an old bus rattled up and they got in. The driver was late, and to make up for time he drove fast. At the bottom of a hill, on a wide sheet of black ice, the bus turned like a balky horse, rocked, steadied, and the driver threw himself over the wheel as if to protect it. An army lorry came down the hill, the first of two. Ilona's mother pulled the baby against her and pulled Ilona's head on her lap.

"Eight killed, including the two drivers," Ilona said.

Here was their folklore, their richness; how many persons have lost their families on a bus and survived to describe the holocaust? No wonder she and Grandfather were still together. If she had not married her child's father, it was because he had not wanted Grandfather to live with them. "You, yes," he had said to Ilona. "Relatives, no." Grandfather nodded, for he was used to hearing this. Her cold sacrifice always came on top of his disapproval.

Well, that was not quite the truth of it, the émigré's mother went on writing. The man who had interceded for them, whom she had felt it was wiser not to refuse, who might be the child's father, had been married for quite a long time.

The old man looked blank and strained. His eyes had become small. He looked Chinese. "Where we lived then was a good place to live with children," he said, perhaps speaking of a quarter fading like the edge of a watercolour into grey apartment blocks. Something had frightened him. He took out a clean pocket handkerchief and held it to his lips.

"Another army lorry took us to the hospital," said Ilona. "Do you know what you were saying?"

He remembered an ambulance. He and his grandchild had been wrapped in blankets, had lain on two stretchers, side by side, fingers locked together. That was what he remembered.

"You said, '*My mother, my mother,*'" she told him.

"I don't think I said that."

Now they are having their usual disagreement, she wrote her son. Lorry or ambulance?

"I heard," said Ilona. "I was conscious."

"I had no reason. If I said, 'My mother,' I was thinking, 'My children.'"

The rainstorm would cover pages more. Her letter had veered off and resembled her thoughts at night. She began to tell him she had trouble sleeping. She had been given a wonderful new drug, but unfortunately it was habit-forming and the doctor would not renew it. The drug gave her a deep sleep, from which she emerged fresh and enlivened, as if she had been swimming. During the sleep she was allowed exact and coloured dreams in which she was a young girl again and men long dead came to visit. They sat amiably discussing their deaths. Her first fiancé, killed in 1943, opened his shirt to show the chest wound. He apologized for having died without warning. He did not know that less than a year later she had married another man. The dead had no knowledge of love beyond the span of their own lives. The next night, she found herself with her son's father. They were standing together buying tickets for a play when she realized he was dead. He stood in his postwar shabbiness, discreet, hidden mind, camouflaged face, and he had ceased to be with the living. Her grief was so cruel that, lest she perish in sleep from the shock of it, someone unseen but conciliating suggested that she trade any person she knew in order to keep him with her. He would never have the misery of knowing that he was dead.

What would her son say to all this? My mother is now at an age when women dream of dead men, he might tell himself; when they begin to choose quite carelessly between the dead and the living. Women are crafty even in their sleep. They know they will survive. Why weep? Why discuss? Why let things annoy you? For a long time she believed he had left because he could not look at her life. Perhaps his going had been as artless, as simple, as he still insisted: he had got his first passport, flown out with a football team, never come back. He was between the dead and the living, a voice on the telephone, an affectionate letter full of English words, a coin rolled and lying somewhere in secret. And she, she was the revered and respected mother of a generous, an attentive, a camouflaged stranger.

Tell me the weather, he still wrote. Tell me the names of streets. She began a new page: Vörösmarty Place, if you remember, is at the beginning of Váci Street, the oldest street in the Old City. In the middle of the Place stands a little park. Our great poet, for whom the Place is named, sits carved in marble. Sculptured figures look gratefully up to him. They are grateful because he is the author of the national anthem. There are plane trees full of sparrows, and there are bus stops, and even a little Métro, the oldest in Europe, perhaps old-fashioned, but practical— it goes to the Zoo, the Fine Arts Museum, the Museum of Decorative Art, the Academy of Music, and the Opera. The old redoubt is there, too, at least one wall of it, backed up to a new building where you go to book seats for concerts. The real face of the redoubt has been in ruins since the end of the war. It used to be Moorish-romantic. The old part, which gave on the Danube, had in her day—no, in her mother's day—been a large concert hall, the reconstruction of which created grave problems because of modern acoustics. At Gerbeaud's the pastries are still the best in Europe, she wrote, and so are the prices. There are five or six little rooms, little marble tables, comfortable chairs. Between the stiff lace curtains and the windowpanes are quite valuable pieces of china. In summer one can sit on the pavement. There is enough space between the plane trees, and the ladies with their elegant hats are not in too much danger from the sparrows. If you come there, you will see younger people, too, and foreigners, and women who wait for foreigners, but most of the customers, yes, most, belong to the magic circle of mothers whose children have gone away. The café opens at ten and closes at nine. It is always crowded. "You can often find me there," she went on, "and without fail every Saturday," as if she might look up and see him draw near, transformed, amnesiac, not knowing her. I hope that I am not in your dreams, she said, because dreams are populated by the silent and the dead, and I still speak, I am alive. I wear a hat with a brim and soft grey gloves. I read their letters in three foreign languages. Thanks to you, I can order an endless succession of little cakes, I can even sip cognac. Will you still know me? I was your mother.

What Is Style?

I do not reread my own work unless I have to; I fancy no writer does. The reason why, probably, is that during the making of the story every line has been read and rewritten and read again to the point of glut. I am unable to "see" the style of the two stories presented here, and would not recognize its characteristics if they were pointed out to me. Once too close, the stories are already too distant. If I read a passage aloud, I am conscious of a prose rhythm easy for me to follow, that must be near to the way I think and speak. It seems to be my only link with a finished work.

The manner of writing, the thread spun out of the story itself, may with time have grown instinctive. I know that the thread must hold from beginning to end, and that I would like it to be invisible. Rereading "Baum, Gabriel" and "His Mother," all I can relate is that they are about loss and bewilderment, that I cannot imagine the people described living with any degree of willingness anywhere but in a city—in spite of Gabriel's imaginings about country life—and that a café as a home more congenial than home appears in both. The atmosphere, particularized, is of a fading world, though such a thing was far from my mind when the stories were written. It may be that the Europe of the nineteen-seventies already secreted the first dangerous sign of nostalgia, like a pervasive mist: I cannot say. And it is not what I have been asked to discuss.

Leaving aside the one analysis closed to me, of my own writing, let me say what style is *not*: it is not a last-minute addition to prose, a charming and universal slipcover, a coat of paint used to mask the failings of a structure. Style is inseparable from structure, part of the conformation of whatever the author has to say. What he says—this is what fiction is about—is that something is taking place and that nothing lasts. Against the sustained tick of a watch, fiction takes the measure of a life, a season, a look exchanged, the turning point, desire as brief as a dream, the grief and terror that after childhood we cease to express. The life, the look, the grief are without permanence. The watch continues to tick where the story stops.

A loose, a wavering, a slipshod, an affected, a false way of transmitting even a fragment of this leaves the reader suspicious: What is this too elaborate or too simple language hiding? What is the author trying to disguise? Probably he doesn't know. He has shown the works of the watch instead of its message. He may be untalented, just as he may be a gifted author who for some deeply private reason (doubt, panic, the pressures of a life unsuited to writing) has taken to rearranging the works in increasingly meaningless patterns. All this is to say that content, meaning, intention and form must make up a whole, and must above all have a reason to be.

There are rules of style. By applying them doggedly any literate, ambitious and determined person should be able to write like Somerset Maugham. Maugham was conscious of his limitations and deserves appreciation on that account: "I knew that I had no lyrical quality, I had a small vocabulary ... I had little gift for metaphors; the original or striking simile seldom occurred to me. Poetic flights and the great imaginative sweep were beyond my powers." He decided, sensibly, to write "as well as my natural defects allowed" and to aim at "lucidity, simplicity and euphony." The chance that some other indispensable quality had been overlooked must have been blanketed by a lifetime of celebrity. Now, of course, first principles are there to be heeded or, at the least, considered with care; but no guided tour of literature, no commitment to the right formula or to good taste (which is changeable anyway) can provide, let alone supplant, the inborn vitality and tension of living prose.

Like every other form of art, literature is no more and nothing less than a matter of life and death. The only question worth asking about a story—or a poem, or a piece of sculpture, or a new concert hall—is, "Is it dead or alive?" If a work of the imagination needs to be coaxed into life, it is better scrapped and forgotten. Working to rule, trying to make a barely breathing work of fiction simpler and more lucid and more euphonious merely injects into the desperate author's voice a tone of suppressed hysteria, the result of what E.M. Forster called "confusing order with orders." And then, how reliable are the rules? Listen to Pablo Picasso's rejection of a fellow-artist: "He looks up at the sky and says, 'Ah, the sky is blue,' and he paints a blue sky. Then he takes another look and says, 'The sky is mauve, too,' and he adds some mauve. The next time he looks he notices a trace of pink, and he adds a little pink." It sounds a proper mess, but Picasso was talking about Pierre Bonnard. As soon as we learn the name, the blues, mauves and pinks acquire a meaning, a reason to be. Picasso was right, but only in theory. In the end, everything depends on the artist himself.

Style in writing, as in painting, is the author's thumbprint, his mark. I do not mean that it establishes him as finer or greater than other writers, though that can happen too. I am thinking now of prose style as a writer's armorial bearings, his name and address. In a privately printed and libellous pamphlet, Colette's first husband, Willy, who had fraudulently signed her early novels, tried to prove she had gone on to plagiarize and plunder different things he had written. As evidence he offered random sentences from work he was supposed to have influenced or inspired. Nothing, from his point of view, could have been more self-defeating. Colette's manner, robust and personal, seems to leap from the page. Willy believed he had taught Colette "everything," and it may have been true—"everything," that is, except her instinct for language, her talent for perceiving the movement of life and a faculty for describing it. He was bound to have influenced her writing; it couldn't be helped. But by the time he chose to print a broadside on the subject, his influence had been absorbed, transmuted and—most humbling for the teacher—had left no visible trace.

There is no such a thing as a writer who has escaped being influenced. I have never heard a professional writer of any quality or standing talk about "pure" style, or say he would not read this or that for fear of corrupting or affecting his own; but I have heard it from would-be writers and amateurs. Corruption—if that is the word—sets in from the moment a child learns to speak and to hear language used and misused. A young person who does not read, and read widely, will never write anything—at least, nothing of interest. From time to time, in France, a novel is published purporting to come from a shepherd whose only influence has been the baaing of lambs on some God-forsaken slope of the Pyrenees. His artless and untampered-with mode of expression arouses the hope that there will be many more like him, but as a rule he is never heard from again. For "influences" I would be inclined to substitute "acquisitions." What they consist of, and amount to, are affected by taste and environment, preferences and upbringing (even, and sometimes particularly, when the latter has been rejected), instinctive selection. The beginning writer has to choose, tear to pieces, spit out, chew up and assimilate as naturally as a young animal—as naturally and as ruthlessly. Style cannot be copied, except by the untalented. It is, finally, the distillation of a lifetime of reading and listening, of selection and rejection. But if it is not a true voice, it is nothing.

Hugh Hood

HUGH HOOD was born in Toronto in 1928 and was educated at the University of Toronto. After a brief period of teaching in the United States, he moved to Montreal, where for many years he has been a professor of English at Université de Montréal. He is working on a *roman fleuve* entitled *The New Age/Le nouveau siècle* which, when complete, will comprise twelve volumes.

Other Works

Flying a Red Kite, (1962) Stories
White Figure, White Ground, (1964) Novel
Around the Mountain: Scenes from Montreal Life (1967) Stories
The Camera Always Lies, (1967) Novel
Strength Down Centre: The Jean Béliveau Story, (1970) Sports Documentary
A Game of Touch, (1970) Novel
The Fruit Man, the Meat Man, and the Manager, (1971) Stories
You Can't Get There From Here, (1972) Novel
The Governor's Bridge Is Closed, (1973) Essays
The Swing in the Garden, (1975) Novel
Dark Glasses, (1976) Stories
A New Athens, (1977) Novel
Selected Stories, (1978)
Reservoir Ravine, (1979) Novel
Scoring: Seymour Segal's Art of Hockey, (1979) Art Criticism
None Genuine Without This Signature, (1980) Stories

Breaking Off

Jupiter Life and Casualty/Canada (with home offices in East Tonawanda, N.Y.) were locked into a term lease in Commerce Court that had been one of the keys to the financing of the complex, four tower floors, the twenty-second to the twenty-fifth: Executive Offices, Finance, Legal Department, Sales, Advertising and Publicity, Computer Centre, Records and Statistics. There was intermittent gossip in the offices about a new building on the 401 service road in Oakville, which scared everybody on junior staff. The move to Oakville would cost half of them their jobs, for it would be a testing commute. The Commerce Court lease, however, was in the opinion of the legal department an ironclad document. It had looked unbreakable when it seemed favourable to Jupiter, and it looked from an unfavourable angle even more likely to hold water. No move seemed imminent. The lease ran through 1987.

Overcrowding was an eternal office menace, which implied continual shuffling round of desks and fragile partitions; small rooms were always being re-assigned to persons in modest authority. Every six months a new wave of design efficiency would sweep through some department, washing away bulletin boards and water coolers, re-arranging the positions of graphs, charts, files. Only the computer banks remained impassive. Very extensive, anchored to special power-cables, they could not be shifted to any area not serviced by reinforced flooring, special shielding, and sophisticated circuitry.

This sempiternal fluxion contrasted sharply with the tone of the chaste and perfectly clean quarters in which it evolved. The office tower was a marvel of simple, natural illumination, efficient heating and cooling. The interior temperature remained at an equable seventy degrees winter and summer, and there was none of the faint susurration of air-conditioners that tore at the nerves of personnel in office complexes completed in the nineteen-sixties and the earlier nineteen-seventies. As far as mere irreducible living conditions went—lighting, heating, smooth silent floor tiling, portability of partitions, colours of walls, durability of door hardware, ease of building maintenance—the tower was an unqualified success. It seemed the correct solution—or anyway one of the possible correct solutions—to problems of inner-city work-force comfort. Overcrowding must be avoided or this elegant solution would suffer a credibility loss. The architect—a western visionary—had stipulated in the final contracts the number of workers allowable per given square-footage of area space according to function. His provisions were rigorous, and the executives felt obliged to observe them.

Sometimes it seemed that in order to keep the four floors functional and elegant they had either to restrict the amount of business done, or overwork their employees. Perpetual juggling of assignments, farming out of a certain quantity of legal work and some publicity consultancies, and regular updating of information storage and retrieval systems, helped in part to preserve an attractive environment, always in delicate balance.

Enormous quantities of paper had to be disposed of daily, because the photocopy centre spewed forth an unending stream of pamphlets, booklets, memoranda running to many pages, and statistical breakdowns of remarkable subtlety and advanced mathematical character, all designed to be disposed of as soon as read, sometimes sooner. This was a part of an ongoing revolution in the technique of office management, which was replacing heavy, unwieldy, bulky filing cabinets, and punch-card or drum-type retrievers, by disposable records issuing from memory-banks of relatively compact physical proportions.

The photocopy centre, for example, tucked away between the computer centre and records and statistics, possessed two distinct copying systems—the small and the large—which were in operation all the time, staffed by two permanent women, and a temporary boy who did nothing but empty the OUT trays as fast as they filled. This boy, or rather this series of boys identical in manner and costume, and facial configuration, for all practical purposes a single specimen of the type, nameless but potent, sometimes found himself inadequate to this rapid flow. Confidential reports often fell to the floor to be covered by piles of other more or less recherché documentation. Information proliferated: knowledge became obscure: wisdom was inconceivable.

When too much paper had accumulated, the young women who operated the copiers, Olive Honeywell and her leg-girl Emmy Ivey, used to have to send a hurry-up call to other department and section heads, beseeching them to come and get it, the latest massive publication, the weekly claims breakdown, monthly policy registration, quarterly statement, annual report. Then the other departments would send around their youngest staff members to bear away what seemed relevant. In this way, Olive and Emmy acquired a wide acquaintance with strong-backed, usually male messengers. Theirs was a useful command post, a kind of redoubt whose walls were solid bricks of heavy white photocopy paper piled in stacks sometimes seven feet high. The photocopy centre had originally stood right out in the open, but over-production had walled it in, and now it was effectively a small cave of fact in which two fatal sisters and a malignant elf plied their shuttles.

They had copiers of the utmost sophistication. The big one could not only copy at unprecedented rates, but could sort the sheets as they burst from the entrails of the reproduction system, spraying pages into individual racks, lining them up, then stapling them. You could set the copier's memory, for example, such that the title page would be copied forty-eight times and distributed in the racks, then the table of contents, the opening page of text, the following pages, the appendices, a regular little book produced miraculously out of nowhere in seconds.

The little copier, Emmy Ivey's special pet, could not do these wonderful things, but it was very quick on single-sheet reproduction. If what was wanted was six hundred copies of two facing pages from *Actuarial Review,* Emmy could have them ready for distribution in five minutes.

Naturally with this production capacity they were up to here in high-quality, expensive, white photocopy paper. Supplies began to be ominously heavy; there was a serious question about weight-distribution. The centre started to spread out after a while. Olive used to say jokingly, "I don't have secretary's spread, but my department does." She certainly did not have the characteristic poor posture and inferior muscle tone of a stenographer chained to a desk. Long practice in sprinting about the confined space available while carrying heavy weights had kept her lissome and markedly underweight, though approaching thirty. As for Emmy, she was a phantom of delight, her head with its bouncy aureole of tightly permed blonde ringlets all that was visible to the exterior world, the entire length of the twenty-third floor, a sea of bent heads at light spacious attractive desks, spreading towards the far region of separate offices where, it was whispered, actuaries and logicians dwelt, and beyond them again in larger rooms, vice-presidents.

From vantage point at the feed-slot of the small copier, Emmy occasionally sallied forth with material wanted immediately, which some person would actually read. For some reason such publications were infrequent and small in print-order. Very rarely were more than fifty copies required of something which would be studied with care; these fifty rarities were invariably circulated to a restricted list of folks who were required to possess literacy, which was comprised of policy-making senior staff and department managers. Emmy could easily distribute an entire edition in a rapid forty-five minute tour of the four floors which the company occupied, sliding single copies into the appropriate IN trays as she passed, like some ministering angel of the Old Testament, a type of Passover messenger delivering saving signs.

She gave much pleasure to those who witnessed her passing. The golden head commanded high visibility; she earned a surprisingly large salary for a young single woman with a high-school education, and spent most of it on her clothes. She was still living at home but thinking about her own apartment. Clothes, potential apartment furnishings, and her stereo and records, were what she spent her earnings on; she had no thought of saving. She wore casual, laid-back styles, wraparound ankle-lengths, the vests of men's suits found in secondhand and Junior League stores, frilled shirtwaists, occasional middy blouses, men's neckties loosely knotted, scarves in figured silks. Before the movie came out, she had achieved an Annie Hall look which was first queried by her bosses, then highly approved of by them, once they recognized it in advertising. Emmy was the office pet.

Often on these peregrinations she would meet one or another of the boys who came to the sequestered photocopy section to pick up heavy piles of stock. Les Pargiter was one of them, from the legal department, the most junior lawyer on their staff, not ashamed to act as a privileged office boy, possessor of two university degrees and unexpectedly youthful looking. Les was always puzzled to find how little his university background meant to Emmy; she had had almost no contact with professional or university people, and their learned attainments meant absolutely zero, zilch, zip to her. Most people she knew were working for a big company with a pension plan and a hospitalization scheme tied into OHIP and offering extra psychiatry as a fringe benefit. She had no knowledge whatsoever of other kinds of lives lived in other parts of the city besides the office or her home on Albany Avenue near the Bloor/Bathurst subway station. Everybody had the same kind of stereo, in the same price range between six hundred and fifteen hundred dollars. Most girls in the office tried to look like her, and she certainly wasn't going out of her way to look for Mister Goodbar.

Basil Mossington was more interesting than Les Pargiter or Motil Panilal or Sandor Ferenczi, though equally from some distant region which her imagination could not penetrate. He lived way off somewhere forty miles across town. When he went home at night he took the Yonge Street line all the way up to Finch, and a bus from there to someplace out back of Black Creek. He worked in Finance, in the budget section, and like Les Pargiter was one of the most junior employees, without Les' advanced professional training. Basil had answered a want-ad to get his job. He had one year at Ryerson behind him; classroom education meant nothing to Basil. He thought that work was better than school. Like Emmy, he enjoyed having money to buy things.

None of the grave questions which twenty-year old people used to ask themselves ever crossed the minds of Emmy and Basil: whether or not they should save up to buy a home—an idea which would have struck either of them as bizarre. Nobody they knew had any idea of doing that. Everybody lived in one-bedroom high-rise apartments, which you could furnish in high style for very little money actually paid down. You could have the ready use of five or six major credit cards. You could pick up what you needed to eat every night after work at a Mac's Milk. You could wear new or secondhand or old clothes strictly according to your taste, as long as you could dig it. Neither of them had thought through this fate, but it was there, discoverable, somewhere in the backs of their heads. Two people with no commitments and twice their individual earnings— an extraordinarily large amount—could have an apartment in a brand-new building with big closets, full-length mirrors, a crystal room-divider between dining and food preparation areas, and a twentieth storey balcony with a view of the lake, posters from Marci Lipman Gallery, colour TV, twenty-one day vacation excursions via Sunflight to Greece or St. Lucia, forever and ever, without having to learn to unlearn anything.

About two months after Basil began to be seriously and steadily aware of Emmy's orbitings, he went to a stylist in the bowels of Toronto-Dominion Centre and had his hair blown and waved, which gave him the look of a pro football player, a cornerback. Hardly anybody at the office noticed the change in hair style, because most of the older guys in Finance had already had it done. Even some of the actuaries were into far-out stylings and disco.

Emmy noticed it. She started stopping beside his desk instead of whizzing past with a brief backwards look over her shoulder and a bob of the head.

"Here's the constant-estimate-adjustment sheet for the third week of the current quarter, and the departmental breakdown, oh, and the extrapolation for the remainder of the quarter, and the . . . let's see, what is this . . . the in-field operations costings, and this is the divisional operations summary with three-previous-year comparison parameters. That's all, I think." Business of looking under arm. "Yes. That's all."

"That's a lot of paper. Don't you ever get tired?"

"I don't know. The whole thing comes to, what is it you've got there?"

"Runs about twenty pages."

"Well, times fifty, eh? Gives you five hundred sheets of paper. I'd be a pretty poor physical specimen if I couldn't carry that much weight, wouldn't I?"

"You look in pretty good shape to me. What are you doing, running? I mean, do you run? Tennis? Do you belong to a health club or something?"

"Well, I don't yet actually, but I'm considering it. I've been thinking about Super Silhouette."

"Super Silhouette is just for girls, I mean women, right?"

"No, it went unisex about last January. A lot of guys go there."

"What are they, mostly gays?"

"I guess there's some gays. I don't really know. I only went the once, with a girlfriend. I noticed mostly black guys."

"Why would that be?"

"I don't know. Maybe they've got more money."

"It could be that, yeah . . . but you haven't joined yet?"

"No. That month I went to a new stereo, a Sansui top of the line. I'm up around fourteen hundred dollars now."

"Who do you like?"

"Queen, Pink Floyd, Kate Bush. I like Leon Redbone too."

"Redbone?"

Emmy giggled. "I have to go. You'd better take those in to Daffy Duck."

They both laughed. Daffy Duck was the head of the Finance Department, called that by everybody who worked for Jupiter because of his heavy lisp in moments of excitement or annoyance. His true name was something quite different. Emmy stood on the tiptoes of her left foot, lining up her pile of papers.

Basil said suddenly. "You look like a bird poised for flight."

"I also own a parrot," she replied unexpectedly.

"You probably get it from him."

"Get what?"

"That look of being up on a branch, ready to fly away."

This remark pleased Emmy. It seemed stirring and romantic, and stayed in her mind, though she didn't exactly think of it as gallant. She didn't know that word, but had an idea of the thing it named, an agreeable and deferential readiness to serve, to protect and defend. She might have called it kid stuff, or male chauvinism, depending on her attitude to herself and to young men, or "class" or "cool" or merely "being nice," the simplest and least precise signal of acceptance and approval. She had no moral vocabulary, but she had a complex moral life, which went on throughout her waking hours without her being in the least aware of what was happening; she lived in a riot of difficult questions and stern judgements, which she could neither propose exactly nor form finally.

She knew that she was doing something to and with Basil which depended on her attractiveness, but she knew she wasn't a tease and didn't want to get serious. She didn't know that the four generations immediately previous to her own had called this "flirting," and if anybody had described her as a flirt she would have felt demurely old-fashioned and girlishly sweet, and she would have been at a total loss to identify a model for her behaviour. The closest she might have come was one of the girls in *Charlie's Angels*, probably Jaclyn Smith, or the Cindy Williams character in *American Graffiti*. She had no language to cover her behaviour, and this deficiency made her self-consciousness very intense.

She often wondered where her life was going, as she grew a bit older but, she felt, no wiser. As the shape of her body changed, grew less girlish and more womanly, thickened slightly at the waist and hips and grew fuller in the bosom, as she stopped being a size-eight, she might expect to change inside too, in her head, but what kind of change should she expect? Would she keep this job? Or become head of the photocopy department when Olive left to get married? As far as Emmy knew, Olive had no such plans. Her life outside the office seemed to consist in going with other girls to places to eat lunch, or have a drink after work; then she vanished into the city and her own mysteries. In three years or five or seven, Olive might disappear for good. Emmy had no way of telling; either of them might outlast the other. It was very unlikely that they would remain where they were until they were old. Nobody like them had done this; there were no old people in the office. Some strange process of selection and elimination kept the visible range of people around her at Jupiter Life no more than thirty-eight at the outside. Almost none of the women in the office was older than, say, thirty-four or -five. Where were all the oldies?

Suppose she were to try and make some sort of connection with Basil or somebody like him. What would that be like? The words "get married to" drifted through her head now and then, but she couldn't connect with them. People still did that, she knew, but what was the point to it? Nobody minded if you lived together two by two, or two guys and a girl, or two girls and two guys, or any of the other possible combinations. She had been in apartments shared by all numbers up to eight, in most of the possible combinations, and nobody minded or cared or paid any attention to who lived there and who didn't or for how long. "Get married to" rang no bells. She knew everything there was to know about IUDs and pills and about the state having no business in the bedrooms of the nation, and cared nothing about these matters. She had been clinically de-sexed by current history.

She was still living with her family in the brick house on Albany Avenue, two blocks north of Bloor. The old-time family structure which had ruled her parents' lives was still highly visible around her. Her grandfather lived in the house; he had the best and biggest bedroom in the place, the front room with the canopied balcony which monopolized the morning sun. This was because he owned the house and allowed his son's family to live there for a moderate rent. Old Mr. Ivey had been a barber with his own shop and four chairs—three lesser barbers in his pay—at the corner of Brunswick and Bloor from around 1928 till just a couple of years ago. He had bought the Albany Avenue house at the bottom of the market in 1933. His wife was dead; one of his boys was dead; the girls were married and living in other parts of the city, but his younger son and his son's wife, two grandsons and young Emmy, were all comfortably installed in his house, earning huge amounts of money and carrying the heating, insurance, and taxes for him, as their rent. The mortgage had been paid off years ago and the book value of the building was now enormous, a far larger amount than old Mr. Ivey had ever imagined himself possessing.

For his granddaughter, this very comfortably-off, dignified, neatly dressed old barber didn't exist. She saw him every night but he wasn't real. She couldn't even begin to guess what his life had been like, or was like now. She could barely understand what her parents said to her, although their sporadic remarks made more sense than her grandfather's disconnected, almost demented—as they seemed to her—observations and suggestions. All the same he had given her Crackers, the parrot, the nicest present she had ever had. She often wondered what he'd been thinking of when he'd bought it for her eighteenth birthday, more than two years ago. Had he always wanted a parrot in the house and picked her birthday as the time to acquire one? It was impossible to say. She loved the parrot, had named it herself, and passed whole evenings watching it and trying to get it to talk. She was certain that it could say its name, "Crackers," and also perhaps "Where's Emmy?" but there was widespread disagreement about this in the family. Her brother Marshall claimed that Crackers had once said, "Come on over!" to him. The notion that her bird said things to Marshall that he didn't say to her troubled Emmy deeply.

Between the kitchen and the dining room in the Ivey house there lay an extra downstairs room, not the living room, which was at the very front of the house, but more of an expanded passageway, a cloakroom or butler's pantry, of whose original function nobody in the family was certain. The house had been built at a time when rather formal dinner service was still customary in well to do families, this room might have been some sort of serving room or buffet. It was difficult to identify. The passage of time had made of it a peculiar no-man's-land where old furniture collected in clumps. There were two prehistoric sofas in there and an ancient Zenith TV with a twelve-inch screen, and among other crowded items an enormous cage, a kind of terraced apartment block for parrots, in which Crackers swung from his perch, making eager noises in the early morning and peaceable split-tongued gurgles in the evening, as the time approached for his retirement to rest. With the installation of the parrot, this room had been definitively identified as Emmy's. It was shady and retired; there was a glass-panelled door through to the dining room and a curtained archway to the hall. Here she used to entertain young men who came calling, and it was a settled matter of family policy to let her strictly alone while these entertainments were proceeding. Her father and mother and even her brothers were aware that the young women of today live lives completely different from those of women in earlier times, freer lives, more self-determinate, void of conditioning.

When Basil Mossington started coming to the house there was none of the low comedy that in times past was often associated with patterns of courtship. For one thing, nobody, not even Emmy and Basil, had any clear idea of whether or not this was a pattern of courtship. They hadn't studied anthropology and didn't know that almost any form of conduct can be a courtship-pattern in the right context. The whole damn' family, the brothers, the retired and withdrawn grandfather, Dad, and vivacious and noisy Mrs. Ivey, knew that they'd better keep their hands off and their tongues still if they didn't want Emmy to disappear from view forever; they knew she'd been buying apartment furniture at odd moments. There was a brand new Simmons Hide-a-Bed and love seat in an oatmeal twill, sitting in that middle room no-man's-land, which Emmy had bought on impulse at a sale. It would look pretty smart in the living-room of a one-bedroom somewhere. It certainly didn't go with any of the other furniture in there, the superannuated chesterfields and hatracks, the parrot cage.

Crackers the parrot supervised Basil and Emmy in strident and vociferous tones, sometimes so like human speech miniaturized that they were hallucinatory. They would be strolling around this room, wondering what it was and what they were supposed to be doing in it, poking at the stuffing of the chesterfields, sofas, divans, davenports, whatever those old relics were, or peering at the backs of books in the ranked wooden bookcases—there seemed to be an almost complete run of

Reader's Digest books, with titles like "Annapurna" and "Kabloona" printed on the spines. Or they might tinker with the old Admiral electric record player and the Mart Kenney records that were strewn about, always in a sleepwalker's blank failure to apperceive what these objects were.

A lot of their time in there was spent in overtures to the parrot, passing him bits of celery or apple, changing his water, trying to stroke his tail feathers, an endearment which he sternly resisted. One night when they let him out at the top of the cage, where he could perch in his "poised-for-flight" stance, Basil began to snort and grunt uncontrollably. At length Emmy realized that he was laughing.

"That's where you learned to stand like that."

"Where? What?"

"He looks just like you, standing on the edge like that."

She wasn't sure how to take this but felt certain that the learning process must go from her to the parrot and not the other way around. After all, she antedated the parrot. She held up a finger with a chunk of apple stuck to the tip. Crackers shifted an uneasy foot and cocked an eye, inclining his head towards the fingertip.

"Shhhh shhhh shhhhhhhh."

"Gwock wock wock. Gwock."

"Come on, little Crackers!"

The bird bent and snatched the fruit in his beak, crushing it audibly.

"Muppetational," exclaimed Basil, and feeling moved by unfamiliar impulse he stepped briskly forward to kiss Emmy on the back of the neck or behind the ear. He remembered seeing this done in a recent movie. But she stepped aside unawares and he found his face pressed against the tiny cold bars of the cage. He was not a surefooted suitor, hardly a suitor at all. One of those fumbling types who don't swing the bat crisply and with attack, he found it hard to ingratiate himself with the Ivey family, not knowing what kind of people they were. The two brothers, Marshall and Clem, were visible but rarely. Marshall, the oldest child, was a chief flight attendant for Air Canada who spent more time over the Caribbean than in Toronto; he had much seniority and flew on preferred routes, always to warm countries. Clem was a recording engineer in a studio on Yorkville Avenue of such technical sophistication that he could give no adequate verbal account of it. He really was an intimate of many recording stars, didn't boast of it, scarcely mentioned that Joni or Carly had been using up some of their tax-break in the studio the day before yesterday.

Mrs. Ivey had perhaps the most unreadable character of them all. She looked to Basil pretty much what the mother of a family ought to look. She prepared meals, and sometimes wore an apron in the kitchen. The first time he came to the house, Mrs. Ivey happened to let fall some observation about games of chance, and Las Vegas. Thinking to make a favourable impression though he had no specific feelings one way or the other, Basil had piously remarked that he held gambling in great disesteem. He thought it a vice, a serious flaw in character, the wish to get something for nothing, an impossible distortion of the real. He would never think of gambling, not he. He had too much respect for his earnings to throw them down the toilet. These last two observations were true.

Rather to his discomfiture it immediately turned out that Mrs. Ivey was an ardent and inveterate horse-player and purchaser of lottery tickets. She followed the *Morning Telegraph* and Jimmy the Greek's sports line religiously. Her great ambition was to get back to Vegas where she had once passed a never-to-be-forgotten week on some excursion flight with hotel and meals included, which Marshall had given her as a Christmas present. She eyed Basil with mistrust. He saw that his half-hearted protestations of what he thought was virtue had gone for nothing.

He was a nervous guy. No matter how hard he tried to keep off coffee when he was going to visit Emmy, he found that he gulped two or three cups of the stuff during his evening meal, then was apt to spend much of the evening wondering where the bathroom was. The coffee had a marked effect on him, especially if his feet were cold, which made these evenings very mixed in the impression they left. If he and Emmy were out somewhere, he always spotted a toilet first thing, in the theatre before the movie started, or at a weird place they used to go to, over near Ossington along Bloor, which had been a Macedonian restaurant for forty-seven years before suddenly metamorphosing itself into an early Toronto copy of a Jackson Heights disco.

It was one strange scene—crowds of people shooting their arms alternately in the air like convulsed wind-up toys—wearing vests and shiny high boots while rhythmic choruses of soprano voices chanted indecipherable syllables which recurred hypnotically. There was an operator on a dais, back in the recesses of the long room which had been the kitchen of the restaurant. Where he sat had been the location of the cookstove and a powerful smell of fries and gravy lingered there, oddly harmonizing with the flickering shadows and the sound of many sliding dancing boots. There was a toilet in this place which Basil detected effortlessly—he had a lightning-quick eye for men's room signs—and the descent to the facility, down a staircase at the side of the room, was magical in the suddenness of the stylistic transformation from the sounds and sights of the late seventies to the conventional stinking basement washroom of those district restaurants called things like New Idea Lunch, Arlington Grill, Osgoode Café, featuring Devon Ice Cream and canned chicken noodle soup, which had been characteristic of the mid-century in the city: standup urinals which dripped and sweated, with G.H. Woods Germicidal cakes of unearthly violet hue strategically seated in their recesses, conventional inscriptions delivering highly unlikely messages, phone numbers, names of theoretically enthusiastic sexual partners.

Basil would have to visit the toilet three or four times in the evening, no matter how much he sweated upstairs. This gave Emmy a peculiar impression of him as a friend actuated by sudden opaque impulses. She didn't know where she stood with him, or when he might disappear somewhere, muttering an unconvincing excuse. He would reappear holding two drinks, but never consumed his. This struck her as odd indeed. She knew nothing about him except what could be picked up in the most casual surveillance in the office, at her home, and in the uncertain shadows of the disco. He seemed a creature of the subway, in the sense that he and millions like him were strung out along the criss-cross of the main subway routes like crystalline atoms clustering around the nodes of the stations. From the Finch station multiple lines of structure shot jaggedly forth towards King City and Richmond Hill, places to which Emmy would never travel, any more than she would visit Madagascar or Tierra del Fuego. When Basil abandoned a paper cup of fruit drink behind a loudspeaker, the act seemed loaded with unreadable significance.

Much later he took her home and sat with her under the watchful eye of the parrot, leaning close to her for moments, then looking wildly around and plucking at the collar of his sweaty shirt. He was terribly uneasy, crossed his legs, stood up and sat down, then murmured endearments which lacked conviction. Towards one in the morning he shot erect and abruptly excused himself, pacing away into the adjacent kitchen with rapid agitated movements. In a moment she heard him running the taps at the sink. There was a pause. The sound of rushing water grew. Perhaps he was looking for a glass.

She pushed through the curtained archway and stuck her head around the frame of the kitchen door. All the lights were on in the room and for a second or two Basil was just a vibrating dark outline in the glare. Then her eyes focussed and she saw him jump back from the edge of the sink with his hands clutched convulsively at his waist. He turned towards her with a smile of frightened guilt.

"Hi," said Emmy.

He brushed the back of his hand across his mouth and cleared his throat. Then he bent his back and stuck his head under the taps, drinking convulsively and getting water in his ears. There was a quiet metallic buzz which she couldn't identify. He turned off the taps and faced her. "Thirsty!" he said.

It wasn't until two or three days had gone by that she worked out the explanation for the extraordinary furtiveness of his manner. He'd been too shy to ask where the toilet was, and she'd surprised him peeing in the sink.

After that she couldn't feel the same, naturally, and she ignored Basil in the office, keeping her head averted in an affected way when she had to pass his desk. He tried to speak to her, smiling in the same way he'd smiled the week before the incident, when she'd considered him attractive and worthwhile, but everything was altered. He seemed much more real to her now, much more there, and distinctly contemptible. The minute he'd emerged from the shadows he'd done something silly. Was everybody going to prove to be like that? Basil started calling her at home, which he'd never done before, and she had to listen to her mother taking the calls.

"I don't want to talk to him."

"Why? What's he done to you? I thought he was a nice boy, a little tight-assed maybe but kind of sexy."

"For goodness' sakes, Mother!"

She wished her mother wouldn't talk in that style; it reminded her too much of Ellen Burstyn and Cybill Shepherd in *The Last Picture Show*. She wasn't a dumb teen-aged tease like the girl in the movie. Her mother wasn't a smart, tough, hard-bitten broad either. The whole recital bored her, and it made her mad when her mother insisted that she speak to the young man.

"No, I'm busy tomorrow night. I'm staying downtown with Olive; we're going to the ballet. And no, no, I'm busy all next week. I'm sorry, no."

He claimed he had a birthday present for her, which he wanted to show her, so she went as far as to agree to meet him after lunch, in the treed space between the towers of Commerce Court, where personnel sometimes sat when the weather was fine. There were potted shrubs and a few struggling plantations of slender maples down there, a pool and a fountain. He sat perched on the edge of a bench and showed her the birthday present, and it really was nice. An excellent piece of costume jewellery, still in the *People's* box, a pin or clip—she didn't examine the fastener—in gilt paste in the shape of a slender, feminine hand and wrist, with long, stylized, tapering fingers, a minute shard of genuine ruby tipped onto the third finger—it was a right hand—to simulate a tiny ring. She thought it might be from one of the better lines of junk jewellery, Coro or Schneiderhan, or perhaps *Nuit de Noel*. He pressed it on her but she wouldn't accept it.

"No, I'm sorry, no, I just couldn't."

"I don't understand."

"I just don't feel about you in that way."

The item probably cost him a hundred dollars, she thought. He put it away in the little blue box—rather a sweet box—and as it was time to get back upstairs they rode the elevator to the Jupiter suite and parted in silence.

Basil came to the photocopy centre now and then in the following weeks, but never when Emmy was there. He seemed to be avoiding her deliberately, which was fine by her; it spared her embarrassment and perplexity. She had survived a first encounter with another live human being with totally confused notions of conduct. When she heard what the man was doing with that stupid pin, or clip, she almost choked.

"Raffling it?"

"Yes, he won it in a contest, he says, and after all he might as well get the money out of it. Fifty cents a ticket or three for a dollar. I bought six, so I've got a pretty good chance."

"But Olive, you don't know where it's come from. It might be stolen. Have you thought of that?"

"He offered to show everybody his receipt for it."

"How could he have a receipt for it if he won it?"

"Well, I don't care. It's a pretty piece and it would look great on my mohair cardigan if it doesn't damage the stitching."

"You seem to think you'll win."

"I'll bet I do," said Olive. "I think I'll buy another dollar's worth of chances. He claims it's worth over a hundred and fifty dollars."

Emmy gritted her teeth, saying nothing more, and, wouldn't you know, Olive did win the raffle, which was strictly on the up-and-up. Daffy Duck did the drawing one Thursday afternoon, lisping and drooling and laughing at Basil, whom he liked. "A wise young man," he kept braying, "a wise young man." He selected the winning ticket from a ceramic bowl which usually adorned his inner office. The event was exceedingly public, and Emmy, who did not attend, was sure that everybody there was laughing at her. They weren't. They knew nothing about her.

Olive Honeywell wore that clip—or pin—around the office for eighteen months, until she quit to get married. Basil Mossington got promoted and vanished. Severed hands, and other separated members, became permanent properties of Emmy's visions.

The Small Birds

By the beginning of June the black flies and mosquitoes were so thick that Marian was trapped on the sunporch. Nobody quite knew why, but if there was one bug in a building it would go straight for her, forsaking all others, and bite or sting or fly around and around her head, making it impossible for her to concentrate on what she was doing, shelling peas or reading *Cosmopolitan* and laughing at it. Sometimes a heavy fly would alight on the crown of her head where the hair parted and exposed her scalp—they were attracted by the natural oil—and she would shiver with repulsion. She might pass the morning swatting and spraying, then sit all afternoon out on the screened sundeck, listening to the radio or reading or watching spring activity on the water. Just before dusk a pair of blue herons would make two or three passes down the lake; often they flew back north with visible fish flopping in their mouths. The loons wouldn't make their appearance until the herons had nested successfully; there might be some rivalry between them or some element of ecological stress. Do herons eat loons?

Purple martins eat mosquitoes, she remembered. Two years ago the boys had cleared away a lot of piled-up brush at the back of the property, near the parking spaces, and had laid down an expanse of sod for a picnic ground. Now there was thick grass and a big picnic table, and a string of Japanese lanterns in the shagged beeches, where there had been nothing but huge split rocks, chipmunks and juniper mulch. She still couldn't go out there till August or September; she'd get bitten to death, and it was no fun. The boys had built a birdhouse for purple martins, widely reputed to keep down mosquitoes, from a design on the vacation page of one of the Saturday papers. They may not have reproduced the shape of the entryways correctly, because flocks of birds who were plainly not purple martins had promptly moved in to stay—there may have been one or two purple martins in the crowd—and the mosquito count continued unnaturally high; there had been a wet runoff and a wet early spring. About the black flies there was simply nothing to be done.

So Marian waited on the sunporch for the later summer and felt pleased at the immensely wide and high view of the lake and the shore which the snugly screened windows allowed. In the old days at her grandparents' cottage at Beelzebub Lake the screens had been made of wire mesh which rusted and broke, leaving sharp, dangerous needle-points projecting around the holes. Wear-and-tear corrupted old-fashioned screening; the new nylon net was an enormous improvement. The filaments of the mesh were extremely fine but also extremely strong; they conceded nothing to wind and weather, and wore for years without corrosion or breakage, and they interfered only minimally with your view. When you got used to looking through them, they blurred and ran together so that instead of an impression of criss-crossing lines, what you got was a vague sense of some impalpable invisible substance run across the surface of your eyes, something like the onset of glaucoma but not so menacing. You were protected from the bugs and you felt like you were right outside. The sundeck projected forward from the cottage on tall stilts and there was about six feet of storage space underneath, open in front and gradually closing at the sides where the rocks, on which the building stood, humped up gradually under the flooring, rising towards the rear. There were old rowboats stored under there, and a lot of plastic sheeting, used to seal the porch windows in the fall, and a sketchy collection of garden tools. Marian's gang didn't make a fetish of gardening at the lake. Now that they had a picnic lawn out back, they were satisfied to share it with martins and swallows and an occasional much-admired pileated woodpecker.

When the cool August nights killed the bugs, Marian would start to go out, but the first two months of summer were hard time; this marshy swampy spring had sentenced her to sixty days. She would know when her incarceration was approaching its end by the phases of the summer light, the gradual progress of June and July to that point about the beginning of August when the sun would dip low enough in the west, in mid-afternoon, to flood the porch with shine and heat and the gleam of the individual ripples as they came onshore brilliantly white, iridescent like oil paint fresh from the tube, thick and creamy. Meanwhile there was shade and coolness on the porch for several hours, and an even glow of lemon colour washed around and through the field of vision. The sun was back behind the cottage at this time of year, until very late in the day; the shady dark green of the evergreens on the property was sunk all day in lemon tone, and in this genial harmony it was possible to pick out individual birds, identify them, almost name them as pets. She would sit there watching the antics of various tumbling, flipping creatures, slowly realizing that they had their daily routines, just like hers and those of the larger birds: the herons and bitterns and gulls and that masterful quartet of crows who woke her every morning with their bellowed threats at enemies far down the lake.

The little birds were if anything more rigorous in their patterns of instinctual behaviour, their cautious short flyways, choice of favourite trees, their aerobatics. It became clear that the orchestration and the melodies of their songs changed from one hour to the next around the clock: waking calls, assertions of territorial right, feeding and mating calls, warnings, shouts of mere fun, information about food, calls to rest. All this was like a musical score. She came to be able to tell the time of day by the mingled harmonies of the birdcalls and the FM radio that sat close to her tuned to CBC-FM until it was time for the Expos' game, just reachable on a distant FM outlet that faded in and out like the small voices of the swallows, occasionally giving a protracted holler like that pair of whip-poor-wills who sometimes exulted at midnight, around by the creek mouth.

Birdcalls, broadcasts, ballgames, how alliterative, she thought, how naturally formed. Like flight. Some of the birds kept doing something in front of her, winding around five particular evergreens, two tamaracks, a spruce, and two dead pines which still stood up stiffly erect with spiny bare branches, twigged in smaller and smaller points towards invisible tips. Sometimes a bird would stand at the very end of a branch, poised airily on a filament of support so dry and stiff and thin that you couldn't make it out, and the bird would seem balanced over nothing. Then it might make a sudden stab at its toes, and curve in rapid flight down from the branch, directly towards the face of the cottage. Marian would stiffen involuntarily, but no bump of small body against plywood siding ever shocked her. Those aerial swings and rushes, ending somewhere under her feet, finally brought her to realize that at least one bird was up to something under the porch.

She began to take a close interest in what was going on, would arrive at her watching post after a late breakfast, just about the time that "Mostly Music" came on the air on the CBC. She began to associate the theme music, and the names of the program's announcer, Bartley MacMillan, and its producer, Roma Angus, with the nesting activities of two specific birds, whom she christened Bartley and Roma, unusual, slightly phantasmagoric names for swallows. They were certainly swallows, but to which sub-group they belonged she could not say. There were the usual bird books in the cottage, rainy-day reading for idle inquirers, but even the superb Peterson line-drawings could not finally make clear to her whether Bartley and Roma were barn swallows or cliff swallows. They didn't seem to have quite the right shape to their tails for barn swallows, but the plumage was OK. There was an extra bar of grey around their bodies, above the wings, that didn't seem correct for cliff swallows. She concluded that they must be barn and/or cliff swallows, Roma and Bartley.

Sometimes she fancied that she could hear the movement of their wings underneath her feet, and the notion disturbed her. If there were to be birds underfoot, what might dwell in the skies? They kept flying right at the cottage, coming hard, at the last moment dipping and vanishing. They were up to something; the radio hummed and burbled; the 1.00 PM news came on, and then the familiar theme and brisk, loving voice of Bob Kerr from Vancouver, with the afternoon broadcast of classical music. He sounded so friendly and likeable that Marian plucked up her spirits, rose from her chair, and sounded the back bedrooms in search of children. Only one was in the building, her daughter Ruth, busy in the bathroom applying an experimental coat of makeup. Ruth was now about thirteen.

"How come we never go down under the cottage like we used to?" said Marian, and Ruth burst out laughing. "We could get up some kind of game with lumps of coal or something." These were bits of dialogue quoted from James Thurber, familiar to everybody in the family and particularly loved by Ruth, a Thurber enthusiast from infancy. She looked over her shoulder at her mother, nodded once, then turned back and squinted at the mirror. "I'll come in a minute." Her eyelid flickered. "Damn!" she exclaimed.

"Language!" said Marian mildly. They both giggled. Ruth wiped a trace of mascara from her lashes and turned to face her mother. Her *maquillage* was elaborate and bizarre, bright plumage. Colourful. Unrestrained.

Marian said, "Did you know that the swallows are nesting under the porch?"

"Everybody knows that but you, Mumma. They've been going in and out for days. You should see them circling around in there."

"Have you found the nest?"

"No, I haven't looked. Do you think we should disturb it?"

"We won't disturb it, darling, we'll just have a little peek. We've had them nesting before, you know. Maybe you won't remember. It must be ten years ago, before we screened in the porch."

"I remember," said Ruth, though she was uncertain about it.

"You would have been just a tiny girl at the time."

To this observation, Ruth would make no rejoinder. The mother and daughter strolled around to the front of the building, and in underneath the open face of the porch. They were now in sunny shade, out of the direct line of the sun, right below the picnic table on the deck. They heard a piece of music come to an end, and then the comfortable voice of the broadcaster explaining the peculiarities of the record, and its loved and special place in his huge—monstrous—collection. The charming, friendly voice, the warmth without glare, the half-light, the absence of insects, the presence of Ruth. Marian felt so well that she almost felt sick.

"Here it is," said Ruth. "In under the floorboards, tucked up on the beam. I think they may be trying to hide it."

"You and your premonitions," said Marian, and they giggled again very quietly. The nest was most cleverly concealed in a corner formed by two main supporting beams roofed in by the plywood flooring of the sundeck. Only an informed seeker or one of the swallows could have spotted it, because the sunlight could never get in there at an angle acute enough to illuminate the crossbeams. It was a small nest, about the circumference of a softball, delicately and precisely put together of pine twigs and juniper needles. Dried now to a russet brown, the juniper shone in shadow.

There were four eggs in the nest, each the size of a green grape, but very different in colour, a pale grey or grey-blue, a colour found in expensive stone ware, neither polished nor shiny, chalky. Ruth pointed at them with an extended forefinger, careful not to touch.

"Yes, four," she muttered almost inaudibly.

"We'd better get out of here," said Marian. "They'll be wanting to get back on the nest." And pat on cue, like the poor cat in the adage, a bird hurtled into the crawl space beside them like a projectile, whizzing past Marian's ear and out through the narrow opening at the side of the cottage with extraordinary speed. Marian stood erect in shocked amazement, and bumped her head noisily and painfully on the firm plywood.

"Fuck!" she expostulated.

Ruth said, "Language!"

The presence of the nest explained the perpetual comings and goings of Roma and Bartley, perhaps of their friends and relations too. It didn't seem possible to Marian that two small birds could give so readily the impression of a crowd. It wasn't that they were noisy; it was that they were around all the time, circling and diving, peeling off in echelon, or sitting motionless in front of her at a ten yards' remove, on bare spiny twigs or hidden in thick pine boughs. Their speed, their surety, their swift instincts, confounded her and caused a terrible commitment to their survival to rise up in her breast. Nothing must happen to them but good, she resolved, and she was desperately, bitterly, dashed to learn from one of her sons that the baby swallows had all died.

"Ohhh, no, don't tell me . . . ," she said.

"I saw the broken shells, Mum. Maybe I shouldn't have said."

Neil could recognize the signs of his mother's genuine sorrow. He took a spoonful of Captain Crunch and shivered; the cream was chilled and the morning fresh. "Why not go and see for yourself?" he said, not unkindly. "I might have been wrong."

"How are the mosquitoes?" she said morosely.

"It's cool. It's cool." So she went.

The fascination of the process, the cycle, pulled her under and into the shade. The nest was visible, but only just, at this hour. There were—oh, damn it—half-shells and little bits of broken shell lying here and there on the rocks, just below the nest. She picked up a half-shell and stuck it on the end of the little finger of her right hand. It looked like a terribly smart cloche hat of the nineteen-twenties, such a chic colour too. She wiggled the finger, then forced herself to peer into the dim light, trying to see what lay in the nest. She was able to make out what looked like a pile of slimy mucous, a kind of muddle of bones and half-formed feathers and semi-liquid greyish matter, without vital form. The look of the mess almost made her gag. She withdrew her head and started back outside. A swallow—possibly Bartley—passed her as she left, heading gracefully towards the nest with something hanging from his beak. This detail didn't light up in her head for several days, well on towards the beginning of July. Those slithery glistening minute exposed tendons, that liquid, the failure of generation. She strove to put the matter from her mind.

And then one Sunday afternoon she received better news. She was monitoring a double-header from Pittsburgh for Neil, Ruth, Daisy and John, who were down at the water. She caught sight of Ruth climbing slowly from the dockside, and called down to her, "Pirates leading by two runs in the third on Parker's double, Moreno and Foli scoring." Ruth turned to relay the news to the beach, and Marian sat down and let herself relax in the sun. Insects buzzed outside the mesh; the broadcasters exchanged rhythmic dialogue, crowd noises in the background, powerfully impressive recurrences of between-innings commercials. Sleep in the heat.

"Mumma Mumma Mumma, they're not dead," shouted Ruth from somewhere underfoot, "they're not dead at all, they're sitting in the nest, oh, they look so funny, come down and look. Hey Mumma!"

Marian roused herself. A huge powerboat passed in front of the cottage, the discharge of its sparkplugs causing a rasping buzz on the radio, like the roar of a power saw.

"Come on Mumma," urged Ruth, "down by the nest." There was thrilling vitality and certainty in the child's call. Marian's shoulders were covered in a fine, light sweat. She trembled and blinked, then trotted out the side door and around to the front of the building, where Ruthie beckoned to her from the crawl space. She was crouched beside the nest making a lot of noise, while Roma and Bartley buzzed around her angrily, trying to drive her off.

"You're frightening the mother," said Marian.

"I know I know I know, but you've got to come and see them this one time; they're so funny with their little heads all in a row."

This description charmed Marian; she decided that one quick examination would not be traumatic. She inclined her head and climbed in under the flooring and there, sure enough, the four nestlings sat piled up on top of one another with very little room—none—to move about. They were an absurd sight, feathers forming thickly, heads almost circular, all in profile. They had minute, whitish-yellow bills, which opened and shut avidly, and they were all, without doubt, very much alive. They bore a farcical resemblance, in their insistence on remaining strictly in profile, to much mediaeval religious art, whether in mosaic, fresco, or painting. Marian was reminded of dozens of groups of saints, viewed in right profile and superimposed one upon the other, with geometrically regular round haloes piled up like gilt coins on a dark plate. Some Biblical incident was insistently recalled, most likely from Ottonian representation in gospel book or fresco. All at once she had it: in the way the pulsing bodies were heaped together, in the pattern of unblinking eyes, working mouths, perfectly round little skulls, the small birds evoked the attitudes of the apostles rocked about in the stern of the fishing boat, as given in traditional pictures of Christ stilling the waves. There was the same awareness that something unexpected was about to take place, and the same profoundly human confusion.

Bartley and Roma screamed in busy anger. Ruth and Marian withdrew. The radio hooted in excitement. Somebody had just got the go-ahead run. The commercial came on:

"Coke adds life, Coca-Cola adds life . . ."

Maybe Bartley and Roma were feeding the kids on Coke; they got bigger and bigger and the nest bulged and began to burst. Once or twice, in ensuing weeks, Marian surprised one of the parents in the act of shoring up the side of the nest, working fresh twigs into a space which threatened nestling-fallout. The grown swallow was perched nervously on the crossbeam, pecking away at shreds of twisted woody stuff, working it into crevices, making everything tight. Under here there was no problem about rainfall. How clever of them, thought Marian, then she remembered that the action was, after all, dictated purely by instinct. The birds could be conceded no moral credit for their sense of parental responsibility. They were always around the nest now, feeding the next generation with bits of matter almost invisibly small. Marian never saw any worms, but was able to identify the act of feeding. The parents would post themselves beside the nest with their backs to her. They would make that funny unmistakable dip of the shoulders. Competitive pipings from the young, almost inaudible. Should be on film, Marian thought, Disney would make a killing with this. She never actually witnessed the passing of food from mouth to mouth.

The small birds grew and survived, crowded and hampered in their movements as they were. How would they learn to fly, Marian wondered. How would they ever find room to move their wings, could they see at all? What could they hear, how receive instruction in the difficult art of self-powered flight? By mid-July crisis impended: there was no more room in the nest. In a day or so they would start falling out, and the nest was balanced over bare, flinty, ancient rock. A fall would make mush of infant bones. She worried, knowing that this was absurd, that the species would perpetuate itself, doubtless with losses according to statistical norms. A couple of the young would fail to negotiate first flight, but so what? We all have to take our chances. It made her laugh to imagine that the sound of classical programming on CBC-FM and the commercials and the baseball broadcasts would form part of the inherited natural sound patterns heard and instinctually assimilated by the next generation of barn or cliff swallows. Maybe the Coca-Cola jingle would turn up in their territorial calls next summer. Fusion of art and nature.

On Saturday, the nineteenth of July, she was lurking near the nest, thinking that she might anticipate some infant attempt at flight, catch the creature if the attempt should go badly. She might retrieve some squeaking Icarus before he hit rock, a basket catch like those the outfielders kept making in National League play, as described in the summer-long sequence of Expos-network broadcasts going on in the swallows' sky. In a bird's mind, the account of the game would seem like the voice of God, superior to the visible order, coming from elsewhere, a something given, part of pure life. She moved over to stand looking at the infants. They were fully formed, she thought, all set to go. Above her on the porch there came one of those irregular interruptions of FM broadcasting, and the game faded away into distant blur of competing FM signals from thousands of miles off. Invisible influences crossed in the upper air. She turned her head to look out from under and then she heard the strange sound, never before, never after.

A swift-running rushing breathy sound, blurring, whistling, like being kissed by the angels, whispering, running past her hair.

When she looked back, the nest was empty.

There was nothing on the rocks.

She began to sniffle, then repressed the impulse.

Now there would be six particular swallows to be picked out of the circling crowd. She wondered if she would be able to recognize them. Could she draw them home by familiar sound? Would the voice of Bob Kerr call them to himself? It seemed a better than fifty-fifty wager. Afternoons on the sunporch lengthened; she began to struggle with binoculars, trying to focus directly on the branches close to the cottage. It ought to be possible to get a look at one of the birds in tight closeup, almost as though perched on the end of the glasses. They were too quick for her; every time she got one of them into focus he or she would dart away, and as she swung the glasses to try and follow the flight, the milky and confusing impressions caused by the nylon screening would make her blink and lose track of the motion.

Eventually Marian's nature studies began to decline in interest. The glasses were more an impediment to observation than anything. She would catch herself mumbling, "I could see perfectly well if it weren't for these damn' glasses." The annoying element of the situation, which she recognized as fundamentally comic, was that the life of the birds grew more fascinating and complex just as she began to be bored with it because of her natural incapacity. This paradoxical relation struck her as exceedingly lifelike. She let the glasses alone after that, content to enjoy the weather.

It was becoming almost aggressively warm and sunny on the sunporch in the August afternoons, when the illumination that flooded the space reached an unmixed golden tone, which it retained very late. It was hot and made you sweat all over, not just in a light perspiration but in big drops which stood out on the forehead, arms and neck, and ran down inside one's bathing suit. Marian felt as though she could almost swim, certainly slither around, in this home-style sauna. She would put her head down on her arms and sit there, wet, hot, solitary and happy.

She kept hearing wings, wings, and the ballgame on the radio and new recordings of ancient instruments playing the infant symphonies of Mozart. Birds all over. Sitting on pine branches right outside, closer. Very close as though listening to baby Mozart or the game fading and returning. Swimming in the heat and the gold light. She moved her head idly, turning a cheek down into her bent elbow and feeling the wet in the hair on the back of her neck, warm sweat on her shoulderblades. Pipings. Soft calls. She lifted her head from her arms and opened and shut her eyes, trying to clear them in the blurring sunshine. The birds clustered just outside, listening to the game in their own space. Marian whispered, "They're all around me." She glanced to the right and caught a glimpse of a young swallow motionless in the corner of her eye. Directly in front of her hovered a plump little dark silhouette, changing size in the wash of intense gold and blue. She blinked and looked again from left to right, picking them out one after another looking in at her and listening, leaning, tiny bright eyes gleaming in at her through the net.

Floating Southwards

As of date of writing, December 1981, I've written ninety-three short stories, all of them published or about to be published, and I've written eight published novels, two early unpublished novels and a bit of a third, and I'm preparing another to be published sometime in 1984. I'm the only Canadian fiction-writer who has done so much in both forms. Richler? Goodish novelist but not much of a story-writer and wouldn't claim to be one. Laurence? Close, but the stories are clearly of secondary importance. Gallant? Primarily a story writer. Munro? Same thing. When I try to think of Canadian fiction writers who have excelled in both forms, my memory throws out the Morley Callaghan card and that's all. Davies? No stories. Aha, what about John Metcalf and Audrey Thomas? There are two writers who have written well in both the longer and shorter forms. I can't think of any more.

My work has divided itself naturally and easily—with a smoothness that always surprises me—into two intimately related, co-operating parts. I have made it a habit for many years to work on a novel in the months from January to May. I'll do a first draft, take the ensuing summer and fall for other matters, then return to the novel the following winter and finish a final draft in May of the second year. For example, I wrote the first draft of *Black and White Keys* from January to May of 1980, and the final draft in the corresponding period of 1981.

In the summers I sail my boat, swim, insulate another bedroom at the cottage, mind my own business—my very favourite pastime. In the fall I'll write three or four stories. Novels: winter and spring. Stories: summer and fall. Sometime or other I ought to sit down with a really competent literary theorist—not a deconstructionist—to see if any constant and specific relation can be found between the two interacting bodies of material, bundles of modalities. What do they have in common and what divides them, *for me*? I suppose that some writers can work easily on a novel and a short story at the same time—there have been times in my life when I did this—but now I instinctively prefer to keep the two enterprises rigorously separate as to time. I did write the opening of *The Swing in the Garden* in October and November one year, and that's the last time I undertook such a thing. I don't see any reason why stories come quicker and better in the fall than in the spring—and of course they don't. I think about my stories all the time I'm writing one or another draft of a novel. I keep a list pinned up beside my table of the next six to eight stories I intend to write, and I see it every morning. Right now, for instance, I'm thinking about three stories I plan to write in the fall of 1982, called "The Blackmailer's Wasted Afternoon," "We Outnumber the Dead," and "Moskowitz's Moustache." My experience has been that when a story gets far enough forward in my head for me to give it a title, I'll proceed at some time or other to write it. I expect to die with six or eight stories quite clear in my head, unwritten simply because I never got around to them. I'd better write the titles down somewhere before I go. Maybe one of my kids will want to carry on the business.

I could easily switch things around and write stories from January to May, and novels from September to December; it isn't the inner demands of form that dictate the arrangement, it's a matter of convenience more than anything else. Mind you, what seems mere convenience may be dictated by deep inner necessity. I like very much (suspiciously much?) to have a very long work to concentrate on through the depths of winter. January through to my birthday (April 30th), those are the times for novels. After Christmas, right at New Year's, you grit your teeth, type out your scenario, and plunge into those heavenly opening pages with all the world of the possible before you; "we were the first that ever burst into that silent sea." There is no feeling quite like that in my experience. Those first sixteen to twenty pages, where you close off so many thought-over likelihoods and begin to see which avenues you will choose to follow, which reject. You refuse all invitations—and what bliss that is—and descend into the depths of the narrative. Writing a novel is a lot like dying, and very much like undergoing deep analysis. Then comes that extraordinary day when you pass the halfway mark in your outline and you perceive that everything from here on will be downhill racing, hazardous and speedy. The last hundred pages of a novel are like being reborn. I suppose novel writing is inwardly a wintertime process. Novels take time.

Stories intensify moments: there's the trace of the difference. I write stories in September, October, November, and I begin to flag in early December when I can sense the next novel-writing exercise looming big in my imaginings and feelings. When I'm writing stories, the year is beginning for me. As I've spent a large part of my life teaching, September is of all months the one in which my life starts all over again.

What it is to write a story in September or October! You only have to look through the sunny warm fully lighted lemon-coloured atmosphere of "The Small Birds" to see what my feelings can give me in mid-September. The story was composed in September of 1980.

Having said this much, I have now to confess that "Breaking Off," the other story included in this anthology, was written in January of 1979, as one of a series of six stories that I wrote from October 1978 to May 1979 to complete the collection *None Genuine Without This Signature.* The story written immediately before "Breaking Off" was "New Country," in December 1978, and the following story, written in February 1979, was, appropriately enough, "February Mama." That brief period was the first for years, and will probably be the last for many more years, in which I was free to work on stories in mid-winter, and the reason is clear. I had taken a year off from novel-writing, something I will likely only be able to do once more in my life, for reasons which will be perfectly clear to readers of *The New Age/Le nouveau siècle.*

If I'm to have my novel-sequence work out according to design, the final volume will have to appear in 1999, if possible on New Year's Eve, when the odometer turns over and we'll have the three zeros showing, two-zero-zero-zero, for only the second time since the beginning of the Christian Era. This is called taking the long view. If I'm to have my novels in the nineties coming out in the odd-numbered years, such that they end with 1999, I'll have to take one more year off sometime around the end of the present decade. At that time I'll probably write a few more stories around the beginning of a year. I hope they turn out like "Breaking Off" and "February Mama."

From these notes you can readily draw three conclusions: 1. I'm obsessed with minute and specific arrangements of form, behaviour very familiar to psychoanalysis; 2. my stories and novels are fitted in and around each other in a very close symbiosis like the yolk and white in one shell. Which is yolk, which egg? You tell me. Every reader has his own opinion. 3. a September story and a January story should show striking differences of form. In fact "The Small Birds" and "Breaking Off" do display very distinct qualities. When I wrote "Breaking Off" I was doing it at a time when I felt like I should be working on long fiction. The story feels novelistic to me. It is the closest I have come to the novella or long story, and is based on a subject I had been mulling over since about 1948, more than thirty years. It is a very heavily charged *donnée,* too large really for the short story form. As I was writing it, I knew that I must condense, squeeze, truncate, compress, elide. As my novels do, this story signals the significance of extremely complex patterns of group behaviour—and linguistic usage—using individual lives as enactments of social forms; the story has embedded in it an ongoing criticism of various types of communication, such as, for example, the strange speech of parrots. I'm not talking about mere social history—any idiot can write social history—and I'm not primarily concerned with the multiplication of observed detail, although many of my critics have said that I am. I mean the way that membership in an army, a church, a big business, a social class, a language group, circulates like arterial blood (ha, a metaphor, no, a simile, anyway an explicit comparison for a change) into personal conduct in such a way as to make of occasional selected individuals immensely expressive representatives of what is happening in their world. Emmy and Basil are representative people in this specific sense, doing representative things. Not trendy things or symbolic things. Here I'm placing myself in a relation with Emerson, in his essay on "Representative Men," and with Scott Fitzgerald, who considered himself all his life to be a man peculiarly endowed with a power to express in his life/work the immense social forces that were swirling around him.

Emerson was somewhat more ready than Fitzgerald to see the source of these forces in the will of the Almighty. To that will I would add the Divine Intelligence which is one with that will, and am happy to trace these currents to such a spring. In "Breaking Off" my central imaginative preoccupation—the powerfully apprehended sensory schema which was lodged in my consciousness as I wrote—is that of an enormous chunk of ice, a part of the glacier, separating itself from the Arctic icecap and floating southwards on the current, gradually diminishing somewhat in size until it becomes an iceberg, smaller than at birth but still immense and capable of destroying the greatest human enterprise. This image is not found in the overt text of the story, except in the implications of the title. The social groups, the language systems, the courtship patterns, which Basil and Emmy share, form a mass like that of the southwards-moving iceberg with nine-tenths of its significance below the surface, but deadly. This isolated chunk of human culture—ourselves in the last third of this century—cannot speak to the times which went before us, cannot hear their voices. "Breaking Off."

The September story "The Small Birds" is much less novelistic, much more characteristically what the textbook twentieth-century story is supposed to be: a compressed single image of a moment of experience so intense as to eternize itself and stand for the significance of many lives, perhaps all lives. It is for such moments that we live. The most important sentence in "The Small Birds" comes close to the end. "Invisible influences crossed in the upper air." I originally wrote "Invisible voices crossed in the upper air," but realized at once that some captious critic would insist that voices are definitively invisible, and so changed the word to "influences," which gives a pleasing suggestion of the in-flowing *(Einfluss)* of spirits, water or grace. "Crossed" fits in nicely too. The story builds up from our apprehension of the presence of spirits, and I don't think that I'll say any more about it. It might be my best story. It might be my only one.

Norman Levine

NORMAN LEVINE was born in Ottawa in 1924. He served with the RCAF during the war and afterwards went to McGill University in Montreal. In 1949 he left Canada and lived in St. Ives, Cornwall, for the next thirty years. He recently returned to Canada and now lives in Toronto. His work has been widely translated, and in Germany his translator is Heinrich Böll.

Other Works

Myssium, (1948) Poetry
The Tight-Rope Walker, (1950) Poetry
The Angled Road, (1952) Novel
Canada Made Me, (1958) Autobiographical Travel Book
One Way Ticket, (1961) Stories
From a Seaside Town, (1970) Novel
I Don't Want To Know Anyone Too Well, (1971) Stories
Selected Stories, (1975)
Thin Ice, (1979) Stories

A Small Piece of Blue

On Thursday morning the train arrived at Sault Ste Marie. Leaving my bag in the left luggage I asked the way to the office of the Algoma Ore Properties. The man in the company's office was tall and wore a loose-fitting summer suit. He had the appearance of an athlete turned salesman. Straight blond hair combed back without a parting, a well-fed face. But there was something deceptive about the way he talked. For his mouth when open seemed unnatural in that position as in those films where animals are made to speak like human beings. I showed him my letter from the Mine Manager. He read it, said I was lucky, for I would be able to get a train out tomorrow.

"There are only two trains that go up a week, Tuesdays and Fridays."

He walked to a large map on the wall. It hung there framed. The bottom had a large blue area marked Lake Superior. Smaller pieces of blue were scattered all over the map.

"The only other way is by seaplane." He tapped a spot in the far right-hand corner. "There won't be a plane till Saturday and if the weather's bad there won't be a plane."

He enjoyed what he had said for he walked away from the map to his desk and offered me a cigarette.

"It'll cost you twenty more dollars to fly in."

It was the way he mentioned money that brought back those classes in salesmanship we had at high school where we had to stand in front of the class and pretend we were selling something while the teacher criticized our technique.

"Besides it's a job," the tall man said, "finding the right lake. There are thousands like them. And the bush pilots are just as likely to put you down on the wrong one."

I said I would take the company's train.

Sault Ste Marie was the kind of place that I had been in before. The quick stay in a small town where I knew that after a few years I would remember very little of it, in this case a zoo. Away from the main street I walked in a residential area. The houses were set back from the sidewalk by lawns; grass, trees, but no flowers. One wooden house with a large veranda had a cardboard sign, *Room To Let,* nailed to a veranda post. Above the bell-button was a metal plate, *L. M. Kalma. Music Teacher. Qualified.* I rang the bell. I could hear the bell ringing inside. But the tall, grey door remained closed. I rang and knocked and waited. A window on the top opened but no one looked out. Then I heard steps.

The woman who opened the door was small. She had a dressing-gown on over a nightdress. Her hair was grey, fuzzy, and held in place by a net. Though it was early afternoon the fact that she had obviously just come out of bed did not seem as startling as her face. The eyes were there. So was the mouth. But where her nose should have been there was a flat surface of scarred flesh with two small holes.

"You caught me undressed."

I told her I wanted a room for one night. She led me upstairs to a bedroom. A square room with a window and a large four-poster bed. "It's a feather bed," she said. "They are much better than spring or rubber. The feathers they sleep with you like another person."

My first impulse was to make some excuse, leave, and find another place.

"The clever doctors, to them I ought to be dead."

She said this without sadness or humour. Then she showed me the bathroom, the light switch, asked me if I liked music, if $1.50 was not too much for the room, and placed on the kitchen table some cold chicken with sliced cucumber that she had taken from the ice-box. She insisted that I sit down and eat. I ate the food and she talked. She talked as if we had known each other for a long time. Like boat-passengers who have been forced into each other's company only for a particular journey and are safe with the knowledge that no matter how much one says or does there is no consequence to be faced. I now found a strong physical attraction to her face.

Later in the evening when I returned with my bag from the station it was difficult to recognize her as the same woman who opened the door. She had on a dark dress instead of a dressing-gown, but her face was different. She wore a false nose attached to a false piece of skin that stretched from one ear to the other and by wearing glasses held it in place. Face powder and rouge generously put on only helped to show the falseness. I preferred the scarred face with the two air holes to this manufactured monstrosity. In her attempt to look normal she looked ugly.

Next morning the train did not begin from the railway station but from a private siding by the Algoma Ore Properties' office. In the coach, besides myself, were four middle-aged Americans dressed in bright lumberjack shirts with fishing gear piled around them. The only other person was the ticket collector who, I discovered later, was also our cook.

The coach was old and of a type I had not seen on either the Canadian National or the Canadian Pacific. The inside was like a worn-out billiard table with large patches eaten out of the green. The seats were hard and uncomfortable. Gas brackets hung from the ceiling. In the centre of the ceiling a light-bulb did not give much light. But we did not go through many tunnels. Travelling into the bush we continually crossed trestle-bridges, curved by small lakes, and moved slowly through miles of pine and soft-wood. By noon the journey had gone on much too long. The total distance was less than a hundred miles north and we had travelled half of it when the ticket collector came and asked me if I wanted some grub. I followed him into his compartment at the head of the coach. One side had deep shelves from the ceiling to the floor and the shelves had tinned goods in them. The ticket collector took a tin from a shelf. He showed me the tin. *Grade A. Specially Selected Ready To Serve Chicken.* "Want this?" he asked. "Go to your seat and I'll call you when she's ready. Here. Have a funny. It's on the house." He went over to the loose papers on top of a bundle. "What do you want? Annie. Tarzan. The Katzenjammer Kids."

A dog barked. In the corner opposite to where we were a cocker spaniel was kept in a large wicker cage.

"She's going the same place as you're going," he said.

I looked out from the small observation window. The train was going through a narrow valley. The earth was banked along the track. We were travelling so slow that it was possible to see the cracks in the soil. The ticket collector put down the chicken tin and filled a bowl with water from a kettle.

"You don't mind if I give her water. Trains give them this thirst."

He made a clucking noise with his tongue and walked over to the wicker basket and put the bowl down so that the dog could reach it.

"She belongs to an engineer at the Mine. He sends her to the Soo whenever she's on heat."

He knelt to the dog and fell over as the coach jolted. Instead of getting up he lay sprawled on the floor and talked to the dog.

"Was it good girl? Eh, my beauty. C'mon tell me—"

I left the ticket collector talking to the dog and returned to my seat with The Katzenjammer Kids and looked out of the window. The first excitement of seeing so much green and trees had passed. The trees were monotonous and I wanted the journey to end. I wondered why I was going to the Mine. Part of it was for the money and the experience. But I felt convinced that there was something else. Four years of lectures and campus enthusiasms had given me an overdose of books and words and examinations. I felt as if I was on a see-saw, stuck to the one side that was raised, where my head was the only part involved in "the goings on." Not that those four years were unpleasant. They only seem a waste of time, looking back.

I did not see the Mine until sundown. From the train it looked like an old ruin on top of a hill where the hills around were without trees or grass. The station was at the bottom of the hill and we stopped by a long wooden platform. The train picked up water. Parcels and crates were moved from the train to the waiting trucks. Then the spaniel, free from the wicker cage, was given to someone in a car. A cream-coloured bus was also by the side of the platform. Some men were inside. I went to the bus. The driver sat like a sparrow over the wheel, a jockey cap on his head. He wore an orange sweater with a large H in green across the front.

"Your name Tree?"

When I said it was he said, "Hop in."

The men by the station were watching the re-union of the spaniel with her owner. There were some guttural jokes made at the spaniel's friskiness, for they knew where she had been. Then the bus backed, turned, and drove off.

We came to a lake with wooden houses on one side. The bus stopped by a General Store. Several men with black lunch-pails climbed in. They called the driver Jack in various accents. He punched small cards that the men held up as they entered the bus. We drove around the lake and up a hill. Above us a steel cable carried large buckets of iron ore from the Mine to the Sinter Plant. We stopped at the top of the hill, beside a wooden building. I asked the driver where the office was. He said to follow him. He carried a mailsack over his shoulder.

"Where you from?"

"Montreal."

"Play ball?"

"A bit."

"What position?"

"I pitch."

He remained silent as we went through a wooden gate and into a frame building partitioned off for several offices. The bus driver dropped the mailsack on the floor and a girl came out of one of the partitions.

"Hi, Glorie. Someone from Montreal." And he went out.

She came to the counter, unsmiling, and took some paper, spread it flat.

"When did you come?"

A skirt and sweater and on her sweater at the neck she wore a black cross.

She took my name, age, and home address. Her eyes moved nervously. Her other features were coarse. When my card was filled out she told me to go to the cookhouse, a building some twenty yards away, and ask for the cook.

I crossed the bare hard-packed ground and saw a man with glasses, stripped to the waist, holding a white apron. He stood by the cookhouse near several large barrels filled with garbage and looked towards the horizon. I asked him if he could tell me where I could find the cook.

"Where you from?" he said with a Scottish accent.

"Montreal."

"Montreal," he said the word slowly, "it's seven years since I've been there. How are *The Canadiens* doing?" Not waiting for a reply he became excited and talked quickly. "The last time I was there I did a food crawl. I started at Pauze's with a dozen oysters then I went to the Bucharest for a steak, Ben's for a smoked-meat sandwich, Chicken Charlie's on St Catherine for spareribs, and ended with spaghetti and meat balls at FDR's and before I caught the midnight train I took a taxi to a place called *Au Lutin qui Bouffe* where somebody blind played a piano while I had frog's legs and my picture taken giving a baby's bottle of milk to a little pig." As spontaneously as he started, he stopped. To cover up his embarrassment he became silent, then formal, as he led me to his cookhouse office.

In his office he issued me a new black lunchpail and I signed a slip for it. He told me to scratch my name on the lunchpail with a nail and that supper was at seven-thirty, so that I still had half an hour to get a place to sleep. We walked outside, through the dining-hall. Unpainted large wooden tables. Benches on both sides. The first table near the door had chairs, and a sign, *Staff Only.*

He showed me a building about fifty yards down the hill.

"Go to room nine, Laddie, and ask for Willie Hare."

The cable stretched over the cookhouse and I could hear it creak as the buckets kept passing overhead. Where the cable crossed between cookhouse and office a steel net was suspended above the ground.

I found number nine in a building smelling of paint. Outside the door a bundle of dirty laundry was tied together by a shirt. Some time passed between my knock and the door being opened. At first I thought he was a boy, then he switched the room light on and I could see that he was old, unshaven, and sleepy. He could not be much more than five feet, a thin frame covered by a dirty white shirt buttoned tight at the neck, collar crumpled, and grey trousers that were too small. He wore no shoes but heavy woollen socks. His fly-buttons were undone.

"My name is Tree. The cook told me that you would let me know where I sleep."

He hesitated, then turned back to the room leaving the door open. He went to a cupboard and pulled out a large piece of cardboard. Then he sat down on his bed and began to examine the large writing on one side of the board.

I looked around the room. It stank of old age. Shelves covered an entire wall. In these shelves: toothpaste, soap, razor blades, shoe laces, and chocolate bars, were propped up in open boxes. Above his bed, pasted to the wall, was a map similar to the one hanging in the company's office in Sault Ste Marie. Covering most of the map were pictures of boxers, hockey players, movie stars, old Christmas cards, pin-up girls, and an old calendar advertising Life Insurance.

"Your's will be number forty-two."

He spoke with difficulty for he had no teeth. They were sunk in a glass of water on the floor by his bed. "You'll have another student in with you later. Tree." And he laughed. "That's an easy one to spell." He

licked the end of the pencil and printed my name large on the cardboard.
"You can get most things from me." He showed me the cupboard built
into the wall where he returned the piece of cardboard. Inside sprawled
hundreds of paper-backed books. "Mystery, cowboy, sex stories, no need
to pay. It'll come off your cheque." He gave me the key to my room and
returned to his bed entering between the sheets fully dressed.

"By the way Tree, where you from?"

"Montreal."

I waited. There was no reply.

As I walked out he called back. "Shut the light."

Number 42 was a square room freshly painted white, with one
window directly opposite the door. Two beds. Two dressers. A naked
light hung from the ceiling. I tried to raise the window but was able to
move it only a few inches. I could see the side of a hill, the sky, and trees.
The outside air tasted cold in my throat.

I unpacked and had put on a sweater and old flannels when I heard a
bell tolling. There was nothing urgent about the sound. Silence. Then the
sound again. I went out of the room and looked out of the window in the
passage. Men were pressed tight to the door of the cookhouse. Others
were running towards it. Suddenly the door opened and those that were
there disappeared inside. By the time I reached the cookhouse the tables
were crowded with men eating. Late-comers, like myself, were running
from one table to the other until we found a place on a bench.

At my table they were speaking German. The only one not speaking
was deformed. He sat opposite me. Stubbles for fingers on a wrist which
was raw. A large red handkerchief, tied around his head, went
underneath his chin. He used this handkerchief to hold his jaw together.
To eat he would loosen the knot above his head and with one stubbled
hand he would slide the food from the table to his mouth while the other
worked the jaw up and down.

"You a Canadian?"

He had bad teeth.

"Yes," I said.

"Look at the monkeys eat."

As a platter of food was placed on the table, often before it reached
the table, bodies pushed, hands snatched whatever they could get. In less
than ten minutes it was all over.

Outside the tramline continued to creak. The men stood waiting by the side of the cookhouse where, on to the main wall, a wooden booth was built. It stuck out like an ear. Steps without handrails led to a door. Someone shouted. "Here he comes." I saw Willie Hare coming from the office towards the cookhouse, his hands full of letters and newspapers. He gave the letters to the first man then went up the ladder to the booth and threw the papers inside. "Shout them out." Another man took the envelopes away from the first man and began to call out names. Letters passed from hand to hand. After all the names had been read out several times the DP's went through them again.

I woke next morning to the sound of blasting followed later by the steady tolling bell. Breakfast was a repetition of the supper last night, except that different faces were at the table. After breakfast I walked over to the office. The manager had not yet arrived. Glorie suggested that I go and see the doctor as I had to have a medical before I could begin work.

The doctor's office (a wooden building as were all the buildings on top of the hill) was a few minutes' walk from the cookhouse. His hours according to a sign were 10-12. I arrived after ten and it was now 11.32 and still no one had arrived. A man with a crew-cut, wearing white shorts and an open shirt approached. I asked him if he was the doctor.

"I'm not that lucky," he said, and walked on.

The doctor arrived at noon. He was the palest person I had so far seen at the Mine. A long head on a tall thin body. His face reminded me of a goat. Straight black hair parted on the side. A thin mouth. It was difficult to guess his age. He could as easily have been in his thirties as in his forties. He opened the door and indicated that I enter.

"They said in the office to come and see you about a medical."

He remained silent, took off his jacket and flung it on to the leather couch that was near his desk. The room was small and stifling. All the windows were closed. Papers were on the floor. A file, like a broken accordion, lay on the floor with papers sticking out from the bellow pockets. A telephone was on the desk. Beside it, piled high on top of each other, were old telephone directories. On the desk a dish had dried apples, over-ripe pears, and an onion sprouting. A green filing cabinet stood against the wall by the window. On top of it several parcels, tied crudely together, had holes in the brown paper as if the rats had been there. A picture of Mickey Mouse was the only bright spot in the room and it hung as a target on a piece of cardboard underneath the eye-chart. There were three chairs and a leather couch to sit on.

"You another student?"

I said I was.

He began to listen to my chest.

"Where you from?"

"McGill."

He looked up, surprised.

"And how is the dear place. Are they still after you asking to give money for some building or drive, writing you letters, telling you how important you are to them—"

"I just graduated," I said.

"You'll get them soon enough."

He did not bother to examine me further but went over to his filing cabinet, unlocked it, and from the back he brought out two large glasses and a half-full bottle of brandy.

"It's all right, Tree. I was there myself. Good time. Best time I ever had."

He poured the glasses nearly full and we drank.

"We must have a re-union. You know you are the first McGill man who has hit this God-forsaken hole. The others at the staff table are a bunch of hicks from all the hick colleges across the country." Then, as if he remembered something, he came and shook my hand.

"My name is Crepeau."

We continued drinking. I told him who on the faculty had died, who had left, and he appeared to be interested when I said a name he knew. The conversation jumped from the campus, to Montreal, to sport, to the different places we had seen. "Look at yourself," he suddenly interrupted, "You talk. You can talk like I can talk. We both can make talk. Talk on anything. They have seen to that. But what good does it do you, or anybody else? They've sandpapered all your rough edges, your instincts, your intuitions, then turned you out with a fake smartness like a car on the assembly line. You happen to be the 1950 model. I was the 1933. The funny thing is we like it."

He stood up.

So did I.

"You'd better sit. You're only here for this summer so you'd better listen. I was like yourself twenty years back, perhaps better. I had first-class honours, won prizes, had an offer to continue research in a San Francisco hospital. But I said to hell with them—"

He opened his arms indicating the untidy room.

"—they don't make it easy for you to be a failure."

Suddenly he seemed to lose interest in what he was saying for he walked to the filing cabinet and from behind it took out an air rifle and a candle. He lit the candle and stood it up on top of the filing cabinet, in front of the crudely wrapped parcels. He broke his rifle and inserted a slug.

"Let's see what kind of shot you are. Go against the far wall and put the flame out."

The distance was about ten yards. I aimed. I missed. He made me try again. This time I hit the candle, knocking it down, but the wick still burned. He tried. His first shot either went through the flame, or very near it, for it flickered. The next one put it out. He returned the rifle to its place and offered me a cigarette.

"I know I'm tight, but it does not matter. What does any one person matter. They come into your world for a while then leave it just as quickly as they entered."

He finished what was in his glass, poured more in and drank it down.

"Don't expect the men to like you. When they find out that you've been to university and have come here it's like telling them that what they believe in is rotten. They work hard to save money so that their kids can go to university, get a degree, and not have to come to places like this. Then they see you here—"

The room was stuffy yet all the windows were shut. I was glad that he stopped talking for I found the atmosphere in the room and the brandy had made me sleepy and I wondered how much longer he would go on before I could excuse myself and leave.

"Use your eyes and you can see a lot," he said. "Everyone else who is here has not come by choice. The DP's are counting the days, marking them off on their calendars until they can get away to Toronto, Montreal, or Winnipeg. Those who work underground stay as long as the bonus makes it worthwhile, then they drift to some other place. A few scarecrows like Willie Hare and Old Harold hang on because the company ruined them as human beings. For fun the men play crap, smuggle hootch, and pin black lace panties on their walls that they get from the Soo."

He stopped talking to drink and fill the glasses again.

"I suppose you'll return to Montreal," he burped and excused himself.

"I don't want any of that kind of civilization. I've contracted out from all of them. I drink, and I write poetry."

He tried to get more brandy out of the bottle but it was empty.

"Sometimes I go to the Soo. The last time I took a case of Scotch, found myself a hotel room, locked the door, and I didn't get out of bed as long as the Scotch lasted."

He went over to his desk, unlocked a drawer, and brought out a leather folder. From it he took a piece of paper.

"I wrote this on my last blow."

All your experiences:
Those bits.
Those pieces you carried away with you.
How long will they last?

At the undertaker she showed me the coffin.
'Oak the best wooden one
Won't last you more than twenty-five years.
It falls away like paper.'

Those bits and pieces you carried away.
How long will they?

He stopped. For some reason he looked embarrassed. He went to his desk and returned the piece of paper to the leather folder.

"I've got a couple of hundred poems. Some day I'll get them put into a nice book and send it to the dear old place with my compliments."

The effort of reading seemed to sober him up for he threw the empty bottle into a large sack by his desk that had something soft in it for there was no sound of the bottle hitting. He picked up his jacket.

"There's no point staying in here."

We went out and walked along the slope of the hill. The bell began to toll for lunch. Grass was burnt. And scattered were small patches of blueberry bushes. We walked on a narrow path sunk in the hard ground following the contour of the hill. I could see the tramline going down but we were too far away to hear the buckets creak although the sound of the bell still reached us. The doctor walked in front.

"Fly in?"

"No. I took the train."

"It only takes an hour to fly in."

"The manager at the Soo told me pilots can't find this lake easy."

"There's only one lake in the bush shaped like ours."

We walked on. The sun was still hot. The bell tolled behind us. And I could now see a gull flying alongside the hill and a small piece of blue locked in the surrounding earth and rock growing larger below. The slope of the land entered the water and split the top quarter in two.

"What does she look like to you," the doctor said.

I stood on a flat rock looking at the lake that I had come by on the bus yesterday.

"To me it's more like a heart."

He said this without waiting to hear what I might say.

We All Begin in a Little Magazine

We live in a small coastal town. And in the summer, when the place is looking its best, it becomes overcrowded with people who have come away from the cities for their annual holiday by the sea. It is then that we leave and go up to London for our holiday.

My wife usually finds a house by looking through *The Times.* In this way we had the house of a man who built hotels in the poor parts of Africa so that wealthy American Negroes could go back to see where their grandparents came from. Another summer it was an architect's house where just about everything was done by push-button control. A third time, it was in a house whose owner was in the middle of getting a divorce—for non-consummation—and wanted to be out of the country.

This June she saw an ad saying: DOCTOR'S HOUSE AVAILABLE IN LONDON FOR THREE WEEKS. REASONABLE RENT. She phoned the number. And we agreed to take it.

The advertised house was central, near South Kensington tube station, not far from the Gardens. The taxi took us from Paddington—how pale people looked in London on a hot summer's day—and brought us to a wide street, stopping in front of a detached all-white house with acacia trees in the front garden. A bottle of warm milk was on the doorstep. I opened the door with the key and brought our cases inside.

The phone was ringing.

"Hello," I said.

"Is this *ABC?*" a youthful voice asked.

"I'm sorry," I said. "You have the wrong number."

"What is your number?"

"Knightsbridge 4231," I said.

"That *is* the number," the voice said.

"There must be some mistake," I said. "This is a doctor's house."

"Is the doctor there?"

"No," I said. "He's on holiday."

"Can I leave a message for him?"

"Are you ill?"

"No," he said. "Tell him that David White rang. David White of Somerset. He has had my manuscript for over six months now. He said he would let me know over a month ago. I have written him four times."

"I'll tell him," I said.

"If he needs more time," the young man said hesitantly, "I don't mind—"

"Okay," I said and hung up.

"I don't know what's going on here," I said to my wife.

But she and the children were busy exploring the rest of the house.

It was a large house and it looked as if it had been lived in. The front room was a children's room with all sorts of games and blackboards and toys and children's books and posters on the walls. There was the sitting-room, the bottom half of the walls were filled with books in shelves. There were more books in the hallway, on the sides of the stairs, and in shelves on every landing. There were three separate baths. A breakfast room where a friendly black cat slept most of the time on top of the oil-fired furnace. And a back garden with a lawn; flowerbeds on the sides; a pond with goldfish, water-lilies; and a copper beech tree at the end.

The phone rang and a shaky voice said:

"May I speak to Doctor Jones?"

"I'm sorry, he's on holiday."

"When will he come back?"

"In three weeks," I said.

"I can't wait that long," the voice said. "I'm going to New York tomorrow."

"Would you," I said, "like to leave a message?"

"I can't hear what you're saying," the voice said. "Can you speak up? I'm a bit deaf and have to wear a hearing aid. The doctors have a cure for this now. If I'd been born two years later I would have been all right."

"I said would you like to leave the doctor a message?"

"I don't think that will do any good," he said. "Could you look in his office and see if he has a poem of mine? It's called 'Goodbye.' If it is in proof, don't bother. I'll wait. But just find out. I'm going over to teach creative writing in night school so I can make some money to come back here. The poem will probably be on the floor."

"Hold on," I said.

I went into the office at the top of the house. The floor was cluttered with papers and magazines and manuscripts with letters and envelopes attached. On a wooden table, a large snap file had correspondence. A box had cheques for small amounts. There were also several pound notes, loose change, a sheet of stamps, and two packages of cigarettes. (How trusting, I thought. The doctor doesn't know us—supposing we were crooks?) There was typing paper, large envelopes, a typewriter, a phone, telephone directories, and some galleys hanging on a nail on a wall. A smaller table had an in-and-out tray to do with his medical work, more letters, and copies of the *Lancet*. The neatest part of the room was the area where stacks of unsold copies of *ABC* were on the floor against the far wall.

"I'm sorry," I said on the phone. "I can't see it."

"Oh," he said. He sounded disappointed.

"Well, tell him that Arnold Mest called. M-E-S-T."

"I've got that," I said.

"Goodbye," he said.

"You won't guess," I told my wife. "The doctor edits a little magazine."

"We can't get away from it," she said.

Early next morning the doorbell woke us. It was the postman. He gave me several bundles. There were letters from different parts of England and Europe and airmail ones from the States, Canada, Australia and South America. There were two review copies of books from publishers. There were other little magazines and what looked like medical journals, and a few bills.

As I put the envelopes and parcels on the chair in the office and saw the copies of *Horizon* and *New Writing*, the runs of *Encounter, London Magazine,* and a fine collection of contemporary books on the shelves right around the room—it brought back a time twenty years ago when I first came over.

There was still the bomb-damage to be seen, the queues, the ration-books, the cigarettes under the counter. And a general seediness in people's clothes. Yet I remember it as one of my happiest times. Perhaps because we were so innocent of what writing involved. A lot of boys and girls had come to London from different parts. And we would meet in certain pubs, in certain restaurants, Joe Lyons, the French pub, Caves de France, the Mandrake. Then go on somewhere else. I remember going over to see another Canadian, from Montreal, who was writing a novel. He had a studio, by the Chelsea football grounds (we could always tell when a goal was scored). I remember best the cold damp winter days with the fog thick—you could just see the traffic lights—and then going inside and having some hot wine by the open fire and talking about writing, what we were writing, and where we had things out. We used to send our stories, optimistically, to the *name* magazines. But that was like taking a ticket in a lottery. It was the little magazines who published us, who gave encouragement and kept us going.

I remember Miss Waters. She was in her late forties, a pale woman with thinning blond hair and a docile tabby cat. She edited a little magazine founded by her great-grandfather. She had photographs of Tennyson on the wall, of Yeats and Dylan Thomas. And wooden pigeon holes, like the sorting room at the post-office, with some of the recent back-issues. She didn't know when I was coming. But she always greeted me with:

"How nice to see you. Do come in."

She walked, ahead, into the dark living-room. Suggested that I take my winter coat off. Then she would bring out a decanter of sherry and fill a glass. Then take out a package of *Passing Clouds,* offer me a cigarette.

I was treated as a writer by this woman when I had very little published. And that did more than anything to keep up morale. And after another sherry, another *Passing Cloud,* and she had asked me what I was working on and seemed very interested in what I said, she told me that her great-grandfather paid Tennyson a thousand pounds for one of his short poems, and two thousand pounds to George Eliot for a short story. (Was she trying to tell me that there was money to be made out of writing?) Then she stood up. And we went into the other room. It was very neat and tidy. Magazines on a table laid out as at a newsagent's, books as in a library.

"Is there anything you would like to review?" she asked.

I would pick a novel or two, or a book of short stories.

Then she would say. "And help yourself to four books from that pile."

That pile consisted of books she didn't want reviewed. She had told me, the first time, to take these books to a bookseller in the Strand who would give me half price for them, and later sell them to the public libraries. But before I could get the money from him I had to sign my name in what looked like a visiting book. And I saw there, above me, the signatures of the leading Sunday and weekly reviewers—they were also selling their review copies for half price.

And I remember how I would come to her place—with the brown envelopes lying behind the door—broke and depressed. And when I left her, I left feeling buoyed up, cheerful. There would be the few pounds from the review copies. Money enough for a hamburger and a coffee and a small cigar. And there was something to do—the books to review. She always paid in advance.

And before Miss Waters there were others. The press officer at the Norwegian Embassy—he ran a Norwegian little magazine, in English, from London. And another one, from India, also in English. My early stories appeared in both. And when I got a copy of the Indian magazine I saw that my Canadian characters had been turned into Indians. And there was another editor who would ask to borrow your box of matches. Then when you got back to your flat you found he had stuffed a pound note inside the box.

They are all gone—like their magazines.

And something has gone with them.

Those carefree days when you wrote when you felt like it. And slept in when you wanted to. And would be sure of seeing others like yourself at noon in certain places.

Now in the morning, after breakfast, I wait for the mail to come. Then I go upstairs and close the door behind me. And I make myself get on with the novel, the new story, or the article which has been commissioned by a well-paying magazine. I take a break for lunch, then come back up here until 4. Once in a while I might take a day off and go on a bus to see what the country is like. I forget that there is so much colour about. Or, for a change, take a train for the day to Plymouth. But otherwise, it is up the stairs to this room. All my energy now goes into work. I light up a small Dutch cigar, and sometimes I talk to myself. I feel reasonably certain now that what I have written will be published. Writing has become my living.

Of course there are still the occasional days when things are going right and the excitement comes back from the work. Not like in those early days when writing and the life we were leading seemed so much to belong together. I had complete faith then in those little magazines. What I didn't know was that what they bred was infectious. They infected a lot of young people with the notion that to be involved with literature was somehow to be involved with the good life. And by the time you learned differently—it was usually too late.

On Friday I had to be up early. In the morning I was to be interviewed in a rowing-boat on the Serpentine for a Canadian television program on the "Brain-Drain." And later I was to meet my publisher for lunch.

It was very pleasant on the water early in the morning. The sun made patterns. People going to work stopped to watch. While I rowed the interviewer, the cameraman, the sound-recordist and their equipment—and was asked why I wasn't living in Canada, and why did I write?

I met my publisher in his club. He is an American, from Boston, bald and short. We had a martini. Then another. Then we went into the dining-room. Smoked salmon followed by duck with wine, then dessert. And ending with brandy and a large Havana cigar.

He asked me what type I would like for the book, could I send him the blurb for the dustjacket? He told me the number of copies they would print, that one of the Sunday papers wanted to run a couple of extracts before publication. He told me some gossip about other writers, publishers and agents. And what was I writing now? And which publishing season would he have it for?

I left him after 4, and caught a taxi back to the house.

"How did it go?" my wife asked.

"Okay," I said. "How was the zoo?"

She began to tell me when we heard a noise. It sounded as if it was coming from the front door. We went to look and surprised a man with a key trying to open the door. He was in his late fifties, short and stocky and wearing a shabby raincoat.

"Is the doc in?" he said timidly.

"No," I said. "He's on holiday."

"Oh," he said. "I've come up from Sussex. I always have a bed here when I come up."

He spoke with an educated accent.

"I'm sorry," I said. "But we have the place for three weeks."

"I always have a bed here when I come up."

"There isn't room," I said.

"My name is George Smith," he said. "*ABC* publish me. I'm a poet."

"How do you do," I said. "We'll be gone in ten days. Come in and have a drink."

While I poured him a brandy, I asked what was the name of his last book.

He said he had enough work for a book and had sent the manuscript to—and here he named a well-known publisher.

"But I haven't heard," he said.

"That's a good sign," I said.

"Perhaps they have lost it," he said. "Or they are, like Doc, on holiday."

He brought out a small tin and took some loose tobacco and began to roll his own cigarette and one for me.

"How long," I asked, "have they had it?"

"Nearly five months," he said.

He finished his brandy. I poured him some more.

"I would ring them up and find out," I said. "Or drop them a line."

"Do you think I should?"

"Yes," I said.

I went to the door to see him out. And instead walked him to the bus stop.

The street was full of mountain ash and red berries were lying on the lawns, the sidewalk, and on the road.

"I had a letter from T. S. Eliot," he said. "I kept it all these years. But I sold it last month to Texas for $50," he said proudly. "My daughter was getting married. And I had to get her a present."

I asked him where he would stay the night.

"I have one or two other places," he said. "I come up about once every six weeks. London is my commercial centre."

I went and bought him a package of cigarettes.

"Thank you," he said.

The red bus came and I watched him get on.

When I got back my wife said:

"Well, do you feel better?"

"No," I said.

It went on like this—right through the time we were there. An assortment of people turned up at the door. There was a young blond girl—she wanted to lick stamps for literature. There were visiting lecturers and professors from American and Canadian and English universities. There were housewives; one said, over the phone, "I'll do anything to get into print." There were long-distance telephone calls. One rang after midnight and woke us up. "Nothing important," the voice said. "I just wanted to have a talk. We usually do now and then. I've had stories in *ABC*."

There was, it seemed, a whole world that depended on the little magazine.

I tried to be out of the house as much as possible. I went to see my agent. He had a cheque for $500, less his commission, waiting for me, for the sale of a story. He took me out for a meal. And we talked about the size of advances, the sort of money paperback publishers were paying these days, the way non-fiction was selling better than fiction. I met other writers in expensive clubs and restaurants. We gossiped about what middle-aged writer was leaving his middle-aged wife to live with a young girl. And what publisher was leaving his firm to form his own house. I was told what magazines were starting—who paid the best.

Then I would come back to the phone ringing, the piles of mail, and people turning up at the door eager to talk about the aesthetics of writing. I didn't mind the young. But it was the men and women who were around my age or older who made me uncomfortable. I didn't like the feeling of superiority I had when I was with them. Or was it guilt? I didn't know.

Meanwhile my wife and kids enjoyed themselves. They went to the Victoria and Albert Museum, the National Gallery, the Tate. And came back with postcard reproductions that they sent to friends. They went to a couple of Proms, to a play, had a day in Richmond Park, Hampton Court, and a boat ride on the Thames.

When the time came to go back—they didn't want to.

But I did.

I had passed through my *ABC* days. And I wanted to get away. Was it because it was a reminder of one's youth? Or of a time which promised more than it turned out to be? I told myself that there was an unreality about it all—that our lives then had no economic base—that it was a time of limbo. But despite knowing these things, I carry it with me. It represents a sort of innocence that has gone.

On the Saturday morning waiting for the taxi to come to take us to Paddington Station—the phone rang. And a young girl's voice wanted to know about her short story.

I said the doctor was away. He would be back later. She ought to ring this evening.

"What time?"

"After nine," I said.

"Have you read the story?" she asked. "What do you think of it?"

"We just rented the house," I said. "We were here for a holiday."

"Oh," she said. "You're not one of us?"

"No," I said.

Then the taxi came. And the driver began to load the cases into the back of the car.

Afterword

I wrote "A Small Piece of Blue" towards the end of 1955 in St Ives, Cornwall. I was waiting to go to Canada in order to do a trip across the country (the trip was to form the backbone of the book *Canada Made Me*) and had made a list of the places I would visit. One of the places was Helen Mine, an iron mine in northern Ontario, where I had worked during the summer of 1948 after graduating from McGill. In the autumn I would return to McGill for my M.A., then go off to England. Meanwhile I had to earn some money. A summer job, in the past, usually meant working in Ottawa, for the government, in an office. But there had been a war. I had been in the RCAF. And I didn't want to go back to what I was used to. So going to work in the mine was also an act of bravado.

I didn't have a clear notion of the story when I started. Only a definite intention—of wanting to show something of what living and working in this iron mine was like. Yet, some of the ingredients in this story came not from the mine but from people and incidents I had met elsewhere.

The woman with no nose—she came from Barnstaple, in North Devon. She was a music teacher and let out a room. I took it for a few months in 1954.

The shooting with the gun, indoors, at a lit candle was told to me about what went on board the French Crabbers, anchored in the bay off St Ives, at night.

The poem that begins:

All your experiences:
Those bits.
Those pieces you carried away with you.
How long will they last?

I wrote that separately, as a poem, in 1952. I had not long been married and we were staying, very briefly, with my wife's parents in London. I remember I was in a pub reading a newspaper. An American professor had come over to England to exhume a tomb to try and prove that Bacon had written Shakespeare's plays. There was another customer in the pub as well. We got talking. He said he worked at an undertakers. And he told me some technical things about his job: what was the best wood to have and how even that didn't last very long . . .

I did not think of these separate pieces as parts of a jigsaw that I had to get to fit in order to make this story. As I remember it, all I wanted was to write a story about the experience of living and working in the mine. And it was the pressure of writing the story that made me remember these disconnected memories. The pressure of writing the story was like a magnet that pulled these pieces from my past. And by the time I came to the part of the doctor I found I had to invent him in order to make the story work.

A few months after finishing "A Small Piece of Blue" I was in northern Ontario again, at Helen Mine. And one of the first things I did was to go to the lake to see if it was shaped like a heart. It wasn't. And I don't know why I expected it to be.

"We All Begin in a Little Magazine" was written in the autumn of 1971. And I remember the circumstances clearly.

I had spent four years (1965–69) writing and revising the novel *From a Seaside Town*. It was published in 1970. Then I made a selection of some of the early stories and most of the recent ones for *I Don't Want To Know Anyone Too Well*. And that was published in 1971. All I had left were a few odd stories I had not included. I tried to earn some money by sending these to Robert Weaver at the CBC. He kept returning them. After returning the same story twice he asked me if I would write a new story for him, as a commission, for his radio series *Anthology*. (Ten years later, in Toronto, he told me it was the first time the CBC had commissioned anyone to write a short story.) I received Weaver's letter in Mordecai Richler's house on Kingston Hill, in Surrey. We had come up from St Ives to stay in his house and have a London holiday, while he and his family went off for a holiday in Ireland. (It was not the first time that Mordecai let us have his house in this way.)

Two years earlier, in the summer of 1969, when I finished the novel, we had come to London for a three-week holiday, and found that the person whose house we had rented ran a little magazine. Somehow being in Mordecai's house surrounded by the books and the magazines that I knew from my past . . . and having been in a previous house in London where the person edited a little magazine . . . then the commission by Robert Weaver who edited *Tamarack Review*—all these combined to get me thinking about my early years in post-war England. The ambitions to be a writer. The life we led. And the difference, now, that I was one. It was this confrontation, of the past with the present, that set off the story.

Like "A Small Piece of Blue," I can pick out bits and pieces taken from a variety of places and times. And George Smith, and his visit, is an invention. But the feeling of the life we lived (and a feeling of that time) before we became writers and painters—it was this that I tried to trap.

And I remember how during that holiday in 1971 deciding, on an impulse, to go and see a painter who had been a good friend in those early years. And who I had not seen since. He was considered, then, one of the most promising young painters in England. A well-known London gallery had promised him a show when he had enough paintings. But that exhibition never did take place . . . I finally traced him to his present address. He wasn't in. I'm sure that if we had met I'd have seen the changes in his face as he would in mine. But in the way of life (the bare rooms with the windows wide open, the paint peeling from the walls, the different bell-buttons by the front door that were not working)—in that he hadn't changed. And, it seemed, that I had.

I sent the manuscript off to Weaver. He (promptly arranged for a new commission) said he liked it. And thought it was "a sad story."

John Metcalf

JOHN METCALF was born in Carlisle, England, in 1938 and emigrated to Canada in 1962. He worked for some years as a school teacher and university lecturer and has been writer-in-residence at the University of New Brunswick, the University of Ottawa, and Concordia University in Montreal. He edits, with Leon Rooke, the annual anthology *Best Canadian Stories*.

Other Works

The Lady Who Sold Furniture, (1970) Stories
Going Down Slow, (1972) Novel
The Teeth of My Father, (1975) Stories
Girl in Gingham, (1978) Novellas
General Ludd, (1980) Novel
Kicking Against the Pricks, (1982) Essays

Gentle As
Flowers Make
the Stones

Fists, teeth clenched, Jim Haine stood naked and shivering staring at the lighted rectangle. He must have slept through the first knocks, the calling. Even the buzzing of the doorbell had made them nervous; he'd had to wad it up with paper days before. The pounding and shouting continued. The male was beginning to dart through the trails between the *Aponogeton crispus* and the blades of the *Echinodorus martii*.

Above the pounding, words: "pass-key," "furniture," "bailiffs."

Lackey!

Lickspittle!

The female was losing colour rapidly. She'd shaken off the feeding fry and was diving and pancaking through the weed-trails.

Hour after hour he had watched the two fish cleaning one of the blades of a Sword plant, watched their ritual procession, watched the female dotting the pearly eggs in rows up the length of the leaf, the milt-shedding male following; slow, solemn, seeming to move without motion, like carved galleons or bright painted rocking-horses.

The first eggs had turned grey, broken down to flocculent slime; the second hatch, despite copper sulphate and the addition of peat extracts, had simply died.

"I know you're in there, Mr. Haine!"

A renewed burst of door-knob rattling.

He had watched the parents fanning the eggs; watched them stand guard. Nightly, during the hatch, he had watched the parents transport the jelly blobs to new hiding places, watched them spitting the blobs onto the underside of leaves to hang glued and wriggling. He had watched the

139

fry become free-swimming, discover the flat sides of their parents, wriggle and feed there from the mucous secretions.

"Tomorrow . . . hands of our lawyers!"

The shouting and vibration stopped too late.

The frenzied Discus had turned on the fry, snapping, engulfing, beaking through their brood.

A sheet of paper slid beneath the door.

He didn't stay to watch the carnage; the flash of the turning fish, the litter floating across the surface of the tank, the tiny commas drifting towards the suction of the filter's mouth.

He went back into his bedroom and worked himself into the sleeping-bag. Four more weeks and they would have lost their tadpole look, growing towards their maturity, becoming disc-shaped.

He studied the All-Island Realties notice. Nasty print. Two months rent. $72.50 per month. $145.00. And two more months before he could apply for the last third of his Arts Bursary. He reached for the largest butt and, staring into the flame of the match, considered his position. A change of abode was indicated. And preferably by evening.

Taking his night-pencil, his Granby Zoo pencil with animal-head pictures, he wrote on the back of the notice *God Rend You, All-Island Realties.* And then doodled. And then found himself writing out again from memory what he had completed the day before.

Into your hands, my father and my mother, I commend
My darling and delight, my little girl
Lest she be frightened by the sudden dark
Or the terrible teeth of the dog who guards your world.

"Your world" was exactly right. No use in fucking about with "Hades" or "Tartarus."

Parvula ne nigras horrescat Erotion umbras
Oraque Tartarei prodigiosa canis.

"Sudden dark" wasn't bad either.

There was a sense of rightness, too, in dividing the sentences of the original into stanzas.

The night had produced no advances on stanza two.

She would have been but six cold winters old if she had lived
Even those few days more;

That could stand. But

Inter tam veteres ludat lasciva patronos,

"patronos," that was the bugger. "Protectors" was impossible; "guardians" too custodial. Something grave was needed, grave yet tender.

"veteres patronos"

His pencil worked loops and curlicues on the paper.

The muffled phone in the kitchen rang twice, stopped, rang again. Pulling on his jeans, he went to answer it.

"Jim? It's Jackie, man."

Jackie's voice dropped to a whisper.

"The Desert Express Is In."

"Good shit?" said Jim.

"Up a tree—you know? A real mindfuck, man."

"Far out," said Jim.

"Hey, and that Gold, man. What a taste! Two tokes and you're wasted!"

"Tonight, man," said Jim.

He hung up the phone and sighed.

"veteres patronos"

veteres patronos

His possessions, by design, fitted into two large cardboard cartons. Kettle and mug. Sleeping-bag and inflatable mattress. Clothes. One picture. Writing materials. An alarm-clock. The few books he had not sold.

He stirred the coffee and Coffeemate together and wandered into the front room. On the table there lay the medium felt pen, the fine, and the fountain-pen. Beside them, the three pads of paper, white, yellow, and pale blue, the porcelain ash-tray, the square of blotting paper, the Edwardian silver matchbox.

He sat at the table drinking the coffee. He tried to visualize the three stanzas of the completed poem on the page. He'd have to supply a title; and at the end, in brackets, "The poet commends the soul of a pet slave girl to his parents who are already in the lower world. Adapted from Martial. *Epigrams. Book V.*34." Less distracting than under the title.

"veteres patronos"

He stared at the aquarium; had only a half of the fry survived—a little half of all his pretty ones—growing to the size of a dime, a quarter, a silver dollar, he could have sold them through Réal to Ideal Import Aquariums for twelve to fifteen dollars each.

With the medium felt pen on white paper he wrote:

Sixty *Symphysodon discus* at a conservative $12.00 = $720.00
Minus $25.00 for the tank
$10.00 for the pump and filter
$30.00 for the breeding fish
$15.00 for weed, tubifex worm, whiteworm,
brine shrimp and *daphnia*.

An inevitable profit of $640.00.

Work was impossible.

He needed money; he needed a place to live.

He began packing his belongings into the two cartons. The $3,500 of his Canada Council grant eroded by child-support payments, eroded by the cling of old habits. He would have to abandon the aquarium and hope that Réal could get it out.

The last of the air from the mattress.

Pevensey!

Pevensey might be good for a $30.00 review. Maybe even $60.00 for a round-up. If he could be trapped. He rolled the mattress and sleeping-bag brooding about the toadish Pevensey. Who had promised to review *The Distance Travelled* and lied.

Lack of space, old boy. Hands were tied.

In his Toad-of-Toad's-Hall tweeds and deerstalker.

In his moustache.

Who weekly reviewed *English Formal Gardens of the Eighteenth Century* or *The Rose Grower's Vade Mecum*, toadish Memoirs of endless toadish Generals.

Opening the freezer compartment of the fridge, he took out the perspex map-case which contained his completed poems and work sheets and wiped off the condensation; he kept them there in case of fire.

The kipper and the cardboard cup of Bar-B-Q Sauce he would leave to All-Island Realties as quit claim and compensation.

"Montreal *Herald*," said the girl. "Entertainments."

"Charles Pevensey, please."

"I'm sorry. He's not in this morning."

"Oh. That's strange. I'd understood he's been trying to contact me. Something about the length of my review."

"Oh," said the girl. "I see. Well, he might be in later. If you could call back at about eleven?"

Could one, he wondered, "beard" a toad?

Hefting his Air Canada bag, he stood looking around the bare white room. He'd shift the cartons after nightfall. The picture. The sleeping-bag would protect it.

A potato-shape in black crayon. A single red eye near the top. Seven orange sprouts. He'd typed underneath:

"Daddy" by Anna Haine (age 2½)

The newsprint was yellowing, the expensive non-glare glass dusty; the top edge of the frame was furred. He wiped it clean with his forefinger.

Orange arms and legs of course, silly Jim.

He tried to recall the name of the girl who'd got it framed for him. A painter sort of girl. Black hair, he remembered.

Frances?

Sonia?

But it was gone.

The Montreal *Herald* building reared concrete and glass. As he walked along toward the main entrance, past the emporia of used office-furniture, the pawn shops, the slum side streets, he wondered, as he often wondered, why he always had a compulsion to lie about his occupation to the people who gave him lifts; why he claimed to be a professor at McGill, a male nurse, a pest-control officer, a journalist.

The escalator conveyed him to the potted palms of Third Floor Reception, the elevator to the Fourth. Below him on the first and second floors, the giant drums and rollers of the *Herald* presses. He smiled at the memory of a wrench-brandishing Charlie Chaplin swimming through the cogs. He turned down the corridor to Entertainments and pushing through the swing doors, walked up the aisle between the desks to Pevensey's corner. The desk was piled with review copies, a hundred more stacked in the window embrasure behind.

He stood irresolute for a few moments and then went into the pen and sat in Pevensey's chair. The clattering typewriters paid no attention. Opposite, on the other side of the room, he noticed another set of swing doors. Glass port holes. He glanced at the top copy-sheet in the folder; a review of *Heraldry and You.* He took three cigarettes from the open package on the desk.

A tall blonde girl was walking up the aisle, looked about twenty, shoulder bag, shades. Legs too thin. She went into the next pen and dropped her bag on the desk. A plaque on the desk said Youth Beat. Her typewriter cover was dotted with stick-on flowers and butterflies. He felt her staring at him.

"Excuse me, sir."

"Umm?"

"Are you looking for someone?"

"What an attractive pendant!" he said, staring at her breasts.

"Oh, thank you."

He turned back to the file of copy.

"Excuse me. . ."

He did his blank look.

"If you're waiting for Mr. Pevensey, I'm afraid. . ."

"Mr. Pevensey!" called Jim.

A tactical blunder.

Pevensey, what looked like a teapot in his hand, glanced, pushed back through the swing doors, disappeared. Jim hurried after him.

"Mr. Pevensey!" he shouted to the echo of the footsteps on the concrete stairs. He ran down and found himself in an empty corridor facing two doors.

"PEV-EN-SEY."

One door led to the cafeteria, the other to the library. The cafeteria was nearly empty; the library girl claimed not to know who Pevensey was. He walked back up the corridor, past the foot of the stairs, found a washroom. Locking himself into a cubicle, he took the Magic Marker from his Air Canada bag and wrote on the wall:

"Charles Pevensey has a PERSONAL subscription to *Reader's Digest.*"

He lowered his trousers and sat.

He needed money.

He needed breakfast.

He needed a place to live.

A downtown breakfast would be more expensive than the Budapest where he usually ate; he liked the Budapest because George, the owner, had gold teeth and always said, "For you, gentlemans?" Today, he decided, would have to be a toast day.

Toast reminded him that it was Monday. He added a note to his list:

"Cantor's Bakery 11.30 pm (if poss.)."
The woman there sold him Friday's Kaiser rolls for 2 cents each. He also needed more tins of Brunswick sardines. Holding steady at 29 cents a tin.

Moving upset him. And he was fond of the Victoria Manor Apartments. He would miss the conversations with Mrs. McGregor who gave him milk and who, on the day he'd moved in six months or so ago, had slipped a note under his door which read:

> They are all FLQ in this building. Signed:
> the Lady Next Door. (Scottish)

And Bernie who ran the F.C.I. Detective Agency on the first floor. He'd miss the stairways which were always jammed with struggling furniture; the conversations with the basement owner of the Harold Quinn School of Music; the showcase outside the Starkman Orthopedic Shoe Company which was full of plaster casts of deformed feet.

The rest of the list read:
Call Réal.
Call McCready.
Night of the Jewish Ladies.

Staying with Myrna would be impossible; she'd want to screw all the time which was wasteful and irritating when he was nearing a possible form. Alan was still shacked up with the Bell Telephone girl.

Carol?

He remembered the last time he'd been forced to use her place. No. Not even for a few days could he live in the maelstrom of *her* emotional life. He remembered how, at her last gasp, she'd sobbed a stanza of Sylvia Plath. Nor, come to think of it, could he stomach her brown rice with bits in, wheat germ salad, and other organic filth. And he definitely wasn't inclined to endure lectures on the power of Sisterhood and the glories of multiple clitoral orgasm.

Remembering a glimpse of her naked in the bathroom, one foot on the rim of the tub, thigh, hip, the creases of her waist suffused in morning sunlight. Pure Bonnard stuff. Painter's work. He wondered if she still brushed her teeth with twigs, still washed her hair with honey.

He strained and grunted.

veteres patronos

He was being too literal. Again. He needed to get further from the text. To preserve. Intact. The main line of. Intent. But let. The.

The outer door banged shut; the bolt of the next cubicle slotted home. Checkered trousers rumpled over a pair of brown shoes.

Inter tam veteres ludat lasciva patronos
Et nomen blaeso garriat ore meum.

"Care!" said Jim.

The brown shoes cleared his throat.

Yes.

Expand it.

She would have been but six cold winters old if she had lived
Even those few days more; so let her walk
And run a child still in your elder care

"You beautiful, *inevitable* bastard!" said Jim.

"Are you okay?" said the brown shoes.

"What?"

Breakfasted on toast and coffee (25 cents) now 12.35 and his guts hollow. Used the counter phone. Professor McCready was teaching; would he care to leave a message. The white globes above the length of the counter reminded him of a night scene. A café. A woman singing. Degas? Renoir?

Just beyond, in that place between night and twilight, not to be pried at, not to be forced, the words were moving in his head.

He walked up towards Dorchester and the Queen Elizabeth Hotel weighing his chances in the lottery of grant renewal. His other two references were certain to be good. He'd sent McCready a xerox of the central poems of *Marriage Suite* now nine days ago along with the Letter of Reference form. Sixteen days to the deadline.

He strolled into the foyer of the Queen Elizabeth and wandered around looking for the notice board. Conventions, Annual Meetings, Associations of. Sometimes, wearing shirt and tie, under buffet conditions, it was possible to lunch or dine with Travel Agents, Furniture Retailers, Pharmaceutical Sales.

In the hardcover Classic Book Store on St. Catherine Street, he checked the number of copies of *The Distance Travelled*, arranged them

more advantageously. He was classified under "Canadiana" and surrounded by Esquimaux and whales.

He strolled back on the other side of the street to the paperback
store and browsed through the literary magazines, off-set and mimeo,
looking for work by his contemporaries. *Edifice, Now, Ssip,* another new
thing from Vancouver called *Up Yours.*

He walked up to the Sheraton and consulted the noticeboard; looked
in at Mansfield Book Mart; checked the Sonesta Hotel.

The same girl answered the phone again. Professor McCready had
just left for the day; would he care to leave a message?

Ten cents.

He copied down McCready's home number from the directory.

Academe—Intercede for us

Standing closed in the phone booth, he stared out at the flow of cars
along Sherbrooke.

Jury of Experts—Compassionately Adjudicate us

Significance of Past Contribution—Justify us

Selling the drugs for Jackie would probably bring him $40.00 or
$50.00 but he resented the waste of time, the endless phone-calls.

The Desert Express Is In.

Poor glazed bastard.

He wondered what peyote looked like; what one *did* with it?
Smoked it? Made an infusion? Ate it? He went back towards Classics to
find out. For all he cared, they could stuff it up their collective fundament.
As he walked along, he constructed arguments:

*Look, man. You've dropped acid. You've done chemicals. Okay. But
this is pure, it's like ORGANIC.*

Or, for the carriage trade,

*It's like acid, but SMOOTH. It's the difference between a bottle of
Brights and a bottle of wine.*

In Classics he gleaned the necessary sales information.

You ate it.

Devotees of the cactus cult are said to be "following the Peyote
Road"—he copied the expression into his notebook. The practice had
spread from Mexico to the Kiowa, Comanche, and Apache Indians.
Ingestion put one in touch with *mana*—the LIFE FORCE. Introspection
resulted. Visions of God, Jesus, and those on the Other Side were
vouchsafed.

The prospect of being forced to stay with Jackie was depressing. In the gloom of obligatory candles he would have to listen to the latest fragment of Jackie's novel—the action of which all took place in Jackie's head during a seven hour freak-out on top of Mount Royal and involved him in varieties of Cosmic Union with stars, planets, and a bi-sexual Cree Guide called Big Bear.

And he, in turn, would have to pay tribute by giving Jackie a copy of his latest verse. He'd already chopped *Howl* into tiny sections. He considered Gerard Manley Hopkins.

> O the mind
> > MIND
> has mountains
> > cliffs
> > of
> > fall
> > SHEER
> nomanfathomed.

It's like a lyric, man. They write themselves.
He resolved to call Carol.
For an hour or more, he stood watching the work on a construction site on Dorchester. He watched the tamping of the dynamite in the rock, watched the crane swing the coir nets and matting into place, waited for the full *crump* and the heave of the matting and then the buckets grubbing out the boulders and the scree. He could feel the words edging closer. He watched until he no longer saw the yellow helmets, the clanking bulldozers, the trucks churning up the muddy slope, until his eyes grew unfocussed.

The end of the afternoon was growing cold. The words hurried him across the approach of the Place du Canada where the wind was clacking the wire halyards against the aluminum flagpoles.

He found an empty table at the back of the Steerarama and sat warming his hands on the coffee cup. Shapes of figures passing beyond the net-curtained windows. Light on the chrome of the cash register. A sheen of light across the polished lino below the cash register, a green square, a red square, part of a green square before the carpet edge.

Et nomen blaeso garriat ore meum.
The horns were long, buffed and lacquered, the colours running

from grey through beige to jet at the points. From the astrakhan middle where the horns were joined hung a card which read:

Our "Famous" Steerburger (6 oz. of Prime Beef)

As he tilted his head, the light ran the horn's curved length.

blaeso garriat demanded "lisping," "stammering."

The gloss had given him,

"And lisp my name with stammering tongue."

Which made the child sound like a cross between a half-wit and Shirley Temple.

"lisping"

"prattle"

"babble"

He stared at the cinnamon Danish in the glass case on the counter. But the Night of the Jewish Ladies had promised refreshments.

Although a bending of the text, a real distortion of meaning even, and swaying on a tightrope over sentimentality, "baby talk" might.

Might.

If it was somehow balanced off.

He smoothed the paper placemat with the edge of his hand and sat staring at the drawing of the smiling waitress.

Bienvenue

He gave her spectacles, a moustache, gaps in her teeth. Suddenly he started to write.

She would have been but six cold winters old if she had lived
Even those few days more; so let her walk
And run a child still in your elder care
And safely play, and tease you with my name in baby talk.

Nodding at what he'd written, he stretched and leaned back. Everything depended now on the resolution of the final stanza. Blondin poised over Niagara had little on this. Lips working, he read the lines through again and again.

Precarious.

The *ands* repetition wasn't bad, wasn't *too* obtrusive in its suggestion of the child. But it was the tension in "tease"; it was only "tease" and its implications that were keeping him aloft.

He found that he was gazing at the cinnamon Danish; he wanted the cinnamon Danish very much. He could feel the pressure of the final stanza, the bulge and push of it in his head. The hunger had turned to hollow pain. Half an hour to his meeting Mrs. Wise on the mezzanine in her russet linen pant suit and carrying a copy of the Montreal *Herald*. A group of young wives, she'd said, meeting in each other's houses, quite informally, to discuss, to listen to speakers, to be stimulated, to broaden horizons.

Now you musn't be modest, Mr. Haine. Quite a few of the girls saw your photograph and the piece about you in the Gazette.

He hoped they'd pay him the $25.00 after the reading and not at some polite interval; he hoped it was sandwiches and not cakes. Sandwiches with meat in.

Or egg.

Or cheese.

He felt an urge to delete the inverted commas on the *Our "Famous" Steerburger* sign with his Magic Marker.

He hoped that payment would be made in cash.

The last time had been cakes.

Seventeen members of the Canadian Authors' Association had gathered in a salon of the Laurentian Hotel. The president had asked everyone to stand one after another to announce their names. Most were hyphenated ladies.

Against their rising conversation, he had read from *The Distance Travelled*. During the last two poems a waiter had wheeled in a trolley of iced cakes and an urn of coffee.

The president, a large lady, had called the meeting to order.

When he'd finished reading, sudden silence ensued.

Answering the president's call for questions, a lady with aggressive orange hair had said,

"Am I right in assuming you've had your work published?"

"Ah, yes."

"And you didn't pay for it?"

"Pay for it?"

"To have it published."

"Oh. No."

"Well my question is—who do you know?"

"Know?"

"In Toronto."

Alone in the cream and gold sitting room, he examined the mantelpiece with its tiny fluted columns, shelves, alcoves, its three inset oval mirrors. He examined the silver-framed bride and groom. He examined the Royal Doulton lady in her windblown crinolines, the knick-knacks, the small copper frying-pan-looking thing that said *A Gift from Jerusalem,* the Royal reclining Doulton lady. Glancing round at the open door, he turned back and peered into the centre mirror to see if hairs were sticking out of his nose.

He sank for a few minutes into the gold plush settee.

The doorbell kept ringing; the litany continued.

Bernice! It's beautiful!

We only finished moving in three weeks ago.

The pair of brass lamps which flanked the settee were in the form of huge pineapples. He touched the prickly brass leaves. The lampshades were covered in plastic. On the long table at the far end of the room, a white tablecloth covered food; he stared at the stacked plates and cups and saucers, at the tablecloth's mysterious humps and hollows. He took a cigarette from the silver box. Which of the little things on the occasional tables, he wondered, were ashtrays? Each time the front door opened, the chandelier above him tinkled.

Oh, Bernice! And quarry-tile in the kitchen too!

Would you like the tour?

And as the tramplings went upstairs, faintly:

master-bedroom ...

cedar-lined. ...

A plump woman wandered in. He nodded and smiled at her. She hesitated in the doorway staring at him. The green Chinese lady gazed from her gilt frame. The plump woman went around the other end of the settee and stood fingering the drapes. He tried to remember the painter's name; Tetchi, Tretchisomething—a name that sounded vaguely like a disease.

"Are you the poet?" said the plump woman.

"Yes, that's right."

He smiled.

"We had a nudist last week," she said.

Panty-hose. Stocking-top. The whites of their thighs.

Seated in the centre of the room on the footstool provided, he read to the assembled ladies. He read from his first Ryerson chapbook.

He read his Dylan orotundities,

In a once more summer time than this.

His Auden atrocities,

Love, now, like light.

He read for 40 minutes, giving them Nature, Time and Love.

The pièce de résistance proved to be lox.

With rye bread. And cream cheese. Salami. Half-sours. Palma ham. Lima bean salad with mint. Devilled eggs and sculptured radishes. The cheese-board afforded Limburger, Gouda, Cheddar, Danish Blue, Feta and Gruyère.

Are poets different than other people?

Salami.

. . . or do you wait for inspiration?

Potato salad.

"No, of course not. It's my pleasure. For. . . ?"

"Bernice."

Jenny. Helen. Shirley. Joan. Ruby.

WITH BEST WISHES.

Nine Distance Travelled *at $6.00 (Author's Discount $2.00)* = $18.00 *Profit.*

"Well, I don't want to sound pompous, but I suppose you'd call it vision."

Radish.

"Pardon?"

". . . was wondering if Bernice had arranged a lift downtown for you? Because I'm leaving soon if you'd like a ride?"

"Over there," she said as they crunched across the gravel. "What my dear husband calls 'the Kraut bucket.'"

He wondered how old she was. Thirty-five. Expensively styled black hair. A year or two more maybe. Her strained skirt rode higher as they slammed the doors. He glanced at the nylon gleam of her thighs. She seemed unconcerned.

"Cigarette?" she said.

He leaned towards the flame. Her perfume was heavy in the car. She blew out smoke in a long sigh.

"I liked your poems," she said.

"Thank you."

"I'm not just saying that. I thought they were really good."

"I really appreciate that."

"You're very polite—a very polite person, aren't you?"

She turned the key and roared the motor.

"What makes you say that?" he said.

She shrugged.

"Nothing."

As they turned out of the drive, she said, "How do you stand it?"

"Stand what?"

"Oh, for Christ's sake!" she said.

He stared at her profile.

"Why do you go then?" he said.

"Stand *what*," she said.

"What the hell did you expect me to say?"

She shrugged and then crushed the cigarette into the ashtray.

"Are you married?"

"No," he said. "Why?"

She turned onto the access road to the Trans-Canada.

"Kids," she said. "My dear husband's dinners. Even Bernice Wise is a vacation."

She snapped on the radio.

They settled into the drive back from Pointe Claire. She drove with angry concentration. The nylon sheen of her thighs green in the glow from the radio dial. The winding and unwinding notes of a harpsichord, the intricate figurings, absolved him from conversation. Mesmeric the rise and fall of headlights, the steady bore of the engine, the weaving patterns of the lanes of traffic; mesmeric the play of light and shadow, the approach and fall of overpasses, the rush of the concrete void. The heater was making him drowsy. The words were drifting. Her gloved hand moved on the gear-shift.

Trying to break free, the swell of words lifting and stirring like pan ice.

Mollia non rigidus caespes tegat ossa, nec illi,
> *Terra, gravis fueris: non fuit illa tibi.*

The final movement of the poem, dear ladies, changing direction, *terra*, changing direction, *terra* in the vocative.

All, all, dear ladies, a question of balance.

"*rigidus caespes*"

"Sod," was ludicrous; he toyed with "rock," "turf" and "stones." He was being trapped into the literal again; the morning at the Montreal *Herald* was repeating itself.

"Charles Pevensey has a PERSONAL subscription to the *Reader's Digest*."

Pleasing.

There was something about the toadlike Pevensey that had been working on his mind all day. An echo of the name's sound. *Epitaph on Salomon Pavy.* Because it was an echo too, he knew, of Ben Jonson. *Epitaph on Elizabeth L. H.*

Pevensey. Pevensey.

Penshurst.

COUPLETS.

It needed couplets. *That* was the connection. The bastard needed couplets. He sat up and patted his pockets, finding a pencil stub in his shirt. His pad was in the Air Canada bag on the back seat. Removing the cigarettes from his package, wrapping them in the silver paper.

"Yes, please," she said.

"What? Oh, sorry."

"Will you light me one?"

As she took it from him, she said, "I'm sorry I was bitchy before."

"That's okay."

"Just one of those days," she said.

He spread the inner part of the packet on his knee and started to write, then scribbled over the words.

The car stopping and starting now. Neon signs. Salada Tea. Traffic lights. Uniroyal Tire.

They turned south onto Decarie heading downtown. Past the first of the restaurants.

"Mr. Haine?"

She glanced in the rear mirror and then smiled at him.

"If you want to write it down," she said.

"What?"

"It's 743-6981."

Gentle as flowers ... he wrote.

"And if a man answers?"

She laughed.

Gentle as flowers make the stones

She pulled into the right-hand lane and took the exit to Queen Mary Road.

"You know something?" she said.

He grunted enquiry, crossing through a word he'd written.

"You've got a cruel mouth. I bet a lot of women have told you that."

"Me, cruel? I'm nice," he said.

"James Haine," she said. "Does anyone call you 'James'?"

"No. Nor Jimmy."

Dare he use "comfort"?

"Actually," she said. "my name isn't Rena. Well, it *is*, but my friends call me Midge."

"Midge?"

"Short for Midgicovsky—from school."

"That's a nice name," he said. "I like that."

"And you *have* got a cruel mouth."

"Oh, Grandmama!"

"What's that meant to mean?"

A girl's name—two syllables.

"You're making me sound like the Big Bad Wolf."

"What?"

"You know. All the better to bite you with sort of stuff."

She laughed.

"Well, you *have*," she said. "And anyway, you don't hear me screaming for help."

That comfort...

"Anyway, I like it," she said. "You're different."

He glanced at the Duc de Lorraine bakery as they turned onto Côte des Neiges. He used to buy warm croissants there in his richer days. Surprise her with coffee, cognac, croissants. After writing all night, walking up in the early morning with the dog before she was awake.

Two syllables.

She braked and changed lanes.

Gentle as flowers make the stones
That comfort Liza's tender bones.

Turning off Côte des Neiges, she took the road leading up to the Mountain.

"It's so beautiful up here at night," she said. "You don't mind, do you? I always come this way on the way home."

On the left the cemetery spreading up the slope for acres behind the black railings; mausoleums, statues, crosses, the dull glimmer of the endless rows of polished marble headstones.

Past Beaver Lake. On to the summit.

She parked the car at the Mount Royal Lookout, silence settling as they gazed over the lights of the city. A ghostly wedge from the revolving sweep of the searchlight on top of Place Ville Marie shone against the cloud bank to their left, shone, disappeared, shone.

"I never get tired of this view," she said.

He nodded.

She sighed.

"Jim?"

As he turned, she stretched across, her arms reaching out for him. She kissed his chin, the corner of his mouth, found his lips. Twisting towards her in the awkwardness of the seat, the gear-shift, he put his arms round her, one hand on a breast.

"Hold me," she whispered.

His back was hurting.

Her mouth was hot and open. Squirming, she reached up and unhooked her brassiere. After a few moments, she pushed her face into his neck.

"That's the sad thing about getting old," she said, her breath hot and moist on his flesh, "having your breasts fall."

"Not old," he mumbled.

She kissed him open-mouthed, then biting gently at his lower lip. She was breathing heavily.

"Get in the back," she whispered.

As they kissed again, her legs were stirring restlessly. His hand moved over nylon. She lifted herself, pulling up her skirt. She stretched out one leg and drew the other up, gasped as his fingers found her.

"We can't," she whispered. "We mustn't."

Her breathing was throaty.

"I'm off the pill and I haven't got anything with me."

His fingers were moving.

"You don't mind?"

She moved her bottom further off the edge of the seat; she was gripping his other arm and making noises.

The side of his face was sweaty against the shiny plastic upholstery. She was arching, arching herself towards him.

Suddenly her body went rigid and she clamped his hand still. They lay quiet, the rate of her breathing slowing. Her eyes were closed; her face slack. He watched the sweep of the searchlight against the cloudbank.

Lie lightly, Earth...

No.

After a minute or so, she moved her legs, easing herself up.

"Mmmm," she sighed.

She pushed him towards the other side. Her hands undoing his belt-buckle, she whispered, "Go on, lie back." She was pushing up his shirt. She lay with her cheek against his stomach and then he felt the heat of her mouth on him. Her hand moving too.

Her hair was stiff, lacquered.

He grunted and she moved her head; sperm pumped onto his stomach.

They lay in silence.

He could feel the sperm getting cold, running down his side, cold on his hip.

"There's some Kleenex in my purse," she said.

She wiped his thigh and stomach, and pulling down his shirt, snuggled up against him, kissing his mouth, his chin, his neck. He stroked her shoulders, back, running his hand down to her buttocks and up again. She pulled herself higher until her cheek was against his.

"Was it good for you, too?" she whispered.

"Mmm."

He felt a mounting excitement.

All, all, dear ladies, a question of balance.

And he'd found it.

His balancing pole, as it were, commas.

COMMAS

No risk of falling now; no staggering run up the incline of a sagging rope.

Earth COMMA *lie lightly on her* COMMA *who* COMMA
Living COMMA *scarcely burdened you.*

Tears were welling in his half-shut eyes, the lights of the city lancing gold and silver along his wet lashes, the poem perfect.

Gentle as flowers make the stones
That comfort Liza's tender bones.
Earth, lie lightly on her, who,
Living, scarcely burdened you.

Feeling his hot tears on her cheek, she lifted her head to look at him.
"You're crying," she whispered. "Don't cry."
She brushed the backs of her fingers against his cheek.
"Jim?"
He stirred, shifting himself of some of her weight.
"Jim?"
She nestled against him.
"You know something?" she said. "You're very sweet."

Single Gents Only

After David had again wrested the heavy suitcase from his father's obstinately polite grip and after he'd bought the ticket and assured his mother he wouldn't lose it, the three of them stood in the echoing booking hall of the railway station. His mother was wearing a hat that looked like a pink felt Christmas Pudding.

David knew that they appeared to others as obvious characters from a church-basement play. His father was trying to project affability or benevolence by moving his head in an almost imperceptible nodding motion while gazing with seeming approval at a Bovril advertisement.

The pink felt hat was secured by a hat-pin which ended in a huge turquoise knob.

Beyond his father's shoulder, looking over the paperbacks on the W.H. Smith stall, was a woman in a sari. David kept under observation the vision of the bare midriff and the ponderous hand of the station clock while pretending to listen to the knit-one-pearl-one of his mother's precepts.

His father eventually made throat-clearing noises and David promptly shook his hand. He stooped to kiss his mother's cheek. Her hat smelled of lavender, her cheek, or possibly neck, of lily-of-the-valley. He assured her the ticket was safe, that he knew where it was; that he'd definitely remember to let her know in the letter for which she'd be waiting if the train had been crowded; if he'd managed to get a seat.

The loud speakers blared into demented announcement, flurrying the pigeons up into the echoing girders. The onslaught of this amplified gargle and richochet coincided with his mother's peroration, which seemed to be, from the odd phrase he caught, a general reworking of the Polonius and Mr Micawber material, warnings against profligacy, going to bed late, burning the candle at both ends, debt, promiscuity, not wearing undershirts, and drink.

She gripped his hand.

He watched her face working.

As the metal voice clicked silent, she was left shouting,

"THE SECRET OF A HAPPY LIFE IS..."

Mortified, David turned his back on the gawping porter.

His father did a throat-clearing.

She continued in a fierce whisper,

"... is to *apportion* your money."

He returned their wavings, watching them until they were safely down into the tiled tunnel which led to the car park, and then lugged his case over to the nearest waste basket into which he dropped the embarrassing paper bag of sandwiches.

With only minutes to go before his train's departure, the barmaid in the Great North-Western Bar and Buffet set before him a double scotch, a half of best bitter, and a packet of Balkan Sobranie cigarettes. Flipping open his new wallet, he riffled the crisp notes with the ball of his thumb. The notes were parchment stiff, the wallet so new it creaked. Smiling, he dismissed the considerable change.

The scotch made him shudder. The aroma of the Sobranie cigarettes as he broke the seal and raised the lid was dark, strange and rich. He was aware of the shape and weight of the wallet in his jacket's inside pocket. Stamped in gold inside the wallet were words which gave him obscure pleasure: *Genuine Bombay Goat*. With a deft flick of his wrist, he extinguished the match and let it fall from a height into the ashtray; the cigarette was stronger than he could have imagined. He raised the half of bitter in surreptitious toast to his reflection behind the bar's bottles. Smoke curling from his nostrils, he eyed the Cypriot barmaid whose upper front teeth were edged in gold.

He sat in a window seat of the empty carriage feeling special, feeling regal, an expansive feeling as physical and filling as indigestion. He crossed his legs, taking care not to blunt the immaculate crease in his trousers, admiring his shined shoes. A mountain of luggage clanked past, steam billowed up over the window, a whistle blew. And then the carriage door opened and a toddler was bundled in from the platform followed by a suitcase and parcels and carrier-bags and its mother. Who hauled in after her an awkward stroller.

Doors slamming down the length of the train.

"Ooh, isn't the gentleman kind!" said the woman to the toddler as David heaved the suitcase up onto the luggage rack.

"And these?" said David.

From one of the carrier-bags, a yellow crocodile made of wood fell onto his head.

The toddler started to struggle and whine as the train pulled out. It was given a banana. It was pasty-looking and on its face was a sort of crust. Old food, perhaps. Possibly a skin disease. It started to mush the banana in its hands.

Turning away, David gazed out over the backs of old jerrybuilt houses, cobbled streets, cemeteries, mouldering buildings housing strange companies found in the hidden parts of towns visible only from trains: *Victoria Sanitation and Brass, Global Furniture and Rattan, Allied Refuse.* Clothes lines. The narrow garden strips behind the houses looking as if receding waters had left there a tideline of haphazard junk.

The train cleared the neat suburbs, the gardens, the playing fields for employees, picked up speed, vistas of distant pit-heads, slag heaps, towering chimneys and kilns spreading palls of ochre smoke, all giving way to fields and hedges, hedges and fields.

Inside his head, like an incantation, David repeated:

The train is thundering south.

Beside the shape of the wallet in his jacket's pocket was the letter from Mrs. Vivian Something, the University's Accommodations Officer. The tone of the letter brusque. He had not replied promptly as he has been instructed so to do and no vacancies now existed in the Men's Halls of Residence. Nor were rooms now available on the Preferred List. Only Alternative Accommodation remained.

274 Jubilee Street.

The morning sunshine strong, the train thundering south, the very address propitious, *Jubilee.*

As the train bore him on towards this future, he found himself rehearsing yet again the kind of person he'd become. What kind of person this was he wasn't really sure, except that he'd known without having to think about it that it wasn't the kind of person who lived in Men's Halls of Residence.

Blasts on its whistle, the train slowing through a small country station.

Nether Hindlop.

On the platform, rolls of fencing wire, wicker crates of racing pigeons, holding a ginger cat in his arms, a porter.

But at the least, he thought, the kind of person who bestowed coins on *grateful* porters. He still blushed remembering how on his last expedition to London he'd tipped a taxi-driver a shilling and the man had said,

"Are you sure you can spare it?"

And later, even more mortifying, after a day in the Tate and National Galleries, he had sat next to a table of very interesting people, obviously artistic, in a crowded café in Soho. He'd listened avidly as they chatted about Victor this and Victor that and he'd realized gradually that Victor must be Victor *Pasmore*. And as they were leaving, the man with the earring had paused by his table and said in a loud voice,

"So glad to have had you with us."

Even though he had been seared with shame and burned even now to think of it, he had in a way been grateful. He admired the rudeness and aggression and the ability to be rude and aggressive *in public*; the realm of books apart, he still considered it the most splendid thing that he had heard another person actually *say*.

But he found it easier to approach what he would become by defining what he was leaving behind. What he most definitely *wasn't*— hideous images came to mind: sachets of dried lavender, Post Office Savings Books, hyacinth bulbs in bowls, the *Radio Times* in a padded leather cover embossed with the words *Radio Times*, Sunday best silver tongs for removing sugar cubes from sugar bowls, plump armchairs.

But *how*, he wondered, his thoughts churning deeper into the same old ruts, *how* did one change from David Hendricks, permanent resident of 37 Manor Way, ex-Library Prefect and winner of a State Scholarship to something more ... more *raffish*.

"Hold a woman by the waist and a bottle by the neck."

Yes.

Somerset Maugham, was it?

Not much of a point of etiquette in his own teetotal home, he thought with great bitterness, where wild festivities were celebrated in Tizer the Appetizer and where women were not held at all.

"*Whoopsee!*" cried the mother.

The toddler was launched towards him, was upon him. He looked down at his trousers. He tried to prise the clenched, slimy fingers from the bunched material.

"There," he said, "there's a good boy ..."

"Not afraid of anything, *she* isn't!" said the woman proudly.

David blushed.

"Proper little tomboy, encha?"

David smiled.

And regarded his ruined knees.

The house stood on a corner; the front of the house faced onto Jubilee Street, the side of the house faced the cemetery on the other side of Kitchener Street. From the coping of the low wall which bounded the cemetery, rusted iron stumps stuck up, presumably the remains of an ornamental fence cut down for munitions during the Second World War. In an aisle of grass between two rows of tombstones, a small brown dog bunched, jerking tail, its eyes anguished.

There were no facing houses on the other side of Jubilee; there was a canal, tidal the driver had told him, connecting with the docks. The tide was out. Seagulls screeched over the glistening banks of mud. The smell came from the canal itself and from the massive redbrick brewery which stood on its far side.

Most of the tiny front garden was taken up by an old motorbike under a tarpaulin.

"*Not* Mr. Porteous?" she said.

"No," said David, "I'm afraid not."

She held the letter down at a distance, her lips moving. Wiry hairs grew on the upper lip. He suddenly blushed remembering that her house had been described as Alternative Accommodation and hoping that she wouldn't be embarrassed or hurt.

Her gross body was divided by the buried string of the grubby pinnafore. Her hair was grey and mannish, short back and sides with a parting, the sort of haircut he'd noticed on mentally defective women in chartered buses. The torn tartan slippers revealed toes.

"They didn't mark that down," she said.

"Pardon?"

"About the back double."

"Double?"

"With the Oxford gentleman."

"Oh," said David. "You mean ... ?"

"Yes," she said. "They should have marked that down."

He manoeuvred his suitcase round the hatstand and bicycle in the gloom of the narrow passage and followed her ponderous rump up the stairs. Reaching for the banister, grunting, she hauled herself onto the dark landing.

Even the air seemed brown.

"This is the bathroom," she said, "and the plumbing."

He sensed her so close behind him that he felt impelled to step inside. The room was narrow and was largely taken up by a claw-foot bathtub. Over the tub, the height of the room and braced to the wall, bulked the monstrous copper tank of an ancient geyser.

She was standing behind him, breathing.

He began to feel hysterical.

The lower part of the tank and the copper spout which swung out over the tub were green with crusty verdigris; water sweating down the copper had streaked the tub's enamel green and yellow. Wet, charred newspaper half-blocked the gas-burners in the geyser's insides.

"If you wanted a bath, it's a shilling," she said, slippers shuffling ahead of him, "with one day's warning."

Following her into the bedroom, he stared at the vast plaster elephant.

Two single beds stood on the brown linoleum. The wallpaper was very pink. Pinned on the wall between the beds was a reproduction cut from a magazine of Annigoni's portrait of Queen Elizabeth.

"You can come and go as you please—the key's on a string in the letterbox—but we don't have visitors."

David nodded.

"I don't hold with young ladies in rooms."

"No, of course," said David, "Quite."

His gaze kept returning to the elephant on the mantelpiece. Inside the crenellated gold of the howdah sat a brown personage in a turquoise Nehru jacket sporting a turban decorated with a ruby.

"Well ..." he said.

Staring at him, doughy face expressionless, she unscrewed a Vicks Nasal Inhaler and, pressing one nostril closed, stuck it up the other.

He politely pretended an interest in the view.

Below him, a staggering fence patched with warped plyboard and rusted lengths of tin enclosed a square of bare, packed earth.

There was a bright orange bit of carrot.

On one of the sheets of tin, it was still possible to make out an advertisement for Fry's Chocolate.

In the middle of this garden sat a disconsolate rabbit.

When the sounds seemed to have stopped, he turned back to face the room. He looked round nodding judiciously, aware even as he was doing it that it was the sort of thing his father did. He had, he realized, no idea of how to conclude these negotiations.

"And this other person? The man from Oxford?"

"Mr. Porteous."

"He's . . . ?"

"We had a telegram."

"Ah," said David, "yes. I see."

"Cooked breakfast and evening meal included," she said, "it's three pound ten."

"Well," said David, contemplating the elephant, "that sounds . . ."

"And I'll trouble you," she said, "in advance."

He shoved the empty suitcase under the bed.

The thin quilt, the sheets, the pillow, all felt cold and damp.

He thought of turning on the gas fire but didn't have a shilling piece; he thought of putting a sweater on.

Jingled the change in his pocket for a bit, inspected the wall paper more closely; the motif was lilac blossoms in pink edged with purple. It was five-thirty. He wondered at what time, and where, this evening meal was served, if "evening meal" meant tea in some form or dinner.

Voices.

Slap of slippers on lino.

He eased his door open a crack.

"Evening Post. Now that should serve her nicely, the Evening Post. Six pages of the Post. Read the newspaper, do you? Not much of a fellow for the reading. Scars, though! Now that's a different story entirely. Did I show you me scars?"

Through the banisters, an old man's head with hanging wings of white hair. Behind him, a stout boy in a brown dressing gown.

The boy stood holding a sponge bag by its string; his calves were white and plump.

"Now there's a dreadful thing!" said the old man who was

scrabbling about on his hands and knees with the sheets of newspaper manufacturing a giant spill. "A dreadful thing! Two hundred homeless. Will you look at that! There, look, and there's a footballer. Follow the football, do you? Fill in the Pools? Never a drop of luck I've had. Spot the Ball? But a raffle, now! A raffle. I fancy the odds in a raffle. A raffle's a more reasonable creature than Spot the Ball."

He disappeared into the bathroom.

The front door slammed shaking the house.

Boots.

"PERCY?"

"WHAT?"

"PERCE!"

"Quick, now!" shouted the old man. "Quick! Holy Mother, she's in full flow!"

Matches shaking from the box, he secured one against his chest and then rasped it into flame. He set fire to the drooping spill.

"BACK, BOY! BACK!"

Body shielded by the door, face averted, he lunged blindly. The expanding sheet of light reminded David of war films. The old man's quavering cry and the explosion were nearly simultaneous.

Brown shoulders blocking the view.

Suddenly from below, at great volume, Paul Anka.

I'M JUST A LONELY BOY ...

The old man was in the smoke stamping on the spill.

Ash, grey and tremulous, floated on the air.

In front of Mrs. Heaney's place at the head of the table stood a bottle of Cream Soda.

The kitchen was silent except for the budgerigar ringing its bell and stropping itself on the cuttlefish. The cooked evening meal was a fried egg, a wafer of cold ham, a quarter of a tomato, and three boiled potatoes.

The slice of ham had an iridescent quality, hints of green and mauve.

In the centre of the oilcloth stood Heinz Ketchup, Cross and Blackwell's Salad Cream, HP Sauce, Branston Pickle, OK Sauce, Daddy's Favourite, A1 Sauce, a bottle of Camp Coffee, and a punctured tin of Nestlé's Evaporated Milk.

Sliced white bread was piled on a plate.

The old man bobbed and fidgeted, darting glances.

The fat boy was called Asa Bregg and was from Manchester and had come to university to study mathematics. Ken, who had acne and a Slim Jim tie and lots of ball-point pens, was an apprentice at Hawker-Siddeley. Percy, presumably Mrs. Heaney's son, glimpsed earlier in overalls, was resplendent in a black teddy-boy suit, white ruffled shirt, and bootlace tie. What forehead he had was covered by a greasy, elaborate wave. He was florid and had very small eyes. The old man was addressed as "Father" but David was unable to decide what this meant.

Cutlery clinked.

Percy belched against the back of his hand.

The old man, whose agitation had been building, suddenly burst out, "Like ham, do you? A nice slice of ham? Tasty slice of ham? Have to go a long way to beat . . ."

"Father!" said Mrs. Heaney.

". . . a nice slice of ham."

"Do you want to go to the cellar!"

Cowed, the old man ducked his head, mumbling.

The budgerigar ejected seeds and detritus.

David studied the havildar or whatever he was on the label of the Camp Coffee bottle.

Mrs. Heaney rose heavily and opened four tins of Ambrosia Creamed Rice slopping them into a saucepan.

Percy said,

"Hey, tosh."

"Pardon?" said David.

"Pass us the slide."

"Pardon? The what?"

Percy stared.

"Margarine," said Ken.

"Oh! Sorry!" said David.

Crouched on the draining-board, the cat was watching the Ambrosia Creamed Rice.

The old man, who'd been increasingly busy with the cruet, suddenly shouted,

"Like trains, do you? Interested in trains? Like the railway, do you? Fond of engines?"

"Father!"

Into the silence, Asa Bregg said,
"*I* am. I'm interested in trains. I collect train numbers."
The old man stared at him.
Even Percy half-turned.
Ken's face lifted from his plate.
Asa Bregg turned bright red.
"I'm a member of the Train-Spotters Club."

Alone in the room that was his, David stared at the plaster elephant. He wondered how they'd got the sparkles in.

After the ham and Ambrosia Creamed Rice, he'd walked the neighbourhood—dark factories across the canal, bomb-sites, news-agents, fish and chips, Primitive Methodist Church, barber, *The Adora Grill,* and had ended up in the *Leighton Arms* where in deepening depression he drank five pints of the stuff manufactured opposite his room, an independent product called George's Glucose Stout.

The pub had been empty except for an old woman drinking Baby Cham and the publican's wife who was knitting and listening to *The Archers.*

At the pub's off-licence, as a gesture of some kind, he'd bought a bottle of cognac.

He arranged on top of the chest of drawers the few books he'd been able to carry, the standard editions of Chaucer and Spenser serving as bookends, and settled himself on the bed with Cottle's *Anglo-Saxon Grammar and Reader.* Skipping over some tiresome introductory guff about anomalous auxiliary and preterite-present verbs and using the glossary, he attempted a line of the actual stuff but was defeated by the conglomeration of diphthongs, thorns and wens; he had a presentiment that Anglo-Saxon was not going to be his cup of tea.

Heavy traffic up the stairs, voices, a strange jangle and clinking. Mrs. Heaney appeared in the doorway and behind her a tall man with blonde hair.

"This is Mr. Porteous," she said, "from Oxford."

"David Hendricks."

"How do you do? Jeremy Porteous. If I could trouble you?" he said, handing the tightly furled umbrella to Mrs. Heaney. He dropped the canvas hold-all on the floor and, slipping off the coiled nylon rope and the jangling karabiners and pitons, tossed them and the duffle coat onto the bed.

He glanced round.

"Splendid," he said. "Splendid. Now in the morning, Mrs.... ah ... Heaney, isn't it? ... I think, *tea*."

"About the rent, Mr. Porteous."

"A matter for discussion, Mrs. Heaney, if you'd be so kind, following breakfast. I've had rather a gruesome day."

And somehow, seconds later, he was closing the door on her.

He smiled.

"There's a person downstairs," he said, "called 'Father'. Seemed to want to know, rather insistently, if I enjoyed travelling by bus."

David grinned.

Advancing on the gas-fire and elephant, Jeremy said, "There's a special name, isn't there, for this chocolate chap? The one on its neck?"

"Mahout," said David.

Seemingly absorbed, Jeremy moved back a pace the better to view the elephant. He had a slight limp, David noticed, and was favouring his right leg.

"Pardon?" said David.

" 'A plate,' " repeated Jeremy, " 'of Spam.' "

David wondered how it was possible to wear a white shirt in combination with an anorak smeared with mud and at the same time look as sauve as the men in the whisky advertisements.

"What are you going to ..." David hesitated "... read at university?"

"Actually," said Jeremy, "I'm supposed to be involved in some research nonsense."

"Oh!" said David. "I'm terribly sorry. I just assumed... What did you do at Oxford?"

"I spent the better part of my time," said Jeremy, still intent on the elephant, "amassing an extraordinarily large collection of photographs of naked eleven-year-old girls with their ankles bound."

David stared at the elegant back.

He could think of absolutely nothing to say.

The gas-fire was making popping noises.

Desperate to break the silence, David said,

"Have you been climbing? Today, I mean?"

"Just toddling about on The Slabs at Llanberis. Are any of these free? I really must rest these shirts."

As he wrestled open a drawer in the chest, the mirrored door of the wardrobe silently opened, the flash of the glass startling him.

"Did you hurt your leg today?" said David, embarrassed still and feeling it necessary to ease the silence. "When you were climbing?"

"I hurt it," said Jeremy, dropping on his bed toothpaste, toothbrush, towel, and a large green book, "not minutes ago, and quite exquisitely, in what is probably referred to as the hall. On a sodding *bicycle*."

He added to his toiletries a pair of flannel pyjamas decorated with blue battle ships.

"Good God!" he said, pulling back the quilt, patting further and further down the bed. "This bed is positively *wet*."

"Mine feels damp, too," said David.

"*Yours* may be damp," said Jeremy. "*Mine* is *wet*."

He hurled the rope and the climbing hardware into a corner.

"Wet!" he shouted, striking the bed with his furled umbrella, "*Wet! Wet! Wet!*"

He seemed almost to vibrate with rage.

He pounded on the lino with the umbrella's ferrule.

"*Can you hear me, Mrs. Heaney? Are you listening, you gravid sow?*"

He stamped so hard the room shook and the wardrobe door swung open.

"WET!"

He glared about him.

He snatched at the string between the beds.

It broke.

With a loud *clung,* the gas-meter turned itself off.

He stood beside the bed with his eyes closed, one arm still rigid in the air holding the snapped string as though he were miming a straphanger in the Underground. Light glinted on the gold and onyx cuff-link. Slowly, very slowly, he lowered the arm. Opening his fingers, he let the length of string fall to the floor. Eyes still closed, he let out his pent breath in a long sigh.

He limped over to the window. He swept aside the yellowed muslin curtains. He wrenched the window high. He limped to the mantel. He hurled the elephant into the night.

David realized that he, too, had been holding his breath.

The edges of the curtains trembled against the black square.

David cleared his throat.

"Would you," he said, reaching under the bed, "would you like a drink?"

"Ummm?" said Jeremy, turning, wiping his hands with a hand-kerchief.

"A drink?"

"Ah, brandy!" said Jeremy. "Good man! It might help in warding off what these beds will doubtless incubate. Sciatica, for a start."

"Lumbago," said David.

"Rheumatoid arthritis," said Jeremy.

"*Mould*," said David.

Jeremy laughed delightedly.

Digging into his hold-all, he came up with a black case that contained telescoping silver drinking cups which, with a twist, separated into small beakers. He caught David's expression and said,

"Yes, a foible, I'm afraid, but I've always been averse to the necks of bottles. Equal in the eyes of God and all that sort of thing, certainly, but would one share one's toothbrush? Well! bung-ho!"

Along the rim of the beaker, David saw the shapes of hall-marks.

"'Lumbago,'" said Jeremy. "Don't you find that certain words make you think of things they don't mean? 'Emolument,' for example. Makes me think of very naked, very fat, black women. Something I read as a stripling about an African king's wives who were kept in pens and fed starchy tubers—so fat they couldn't get up—just rolled around—and *oiled* all over, rather like . . ." his hands sketched a shape ". . . rather like immense *seals* . . . What was I starting to say?"

"Lumbago," said David.

"Yes," said Jeremy. "I wonder why?"

There was a silence.

"So!" said Jeremy.

David nodded.

Jeremy held out his cup.

"What are you going to do?" said David.

"In the morning," said Jeremy, "we shall fold our tents. What was that woman called?"

"Mrs. Heaney?"

"No. The lodgings woman."

"The Accommodations Officer?"

"She's the one. Cornbury? Crownbury? We shall proceed against her."

"But I thought—well, from her letter, that there *wasn't* anywhere else."

"Nonsense."

"Are you just *allowed* to leave a . . . ?"

"*Who*," demanded Jeremy, "who got us into this—this *lazar house* in the first place? The responsibility is purely hers. We shall question her judgement with indignation and bitterness."

"But . . ."

"With *voluble* indignation and bitterness. We shall demand reparations. *Silver*," he said, "is so comforting to the touch, isn't it?"

David held up the brandy bottle.

"Well," said Jeremy, "*yes*."

"But you see . . ." said David.

"See what?"

"I paid her a week's rent."

"Always," said Jeremy, "try to *postpone* payment. On the other hand," he said judiciously, "never bilk."

"Well," said David, "now that you've . . . I mean, she's not likely to return my . . ."

"Life," said Jeremy climbing into his pyjama bottoms, "is very much a *balancing*, a trading-off of this against that. It's a simple question, surely? The question is: Are you the sort of person who lives in a place like this? To which," he said, working a khaki sweater down over his pyjama top, "one hopes there can be but one reply."

He reassembled the bed and spread his duffle coat over the quilt and on the duffle coat spread two sweaters and his rope.

"I find sleep impossible," he said, "without *weight*."

Whistling "We Plough the Fields and Scatter," he went out with toothbrush and towel.

David sat on the bed enjoying the brandy, enjoying the weight and balance of the silver cup, savouring Jeremy's use of the word: *we*. Thinking about the amazing fluctuations of the long day, he decided that the flavour of events was exactly caught in the casual connective of biblical narrative: *And it came to pass . . .*

The wallpaper made him feel as if he were sitting inside a friendly pink cave.

He was, he realized, drunk.

Jeremy returned whistling the hymn about those in peril on the sea and started to work himself under the layers of bedding. He asked David to pass him the book, a large-paper edition of *The Wind in the Willows* with illustrations by Ernest Shepard.

"I say," said Jeremy. "Would you . . . I mean, would it be a terrible imposition?"

"Would what?"

"Just to read a few paragraphs?"

"I haven't read this," said David, "since I was a child."

"Oh, but you should!" said Jeremy with great earnestness. "It never lets you down."

"From the beginning?"

"No," said Jeremy. "Let me think. Oh, this is *lovely*! There's the field mice singing carols to Ratty and Mole at 'Mole End'—that's always very nice. But . . . *I* know! Let's have the part where Ratty and Mole go to visit Toad. Remember? Where the motor-car wrecks Toad's caravan? Yes, Here it is."

He passed over the book.

He closed his eyes, composed his hands.

"Most kind of you."

David began.

The old grey horse, dreaming, as he plodded along, of his quiet paddock, in a new raw situation such as this simply abandoned himself to his natural emotions. Rearing, plunging, backing steadily, in spite of all the Mole's efforts at his head, and all the Mole's lively language directed at his better feelings, he drove the cart backwards towards the deep ditch at the side of the road. It wavered an instant—then there was a heart-rendering crash—and the canary-coloured cart, their pride and joy, lay on its side in the ditch, an irredeemable wreck . . .

Toad sat straight down in the middle of the dusty road, his legs stretched out before him, and stared fixedly in the direction of the disappearing motor-car. He breathed short, his face wore a placid, satisfied expression, and at intervals he faintly murmured "Poop-poop!"

The Mole was busy trying to quiet the horse, which he succeeded in doing after a time. Then he went to look at the cart, on its side in the ditch. It was indeed a sorry sight . . .

The Rat came to help him, but their united efforts were not sufficient to right the cart. "Hi! Toad!" they cried. "Come and bear a hand, can't you!"

David, turning the page, glanced over at Jeremy. His eyes were closed, his breathing deepening.

Glorious, stirring sight!" murmured Toad, never offering to move. "The poetry of motion! The real way to travel! The only way to travel!

Here today—in next week tomorrow! Villages skipped, towns and cities jumped—always somebody else's horizon! O bliss! O poop-poop! O my! O my!"

"O stop *being an ass, Toad!"* cried the Mole *despairingly.*

"And to think I never *knew!" went on the Toad in a dreamy monotone.*

David looked up.

With a long sigh, Jeremy had turned on his side.

His breathing deepened into a snore.

The coiled rope was balanced on the hump of his shoulder.

"*All those wasted years,"* David continued, reading aloud in the pink bedroom, "*that lie behind me, I never knew, never even* dreamt! *But* now—*but now that I know, now that I fully realize! O what a flowery track lies spread before me, henceforth! What dust-clouds shall spring up behind me as I speed on my reckless way!"*

Jeremy's exhalations were a faint, breathy whistle.

David closed the book.

The edges of the curtains trembled against the black square of the open window.

He switched off the light.

He pulled the quilt up to his chin and lay in the darkness listening.

Somewhere far distant in the night, in the docks perhaps, perhaps slipping its moorings and preparing to move out down the river to the sea, a ship was sounding and sounding.

Building Castles

The short story demands compression and concision, and for years now one of my pleasures has been playing with ways of creating characters quickly and vividly—ways that are analogous to caricature in the visual arts. Critics tend to look down a little on caricature as being somehow a trifle crude, an attitude that probably derives from E. M. Forster's influential book *Aspects of the Novel*. Caricature, say the critics, is an art of simplification, and they seem to suggest that simplification implies "simple." I couldn't disagree more. Caricature is an art of essences, of telling detail seized upon and inflated in the way that cartoonists seized upon Nixon's nose, in the way that African carvings of European colonial authorities are always marked by an exaggeration of the most important features—helmets, buttons, medals and weapons.

E. M. Forster's division of characters into "round" and "flat" seems to me to be propaganda for a type of writing he preferred—the "psychological" exploration. But *all* characters in fiction are artificial constructions; "round" characters are merely constructed *in a different way* from "flat" characters. They are no more "real"—and in my opinion often less so. Falstaff, say, is more vivid to me than any of the characters in *A Passage To India*.

David's mother in *Single Gents Only* is swiftly drawn; she is reduced to the hat that she is wearing, a hat which strikes David as both comic and embarrassing. Her familiar monologues are reduced to "the knit-one-pearl-one of his mother's precepts." Yet at the same time, stories should always have imaginative *density;* literary caricatures are not heavy black strokes on blank paper but heavy lines against a background that *suggests* the complexity and detail of a life. And so David's mother is further suggested by the inexpensive and rather old-fashioned scents or colognes she wears and by her reported monologue and almost pointless desire to know whether David secured a seat on the train. Familiar obsessions and anxieties. His mother is further suggested by the "hideous images" that later come to his mind: "sachets of dried lavender, Post Office Savings Books, hyacinth bulbs in bowls, the *Radio Times* in a padded leather cover embossed with the words *Radio Times,* Sunday best silver tongs for removing sugar cubes from sugar bowls, plump armchairs."

This is not, of course, a simple list. The deliberation of the repetitions and such words as "padded" and "plump" are intended to suggest a stifling comfort and, from David's point of view, a stultifying pointlessness.

The old high school divisions into plot, characters, setting and theme are false divisions and a genuine barrier to understanding stories. Settings suggest character. The description of the surroundings of the Jubilee Street house foreshadows, if you will, horrors to come, but it is also an integral part of the caricature of Mrs. Heaney herself. I worked for a long time over the cadences of this description:

> The house stood on a corner; the front of the house faced onto Jubilee Street, the side of the house faced the cemetery on the other side of Kitchener Street. From the coping of the low wall which bounded the cemetery, rusted iron stumps stuck up, presumably the remains of an ornamental fence cut down for munitions during the Second World War. In an aisle of grass between two rows of tombstones, a small brown dog bunched, jerking tail, its eyes anguished.

I was pleased with the *sound* of "rusted iron stumps stuck up," pleased with the harshness of five stresses in a row. I also liked the *awkwardness* of the sentence about the dog. If the sentence had run in what seems the normal way,

> ". . . a small brown dog bunched, tail jerking . . ."

I'd have lost the sudden close focus that the unnatural placing of "jerking" delivers.

It's a difficult truth to grasp that *speech* creates character much faster than description. Speech itself strongly suggests physical appearance. When I wanted to sketch in the batty old man I wasted a lot of time working and reworking clever descriptive phrases before realizing that his essence was a slightly demented garrulousness. As soon as I started to *listen* to him, he became visible. But I didn't see him in sharp focus until I realized that his voice was Irish.

The whole of the section describing the "cooked evening meal" is an extended exercise in caricature. It has the feel of an A. B. Price cartoon—a master of grotty detail. It starts with a bottle of Cream Soda *standing for* Mrs. Heaney herself. The ghastly array of sauce bottles is "shorthand," if you will, for a much longer description of this Hogarthian crew.

The garish plaster elephant, perhaps won at a fairground, while very much *there* as a physical object, also stands as an embodiment of the ethos of the Heaney menage.

Setting or characterization?

All this material prepares for the advent of Jeremy. He is created almost entirely through dialogue and silences. His remark about little girls *with bound ankles* was once actually made to me by an upper-class young Englishman; it left me, like David, at a loss for words. When I started writing the story I knew what general *shape* the story would have, but the idea of using a passage from *The Wind in the Willows* was a sudden gift. Or perhaps the result of intense, imaginative concentration. It is entirely consonant with Jeremy's character, of course, and Toad himself suggests Jeremy's rather naughty inventiveness. Toad also suggests something of the spirit that David wishes for his own life.

Where does Jeremy come *from?* In part, he's imagined. Something of him is a portrait of a friend of mine. And like most figures in fiction, he's descended from earlier figures in fiction—in this case from Sebastian and his teddy-bear in Waugh's *Brideshead Revisited.*

Character and the emotional relationships between characters can be conveyed in ways far less obvious than the broad strokes I've been talking about. The very rhythms of sentences convey emotions. Consider the first sentence of "Single Gents Only"; it is deliberately anticlimactic. It builds, by delay, to no point at all, to *standing,* to silence. David's detachment from his mother is also suggested in: "He stooped to kiss his mother's cheek. Her hat smelled of lavender, her cheek, or possibly neck, of lily-of-the-valley." It's the "or possibly neck" with its parenthetic commas which is telling and comic.

Well written stories are as complex as poems and it's hopeless to approach a story as if it were, say, newspaper prose. A good story needs savouring. The one phrase in this story which pleases me more than any other is one in a list of things seen from the train window. That phrase is:

"the playing fields for employees."

The hints of rhyme and near-repetitions of sound are wonderfully suggestive of the confines from which David is escaping.

Gentle As Flowers Make the Stones also has its share of caricatures; Mr. Pevensey is an obvious example, but there are more complicated performances. Pevensey, by the way, is a portrait of a real person, now dead. It's a caricature of John Richmond, who used to be the bookpage editor on the Montreal *Star*. The caricature was widely recognized and Richmond, reportedly enraged, "blacklisted" me. And I thought I was being *charitable*.

Consider the following passage:

Alone in the cream and gold sitting room, he examined the mantelpiece with its tiny fluted columns, shelves, alcoves, its three inset oval mirrors. He examined the silver-framed bride and groom. He examined the Royal Doulton lady in her windblown crinolines, the knick-knacks, the small copper frying-pan-looking thing that said *A Gift from Jerusalem,* the Royal reclining Doulton lady. Glancing round at the open door, he turned back and peered into the centre mirror to see if hairs were sticking out of his nose.

He sank for a few minutes into the gold plush settee.

The doorbell kept ringing; the litany continued.

Bernice! It's beautiful!

We only finished moving in three weeks ago.

The pair of brass lamps which flanked the settee were in the form of huge pineapples. He touched the prickly brass leaves. The lampshades were covered in plastic. On the long table at the far end of the room, a white tablecloth covered food; he stared at the stacked plates and cups and saucers, at the tablecloth's mysterious humps and hollows. He took a cigarette from the silver box. Which of the little things on the occasional tables, he wondered, were ashtrays? Each time the front door opened, the chandelier above him tinkled.

Oh, Bernice! And quarry-tile in the kitchen too!

Would you like the tour?

And as the tramplings went upstairs, faintly:

master-bedroom ...

cedar-lined ...

A plump woman wandered in. He nodded and smiled at her. She hesitated in the doorway staring at him. The green Chinese lady gazed from her gilt frame. The plump woman went around the other end of the settee and stood fingering the drapes. He tried to remember the painter's name; Tetchi, Tretchisomething—a name that sounded vaguely like a disease.

"Are you the poet?" said the plump woman.

"Yes, that's right."

He smiled.

"We had a nudist last week," she said.

The description of objects and furnishings exists for its own sake, of course, but it also functions as a description of Bernice. And as the things are seen more or less through the poet's eyes, the description *also* functions as a portrait of the poet himself. "Setting" and "character," then, are not divisible; three differing sets of information are being delivered simultaneously.

The overheard fragments of conversation are set in italic (unconventionally) for a variety of reasons: because the speech is not directed to him, because the speakers are not visible, because italic seems to suggest, in this context, faintness and distance, and because italic here somehow suggests *prattle*.

I would claim, you see, that the use of italic is, in itself, an aspect of characterization.

The word "litany" ironically suggests something of the women's values while also suggesting a ritual, almost mechanical, quality in the conversation.

The invented word "tramplings" does triple duty. I wanted the idea of trampling feet and the idea of *weight* that that implies—the idea that these young women are not exactly sylph-like—and I also wanted a faint suggestion of "little tramps."

The ornate mantelpiece with its "silver-framed bride and groom" and its conventionally "beautiful" knick-knacks—which as a whole suggests Bernice and her life and the lives of her friends and which, through the language used to describe it, reveals something of the poet's sensibility—is set up for the contrast with the poet's peering into one of its mirrors to see if "hairs were sticking out of his nose."

What is the effect, in context, of "Royal reclining Doulton lady"?

The sentence rhythms in the paragraph before the final dialogue are deliberately flat and, as Stephen Potter would say, "plonking." They suggest that the poet and the plump woman have nothing to say to each other. By building, and extending, *silence,* they sketch in another line.

These bits and pieces, then, are just a very few of my pleasures. Writing is very hard work but at the same time it is delightful play. When I think about the act of writing, I often think it's like the play of small children on the beach absorbed in building sandcastles and towns with roads and tunnels all decorated with flags made from popsicle sticks and bits of cigarette packets.

And then the wonderful application of water.

Writing stories has something about it of that tranced pleasure, and

I'm convinced that if readers are to share fully in the delight of writing they must be prepared to play *with* writers; they must launch a car through the tunnel to judge the banking and texture of the sand. Does it need more water? They must pat and stroke and probe. They must roll up trousers, tuck skirts into knickers, get down on hands and knees, and muck about.

Alice Munro

ALICE MUNRO was born in 1931 in Wingham, Ontario. She lived for many years in Vancouver and Victoria but has now returned to southern Ontario, the setting of much of her fiction. She has twice been awarded Canada's highest literary honour, the Governor General's Award.

Other Works

Dance of the Happy Shades, (1968) Stories
Lives of Girls and Women, (1971) Novel
Something I've Been Meaning To Tell You, (1974) Stories
Who Do You Think You Are?, (1978) Stories

Royal Beatings

Royal Beating. That was Flo's promise. You are going to get one Royal
Beating.

The word Royal lolled on Flo's tongue, took on trappings. Rose had
a need to picture things, to pursue absurdities, that was stronger than the
need to stay out of trouble, and instead of taking this threat to heart she
pondered: how is a beating royal? She came up with a tree-lined avenue, a
crowd of formal spectators, some white horses and black slaves. Someone
knelt, and the blood came leaping out like banners. An occasion both
savage and splendid. In real life they didn't approach such dignity, and it
was only Flo who tried to supply the event with some high air of
necessity and regret. Rose and her father soon got beyond anything
presentable.

Her father was king of the royal beatings. Those Flo gave never
amounted to much; they were quick cuffs and slaps dashed off while her
attention remained elsewhere. You get out of my road, she would say.
You mind your own business. You take that look off your face.

They lived behind a store in Hanratty, Ontario. There were four of
them: Rose, her father, Flo, Rose's young half brother Brian. The store
was really a house, bought by Rose's father and mother when they
married and set up here in the furniture and upholstery repair business.
Her mother could do upholstery. From both parents Rose should have
inherited clever hands, a quick sympathy with materials, an eye for the
nicest turns of mending, but she hadn't. She was clumsy, and when
something broke she couldn't wait to sweep it up and throw it away.

Her mother had died. She said to Rose's father during the
afternoon, "I have a feeling that is so hard to describe. It's like a boiled egg
in my chest, with the shell left on." She died before night, she had a blood
clot on her lung. Rose was a baby in a basket at the time, so of course
could not remember any of this. She heard it from Flo, who must have
heard it from her father. Flo came along soon afterwards, to take over

Rose in the basket, marry her father, open up the front room to make a grocery store. Rose, who had known the house only as a store, who had known only Flo for a mother, looked back on the sixteen or so months her parents spent here as an orderly, far gentler and more ceremonious time, with little touches of affluence. She had nothing to go on but some egg cups her mother had bought, with a pattern of vines and birds on them, delicately drawn as if with red ink; the pattern was beginning to wear away. No books or clothes or pictures of her mother remained. Her father must have got rid of them, or else Flo would. Flo's only story about her mother, the one about her death, was oddly grudging. Flo liked the details of a death: the things people said, the way they protested or tried to get out of bed or swore or laughed (some did those things), but when she said that Rose's mother mentioned a hard-boiled egg in her chest she made the comparison sound slightly foolish, as if her mother really was the kind of person who might think you could swallow an egg whole.

Her father had a shed out behind the store, where he worked at his furniture repairing and restoring. He caned chair seats and backs, mended wickerwork, filled cracks, put legs back on, all most admirably and skillfully and cheaply. That was his pride: to startle people with such fine work, such moderate, even ridiculous charges. During the Depression people could not afford to pay more, perhaps, but he continued the practice through the war, through the years of prosperity after the war, until he died. He never discussed with Flo what he charged or what was owing. After he died she had to go out and unlock the shed and take all sorts of scraps of paper and torn envelopes from the big wicked-looking hooks that were his files. Many of these she found were not accounts or receipts at all but records of the weather, bits of information about the garden, things he had been moved to write down.

> *Ate new potatoes 25th June. Record.*
> *Dark Day, 1880's, nothing supernatural. Clouds of ash from forest fires.*
> *Aug 16, 1938. Giant thunderstorm in evng. Lightning str. Pres. Church, Turberry Twp. Will of God?*
> *Scald strawberries to remove acid.*
> *All things are alive. Spinoza.*

Flo thought Spinoza must be some new vegetable he planned to grow, like broccoli or eggplant. He would often try some new thing. She showed the scrap of paper to Rose and asked, did she know what Spinoza was? Rose did know, or had an idea—she was in her teens by that time—but she replied that she did not. She had reached an age where she thought she could not stand to know any more, about her father, or about Flo; she pushed any discovery aside with embarrassment and dread.

There was a stove in the shed, and many rough shelves covered with cans of paint and varnish, shellac and turpentine, jars of soaking brushes and also some dark sticky bottles of cough medicine. Why should a man who coughed constantly, whose lungs took in a whiff of gas in the War (called, in Rose's earliest childhood, not the First, but the Last, War) spend all his days breathing fumes of paint and turpentine? At the time, such questions were not asked as often as they are now. On the bench outside Flo's store several old men from the neighbourhood sat gossiping, drowsing, in the warm weather, and some of these old men coughed all the time too. The fact is they were dying, slowly and discreetly, of what was called, without any particular sense of grievance, "the foundry disease." They had worked all their lives at the foundry in town, and now they sat still, with their wasted yellow faces, coughing, chuckling, drifting into aimless obscenity on the subject of women walking by, or any young girl on a bicycle.

From the shed came not only coughing, but speech, a continual muttering, reproachful or encouraging, usually just below the level at which separate words could be made out. Slowing down when her father was at a tricky piece of work, taking on a cheerful speed when he was doing something less demanding, sandpapering or painting. Now and then some words would break through and hang clear and nonsensical on the air. When he realized they were out, there would be a quick bit of cover-up coughing, a swallowing, an alert, unusual silence.

"Macaroni, pepperoni, Botticelli, beans—"

What could that mean? Rose used to repeat such things to herself. She could never ask him. The person who spoke these words and the person who spoke to her as her father were not the same, though they seemed to occupy the same space. It would be the worst sort of taste to acknowledge the person who was not supposed to be there; it would not be forgiven. Just the same, she loitered and listened.

The cloud-capped towers, she heard him say once.

"The cloud-capped towers, the gorgeous palaces."

That was like a hand clapped against Rose's chest, not to hurt, but astonish her, to take her breath away. She had to run then, she had to get away. She knew that was enough to hear, and besides, what if he caught her? It would be terrible.

This was something the same as bathroom noises. Flo had saved up, and had a bathroom put in, but there was no place to put it except in a corner of the kitchen. The door did not fit, the walls were only beaverboard. The result was that even the tearing of a piece of toilet paper, the shifting of a haunch, was audible to those working or talking or eating in the kitchen. They were all familiar with each other's nether voices, not only in their more explosive moments but in their intimate sighs and growls and pleas and statements. And they were all most prudish people. So no one ever seemed to hear, or be listening, and no reference was made. The person creating the noises in the bathroom was not connected with the person who walked out.

They lived in a poor part of town. There was Hanratty and West Hanratty, with the river flowing between them. This was West Hanratty. In Hanratty the social structure ran from doctors and dentists and lawyers down to foundry workers and factory workers and draymen; in West Hanratty it ran from factory workers and foundry workers down to large improvident families of casual bootleggers and prostitutes and unsuccessful thieves. Rose thought of her own family as straddling the river, belonging nowhere, but that was not true. West Hanratty was where the store was and they were, on the straggling tail end of the main street. Across the road from them was a blacksmith shop, boarded up about the time the war started, and a house that had been another store at one time. The Salada Tea sign had never been taken out of the front window; it remained as a proud and interesting decoration though there was no Salada Tea for sale inside. There was just a bit of sidewalk, too cracked and tilted for roller-skating, though Rose longed for roller skates and often pictured herself whizzing along in a plaid skirt, agile and fashionable. There was one street light, a tin flower; then the amenities gave up and there were dirt roads and boggy places, front-yard dumps and strange-looking houses. What made the houses strange-looking were the attempts to keep them from going completely to ruin. With some the attempt had never been made. These were grey and rotted and leaning over, falling into a landscape of scrub hollows, frog ponds, cattails and nettles. Most houses, however, had been patched up with tarpaper, a few fresh shingles, sheets of tin, hammered-out stovepipes, even cardboard. This was, of course, in the days before the war, days of what would later be legendary poverty, from which Rose would remember mostly low-down things—serious-looking anthills and wooden steps, and a cloudy, interesting, problematical light on the world.

There was a long truce between Flo and Rose in the beginning. Rose's nature was growing like a prickly pineapple, but slowly, and secretly, hard pride and scepticism overlapping, to make something surprising even to herself. Before she was old enough to go to school, and while Brian was still in the baby carriage, Rose stayed in the store with both of them—Flo sitting on the high stool behind the counter, Brian asleep by the window; Rose knelt or lay on the wide creaky floorboards working with crayons on pieces of brown paper too torn or irregular to be used for wrapping.

People who came to the store were mostly from the houses around. Some country people came too, on their way home from town, and a few people from Hanratty, who walked across the bridge. Some people were always on the main street, in and out of stores, as if it was their duty to be always on display and their right to be welcomed. For instance, Becky Tyde.

Becky Tyde climbed up on Flo's counter, made room for herself beside an open tin of crumbly jam-filled cookies.

"Are these any good?" she said to Flo, and boldly began to eat one. "When are you going to give us a job, Flo?"

"You could go and work in the butcher shop," said Flo innocently. "You could go and work for your brother."

"Roberta?" said Becky with a stagey sort of contempt. "You think I'd work for him?" Her brother who ran the butcher shop was named Robert but often called Roberta, because of his meek and nervous ways. Becky Tyde laughed. Her laugh was loud and noisy like an engine bearing down on you.

She was a big-headed loud-voiced dwarf, with a mascot's sexless swagger, a red velvet tam, a twisted neck that forced her to hold her head on one side, always looking up and sideways. She wore little polished high-heeled shoes, real lady's shoes. Rose watched her shoes, being scared of the rest of her, of her laugh and her neck. She knew from Flo that Becky Tyde had been sick with polio as a child, that was why her neck was twisted and why she had not grown any taller. It was hard to believe that she had started out differently, that she had ever been normal. Flo said she was not cracked, she had as much brains as anybody, but she knew she could get away with anything.

"You know I used to live out here?" Becky said, noticing Rose. "Hey! What's-your-name! Didn't I used to live out here, Flo?"

"If you did it was before my time," said Flo, as if she didn't know anything.

"That was before the neighbourhood got so downhill. Excuse me saying so. My father built his house out here and he built his slaughterhouse and we had half an acre of orchard."

"Is that so?" said Flo, using her humouring voice, full of false geniality, humility even. "Then why did you ever move away?"

"I told you, it got to be such a downhill neighbourhood," said Becky. She would put a whole cookie in her mouth if she felt like it, let her cheeks puff out like a frog's. She never told any more.

Flo knew anyway, as who didn't. Everyone knew the house, red brick with the veranda pulled off and the orchard, what was left of it, full of the usual outflow—car seats and washing machines and bedsprings and junk. The house would never look sinister, in spite of what had happened in it, because there was so much wreckage and confusion all around.

Becky's old father was a different kind of butcher from her brother according to Flo. A bad-tempered Englishman. And different from Becky in the matter of mouthiness. His was never open. A skinflint, a family tyrant. After Becky had polio he wouldn't let her go back to school. She was seldom seen outside the house, never outside the yard. He didn't want people gloating. That was what Becky said, at the trial. Her mother was dead by that time and her sisters married. Just Becky and Robert at home. People would stop Robert on the road and ask him, "How about your sister, Robert? Is she altogether better now?"

"Yes."

"Does she do the housework? Does she get your supper?"

"Yes."

"And is your father good to her, Robert?"

The story being that the father beat them, had beaten all his children and beaten his wife as well, beat Becky more now because of her deformity, which some people believed he had caused (they did not understand about polio). The stories persisted and got added to. The reason that Becky was kept out of sight was now supposed to be her pregnancy, and the father of the child was supposed to be her own father. Then people said it had been born, and disposed of.

"What?"

"Disposed of," Flo said. "They used to say go and get your lamb chops at Tyde's, get them nice and tender! It was all lies in all probability," she said regretfully.

Rose could be drawn back—from watching the wind shiver along the old torn awning, catch in the tear—by this tone of regret, caution, in Flo's voice. Flo telling a story—and this was not the only one, or even the most lurid one, she knew—would incline her head and let her face go soft and thoughtful, tantalizing, warning.

"I shouldn't even be telling you this stuff."

More was to follow.

Three useless young men, who hung around the livery stable, got together—or were got together, by more influential and respectable men in town—and prepared to give old man Tyde a horsewhipping, in the interests of public morality. They blacked their faces. They were provided with whips and a quart of whisky apiece, for courage. They were: Jelly Smith, a horse-racer and a drinker; Bob Temple, a ball-player and strongman; and Hat Nettleton, who worked on the town dray, and had his nickname from a bowler hat he wore, out of vanity as much as for the comic effect. (He still worked on the dray, in fact; he had kept the name if not the hat, and could often be seen in public—almost as often as Becky Tyde—delivering sacks of coal, which blackened his face and arms.) That should have brought to mind his story, but didn't. Present time and past, the shady melodramatic past of Flo's stories, were quite separate, at least for Rose. Present people could not be fitted into the past. Becky herself, town oddity and public pet, harmless and malicious, could never match the butcher's prisoner, the cripple daughter, a white streak at the window: mute, beaten, impregnated. As with the house, only a formal connection could be made.

The young men primed to do the horsewhipping showed up late, outside Tyde's house, after everybody had gone to bed. They had a gun, but they used up their ammunition firing it off in the yard. They yelled for the butcher and beat on the door; finally they broke it down. Tyde concluded they were after his money, so he put some bills in a handkerchief and sent Becky down with them, maybe thinking those men would be touched or scared by the sight of a little wry-necked girl, a dwarf. But that didn't content them. They came upstairs and dragged the butcher out from under his bed, in his nightgown. They dragged him outside and stood him in the snow. The temperature was four below zero, a fact noted later in court. They meant to hold a mock trial but they could not remember how it was done. So they began to beat him and kept beating him until he fell. They yelled at him, *Butcher's meat!* and continued beating him while his nightgown and the snow he was lying in turned red. His son Robert said in court that he had not watched the beating. Becky said that Robert had watched at first but had run away and hid. She herself had watched all the way through. She watched the men leave at last and her father make his delayed bloody progress through the snow and up the steps of the veranda. She did not go out to help him, or open the door until he got to it. Why not? she was asked in court, and she said she did not go out because she just had her nightgown on, and she did not open the door because she did not want to let the cold into the house.

Old man Tyde then appeared to have recovered his strength. He sent Robert to harness the horse, and made Becky heat water so that he could wash. He dressed and took all the money and with no explanation to his children got into the cutter and drove to Belgrave where he left the horse tied in the cold and took the early morning train to Toronto. On the train he behaved oddly, groaning and cursing as if he was drunk. He was picked up on the streets of Toronto a day later, out of his mind with fever, and was taken to a hospital, where he died. He still had all the money. The cause of death was given as pneumonia.

But the authorities got wind, Flo said. The case came to trial. The three men who did it all received long prison sentences. A farce, said Flo. Within a year they were all free, had all been pardoned, had jobs waiting for them. And why was that? It was because too many higher-ups were in on it. And it seemed as if Becky and Robert had no interest in seeing justice done. They were left well-off. They bought a house in Hanratty. Robert went into the store. Becky after her long seclusion started on a career of public sociability and display.

That was all. Flo put the lid down on the story as if she was sick of it. It reflected no good on anybody.

"Imagine," Flo said.

Flo at this time must have been in her early thirties. A young woman. She wore exactly the same clothes that a woman of fifty, or sixty, or seventy, might wear: print housedresses loose at the neck and sleeves as well as the waist; bib aprons, also of print, which she took off when she came from the kitchen into the store. This was a common costume at the time, for a poor though not absolutely poverty-stricken woman; it was also, in a way, a scornful deliberate choice. Flo scorned slacks, she scorned the outfits of people trying to be in style, she scorned lipstick and permanents. She wore her own black hair cut straight across, just long enough to push behind her ears. She was tall but fine-boned, with narrow wrists and shoulders, a small head, a pale, freckled, mobile, monkeyish face. If she had thought it worthwhile, and had the resources, she might have had a black-and-pale, fragile, nurtured sort of prettiness; Rose realized that later. But she would have to have been a different person altogether; she would have to have learned to resist making faces, at herself and others.

Rose's earliest memories of Flo were of extraordinary softness and hardness. The soft hair, the long, soft, pale cheeks, soft almost invisible fuzz in front of her ears and above her mouth. The sharpness of her knees, hardness of her lap, flatness of her front.

When Flo sang:

Oh the buzzin' of the bees in the cigarette trees
And the soda-water fountain ...

Rose thought of Flo's old life before she married her father, when she worked as a waitress in the coffee shop in Union Station, and went with her girl friends Mavis and Irene to Centre Island, and was followed by men on dark streets and knew how pay-phones and elevators worked. Rose heard in her voice the reckless dangerous life of cities, the gum-chewing sharp answers.

And when she sang:

Then slowly, slowly, she got up
And slowly she came nigh him
And all she said, that she ever did say,
Was young man I think, you're dyin'!

Rose thought of a life Flo seemed to have had beyond that, earlier than that, crowded and legendary, with Barbara Allen and Becky Tyde's father and all kinds of old outrages and sorrows jumbled up together in it.

The royal beatings. What got them started?

Suppose a Saturday, in spring. Leaves not out yet but the doors open to the sunlight. Crows. Ditches full of running water. Hopeful weather. Often on Saturdays Flo left Rose in charge of the store—it's a few years now, these are the years when Rose was nine, ten, eleven, twelve—while she herself went across the bridge to Hanratty (going uptown they called it) to shop and see people, and listen to them. Among the people she listened to were Mrs. Lawyer Davies, Mrs. Anglican Rector Henley-Smith, and Mrs. Horse-Doctor McKay. She came home and imitated them at supper: their high-flown remarks, their flibberty voices. Monsters, she made them seem; of foolishness, and showiness, and self-approbation.

When she finished shopping she went into the coffee shop of the Queen's Hotel and had a sundae. What kind? Rose and Brian wanted to know when she got home, and they would be disappointed if it was only pineapple or butterscotch, pleased if it was a Tin Roof, or Black and White. Then she smoked a cigarette. She had some ready-rolled, that she carried with her, so that she wouldn't have to roll one in public. Smoking was the one thing she did that she would have called showing off in anybody else. It was a habit left over from her working days, from Toronto. She knew it was asking for trouble. Once the Catholic priest came over to her right in the Queen's Hotel, and flashed his lighter at her before she could get her matches out. She thanked him but did not enter into conversation, lest he should try to convert her.

Another time, on the way home, she saw at the town end of the bridge a boy in a blue jacket, apparently looking at the water. Eighteen, nineteen years old. Nobody she knew. Skinny, weakly looking, something the matter with him, she saw at once. Was he thinking of jumping? Just as she came up even with him, what does he do but turn and display, holding his jacket open, also his pants. What he must have suffered from the cold, on a day that had Flo holding her coat collar tight around her throat.

When she first saw what he had in his hand, Flo said, all she could think of was, what is he doing out here with a baloney sausage?

She could say that. It was offered as truth; no joke. She maintained that she despised dirty talk. She would go out and yell at the old men sitting in front of her store.

"If you want to stay where you are you better clean your mouths out!"

Saturday, then. For some reason Flo is not going uptown, has decided to stay home and scrub the kitchen floor. Perhaps this has put her in a bad mood. Perhaps she was in a bad mood anyway, due to people not paying their bills, or the stirring-up of feelings in spring. The wrangle with Rose has already commenced, has been going on forever, like a dream that goes back and back into other dreams, over hills and through doorways, maddeningly dim and populous and familiar and elusive. They are carting all the chairs out of the kitchen preparatory to the scrubbing, and they have also got to move some extra provisions for the store, some cartons of canned goods, tins of maple syrup, coal-oil cans, jars of vinegar. They take these things out to the woodshed. Brian who is five or six by this time is helping drag the tins.

"Yes," says Flo, carrying on from our lost starting-point. "Yes, and that filth you taught to Brian."

"What filth?"

"And he doesn't know any better."

There is one step down from the kitchen to the woodshed, a bit of carpet on it so worn Rose can't ever remember seeing the pattern. Brian loosens it, dragging a tin.

"Two Vancouvers," she says softly.

Flo is back in the kitchen. Brian looks from Flo to Rose and Rose says again in a slightly louder voice, an encouraging sing-song, "Two Vancouvers—"

"Fried in snot!" finishes Brian, not able to control himself any longer.

"Two pickled arseholes—"

"—tied in a knot!"

There it is. The filth.

Two Vancouvers fried in snot!
Two pickled arseholes tied in a knot!

Rose has known that for years, learned it when she first went to school. She came home and asked Flo, what is a Vancouver?

"It's a city. It's a long ways away."

"What else besides a city?"

Flo said, what did she mean, what else? How could it be fried, Rose said, approaching the dangerous moment, the delightful moment, when she would have to come out with the whole thing.

"Two Vancouvers fried in snot!/Two pickled arseholes tied in a knot!"

"You're going to get it!" cried Flo in a predictable rage. "Say that again and you'll get a good clout!"

Rose couldn't stop herself. She hummed it tenderly, tried saying the innocent words aloud, humming through the others. It was not just the words snot and arsehole that gave her pleasure, though of course they did. It was the pickling and tying and the unimaginable Vancouvers. She saw them in her mind shaped rather like octopuses, twitching in the pan. The tumble of reason; the spark and spit of craziness.

Lately she has remembered it again and taught it to Brian, to see if it has the same effect on him, and of course it has.

"Oh, I heard you!" says Flo. "I heard that! And I'm warning you!"

So she is. Brian takes the warning. He runs away, out the woodshed door, to do as he likes. Being a boy, free to help or not, involve himself or not. Not committed to the household struggle. They don't need him anyway, except to use against each other, they hardly notice his going. They continue, can't help continuing, can't leave each other alone. When they seem to have given up they were really just waiting and building up steam.

Flo gets out the scrub pail and the brush and the rag and the pad for her knees, a dirty red rubber pad. She starts to work on the floor. Rose sits on the kitchen table, the only place left to sit, swinging her legs. She can feel the cool oilcloth, because she is wearing shorts, last summer's tight faded shorts dug out of the summer-clothes bag. They smell a bit mouldy from winter storage.

Flo crawls around underneath, scrubbing with the brush, wiping with the rag. Her legs are long, white and muscular, marked all over with blue veins as if somebody had been drawing rivers on them with an indelible pencil. An abnormal energy, a violent disgust, is expressed in the chewing of the brush at the linoleum, the swish of the rag.

What do they have to say to each other? It doesn't really matter. Flo speaks of Rose's smart-aleck behaviour, rudeness and sloppiness and conceit. Her willingness to make work for others, her lack of gratitude. She mentions Brian's innocence, Rose's corruption. Oh, don't you think you're somebody, says Flo, and a moment later, Who do you think you are? Rose contradicts and objects with such poisonous reasonableness and mildness, displays theatrical unconcern. Flo goes beyond her ordinary scorn and self-possession and becomes amazingly theatrical herself, saying it was for Rose that she sacrificed her life. She saw her father saddled with a baby daughter and she thought, what is that man going to do? So she married him, and here she is, on her knees.

At that moment the bell rings, to announce a customer in the store. Because the fight is on, Rose is not permitted to go into the store and wait on whoever it is. Flo gets up and throws off her apron, groaning—but not communicatively, it is not a groan whose exasperation Rose is allowed to share—and goes in and serves. Rose hears her using her normal voice.

"About time! Sure is!"

She comes back and ties on her apron and is ready to resume.

"You never have a thought for anybody but your ownself! You never have a thought for what I'm doing."

"I never asked you to do anything. I wished you never had. I would have been a lot better off."

Rose says this smiling directly at Flo, who has not yet gone down on her knees. Flo sees the smile, grabs the scrub rag that is hanging on the side of the pail, and throws it at her. It may be meant to hit her in the face but instead it falls against Rose's leg and she raises her foot and catches it, swinging it negligently against her ankle.

"All right," says Flo. "You've done it this time. All right."

Rose watches her go to the woodshed door, hears her tramp through the woodshed, pause in the doorway, where the screen door hasn't yet been hung, and the storm door is standing open, propped with a brick. She calls Rose's father. She calls him in a warning, summoning voice, as if against her will preparing him for bad news. He will know what this is about.

The kitchen floor has five or six different patterns of linoleum on it. Ends, which Flo got for nothing and ingeniously trimmed and fitted together, bordering them with tin strips and tacks. While Rose sits on the table waiting, she looks at the floor, at this satisfying arrangement of rectangles, triangles, some other shape whose name she is trying to remember. She hears Flo coming back through the woodshed, on the creaky plank walk laid over the dirt floor. She is loitering, waiting, too. She and Rose can carry this no further, by themselves.

Rose hears her father come in. She stiffens, a tremor runs through her legs, she feels them shiver on the oilcloth. Called away from some peaceful, absorbing task, away from the words running in his head, called out of himself, her father has to say something. He says, "Well? What's wrong?"

Now comes another voice of Flo's. Enriched, hurt, apologetic, it seems to have been manufactured on the spot. She is sorry to have called him from his work. Would never have done it, if Rose was not driving her to distraction. How to distraction? With her back-talk and impudence and her terrible tongue. The things Rose has said to Flo are such that, if Flo had said them to her mother, she knows her father would have thrashed her into the ground.

Rose tries to butt in, to say this isn't true.

What isn't true?

Her father raises a hand, doesn't look at her, says, "Be quiet."

When she says it isn't true, Rose means that she herself didn't start this, only responded, that she was goaded by Flo, who is now, she believes, telling the grossest sort of lies, twisting everything to suit herself. Rose puts aside her other knowledge that whatever Flo has said or done, whatever she herself has said or done, does not really matter at all. It is the struggle itself that counts, and that can't be stopped, can never be stopped, short of where it has got to, now.

Flo's knees are dirty, in spite of the pad. The scrub rag is still hanging over Rose's foot.

Her father wipes his hands, listening to Flo. He takes his time. He is slow at getting into the spirit of things, tired in advance, maybe, on the verge of rejecting the role he has to play. He won't look at Rose, but at any sound or stirring from Rose, he holds up his hand.

"Well we don't need the public in on this, that's for sure," Flo says, and she goes to lock the door of the store, putting in the store window the sign that says "Back Soon," a sign Rose made for her with a great deal of fancy curving and shading of letters in black and red crayon. When she comes back she shuts the door to the store, then the door to the stairs, then the door to the woodshed.

Her shoes have left marks on the clean wet part of the floor.

"Oh, I don't know," she says now, in a voice worn down from its emotional peak. "I don't know what to do about her." She looks down and sees her dirty knees (following Rose's eyes) and rubs at them viciously with her bare hands, smearing the dirt around.

"She humiliates me," she says, straightening up. There it is, the explanation. "She humiliates me," she repeats with satisfaction. "She has no respect."

"I do not!"

"Quiet, you!" says her father.

"If I hadn't called your father you'd still be sitting there with that grin on your face! What other way is there to manage you?"

Rose detects in her father some objections to Flo's rhetoric, some embarrassment and reluctance. She is wrong, and ought to know she is wrong, in thinking that she can count on this. The fact that she knows about it, and he knows she knows, will not make things any better. He is beginning to warm up. He gives her a look. This look is at first cold and challenging. It informs her of his judgement, of the hopelessness of her position. Then it clears, it begins to fill up with something else, the way a spring fills up when you clear the leaves away. It fills with hatred and pleasure. Rose sees that and knows it. Is that just a description of anger, should she see his eyes filling up with anger? No. Hatred is right. Pleasure is right. His face loosens and changes and grows younger, and he holds up his hand this time to silence Flo.

"All right," he says, meaning that's enough, more than enough, this part is over, things can proceed. He starts to loosen his belt.

Flo has stopped anyway. She has the same difficulty Rose does, a difficulty in believing that what you know must happen really will happen, that there comes a time when you can't draw back.

"Oh, I don't know, don't be too hard on her." She is moving around nervously as if she has thoughts of opening some escape route. "Oh, you don't have to use the belt on her. Do you have to use the belt?"

He doesn't answer. The belt is coming off, not hastily. It is being grasped at the necessary point. *All right you.* He is coming over to Rose. He pushes her off the table. His face, like his voice, is quite out of character. He is like a bad actor, who turns a part grotesque. As if he must savour and insist on just what is shameful and terrible about this. That is not to say he is pretending, that he is acting, and does not mean it. He is acting, and he means it. Rose knows that, she knows everything about him.

She has since wondered about murders, and murderers. Does the thing have to be carried through, in the end, partly for the effect, to prove to the audience of one—who won't be able to report, only register, the lesson—that such a thing can happen, that there is nothing that can't happen, that the most dreadful antic is justified, feelings can be found to match it?

She tries again looking at the kitchen floor, that clever and comforting geometrical arrangement, instead of looking at him or his belt. How can this go on in front of such daily witnesses—the linoleum, the calendar with the mill and creek and autumn trees, the old accommodating pots and pans?

Hold out your hand!

Those things aren't going to help her, none of them can rescue her. They turn bland and useless, even unfriendly. Pots can show malice, the patterns of linoleum can leer up at you, treachery is the other side of dailiness.

At the first, or maybe the second, crack of pain, she draws back. She will not accept it. She runs around the room, she tries to get to the doors. Her father blocks her off. Not an ounce of courage or of stoicism in her, it would seem. She runs, she screams, she implores. Her father is after her, cracking the belt at her when he can, then abandoning it and using his hands. Bang over the ear, then bang over the other ear. Back and forth, her head ringing. Bang in the face. Up against the wall and bang in the face again. He shakes her and hits her against the wall, he kicks her legs. She is incoherent, insane, shrieking. *Forgive me! Oh please, forgive me!*

Flo is shrieking too. *Stop, stop!*

Not yet. He throws Rose down. Or perhaps she throws herself down. He kicks her legs again. She has given up on words but is letting out a noise, the sort of noise that makes Flo cry, *Oh, what if people can hear her?* The very last-ditch willing sound of humiliation and defeat it is, for it seems Rose must play her part in this with the same grossness, the same exaggeration, that her father displays, playing his. She plays his victim with a self-indulgence that arouses, and maybe hopes to arouse, his final, sickened contempt.

They will give this anything that is necessary, it seems, they will go to any lengths.

Not quite. He has never managed to really injure her, though there are times, of course, when she prays that he will. He hits her with an open hand, there is some restraint in his kicks.

Now he stops, he is out of breath. He allows Flo to move in, he grabs Rose up and gives her a push in Flo's direction, making a sound of disgust. Flo retrieves her, opens the stair door, shoves her up the stairs.

"Go on up to your room now! Hurry!"

Rose goes up the stairs, stumbling, letting herself stumble, letting herself fall against the steps. She doesn't bang her door because a gesture like that could still bring him after her, and anyway, she is weak. She lies on the bed. She can hear through the stovepipe hole Flo snuffling and remonstrating, her father saying angrily that Flo should have kept quiet then, if she did not want Rose punished she should not have recommended it. Flo says she never recommended a hiding like that.

They argue back and forth on this. Flo's frightened voice is growing stronger, getting its confidence back. By stages, by arguing, they are being drawn back into themselves. Soon it's only Flo talking; he will not talk any more. Rose has had to fight down her noisy sobbing, so as to listen to them, and when she loses interest in listening, and wants to sob some more, she finds she can't work herself up to it. She has passed into a state of calm, in which outrage is perceived as complete and final. In this state events and possibilities take on a lovely simplicity. Choices are mercifully clear. The words that come to mind are not the quibbling, seldom the conditional. Never is a word to which the right is suddenly established. She will never speak to them, she will never look at them with anything but loathing, she will never forgive them. She will punish them; she will finish them. Encased in these finalities, and in her bodily pain, she floats in curious comfort, beyond herself, beyond responsibility.

Suppose she dies now? Suppose she commits suicide? Suppose she runs away? Any of these things would be appropriate. It is only a matter of choosing, of figuring out the way. She floats in her pure superior state as if kindly drugged.

And just as there is a moment, when you are drugged, in which you feel perfectly safe, sure, unreachable, and then without warning and right next to it a moment in which you know the whole protection has fatally cracked, though it is still pretending to hold soundly together, so there is a moment now—the moment, in fact, when Rose hears Flo step on the stairs—that contains for her both present peace and freedom and a sure knowledge of the whole down-spiralling course of events from now on.

Flo comes into the room without knocking, but with a hesitation that shows it might have occurred to her. She brings a jar of cold cream. Rose is hanging on to advantage as long as she can, lying face down on the bed, refusing to acknowledge or answer.

"Oh come on," Flo says uneasily. "You aren't so bad off, are you? You put some of this on and you'll feel better."

She is bluffing. She doesn't know for sure what damage has been done. She has the lid off the cold cream. Rose can smell it. The intimate, babyish, humiliating smell. She won't allow it near her. But in order to avoid it, the big ready clot of it in Flo's hand, she has to move. She scuffles, resists, loses dignity, and lets Flo see there is not really much the matter.

"All right," Flo says. "You win. I'll leave it here and you can put it on when you like."

Later still a tray will appear. Flo will put it down without a word and go away. A large glass of chocolate milk on it, made with Vita-Malt from the store. Some rich streaks of Vita-Malt around the bottom of the glass. Little sandwiches, neat and appetizing. Canned salmon of the first quality and reddest colour, plenty of mayonnaise. A couple of butter tarts from a bakery package, chocolate biscuits with a peppermint filling. Rose's favourites, in the sandwich, tart and cookie line. She will turn away, refuse to look, but left alone with these eatables will be miserably tempted, roused and troubled and drawn back from thoughts of suicide or flight by the smell of salmon, the anticipation of crisp chocolate, she will reach out a finger, just to run it around the edge of one of the sandwiches (crusts cut off!) to get the overflow, get a taste. Then she will decide to eat one, for strength to refuse the rest. One will not be noticed. Soon, in helpless corruption, she will eat them all. She will drink the chocolate milk, eat the tarts, eat the cookies. She will get the malty syrup out of the bottom of the glass with her finger, though she sniffles with shame. Too late.

Flo will come up and get the tray. She may say, "I see you got your appetite still," or "Did you like the chocolate milk, was it enough syrup in it?" depending on how chastened she is feeling, herself. At any rate, all advantage will be lost. Rose will understand that life has started up again, that they will all sit around the table eating again, listening to the radio news. Tomorrow morning, maybe even tonight. Unseemly and unlikely as that may be. They will be embarrassed, but rather less than you might expect considering how they have behaved. They will feel a queer lassitude, a convalescent indolence, not far off satisfaction.

One night after a scene like this they were all in the kitchen. It must have been summer, or at least warm weather, because her father spoke of the old men who sat on the bench in front of the store.

"Do you know what they're talking about now?" he said, and nodded his head towards the store to show who he meant, though of course they were not there now, they went home at dark.

"Those old coots," said Flo. "What?"

There was about them both a geniality not exactly false but a bit more emphatic than was normal, without company.

Rose's father told them then that the old men had picked up the idea somewhere that what looked like a star in the western sky, the first star that came out after sunset, the evening star, was in reality an airship hovering over Bay City, Michigan, on the other side of Lake Huron. An American invention, sent up to rival the heavenly bodies. They were all in agreement about this, the idea was congenial to them. They believed it to be lit by ten thousand electric light bulbs. Her father had ruthlessly disagreed with them, pointing out that it was the planet Venus they saw, which had appeared in the sky long before the invention of an electric light bulb. They had never heard of the planet Venus.

"Ignoramuses," said Flo. At which Rose knew, and knew her father knew, that Flo had never heard of the planet Venus either. To distract them from this, or even apologize for it, Flo put down her teacup, stretched out with her head resting on the chair she had been sitting on and her feet on another chair (somehow she managed to tuck her dress modestly between her legs at the same time), and lay stiff as a board, so that Brian cried out in delight, "Do that! Do that!"

Flo was double-jointed and very strong. In moments of celebration or emergency she would do tricks.

They were silent while she turned herself around, not using her arms at all but just her strong legs and feet. Then they all cried out in triumph, though they had seen it before.

Just as Flo turned herself Rose got a picture in her mind of that airship, an elongated transparent bubble, with its strings of diamond lights, floating in the miraculous American sky.

"The planet Venus!" her father said, applauding Flo. "Ten thousand electric lights!"

There was a feeling of permission, relaxation, even a current of happiness, in the room.

Years later, many years later, on a Sunday morning, Rose turned on the radio. This was when she was living by herself in Toronto.

Well sir.

It was a different kind of a place in our day. Yes it was.

It was all horses then. Horses and buggies. Buggy races up and down the main street on the Saturday nights.

"Just like the chariot races," says the announcer's, or interviewer's, smooth encouraging voice.

I never seen a one of them.

"No sir, that was the old Roman chariot races I was referring to. That was before your time."

Musta been before my time. I'm a hunerd and two years old.

"That's a wonderful age, sir."

It is so.

She left it on, as she went around the apartment kitchen, making coffee for herself. It seemed to her that this must be a staged interview, a scene from some play, and she wanted to find out what it was. The old man's voice was so vain and belligerent, the interviewer's quite hopeless and alarmed, under its practiced gentleness and ease. You were surely meant to see him holding the microphone up to some toothless, reckless, preening centenarian, wondering what in God's name he was doing here, and what would he say next?

"They must have been fairly dangerous."

What was dangerous?

"Those buggy races."

They was. Dangerous. Used to be the runaway horses. Used to be a-plenty of accidents. Fellows was dragged along on the gravel and cut their face open. Wouldna matter so much if they was dead. Heh.

Some of them horses was the high-steppers. Some, they had to have the mustard under their tail. Some wouldn step out for nothin. That's the thing it is with the horses. Some'll work and pull till they drop down dead and some wouldn pull your cock out of a pail of lard. Hehe.

It must be a real interview after all. Otherwise they wouldn't have put that in, wouldn't have risked it. It's all right if the old man says it. Local colour. Anything rendered harmless and delightful by his hundred years.

Accidents all the time then. In the mill. Foundry. Wasn't the precautions.

"You didn't have so many strikes then, I don't suppose? You didn't have so many unions?"

Everybody taking it easy nowadays. We worked and we was glad to get it. Worked and was glad to get it.

"You didn't have television."

Didn't have no TV. Didn't have no radio. No picture show.

"You made your own entertainment."

That's the way we did.

"You had a lot of experiences young men growing up today will never have."

Experiences.

"Can you recall any of them for us?"

I eaten groundhog meat one time. One winter. You wouldna cared for it. Heh.

There was a pause, of appreciation, it would seem, then the announcer's voice saying that the foregoing had been an interview with Mr. Wilfred Nettleton of Hanratty, Ontario, made on his hundred and second birthday, two weeks before his death, last spring. A living link with our past. Mr. Nettleton had been interviewed in the Wawanash County Home for the Aged.

Hat Nettleton.

Horsewhipper into centenarian. Photographed on his birthday, fussed over by nurses, kissed no doubt by a girl reporter. Flash bulbs popping at him. Tape recorder drinking in the sound of his voice. Oldest resident. Oldest horsewhipper. Living link with our past.

Looking out from her kitchen window at the cold lake, Rose was longing to tell somebody. It was Flo who would enjoy hearing. She thought of her saying *Imagine!* in a way that meant she was having her worst suspicions gorgeously confirmed. But Flo was in the same place Hat Nettleton had died in, and there wasn't any way Rose could reach her. She had been there even when that interview was recorded, though she would not have heard it, would not have known about it. After Rose put her in the Home, a couple of years earlier, she had stopped talking. She had removed herself, and spent most of her time sitting in a corner of her crib, looking crafty and disagreeable, not answering anybody, though she occasionally showed her feelings by biting a nurse.

Who Do You Think You Are?

There were some things Rose and her brother Brian could safely talk about, without running aground on principles or statements of position, and one of them was Milton Homer. They both remembered that when they had measles and there was a quarantine notice put up on the door—this was long ago, before their father died and before Brian went to school—Milton Homer came along the street and read it. They heard him coming over the bridge and as usual he was complaining loudly. His progress through town was not silent unless his mouth was full of candy; otherwise he would be yelling at dogs and bullying the trees and telephone poles, mulling over old grievances.

"And I did not and I did not and I did not!" he yelled, and hit the bridge railing.

Rose and Brian pulled back the quilt that was hung over the window to keep the light out, so they would not go blind.

"Milton Homer," said Brian appreciatively.

Milton Homer then saw the notice on the door. He turned and mounted the steps and read it. He could read. He would go along the main street reading all the signs out loud.

Rose and Brian remembered this and they agreed that it was the side door, where Flo later stuck on the glassed-in porch; before that there was only a slanting wooden platform, and they remembered Milton Homer standing on it. If the quarantine notice was there and not on the front door, which led into Flo's store, then the store must have been open; that seemed odd, and could only be explained by Flo's having bullied the Health Officer. Rose couldn't remember; she could only remember Milton Homer on the platform with his big head on one side and his fist raised to knock.

"Measles, huh?" said Milton Homer. He didn't knock, after all; he stuck his head close to the door and shouted, "Can't scare me!" Then he turned around but did not leave the yard. He walked over to the swing, sat down, took hold of the ropes and began moodily, then with mounting and ferocious glee, to give himself a ride.

"Milton Homer's on the swing, Milton Homer's on the swing!" Rose shouted. She had run from the window to the stairwell.

Flo came from wherever she was to look out the side window.

"He won't hurt it," said Flo surprisingly. Rose had thought she would chase him with the broom. Afterwards she wondered: could Flo have been frightened? Not likely. It would be a matter of Milton Homer's privileges.

"I can't sit on the seat after Milton Homer's sat on it!"

"You! You go on back to bed."

Rose went back into the dark smelly measles room and began to tell Brian a story she thought he wouldn't like.

"When you were a baby, Milton Homer came and picked you up."

"He did not."

"He came and held you and asked what your name was. I remember."

Brian went out to the stairwell.

"Did Milton Homer come and pick me up and ask what my name was? Did he? When I was a baby?"

"You tell Rose he did the same for her."

Rose knew that was likely, though she hadn't been going to mention it. She didn't really know if she remembered Milton Homer holding Brian, or had been told about it. Whenever there was a new baby in a house, in that recent past when babies were still being born at home, Milton Homer came as soon as possible and asked to see the baby, then asked its name, and delivered a set speech. The speech was to the effect that if the baby lived, it was to be hoped it would lead a Christian life, and if it died, it was to be hoped it would go straight to Heaven. The same idea as baptism, but Milton did not call on the Father or the Son or do any business with water. He did all this on his own authority. He seemed to be overcome by a stammer he did not have at other times, or else he stammered on purpose in order to give his pronouncements more weight. He opened his mouth wide and rocked back and forth, taking up each phrase with a deep grunt.

"And *if* the Baby—*if* the Baby—*if* the Baby—*lives*—"

Rose would do this years later, in her brother's living room, rocking back and forth, chanting, each *if* coming out like an explosion, leading up to the major explosion of *lives*.

"He will live a—good life—and he will—and he will—and he will—*not* sin. He will lead a *good life*—a *good life*—and he will *not sin*. He will *not sin!*"

"And if the baby—if the baby—if the baby—*dies*—"

"Now that's enough. That's enough, Rose," said Brian, but he laughed. He could put up with Rose's theatrics when they were about Hanratty.

"How can you remember?" said Brian's wife Phoebe, hoping to stop Rose before she went on too long and roused Brian's impatience. "Did you see him do it? That often?"

"Oh no," said Rose, with some surprise. "I didn't see him do it. What I saw was Ralph Gillespie *doing* Milton Homer. He was a boy in school. Ralph."

Milton Homer's other public function, as Rose and Brian remembered it, was to march in parades. There used to be plenty of parades in Hanratty. The Orange Walk, on the Twelfth of July; the High School Cadet Parade, in May; the schoolchildren's Empire Day Parade, the Legion's Church Parade, the Santa Claus Parade, the Lions Club Old-Timers' Parade. One of the most derogatory things that could be said about anyone in Hanratty was that he or she was fond of parading around, but almost every soul in town—in the town proper, not West Hanratty, that goes without saying—would get a chance to march in public in some organized and approved affair. The only thing was that you must never look as if you were enjoying it; you had to give the impression of being called forth out of preferred obscurity, ready to do your duty and gravely preoccupied with whatever notions the parade celebrated.

The Orange Walk was the most splendid of all the parades. King Billy at the head of it rode a horse as near pure white as could be found, and the Black Knights at the rear, the noblest rank of Orangemen— usually thin, and poor, and proud and fanatical old farmers—rode dark horses and wore the ancient father-to-son top hats and swallow-tail coats. The banners were all gorgeous silks and embroideries, blue and

gold, orange and white, scenes of Protestant triumph, lilies and open
Bibles, mottoes of godliness and honour and flaming bigotry. The ladies
came beneath their sunshades, Orangemen's wives and daughters all
wearing white for purity. Then the bands, the fifes and drums, and gifted
step-dancers performing on a clean hay-wagon as a movable stage.

Also, there came Milton Homer. He could show up anywhere in the
parade and he varied his place in it from time to time, stepping out
behind King Billy or the Black Knights or the step-dancers or the shy
orange-sashed children who carried the banners. Behind the Black
Knights he would pull a dour face, and hold his head as if a top hat was
riding on it; behind the ladies he wiggled his hips and diddled an
imaginary sunshade. He was a mimic of ferocious gifts and terrible
energy. He could take the step-dancers' tidy show and turn it into an
idiot's prance, and still keep the beat.

The Orange Walk was his best opportunity, in parades, but he was
conspicuous in all of them. Head in the air, arms whipping out, snootily
in step, he marched behind the commanding officer of the Legion. On
Empire Day he provided himself with a Red Ensign and a Union Jack,
and kept them going like whirligigs above his head. In the Santa Claus
parade he snatched candy meant for children; he did not do it for a joke.

You would think that somebody in authority in Hanratty would
have put an end to this. Milton Homer's contribution to any parade was
wholly negative; designed, if Milton Homer could have designed
anything, just to make the parade look foolish. Why didn't the organizers
and the paraders make an effort to keep him out? They must have
decided that was easier said than done. Milton lived with his two old-
maid aunts, his parents being dead, and nobody would have liked to ask
the two old ladies to keep him home. It must have seemed as if they had
enough on their hands already. How could they keep him in, once he had
heard the band? They would have to lock him up, tie him down. And
nobody wanted to haul him out and drag him away once things began.
His protests would have ruined everything. There wasn't any doubt that
he would protest. He had a strong, deep voice and he was a strong man,
though not very tall. He was about the size of Napoleon. He had kicked
through gates and fences when people tried to shut him out of their
yards. Once he had smashed a child's wagon on the sidewalk, simply
because it was in his way. Letting him participate must have seemed the
best choice, under the circumstances.

Not that it was done as the best of bad choices. Nobody looked askance at Milton in a parade; everybody was used to him. Even the Commanding Officer would let himself be mocked, and the Black Knights with their old black grievances took no notice. People just said, "Oh, there's Milton," from the sidewalk. There wasn't much laughing at him, though strangers in town, city relatives invited to watch the parade, might point him out and laugh themselves silly, thinking he was there officially and for purposes of comic relief, like the clowns who were actually young businessmen, unsuccessfully turning cartwheels.

"Who is that?" the visitors said, and were answered with nonchalance and a particularly obscure sort of pride.

"That's just Milton Homer. It wouldn't be a parade without Milton Homer."

"The village idiot," said Phoebe, trying to comprehend these things, with her inexhaustible unappreciated politeness, and both Rose and Brian said that they had never heard him described that way. They had never thought of Hanratty as a village. A village was a cluster of picturesque houses around a steepled church on a Christmas card. Villagers were the costumed chorus in the high school operetta. If it was necessary to describe Milton Homer to an outsider, people would say that he was "not all there." Rose had wondered, even at that time, what was the part that wasn't there? She still wondered. Brains, would be the easiest answer. Milton Homer must surely have had a low I.Q. Yes; but so did plenty of people, in Hanratty and out of it, and they did not distinguish themselves as he did. He could read without difficulty, as shown in the case of the quarantine sign; he knew how to count his change, as evidenced in many stories about how people had tried to cheat him. What was missing was a sense of precaution, Rose thought now. Social inhibition, though there was no such name for it at that time. Whatever it is that ordinary people lose when they are drunk, Milton Homer never had, or might have chosen not to have—and this is what interests Rose—at some point early in life. Even his expressions, his everyday looks, were those that drunks wear in theatrical extremity—goggling, leering, drooping looks that seemed boldly calculated, and at the same time helpless, involuntary; is such a thing possible?

The two ladies Milton Homer lived with were his mother's sisters.

They were twins; their names were Hattie and Mattie Milton, and they were usually called Miss Hattie and Miss Mattie, perhaps to detract from any silly sound their names might have had otherwise. Milton had been named after his mother's family. That was a common practice, and there was probably no thought of linking together the names of two great poets. That coincidence was never mentioned and was perhaps not noticed. Rose did not notice it until one day in high school when the boy who sat behind her tapped her on the shoulder and showed her what he had written in his English book. He had stroked out the word *Chapman's* in the title of a poem and inked in the word *Milton,* so that the title now read: *On First Looking into Milton Homer.*

Any mention of Milton Homer was a joke, but this changed title was also a joke because it referred, rather weakly, to Milton Homer's more scandalous behaviour. The story was that when he got behind somebody in a line-up at the Post Office or a movie theatre, he would open his coat and present himself, then lunge and commence rubbing. Though of course he wouldn't get that far; the object of his passion would have ducked out of his way. Boys were said to dare each other to get him into position, and stay close ahead of him until the very last moment, then jump aside and reveal him in dire importunity.

It was in honour of this story—whether it was true or not, had happened once, under provocation, or kept happening all the time—that ladies crossed the street when they saw Milton coming, that children were warned to stay clear of him. *Just don't let him monkey around* was what Flo said. He was allowed into houses on those ritual occasions when there was a new baby—with hospital births getting commoner, those occasions diminished—but at other times the doors were locked against him. He would come and knock, and kick the door panels, and go away. But he was let have his way in yards, because he didn't take things, and could do so much damage if offended.

Of course, it was another story altogether when he appeared with one of his aunts. At those times he was hangdog-looking, well-behaved; his powers and his passions, whatever they were, all banked and hidden. He would be eating candy the aunt had bought him, out of a paper bag. He offered it when told to, though nobody but the most greedy person alive would touch what might have been touched by Milton Homer's fingers or blessed by his spittle. The aunts saw that he got his hair cut; they did their best to keep him presentable. They washed and ironed and mended his clothes, sent him out in his raincoat and rubbers, or knitted cap and muffler, as the weather indicated. Did they know how he conducted himself when out of their sight? They must have heard, and if they heard they must have suffered, being people of pride and Methodist morals. It was their grandfather who had started the flax mill in Hanratty and compelled all his employees to spend their Saturday nights at a Bible Class he himself conducted. The Homers, too, were decent people. Some of the Homers were supposed to be in favour of putting Milton away but the Milton ladies wouldn't do it. Nobody suggested they refused out of tender-heartedness.

"They won't put him in the Asylum, they're too proud."

Miss Hattie Milton taught at the high school. She had been teaching there longer than all the other teachers combined and was more important than the Principal. She taught English—the alteration in the poem was the more daring and satisfying because it occurred under her nose—and the thing she was famous for was keeping order. She did this without apparent effort, through the force of her large-bosomed, talcumed, spectacled, innocent and powerful presence, and her refusal to see that there was any difference between teen-agers (she did not use the word) and students in Grade Four. She assigned a lot of memory work. One day she wrote a long poem on the board and said that everyone was to copy it out, then learn it off by heart, and the next day recite it. This was when Rose was in her third or fourth year at high school and she did not believe these instructions were to be taken literally. She learned poetry with ease; it seemed reasonable to her to skip the first step. She read the poem and learned it, verse by verse, then said it over a couple of times in her head. While she was doing this Miss Hattie asked her why she wasn't copying.

Rose replied that she knew the poem already, though she was not perfectly sure that this was true.

"Do you really?" said Miss Hattie. "Stand up and face the back of the room."

Rose did so, trembling for her boast.

"Now recite the poem to the class."

Rose's confidence was not mistaken. She recited without a hitch. What did she expect to follow? Astonishment, and compliments, and unaccustomed respect?

"Well, you may know the poem," Miss Hattie said, "but that is no excuse for not doing what you were told. Sit down and write it in your book. I want you to write every line three times. If you don't get finished you can stay after four."

Rose did have to stay after four, of course, raging and writing while Miss Hattie got out her crocheting. When Rose took the copy to her desk Miss Hattie said mildly enough but with finality, "You can't go thinking you are better than other people just because you can learn poems. Who do you think you are?"

This was not the first time in her life Rose had been asked who she thought she was; in fact the question had often struck her like a monotonous gong and she paid no attention to it. But she understood, afterwards, that Miss Hattie was not a sadistic teacher; she had refrained from saying what she now said in front of the class. And she was not vindictive; she was not taking revenge because she had not believed Rose and had been proved wrong. The lesson she was trying to teach here was more important to her than any poem, and one she truly believed Rose needed. It seemed that many other people believed she needed it, too.

The whole class was invited, at the end of the senior year, to a lantern slide show at the Miltons' house. The lantern slides were of China, where Miss Mattie, the stay-at-home twin, had been a missionary in her youth. Miss Mattie was very shy, and she stayed in the background, working the slides, while Miss Hattie commented. The lantern slides showed a yellow country, much as expected. Yellow hills and sky, yellow people, rickshaws, parasols, all dry and papery-looking, fragile, unlikely, with black zigzags where the paint had cracked, on the temples, the roads and faces. At this very time, the one and only time Rose sat in the Miltons' parlour, Mao was in power in China and the Korean War was underway, but Miss Hattie made no concessions to history, any more than she made concessions to the fact that the members of her audience were eighteen and nineteen years old.

"The Chinese are heathens," Miss Hattie said. "That is why they have beggars."

There was a beggar, kneeling in the street, arms outstretched to a rich lady in a rickshaw, who was not paying any attention to him.

"They do eat things we wouldn't touch," Miss Hattie said. Some Chinese were pictured poking sticks into bowls. "But they eat a better diet when they become Christians. The first generation of Christians is an inch and a half taller."

Christians of the first generation were standing in a row with their mouths open, possibly singing. They wore black and white clothes.

After the slides, plates of sandwiches, cookies, tarts were served. All were home-made and very good. A punch of grape juice and ginger-ale was poured into paper cups. Milton sat in a corner in his thick tweed suit, a white shirt and a tie, on which punch and crumbs had already been spilled.

"Some day it will just blow up in their faces," Flo had said darkly, meaning Milton. Could that be the reason people came, year after year, to see the lantern slides and drink the punch that all the jokes were about? To see Milton with his jowls and stomach swollen as if with bad intentions, ready to blow? All he did was stuff himself at an unbelievable rate. It seemed as if he downed date squares, hermits, Nanaimo bars and fruit drops, butter tarts and brownies, whole, the way a snake will swallow frogs. Milton was similarly distended.

Methodists were people whose power in Hanratty was passing, but slowly. The days of the compulsory Bible Class were over. Perhaps the Miltons didn't know that. Perhaps they knew it but put a heroic face on their decline. They behaved as if the requirements of piety hadn't changed and as if its connection with prosperity was unaltered. Their brick house, with its overstuffed comfort, their coats with collars of snug dull fur, seemed proclaimed as a Methodist house, Methodist clothing, inelegant on purpose, heavy, satisfactory. Everything about them seemed to say that they had applied themselves to the world's work for God's sake, and God had not let them down. For God's sake the hall floor shone with wax around the runner, the lines were drawn perfectly with a straight pen in the account book, the begonias flourished, the money went into the bank.

But mistakes were made, nowadays. The mistake the Milton ladies made was in drawing up a petition to be sent to the Canadian Broadcasting Corporation, asking for the removal from the air of the programs that interfered with church-going on Sunday nights: Edgar Bergen and Charlie McCarthy; Jack Benny; Fred Allen. They got the minister to speak about their petition in church—this was in the United

Church, where Methodists had been outnumbered by Presbyterians and Congregationalists, and it was not a scene Rose witnessed, but had described to her by Flo—and afterwards they waited, Miss Hattie and Miss Mattie, one on each side of the outgoing stream, intending to deflect people and make them sign the petition, which was set up on a little table in the church vestibule. Behind the table Milton Homer was sitting. He had to be there; they never let him get out of going to church on Sunday. They had given him a job to keep him busy; he was to be in charge of the fountain pens, making sure they were full and handing them to signers.

That was the obvious part of the mistake. Milton had got the idea of drawing whiskers on himself, and had done so, without the help of a mirror. Whiskers curled out over his big sad cheeks, up towards his bloodshot foreboding eyes. He had put the pen in his mouth, too, so that ink had blotched his lips. In short, he had made himself so comical a sight that the petition which nobody really wanted could be treated as a comedy, too, and the power of the Milton sisters, the flax-mill Methodists, could be seen as a leftover dribble. People smiled and slid past; nothing could be done. Of course the Milton ladies didn't scold Milton or put on any show for the public, they just bundled him up with their petition and took him home.

"That was the end of them thinking they could run things," Flo said. It was hard to tell, as always, what particular defeat—was it that of religion or pretension?—she was so glad to see.

The boy who showed Rose the poem in Miss Hattie's own English class in Hanratty high school was Ralph Gillespie, the same boy who specialized in Milton Homer imitations. As Rose remembered it, he hadn't started on the imitations at the time he showed her the poem. They came later, during the last few months he was in school. In most classes he sat ahead of Rose or behind her, due to the alphabetical closeness of their names. Beyond this alphabetical closeness they did have something like a family similarity, not in looks but in habits or tendencies. Instead of embarrassing them, as it would have done if they had really been brother and sister, this drew them together in helpful conspiracy. Both of them lost or mislaid, or never adequately provided themselves with, all the pencils, rulers, erasers, pen-nibs, ruled paper, graph paper, the compass, dividers, protractor, necessary for a successful school life; both of them were sloppy with ink, subject to spilling and blotting mishaps; both of them were negligent about doing homework but panicky about not having done it. So they did their best to help each other out, sharing whatever supplies they had, begging from their more provident neighbours, finding someone's homework to copy. They developed the comradeship of captives, of soldiers who have no heart for the campaign, wishing only to survive and avoid action.

That wasn't quite all. Their shoes and boots became well acquainted, scuffling and pushing in friendly and private encounter, sometimes resting together a moment in tentative encouragement; this mutual kindness particularly helped them through those moments when people were being selected to do mathematics problems on the blackboard.

Once Ralph came in after noon hour with his hair full of snow. He leaned back and shook the snow over Rose's desk, saying, "Do you have those dandruff blues?"

"No. Mine's white."

This seemed to Rose a moment of some intimacy, with its physical frankness, its remembered childhood joke. Another day at noon hour, before the bell rang, she came into the classroom and found him, in a ring of onlookers, doing his Milton Homer imitation. She was surprised and worried; surprised because his shyness in class had always equalled hers and had been one of the things that united them; worried that he might not be able to bring it off, might not make them laugh. But he was very good; his large, pale, good-natured face took on the lumpy desperation of Milton's; his eyes goggled and his jowls shook and his words came out in a hoarse hypnotized singsong. He was so successful that Rose was amazed, and so was everybody else. From that time on Ralph began to do imitations; he had several, but Milton Homer was his trademark. Rose never quite got over a comradely sort of apprehension on his behalf. She had another feeling as well, not envy but a shaky sort of longing. She wanted to do the same. Not Milton Homer; she did not want to do Milton Homer. She wanted to fill up in that magical, releasing way, transform herself; she wanted the courage and the power.

Not long after he started publicly developing these talents he had, Ralph Gillespie dropped out of school. Rose missed his feet and his breathing and his finger tapping her shoulder. She met him sometimes on the street but he did not seem to be quite the same person. They never stopped to talk, just said hello and hurried past. They had been close and conspiring for years, it seemed, maintaining their spurious domesticity, but they had never talked outside of school, never gone beyond the most formal recognition of each other, and it seemed they could not, now. Rose never asked him why he had dropped out; she did not even know if he had found a job. They knew each other's necks and shoulders, heads and feet, but were not able to confront each other as full-length presences.

After a while Rose didn't see him on the street any more. She heard that he had joined the Navy. He must have been just waiting till he was old enough to do that. He had joined the Navy and gone to Halifax. The war was over, it was only the peacetime Navy. Just the same it was odd to think of Ralph Gillespie, in uniform, on the deck of a destroyer, maybe firing off guns. Rose was just beginning to understand that the boys she knew, however incompetent they might seem, were going to turn into men, and be allowed to do things that you would think required a lot more talent and authority than they could have.

There was a time, after she gave up the store and before her arthritis became too crippling, during which Flo went out to Bingo games and sometimes played cards with her neighbours at the Legion Hall. When Rose was home on a visit conversation was difficult, so she would ask Flo about the people she saw at the Legion. She would ask for news of her own contemporaries, Horse Nicholson, Runt Chesterton, whom she could not really imagine as grown men; did Flo ever see them?

"There's one I see and he's around there all the time. Ralph Gillespie."

Rose said that she had thought Ralph Gillespie was in the Navy.

"He was too but he's back home now. He was in an accident."

"What kind of accident?"

"I don't know. It was in the Navy. He was in a Navy hospital three solid years. They had to rebuild him from scratch. He's all right now except he walks with a limp, he sort of drags the one leg."

"That's too bad."

"Well, yes. That's what I say. I don't hold any grudge against him but there's some up there at the Legion that do."

"Hold a grudge?"

"Because of the pension," said Flo, surprised and rather contemptuous of Rose for not taking into account so basic a fact of life, and so natural an attitude, in Hanratty. "They think, well, he's set for life. I say he must've suffered for it. Some people say he gets a lot but I don't believe it. He doesn't need much, he's all on his own. One thing, if he suffers pain he don't let on. Like me. I don't let on. Weep and you weep alone. He's a good darts player. He'll play anything that's going. And he can imitate people to the life."

"Does he still do Milton Homer? He used to do Milton Homer at school."

"He does him. Milton Homer. He's comical at that. He does some others too."

"Is Milton Homer still alive? Is he still marching in parades?"

"Sure he's still alive. He's quietened down a lot, though. He's out there at the County Home and you can see him on a sunny day down by the highway keeping an eye on the traffic and licking up an ice cream cone. Both the old ladies is dead."

"So he isn't in the parades any more?"

"There isn't the parades to be in. Parades have fallen off a lot. All the Orangemen are dying out and you wouldn't get the turnout, anyway, people'd rather stay home and watch their TV."

On later visits Rose found that Flo had turned against the Legion.

"I don't want to be one of those old crackpots," she said.

"What old crackpots?"

"Sit around up there telling the same stupid yarns and drinking beer. They make me sick."

This was very much in Flo's usual pattern. People, places, amusements, went abruptly in and out of favour. The turnabouts had become more drastic and frequent with age.

"Don't you like any of them any more? Is Ralph Gillespie still going there?"

"He still is. He likes it so well he tried to get himself a job there. He tried to get the part-time bar job. Some people say he got turned down because he already has got the pension but I think it was because of the way he carries on."

"How? Does he get drunk?"

"You couldn't tell if he was, he carries on just the same, imitating, and half the time he's imitating somebody that the newer people that's come to town, they don't know even who the person was, they just think it's Ralph being idiotic."

"Like Milton Homer?"

"That's right. How do they know it's supposed to be Milton Homer and what was Milton Homer like? They don't know. Ralph don't know when to stop. He Milton Homer'd himself right out of a job."

After Rose had taken Flo to the County Home—she had not seen Milton Homer there, though she had seen other people she had long believed dead—and was staying to clean up the house and get it ready for sale, she herself was taken to the Legion by Flo's neighbours, who thought she must be lonely on a Saturday night. She did not know how to refuse, so she found herself sitting at a long table in the basement of the hall, where the bar was, just at the time the last sunlight was coming across the fields of beans and corn, across the gravel parking lot and through the high windows, staining the plywood walls. All around the walls were photographs, with names lettered by hand and taped to the frames. Rose got up to have a look at them. The Hundred and Sixth, just before embarkation, 1915. Various heroes of that war, whose names were carried on by sons and nephews, but whose existence had not been known to her before. When she came back to the table a card game had started. She wondered if it had been a disruptive thing to do, getting up to look at the pictures. Probably nobody ever looked at them; they were not for looking at; they were just there, like the plywood on the walls. Visitors, outsiders, are always looking at things, always taking an interest, asking who was this, when was that, trying to liven up the conversation. They put too much in; they want too much out. Also, it could have looked as if she was parading around the room, asking for attention.

A woman sat down and introduced herself. She was the wife of one of the men playing cards. "I've seen you on television," she said. Rose was always a bit apologetic when somebody said this; that is, she had to control what she recognized in herself as an absurd impulse to apologize. Here in Hanratty the impulse was stronger than usual. She was aware of having done things that must seem high-handed. She remembered her days as a television interviewer, her beguiling confidence and charm; here as nowhere else they must understand how that was a sham. Her acting was another matter. The things she was ashamed of were not what they must think she was ashamed of; not a flopping bare breast, but a failure she couldn't seize upon or explain.

This woman who was talking to her did not belong to Hanratty. She said she had come from Sarnia when she was married, fifteen years ago.

"I still find it hard to get used to. Frankly I do. After the city. You look better in person than you do in that series."

"I should hope so," said Rose, and told about how they made her up. People were interested in things like that and Rose was more comfortable, once the conversation got on to technical details.

"Well, here's old Ralph," the woman said. She moved over, making room for a thin, grey-haired man holding a mug of beer. This was Ralph Gillespie. If Rose had met him on the street she would not have recognized him, he would have been a stranger to her, but after she had looked at him for a moment he seemed quite unchanged to her, unchanged from himself at seventeen or fifteen, his grey hair which had been light brown still falling over his forehead, his face still pale and calm and rather large for his body, the same diffident, watchful, withholding look. But his body was thinner and his shoulders seemed to have shrunk together. He wore a short-sleeved sweater with a little collar and three ornamental buttons; it was light-blue with beige and yellow stripes. This sweater seemed to Rose to speak of aging jauntiness, a kind of petrified adolescence. She noticed that his arms were old and skinny and that his hands shook so badly that he used both of them to raise the glass of beer to his mouth.

"You're not staying around here long, are you?" said the woman who had come from Sarnia.

Rose said that she was going to Toronto tomorrow, Sunday, night.

"You must have a busy life," the woman said, with a large sigh, an honest envy that in itself would have declared out-of-town origins.

Rose was thinking that on Monday at noon she was to meet a man for lunch and to go to bed. This man was Tom Shepherd, whom she had known for a long time. At one time he had been in love with her, he had written love letters to her. The last time she had been with him, in Toronto, when they were sitting up in bed afterwards drinking gin and tonic—they always drank a good deal when they were together—Rose suddenly thought, or knew, that there was somebody now, some woman he was in love with and was courting from a distance, probably writing letters to, and that there must have been another woman he was robustly bedding, at the time he was writing letters to her. Also, and all the time, there was his wife. Rose wanted to ask him about this; the necessity, the difficulties, the satisfactions. Her interest was friendly and uncritical but she knew, she had just enough sense to know, that the question would not do.

The conversation in the Legion had turned on lottery tickets, Bingo games, winnings. The men playing cards—Flo's neighbour among them—were talking about a man who was supposed to have won ten thousand dollars, and never publicized the fact, because he had gone bankrupt a few years before and owed so many people money.

One of them said that if he had declared himself bankrupt, he didn't owe the money any more.

"Maybe he didn't owe it then," another said. "But he owes it now. The reason is, he's got it now."

This opinion was generally favoured.

Rose and Ralph Gillespie looked at each other. There was the same silent joke, the same conspiracy, comfort; the same, the same.

"I hear you're quite a mimic," Rose said.

That was wrong; she shouldn't have said anything. He laughed and shook his head.

"Oh, come on. I hear you do a sensational Milton Homer."

"I don't know about that."

"Is he still around?"

"Far as I know he's out at the County Home."

"Remember Miss Hattie and Miss Mattie? They had the lantern slide show at their house."

"Sure."

"My mental picture of China is still pretty well based on those slides."

Rose went on talking like this, though she wished she could stop. She was talking in what elsewhere might have been considered an amusing, confidential, recognizably and meaninglessly flirtatious style. She did not get much response from Ralph Gillespie, though he seemed attentive, even welcoming. All the time she talked, she was wondering what he wanted her to say. He did want something. But he would not make any move to get it. Her first impression of him, as boyishly shy and ingratiating, had to change. That was his surface. Underneath he was self-sufficient, resigned to living in bafflement, perhaps proud. She wished that he would speak to her from that level, and she thought he wished it, too, but they were prevented.

But when Rose remembered this unsatisfactory conversation she seemed to recall a wave of kindness, of sympathy and forgiveness, though certainly no words of that kind had been spoken. That peculiar shame which she carried around with her seemed to have been eased. The thing she was ashamed of, in acting, was that she might have been paying attention to the wrong things, reporting antics, when there was always something further, a tone, a depth, a light, that she couldn't get and wouldn't get. And it wasn't just about acting she suspected this. Everything she had done could sometimes be seen as a mistake. She had never felt this more strongly than when she was talking to Ralph Gillespie, but when she thought about him afterwards her mistakes appeared unimportant. She was enough a child of her time to wonder if what she felt about him was simply sexual warmth, sexual curiosity; she did not think it was. There seemed to be feelings which could only be spoken of in translation; perhaps they could only be acted on in translation; not speaking of them and not acting on them is the right course to take because translation is dubious. Dangerous, as well.

For these reasons Rose did not explain anything further about Ralph Gillespie to Brian and Phoebe when she recalled Milton Homer's ceremony with babies or his expression of diabolical happiness on the swing. She did not even mention that he was dead. She knew he was dead because she still had a subscription to the Hanratty paper. Flo had given Rose a seven-year subscription on the last Christmas when she felt obliged to give Christmas presents; characteristically, Flo said that the paper was just for people to get their names in and hadn't anything in it worth reading. Usually Rose turned the pages quickly and put the paper in the firebox. But she did see the story about Ralph which was on the front page.

FORMER NAVY MAN DIES

Mr. Ralph Gillespie, Naval Petty Officer, retired, sustained fatal head injuries at the Legion Hall on Saturday night last. No other person was implicated in the fall and unfortunately several hours passed before Mr. Gillespie's body was discovered. It is thought that he mistook the basement door for the exit door and lost his balance, which was precarious due to an old injury suffered in his naval career which left him partly disabled.

The paper went on to give the names of Ralph's parents, who were apparently still alive, and of his married sister. The Legion was taking charge of the funeral services.

Rose didn't tell this to anybody, glad that there was one thing at least she wouldn't spoil by telling, though she knew it was lack of material as much as honourable restraint that kept her quiet. What could she say about herself and Ralph Gillespie, except that she felt his life, close, closer than the lives of men she'd loved, one slot over from her own?

What Is Real?

Whenever people get an opportunity to ask me questions about my writing, I can be sure that some of the questions asked will be these:

"Do you write about real people?"

"Did those things really happen?"

"When you write about a small town are you really writing about Wingham?" (Wingham is the small town in Ontario where I was born and grew up, and it has often been assumed, by people who should know better, that I have simply "fictionalized" this place in my work. Indeed, the local newspaper has taken me to task for making it the "butt of a soured and cruel introspection.")

The usual thing, for writers, is to regard these either as very naive questions, asked by people who really don't understand the difference between autobiography and fiction, who can't recognize the device of the first-person narrator, or else as catch-you-out questions posed by journalists who hope to stir up exactly the sort of dreary (and to outsiders, slightly comic) indignation voiced by my home-town paper. Writers answer such questions patiently or crossly according to temperament and the mood they're in. They say, no, you must understand, my characters are composites; no, those things didn't happen the way I wrote about them; no, of course not, that isn't Wingham (or whatever other place it may be that has had the queer unsought-after distinction of hatching a writer). Or the writer may, riskily, ask the questioners what is real, anyway? None of this seems to be very satisfactory. People go on asking these same questions because the subject really does interest and bewilder them. It would seem to be quite true that they don't know what fiction is.

And how could they know, when what it is, is changing all the time, and we differ among ourselves, and we don't really try to explain because it is too difficult?

What I would like to do here is what I can't do in two or three sentences at the end of a reading. I won't try to explain what fiction is, and what short stories are (assuming, which we can't, that there is any fixed thing that it is and they are), but what short stories are to me, and how I write them, and how I use things that are "real." I will start by explaining how I read stories written by other people. For one thing, I can start reading them anywhere; from beginning to end, from end to beginning, from any point in between in either direction. So obviously I don't take up a story and follow it as if it were a road, taking me somewhere, with views and neat diversions along the way. I go into it, and move back and forth and settle here and there, and stay in it for a while. It's more like a house. Everybody knows what a house does, how it encloses space and makes connections between one enclosed space and another and presents what is outside in a new way. This is the nearest I can come to explaining what a story does for me, and what I want my stories to do for other people.

So when I write a story I want to make a certain kind of structure, and I know the feeling I want to get from being inside that structure. This is the hard part of the explanation, where I have to use a word like "feeling," which is not very precise, because if I attempt to be more intellectually respectable I will have to be dishonest. "Feeling" will have to do.

There is no blueprint for the structure. It's not a question of, "I'll make this kind of house because if I do it right it will have this effect." I've got to make, I've got to build up, a house, a story, to fit around the indescribable "feeling" that is like the soul of the story, and which I must insist upon in a dogged, embarrassed way, as being no more definable than that. And I don't know where it comes from. It seems to be already there, and some unlikely clue, such as a shop window or a bit of conversation, makes me aware of it. Then I start accumulating the material and putting it together. Some of the material I may have lying around already, in memories and observations, and some I invent, and some I have to go diligently looking for (factual details), while some is dumped in my lap (anecdotes, bits of speech). I see how this material might go together to make the shape I need, and I try it. I keep trying and seeing where I went wrong and trying again.

I suppose this is the place where I should talk about technical problems and how I solve them. The main reason I can't is that I'm never sure I do solve anything. Even when I say that I see where I went wrong, I'm being misleading. I never figure out how I'm going to change things, I never say to myself, "That page is heavy going, that paragraph's clumsy, I need some dialogue and shorter sentences." I feel a part that's wrong, like a soggy weight; then I pay attention to the story, as if it were really happening somewhere, not just in my head, and in its own way, not mine. As a result, the sentences may indeed get shorter, there may be more dialogue, and so on. But though I've tried to pay attention to the story, I may not have got it right; those shorter sentences may be an evasion, a mistake. Every final draft, every published story, is still only an attempt, an approach, to the story.

I did promise to talk about using reality. "Why, if Jubilee isn't Wingham, has it got Shuter Street in it?" people want to know. Why have I described somebody's real ceramic elephant sitting on the mantelpiece? I could say I get momentum from doing things like this. The fictional room, town, world, needs a bit of starter dough from the real world. It's a device to help the writer—at least it helps me   but it arouses a certain baulked fury in the people who really do live on Shuter Street and the lady who owns the ceramic elephant. "Why do you put in something true and then go on and tell lies?" they say, and anybody who has been on the receiving end of this kind of thing knows how they feel.

"I do it for the sake of my art and to make this structure which encloses the soul of my story, that I've been telling you about," says the writer. "That is more important than anything."

Not to everybody, it isn't.

So I can see there might be a case, once you've written the story and got the momentum, for going back and changing the elephant to a camel (though there's always a chance the lady might complain that you made a nasty camel out of a beautiful elephant), and changing Shuter Street to Blank Street. But what about the big chunks of reality, without which your story can't exist? In the story *Royal Beatings*, I use a big chunk of reality: the story of the butcher, and of the young men who may have been egged on to "get" him. This is a story out of an old newspaper; it really did happen in a town I know. There is no legal difficulty about using it because it has been printed in a newspaper, and besides, the people who figure in it are all long dead. But there is a difficulty about offending people in that town who would feel that use of this story is a deliberate exposure, taunt and insult. Other people who have no connection with the real happening would say, "Why write about anything so hideous?" And lest you think that such an objection could only be raised by simple folk who read nothing but Harlequin Romances, let me tell you that one of the questions most frequently asked at universities is, "Why do you write about things that are so depressing?" People can accept almost any amount of ugliness if it is contained in a familiar formula, as it is on television, but when they come closer to their own place, their own lives, they are much offended by a lack of editing.

There are ways I can defend myself against such objections. I can say, "I do it in the interests of historical reality. That is what the old days were really like." Or, "I do it to show the dark side of human nature, the beast let loose, the evil we can run up against in communities and families." In certain countries I could say, "I do it to show how bad things were under the old system when there were prosperous butchers and young fellows hanging around livery stables and nobody thought about building a new society." But the fact is, the minute I say *to show* I am telling a lie. I don't do it to show anything. I put this story at the heart of my story because I need it there and it belongs there. It is the black room at the centre of the house with all other rooms leading to and away from it. That is all. A strange defence. Who told me to write this story? Who feels any need of it before it is written? I do. I do, so that I might grab off this piece of horrid reality and install it where I see fit, even if Hat Nettleton and his friends were still around to make me sorry.

The answer seems to be as confusing as ever. Lots of true answers are. Yes and no. Yes, I use bits of what is real, in the sense of being really there and really happening, in the world, as most people see it, and I transform it into something that is really there and really happening, in my story. No, I am not concerned with using what is real to make any sort of record or prove any sort of point, and I am not concerned with any methods of selection but my own, which I can't fully explain. This is quite presumptuous, and if writers are not allowed to be so—and quite often, in many places, they are not—I see no point in the writing of fiction.

Leon Rooke

LEON ROOKE was born in North Carolina in 1934 and has lived for years now in Victoria, British Columbia, where he teaches from time to time at the University of Victoria. His fiction has been widely published in Canadian and American magazines, and his plays have been produced professionally in Vancouver and New York.

Other Works

Last One Home Sleeps in the Yellow Bed, (1968) Stories
The Love Parlour, (1977) Stories
The Broad Back of the Angel, (1978) Stories
Cry Evil, (1980) Stories
Fat Woman, (1980) Novel
Death Suite, (1981) Stories
The Magician in Love, (1981) Stories

Winter
Is Lovely,
Isn't Summer Hell

He wondered did she wash her hands before she fall in love. Whatever he wanted he got but mostly that was because he know what he want. Her, for instance. But up to that time he only have dreams of her. My Dream Girl, he say to friends, she like this: and he slice his hands through the air like what he really want is a Coca-Cola bottle. Next thing he know it have happened but *how* it have happened he slow to realize: he married, or mostly near to it. He have her pregnant and everybody choose to hope she is. Married, that is.

You my ideal, more than once he tell her this. What is a poor girl her age to think?

You my ideal! You Something Else!

That kind of talk turn her head.

You not bad yourself, she say.

But still he hesitate. *What's the matter, honey?*—she find herself asking him that question over and over.

Things on my mind.

That is how he try to weasel out of it. *Got me some Man-stuff to think about.* A thousand times he tell her this, and drift right away from her. Leave her standing right where she stand, trying to figure out what she have done to put him in this mood.

Take care yourself, I see you soon.

The truth is, he confused. He up to his eyebrows in trouble and don't know which way to turn. He rue the day. That is what you hear him mumbling to himself sometime as he haunch up his shoulders and slouch along. *Rue the Day! God in Heaven, I rue the day!* His friends see him coming down the street they shout out *How's the Daddy!* and double-over laughing till their sides ache.

Otherwise, he the same as them. That is his trouble, that *otherwise*. Otherwise, he be out shooting pool, having a good time, not a care in the world the same as them. Now instead she a drain on the system, she Trouble with a capital T, and he rue the day.

Back up a minute. Don't forget the fun they have at the start. After their first meeting all memory of it is filled with love. Even if he tell her she have to check up on her hygiene. *Joy,* that was it! They have a new world all their own. People on the street they see them coming they break out into big grins, they say "You two are snug as bugs in the rug, you are stuck together with Elmer's glue." You see one coming you see the other, everybody happy.

He happy too. Up to the time she can take it no more, she grab him by the sleeve to say "I can take it no more, I got a baby on the way, when we getting married, you hear?" Up to that time she have moved him to do all manner of things he have never thought of before. She have touch him where he live. He even write her a poem.

"Let's hear it," she say.

But it turn out to be a poem about Winter not about Love like she expect. "Let's hear it anyway," she say, and fold her arms over her stomach and wait. "Show me your stuff," she say.

"Winter!" he shout out good and loud, making sure she have the title right. *"Winter,* by Thomas M. Jones!

> *The season come but once a year,*
> *the reason we will never know."*

He sit back down. That is all.

"Is that all?" she ask.

"That is all," he say. He squirm in the seat and wait for the praise. It is then that because she like him so much she look at him a long time before she get a hold of herself to say: "I can take it no more, I got a baby on the way, when we getting married, you hear?"

What he do is he stare at her hands like that is where the harm have been done.

"You have to check up on your hygiene!" he suddenly shout, and his face it is a blanket of woe from that minute on.

She have her feelings hurt. "I can do better than you right on the spot!" she yell back at him. And she twist up from her seat, drop her hands by the side, and scream out across the yard, *"Winter,* by Miss Ruby Lee Tucker, 16 years old:

> *The season is not very gay*
> *because the birds all fly away*
> *the lawn lose it summer colour*
> *and take on a winter cover. . . .*

Snakeshit, ha!" she say, and sit back down knowing she have captured the heart of the subject.

For a long time they do not speak about anything, the cat have their tongues, you can feel their cold hearts a mile away.

Then he tie a loop in his shoelace, he gets up, and to make sure his goal is clear to Miss Ruby Lee Tucker he say: "I am going."

She don't say nothing, her eyes just burn a hole in the floor.

"I'll be taking off now," he say.

She kick out at him a small kick, but he skip away.

She look up at him and she ask in a mad voice, "What have I done?"

"Nothing that I know of," he say.

She ask is that all he have to say.

He sit back down, he take her hand a minute then he throw it down and once more stand. "No," he say, "I can't get married."

"Why not?" she say, "you already married?"

"No," he say, "but my brother is."

For the evening that settle the matter. What's done is done, what's said is said, no longer does hope and joy rule in the human breast. He goes off the porch, she goes inside, he goes his separate ways and means home.

Everybody is sad, everybody is glum. Her mama will say "There—there, honey, the worse ain't yet come to worse, you still have your health," and her daddy will say "I always said that boy was no good, none of them Jones ever was," and the friends and neighbours on the street they are sad with regret thinking how hard young love is and maybe a little relieved thinking it is all out of their hands.

Pretty soon word is come that he is seen hanging around. One time he is seen riding by in a car and he toots three times on the horn and everyone wonders whose car he have and how much rubber he lose squealing the tires. Another time he is seen in the alley across the street watching the front door and one time her mama say she heard a noise at the girl's window but she can't for certain say it was him.

All the time a few people are saying maybe he have another girl and shake their heads worried-like or maybe even say they knew what he wanted in the first place from poor Ruby Lee and boys these days they are just no good.

First thing anybody know the romance is on again.

They is back on the street hand in hand, smiling hello to everyone, denying any trouble ever come between them.

The days pass, they are always together, they are tight folks say as skin on skin, couldn't pry them apart with a crowbar.

Before anybody is the wiser he have rented a room in the next block and she have moved in with him.

In time she come to think she married already and you would guess he thought the same, though that is not always the case. To speak in a nutshell sometime she remember how he have hurt her and what is more the baby is about to come due.

"How come you won't make it legal?" she wants to know.

"Marriage," he say, "is a serious step, besides, I am scared of it."

"And what you think that step you done already took was, Mr. Shakespeare?" she say, and she will put her hands under her stomach and lift the hidden baby up at him. What he thinks is that she like to throw his poetic feeling up to his face in crucial times like this, she never let him forget a thing or have a minute's peace.

"Keep talking to me that way," he will tell her, "and I'm going to be busting you one."

"You hit me," she say, "and I'll have Johnny-law on your tail before you can spit."

He tell her she know he wouldn't hit no woman, he don't believe in that sort of thing.

She say that if so his name must not be Jones because she never heard of a Jones yet who didn't knock women around.

"That's a lie," he claim.

And sometimes if she is tired she will let the subject drop. She will put the dinner on the table and if he likes it he will eat it and tell her she sure can cook. Later on about bedtime it will cross her mind to tell him this: "If my first-born Leroy ever find out we ain't wed then you better watch out because one of us or both is bound to kill you sure."

It is at such times that he set his jaw and blink his eye and try to think real hard. The whole situation it seem to him is a new ballgame, he have not yet figured out quite how he come to be here sharing this room with Ruby Lee and her first-born child Leroy by another man. He have to spend a minute checking up on his own history just as he have told Ruby Lee she ought to take time off sometime to check up on her hygiene. It is not that he not know about the child it is just that it never cross his mind to think the child will come live with them, mostly because through all their courting days when they want to go out they go out alone with no unruly child tagging at the heels. Say they are going to a movie or to meet up with some friends or only if they are taking only a short stroll up or down the road her parents would always say, "No, you young folks don't want no youngan' tagging along, Leroy's natural place is here with us, we don't mind, you two young folks just scoot along and enjoy yourselves."

So he have never had to contend with no spoiled brat before.

He never before have his freedom robbed by no four-year-old who don't even have the manners to say thanks.

"You are not being daddy enough to him," she will say, and sometimes if he is already in a bad mood he will pick up a chair and smash it against a wall the same way his own daddy would, and even if later on he is sorry for his yelling and screaming and upsetting everyone he is mostly sorry for himself because he know he can't help himself, the problem is bigger than him.

"I will make it up to you," he will say to her once they are wrapped up in the bed. "You know I am good as my word, I will be a good daddy to him yet."

"You are mean," she will say, "just mean, you don't have no sense now and you never had none." And she will keep on talking through the night in that soft fierce voice, she will not let him forget what a fine ignoble rat he is.

She will let the brat sleep, yes sir, but not him. She roll over to the wall, poking her hind-part out at him, complaining of the hot and cold spells she suffer from, complaining of the cramps she have, biting on the pillow because she have no lawful name, telling him she does not care for herself it is the unborn child she is thinking of. "He's a boy and he grows up he won't be able to get no job, folks will poke fun at him. Say she's a girl, everyone will say she's a tramp, they will look down on her and boys will take what they can get and she'll be no better than what they say because she'll know she never had no lawful name. I hope that makes you proud, I'll be happy when you dead, me, you are lower than the low."

He gets mad and sorry too, he sorry for both of them as his mind drift back through all the time that have got him in this present mess, but what he find himself saying is he wonder if she ever going to wash her hands before she die, he wonder if the day will ever come when she check up on her hygiene—"Just once," he say, "without me reminding you."

She let out a gasp the same way she have done every other time he make this cruel remark and when he move to put his arms around her out of pity or love whatever the case she most goes through the wall into the next room where there is nothing but stairs going down, all to get away from him.

"Go to hell!" he say, his feelings hurt.

"It's where I am," she cry. "It's where I been!"

Gone are the days of the poetry-making. Gone are the days of the big smiles, of these two together tight as skin on skin.

She going to drive him away, some day, with her nagging; others say the fault is him. Them Jones, you know, they think they too good for any girl.

It's her mama's fault, some say, raising her like that, while some others say it's nobody's fault, folks will be folks, you can't blame young people just following a natural human urge.

"Give them time, they work it out, they still young."

"If they don't they ain't the first and I reckon they won't be the last."

Jones he walk around with his head down, nobody can get a kind word out of him except maybe Ruby Lee's first-born tagging along after him though nobody heard the boy calling him daddy yet.

Gone are the days. In them days he know what he want and he rove about the dark street to find it, wondering where in name of heaven she keep herself. Not Ruby Lee just the mystery girl who he can love who will love him. He come upon her finally and certainly for sure, he tell himself, that Ruby Lee she's the one I been looking for, she will fit the bill. Having her is better than having the dream, that much for sure. Better than searching out the lonely nights, looking for something to do, hunting for someone to do it with. Better certainly than waiting for your life to start and all the time doubting it will. So there she was that first night standing against the wall at the Shoo Fly Inn, standing there grinning at him, and he skip over feeling pretty good, giving her a smile, saying "Are you looking for me?" and she speak right up, she say "I'm looking *at* you" and give a little dip to her head and goes right on looking.

And that is how it begin, they have a good time, they can see they are made for each other. He do not know then what is going to happen next, all the same he is in his own mind ready for it, everyone can see he is flying high, he have found out what love is.

Hard to think now when he stop to think about it what is on his mind when he make up a poem called *Winter,* which he never forget and which even now he remember somehow—*the season come but once a year, the reason we will never know.* When he think of it he think his life is behind him, he wonder if he have thrown it all away and ruined Ruby Lee's life in the bargain, never mind for a minute her first-born who it turn out is not so spoiled after all, not a bad little boy come to think of it if anyone ever give him the chance. "You a nice-looking boy," he will sometime say to him, "you got a good heart."

And the boy will run fast to tell his mama what the man who is not his daddy say. And the days for a time they will be good, the old loving days will return, for a time they will think they forget. But the bad news it broods in the heart, it hang between them like the calendar on the door which tell them which day is which. He will not be putting it into words, but what he want most is a love like he feel when he only have a dream of what love is. To make a long story short that is one reason he have for not marrying her at the start. That she want to marry him because she is pregnant, not because she is in love with him. That got nothing to do with it, so he think. Love, that is what he is saving himself for and nothing else. No sir! He like to tell her that. He like to and any day now he think he will.

"We be married a long time ago, you not be holding a knife at my throat. We be hitched up and have a world all our own you not always be trying to tell me what's what, always trying to get the best of me."

"I never," she say, "I never did."

"Snakespit, ha-ha, tell me another one."

"Well you can forget about it now," she say, "I not marry you now you be the last man on earth."

"Yes," he say, "well, with your bad hygiene I be surprised you ever catch anyone."

Funny thing though, she have just come from the bath and his words not hurt at all this time. It finally begin to dawn on her mind that Mr. Thomas M. Jones is crazy on the subject. Frankly up to this moment his preoccupation with soap and water have always been a riddle to her.

"Well, may be," she tell him, "you Joneses wash three times a day, but that don't keep you from being the dirty one around here."

The truth is who is right and wrong is hard to tell. Even the little child can see that it seem to change from day to day. Still that don't keep people from putting their two cents in. Her mama and daddy for instance coax her to come on home, stop living with the fool, being an unwed mother with an orphan child or two is no disgrace these days and may in fact be the best thing. What his folks say is Tom it is clear you two don't get along, we don't say you shouldn't marry her, we don't say you should, all we say is she got herself in this fix and as the evidence shows not for the first time, although we agree with you that her little man is a lovely boy and you'll never hear us say a word against him.

Parents can't help being parents, they say whatever parents say.

"We work it out," he tell her, "one day you know we will."

But she is not speaking to him these days, she cook his dinner when he come home from work and put the plate in front of him and he eats, but she will not eat with him. In bed at night she sleep with one eye open, a knife in her hand and her face to the wall. He feel his manhood is at stake and he drop a warm hand on her hip, he let it stay there though he hardly dare to breathe. Ah, he think finally to himself, she is close to sleep or playing possum, may be now I have her in a friendly mood. He think to let his hand sneak up, wanting her big warmth to hold, but the very second he lift his finger to test out this idea she fling off the cover with a blood-curdling shriek and leap from the bed like someone have stuck a burning stick to her. And the next hour she will spend sitting in the cold drafty hall where other roomers in the house have to walk around her to get home and if they think to stop and pass the time she will bite off their heads.

"Ruby Lee," they will say, "you are waiting for a bus? You a mother-to-be, you do nothing but harm to yourself sitting out here in the drafty hall."

"Drop dead," she will say, "I ain't studying you."

At last he will come out, he will drag out with the one blanket they own and drape it over her, he will sit down beside her but not too close saying something like "How you doing?" or "Ain't you froze?" and in a little while when her temper is cooled she will head back inside with him or she won't. Most likely she won't.

She will walk the dark street, folks coming up to her they will say,

"Child, how come you out alone on a night like this, this a rough neighbourhood, you going to git your throat slit."

"What I care?" she say, "go on about your business, stop bothering me."

But folks stop her anyway, even the worse kind; they can see she down on her luck, that her chin is scraping concrete and she don't have a way to turn.

"Prop yourself up, girl," they say, "every cloud have a lining of some kind, your luck bound to turn."

"Zipper your mouth," she tell these good-intentioned people, "I am going to end it all and jump from the first bridge I come to."

But she is just talking to keep her spirit up, she don't mean herself no harm. She sooner run naked through the street or burn her feet on hot sand than hurt one hair of that unborn baby's head. Already she got the periodic pain, the dizzy spell; already she can squeeze watery milk from her breasts, she can make the baby move inside her almost on command. What she dream of these dark nights is that the baby will come and be nestled all snug in her arms and she will wake up in a sun-lit room to find her folks and his standing in their best clothes at the door of the white bed, every one of them whispering *Ain't he the prettiest thing! He look just like his Mama, just like his Daddy!* and everyone will argue about that a while. Good dreamy music will be playing on her bedside radio her special request, something like *Deep River* or *If You Want Me Baby Don't Throw The Chicken On the Floor*, and a tall man in a blue suit will step forward to yank her toe saying *Ruby Lee, do you take this man?* And she will say *I reckon so*, and the man will next turn to Thomas M. Jones with his back to the wall and he will say *Boy, take your hands out of your pockets and come up here, can't you see I'm talking to you?* Thomas M. Jones will poke his way forward, he will dither and dab and look to escape, but when the man in the suit get down to business and next say *Do you take this bride?* the hard-headed S.O.B. Jones will find it in his heart to say *I do I do I think I do.* He will say this until he git the hang of it and then he will shout it out, *Oh indeed I do!* and he will go on shouting it over and over until everyone have to tell him to shut up his mouth. And like that she will snuggle up to her sweet baby child and turn back at last to sleep with all her heartache gone. The good part and the bad part of her life will be split in half, churning on each side but with a road the bride and groom can walk that is big and high and wide and stretching all the way to the other side exactly like the Red Sea which in fact was nothing in the history of the world before it divide.

That was the dream she have. Now that dream have come and gone and since it went she have had a thousand more—and yet still her story and his go on.

"You are just like your Daddy," these days she can tell both her boys. "You are plain hard-headed and always up to something and not worth the clothes you wear, but me and him will keep you I guess until something better comes along."

So it is that each night now the boys can drop off to sleep snug and warm and no doubt wondering whose side of the story they going to hear tomorrow. Wondering what going to happen next. Feeling how the story of one is the story of them all and wondering why if this is so they remain so fearful of how their own fortune going to fall.

The Problem
Shop

"Ar-Salar-Saloam, of no fixed address and a blight on the soul of this town since you first came to birth, as witnesses against you have put in a No Show and as the Crown's Attorney has thrown up his hands in disgust and had not a shred of evidence in the first place, I have no choice but to declare you a free bird. I want it known, however, by you and by all present that if you ever again appear in my court I shall throw the book at you, guilty or otherwise. You are a reprehensible creature without, so far as I can tell, a single redeeming human trait. You are the bottom of the barrel and in my estimation would frankly be better off hung by the neck. Now get out of here!"

Ar-Salar-Saloam, the case against him so miraculously concluded, left the judge's chambers where these harsh words had been uttered, and walked out into a muggy Victoria day, to head back to his old stomping grounds in the up-and-coming but still derelict area forming the heart of the old city, the part the bloody English hadn't yet ruined with their tea shoppes and cutesy knick-knack tourist joints.

His child-bride Auriole met him on the steps.

"You old dog!" she exclaimed, smiling, cuffing him hard on the shoulder—"I thought you'd be dead by now!"

To her surprise Ar-Salar-Saloam did not cuff her back. Nor did he speak. He trudged on miserably up the street, looking at his shoes—in what she would call *one of his moods.*

"The reason I didn't visit you," Auriole said brightly, catching up, "is I been busy, real busy, it's been real hard on me out here, not knowing which way to turn."

Ar Salar Saloam stumbled on. The way his head hung, the way he slouched, his long arms dangling and his shoes flopping stiffly against

239

the sidewalk, he looked like a man with deep problems—a fact which even occurred to Auriole.

She hung back, biting her nails, wishing he'd git with it.

"Git with it, Dipstick!" she called.

But Ar-Salar-Saloam was already turning the corner.

She found him a few seconds later down on Douglas Street, leaning with his head against a store-front glass, his shoulders scrunched up around his ears and his hands shoved so straight and deep into his pockets that his pants were practically off his hips. She sidled up beside him, silent now, in a mood herself—and for a minute or two both stared at a window poster which had on it the picture of an airplane looking like some kind of bloated python snake, with its front part tied up in a fat knot. THANK GOD IT'S ONLY A MOTION PICTURE, the banner under it read.

Occasional Nudity, the B.C. Censor warned. *Too much swearing. Overall, a negative moral vision curiously copesetic...*

"I seen not one movie," Auriole declared in a lively voice. "I seen not one movie the whole time you were in jail. That's how busy I been!"

Whether responding to this claim or to something revolting in his own nature, Ar-Salar-Saloam's reaction was most curious. With a groan loud enough to startle several passers-by, his body went rigid, he balled up his fists and screwed up his eyes and swayed high up on his toes; Auriole thought he was going to smash his head right through the plate-glass window. She bent her knees, getting set to take off: *"Do it!"* she urged in a fierce whisper. *"Do it! We be to hell and gone before anyone even know what happened!"*

But Ar-Salar-Saloam did nothing of the sort. He straightened up, sighing, shaking off whatever rigours had possessed him, fixing his sad eyes first on Auriole then on the grey street behind her.

They moved on.

To cheer him up Auriole began telling him of all the groovy people she'd met while he'd been locked up. "Great guys!" she said. "Real neat!" A lot of them, she said, would be down at The King's Tattoo this very minute—"probably happy to buy you a suds or two if you've got a real thirst on like I have."

But Ar-Salar-Saloam was off in dreamland or black hole, not even listening to her.

They arrived at Government Street where the Empress Hotel and the Parliament Building hove suddenly into view, like an old and noble but enfeebled couple come together for one last look at the world before going off to gas themselves for what it and they had come to.

They passed on, Auriole chattering, Ar-Salar-Saloam in gloom, looking at her and the city with a mood of puzzled yet serenely elegiac scorn, moving in a stiff-legged gait, his shoulders bent—much as if he had spent the past six months sitting on his knees in a dark corner.

"Is it that old lady bugging you?" asked Auriole. "Is it you thinking it was your fault that old lady croaked?"

Ar-Salar-Saloam's head slid lower. "I never laid a hand on her," he grumbled, his eyes hooded.

Auriole was rapidly losing her own good edge. She wished he would shape up. She had her own troubles, heaps worse than his, and if this is what marriage was—walking around town to no purpose and with your tongue hanging out—she'd best call it quits right now. Without her hit earlier in the day to boost her along she'd have given him a good dressing-down the minute she saw him. She hadn't shed family and school—hadn't come to the ripe age of sixteen—to put up now with anyone messing round with her good times.

But she was afraid he'd hit her if she said any of this, so she decided to keep her trap shut.

At Johnson Street Ar-Salar-Saloam turned, and they went on down to the water: past the string of junk and pawn shops, past the flop-house rooms, past the littered alleys and dusty doorways where on more agreeable days winos would have been clutching at their sleeves—went on past even The King's Tattoo. Past Man Tung Yi's Foot Parlour, past the City Parkade and the Upper Room and Lum's Foam Factory. Went on past Sally Ann whose great blue three-storey building stood guard over this seedy part of Flower Town like a great blue angel not about to forget which side of the bread her butter came from. Went on down to the water.

"How's it feel to be back in civilization?" chirped Auriole.

Ar-Salar-Saloam gave no answer. Mouth open, his legs wide and bent, he was gawking at something way up in the sky.

The Johnson Street bridge was up, and under its black open tongues, just then passing through towards its anchorage in the Inner Harbour, slid a magnificent long white schooner—banners flying, slicing speedily through the black water, its three huge masts looming higher even than the grey city rim and cold mountain range beyond.

"It's *BEAUTIFUL!*" cried Ar-Salar-Saloam, suddenly beaming, dancing a little jig—"What I wouldn't give to have me one of them!"

"Be a good place to dope up," agreed Auriole, her manner solemn. With a short plump finger the colour of dry seaweed she was busy raking over a number of coins in her palm.

"Dollar forty," she announced—"Plenty enough for two drafts at the Tattoo. Let's go."

But Ar-Salar-Saloam stood with closed eyes, his head thrust back and rhythmically swaying, his expression momentarily blissful—as if from some place far removed from his present location music of divine and tranquil nature was somehow flowing through to him.

"My throat needs wetting," whined Auriole, tugging at an arm— "Are you coming or staying?"

Only after the bridge had cranked down and the line of waiting cars had bolted off to wherever it was their drivers were going—only after the beautiful ship had sailed on—did Auriole get him moving.

They had taken no more than a few dozen paces, however, when Ar-Salar-Saloam halted in his tracks. "What's that?" he demanded. "That up there. What is it?"

Auriole followed the line of his outstretched arm.

"That's the new disco," Auriole told him. She didn't tell him that she had been there the last seventeen nights and that it was the swinginist place inside of a thousand miles. What she told him was: "I hear it's real good."

"I don't care about no disco," replied Ar-Salar-Saloam sullenly. "What I mean is that sign in the window next to it."

"You mean the one with the red hand on a stick pointing around the corner?"

Ar-Salar-Saloam said yeah, that's the one he meant.

Stenciled along the length of the red hand were the words NO PROBLEMS TOO BIG. SEE US FOR SATISFACTION.

"That's Fisheye's new place," Auriole informed him. "He's gone into business. Doing real good, I hear."

"Fisheye!" muttered Ar-Salar-Saloam. "Imagine that!"

Further on up the street, painted on another dusty upper window, was another sign, this one reading IN A RUT? SEE THE PROBLEM SHOP— and in smaller letters, B. Fisheye, prop.

" 'Prop' means he owns it," Auriole explained.

"Oh God in heaven, you think I don't know that?"

"Your face was all screwed up, how could I tell? Stop picking on me."

Auriole pouted. She stared at Ar-Salar-Saloam, hating him, figuring she'd never in her whole life had such a hum-drum, no-account day as this one was turning out to be. He was proving just one big headache and she wished he'd never got out of jail. Then she could be down at The King's Tattoo, having herself a good time.

She wished she had herself a cigarette, or at least some chewing gum.

"I got me a real nicotine fit on," she now told Ar-Salar-Saloam. "You don't want to buy me a pack of Players, do you?"

"I done quit," Ar-Salar-Saloam said.

Auriole backed slowly away from him, filled with rage: her lips puckered, her eyes narrowed. She made up her mind: "I'm cutting out!" she cried. "You can do what you want from here on out! I'm fed up with you! I'm going where I'm appreciated, going to have me some fun!"

Thinking surely he would knock her teeth out, she spat and kicked at him, then sucked in her breath and broke away in a fast run.

A few seconds later she disappeared behind the nearby battered door of The King's Tattoo.

Oh little Auriole, thought Ar-Salar-Saloam, only an inch away from sinking down to weep in his solitude: *All you can think of is having your fun. Life don't mean no more to you than having your glass of beer and your weeds and a place to throw down your head. You are one of the world's lucky ones, and what I wouldn't give to be that way again...*

Poor me, thought Ar-Salar-Saloam. Even so, he wiped his eyes and took a deep breath and locked his shoulders—and trudged on. Onward into gloom. Pedestrians walking two and three abreast parted for him, alert for sudden moves, sensing something menacing and alien in his hooded stare, his scowls, his periodic groans.

Oh, Auriole, he thought, *why me?*

Onward, ever onward into misery, into the odious future. Into remorse and the black pit, into melancholy and hopeless sorrow—hopeless because the further along he ventured the more convinced he became that his was a route allowing no turnarounds. *Problems,* he thought, *so many problems, which way do I turn?* He had no idea what his problem was, only that it was a thing so indeterminate and insuppressible, so vast and impenetrable, that when he was able to glimpse it at all what he was put in mind of was a giant and spidery creature that crawled up out of his ears to drop its black hairy legs over his eyes and spin out its sticky black glue over his body head to foot.

Worse yet, all this, he knew, was exactly what he deserved. It was what Ar-Salar-Saloam had been coming to all these years.

Four people were in the waiting room at Fisheye's Problem Shop, five if you counted the dingy-attired man dozing under the iron hat tree in the far corner, six if you counted the proprietor himself. Not nearly as many as Ar-Salar-Saloam had expected. Not for a Fisheye operation. Not with all the troubles loose in this world.

Ar-Salar-Saloam took his place in line.

The real business, he figured, must be going on in a back room. A man with Fisheye's reputation for the fast buck wouldn't be wasting his time on no two-cents operation.

But there was Fisheye at his desk, with a yellow pencil stuck through his mouth and another lodged over his ear, looking as cheerful as you please.

I am the Antichrist, Ar-Salar-Saloam heard someone saying.

The establishment had been fitted out to look something like a church holding-station, with pew-like seats off to the left for the anxious to sit on. Near where the man was sleeping, bolted to the floor, was a stained plywood money-drop box with the words GIVE TO THE NEEDY stamped on its sides. Someone had spray-painted LOVE IS POWER on the side wall. A printed sign off to the right said HOPE I$ BETTER THAN MONEY IN THE BANK. The straw mat by the entrance door said TAKE A LOAD OFF YOUR FEET.

Fly-by-night but not *too* fly-by-night, Ar-Salar-Saloam reasoned.

I am the Antichrist, he heard again. He peered forward and saw that the person speaking was a dumpy, truck-looking woman at the head of the line. Fisheye seemed to be having some trouble with her.

Behind Fisheye, tacked to the wall with masking tape, was a large poster of Mt. St. Helens emitting steam. Next to it was a cardboard print of some yellow flowers in a jug, all sweepy-swirly like the painter had taken his broom to it. It was hanging wrong, and Ar-Salar-Saloam resisted an urge to go and make it right.

A half-dozen carpet remnants of various sizes and colours and weaves had been tossed about the floor.

A fine white mist drifted down from the ceiling.

This gave Ar-Salar-Saloam an eerie feeling, and for the first time he wondered if he had come to the wrong place.

The woman up front continued to rage. "I am the Antichrist!" she shouted.

"You are a pile of you-know-what," Ar-Salar-Saloam heard Fisheye tell her. "Stand aside!"

"That is no way to talk to the Antichrist!" stormed the woman, beating her purse on Fisheye's shaky desk. Papers fluttered to the floor; as Fisheye bent to retrieve them the woman moved over and stood on them. "I am the Antichrist!" she said again. "Do something!" Her face was bloated, the skin purple, as if she had just stepped into a vat of crushed grapes.

Fisheye, too, was losing his temper. "This is a problem shop," he yelled, "what's your problem?" With a rolled newspaper he swatted at the woman's legs until he got his papers back. "Stand aside!" he commanded. "Move on!"

Others in front of Ar-Salar-Saloam were raising their voices as well, saying "Yeah!" and "Git the lead out!" and "We got problems too!" The woman fumed. She banged her purse against the desk and said she was the Antichrist and had her rights the same as anybody else. The dust sifting down from the ceiling seemed to thicken: Ar-Salar-Saloam could see it on the shoulders of the person in front of him, and on the floor in the Antichrist woman's shoeprints as she strode up and down.

Ar-Salar-Saloam trembled; suddenly he felt fearful of his own sanity, wondering whether this strange snowfall was not altogether imagined. It seemed to him that, far from decreasing his troubles, The Problem Shop was only adding to them. A noise behind him made him turn: a small ragged boy, no more than eight or nine, stood poised in the doorway, sobbing wildly. *"Mama Mama Mama,"* wept the boy, *"When will you come home?"*

Ar-Salar-Saloam's own eyes dampened; sobs caught in his throat; the fine white mist went momentarily static, glistening; his knees weakened. He felt himself lifted out of The Problem Shop, transported back to his own stinging childhood: *he* was the boy in the doorway weeping for his lost mother.

Yes, and his mama—worse luck—never *had* come home. She had sent a wire from Reno, saying *Las Vegas next, I'm fed up with working finger to bone, try your Daddy or the church.*

This ragged boy was lucky, he had a mother to look after him. One who could teach him—if not love—then obedience and respect. The Antichrist woman had given up arguing with Fisheye to storm at the miserable boy, to cuff him and shake him, to beat her lessons into his head. *"Get out of here!"* she shrieked. *"I told you never to leave your room! I told you never to bother me while I was doing my work! Am I not the Antichrist?"*

"Yes, Mama," sobbed the throttled boy, "you are the Antichrist."

She ripped at his ear, smacked him hard on the fanny, and slung him back hard against the door. The boy crumpled down, groaning.

"You are, Mama," he whimpered, "I know you are."

"There!" she shouted, turning on Ar-Salar-Saloam and everyone else in the room—"There, you heard my boy! Now you know I am as I say I am!" Her mottled face glistened with perspiration, her glare was furious and would admit no denials. "Tell them again!" she shrieked, spreading her thick legs wide, sweeping both arms high above her head in a victory pose. Cords rippled in her throat; her full bosom heaved.

The boy dragged himself up, to clutch at her: *"Oh, Mama,"* he moaned. *"Oh Mama, come home! Oh Mama, let us take care of you!"* His hands wrapped about her ankles; he slobbered at her feet. *"You are, Mama. You are the Antichrist."*

The woman relented. Her fierce gaze swept over all in the room, she gave the boy another slap or two, but she relented all the same. She was content at last to let the shivering boy hug her knees.

"So long as you understand," she told the silent group. "So long as you know whose problems come first around here!"

The fine white mist leaking from the ceiling appeared to lift and thin; Fisheye's desk chair let out a nasty squeak; over in the far corner the sleeping man was waking up, rubbing knuckles into his swollen eyes and wiping an open hand across the black stubble of his chin.

The Antichrist woman allowed the boy to lead her reluctantly out. Everyone breathed again.

Half-an-hour later Ar-Salar-Saloam was no nearer to having his problems solved. He did not know what to think, and was ready—as he admitted to the now near-empty room—to throw in the towel.

"I'm on my last lap," he told Fisheye, as it came his turn to stand before the proprietor's desk.

Fisheye was scraping a knife blade under his nails, and did not even consent to look up at him.

A few seconds before, with all clients gone except for Ar-Salar-Saloam, the once-sleeping man had got up and bolted the entrance door.

"My goose is cooked," Ar-Salar-Saloam tried again.

Fisheye gave no indication that he heard. He closed his knife and rolled back in his chair and opened a desk drawer. From inside he pulled out a small sign and when he had placed it on the desk Ar-Salar-Saloam saw that it read GONE FOR COFFEE.

To Ar-Salar-Saloam this seemed too much. He wanted to break down and cry, but instead he squared his shoulders and tried again.

"What's that mean?" he asked.

Finally Fisheye looked at him. His expression registered no opinion one way or another—either of his own actions or of Ar-Salar-Saloam's timid insistance on service. He seemed, with his blue empty eyes, to be looking at something totally to the other side of Ar-Salar-Saloam. He seemed totally disinterested.

"Gone for coffee," he now said—pausing, standing up, reaching for his hat—"It's plain English, can't you read?"

The black pit opened up in Ar-Salar-Saloam's stomach and from there quickly spread. His eyes swirled. One minute he was staring at Fisheye's bland countenance and the next second a full wall of black was where Fisheye had been.

Ar-Salar-Saloam's knees buckled; he sagged down.

The black wall came with him and in another second or two it enlarged to cover everything.

"*You got problems, son,*" someone was saying.

It seemed to Ar-Salar-Saloam, grimacing as pain shot up through his head, that it was his own Daddy's voice speaking to him from the grave.

Oh no, Daddy, not me, not Ar-Salar-Saloam. Your little boy can take care of himself, he has not a care in the world.

This time it was his own voice saying this, yet he knew he had not spoken.

It occurred to him that at last his troubles were over, that he had passed over to the other side.

"Wake up, son," another voice said—"No deadbeats allowed, where you're going."

Ar-Salar-Saloam opened his eyes. The darkness swirled away and in its place there came a rippling tide, a white rippling mist . . . which then cleared and in the clearing, standing with his back to him as he squared-off the scrub-broom print of yellow flowers in a jug, was the once-sleeping man who had earlier bolted the door. Fisheye was gone. His papers had been put away, his desk top clear and shiny now except for one small notepad and two gnawed pencils neatly aligned side by side.

"A hired hand, son," the man explained. "Got to have their coffee breaks, their little privileges—union, you know."

Speechless, Ar-Salar-Saloam studied him. The man was older than he had previously appeared, and had a kindly look, although one faintly cavalier. An unlit fag drooped from his lips, and he stood with his hands in his coat pockets, in half-smile, but shaking his legs as if he had just wet himself.

"My own little problem," he sheepishly admitted. "All of us got to have something."

Ar-Salar-Saloam shook the cobwebs out of his head. The man was clearly a lunatic—maybe worse. Yet he swept aggressively forth, throwing out a hand which Ar-Salar-Saloam accepted in his own limp paw.

"That's right," the man smiled, "you're looking at the brains behind this outfit! You got problems, you come to the right place. Take a load off your feet. I can make no guarantees, but I think I can say that if your heart's in the right place you're as good as cured." He thumped his chest, chuckling, dropping down into the empty chair. "Old Fisheye," he said, "always got his sights on the clock. But I value him, don't get me wrong. He's good at weeding out the snowflakes. Knows his job."

Ar-Salar-Saloam cowered; his inclination was to hit and run.

"Speak up!" continued the man. "I find it pays to get right down to peanuts, no beating around the bush. I can't read minds, you know. What brings a bright-looking fellow like yourself to The Problem Shop?"

Ar-Salar-Saloam could not figure where to begin. It was as if all his problems had flown right out of his head.

"That Antichrist woman," said the man, "is she what's got your tongue? You thinking we can't deliver?" He cast his head down in a state of momentary melancholy, as if sensing that Ar-Salar-Saloam was accusing him of falling down on the job. "With some it takes time," he said, his voice low, caressing fur: "Not everybody can expect relief overnight, ours is not a Magic Shop, you know." He came up smiling, however, casting a mischievous glance over Ar-Salar-Saloam's intent head: "No, for that you have to look elsewhere."

Ar-Salar-Saloam mumbled "Oh yeah, I know what you mean,"— although totally at a loss to understand either what the man was saying or what he himself felt.

A deep pool, he thought, *that's what I've fell into. I've got to get myself out of here.*

"All the same," the man now said, rising, shaking his head at the mystery of it all "All the same, she's a case, that Antichrist woman. After a hard day like this one I'm half-willing to slit her throat." He fell silent, moping, mulling the issue over.

Too worried about the business, considered Ar-Salar-Saloam, *to give any little thought to me. Rue the day I come in here.*

"Still," the man said, reflecting, striding to a closet door behind the desk—"Still, she's got the boy. We've done that much at least for her."

Ar-Salar-Saloam wisely kept his silence. *Too much going on around here,* he thought. *Too much I don't understand. I'm out of my element in this zoo.*

"What's your name?" he managed. "Who are you?"

"Some folks call me Captain. The Captain, Cap, Old Salt—take your pick."

Ar-Salar-Saloam was watching the ceiling. The white powdery stuff was beginning to sift down again.

"My costume," the Captain said. "Clothes make the man." He had taken from the closet some kind of blue yachtsman's coat, and was pulling it on. It had a gold fringe on the sleeves and a big blue and gold crest on the pocket which said in rounded letters THE PROBLEM SHOP, and a logo that resembled a parking meter.

"How do I look?"

He looked pretty sharp. He looked what Auriole would call a *lulu,* with maybe a touch too many limp shoes thrown in.

But Ar-Salar-Saloam didn't tell him that. "You'll do," he said.

"You're like a lot of people, son," the Captain off-handedly observed: "Too stingy with the praise." He coughed, yanking out a soiled handkerchief, blowing his nose. "Let's get out of here. This damned white stuff is killing me. Sinus, you know."

The stairway leading down from The Problem Shop was drab and dingy, unlit except for one naked light bulb flecked with paint. The walls were peeling. The boards creaked. At the bottom a garbage can had been overturned and soup cans and gnawed bones and small balls of cooked rice littered the floor. The moment they hit daylight the Captain came to an abrupt halt.

"Well, my boy," he said, "which way will it be? Right or left?"

Ar-Salar-Saloam was buffaloed. He had hoped that if anyone knew the way this peculiar creature would.

"Or are you the kind that goes whichever way you're pointed? Is that your problem, son?"

Ar-Salar-Saloam dropped his shoulders and shuffled his feet, giving the Captain the full force of his hooded stare. The Captain's mind moved too fast; it took too many devious turns. Ar-Salar-Saloam was beginning to think he was some kind of Show Off, a Dink.

"Spell it out, son. Let me hear in your own words what's troubling you."

Ar-Salar-Saloam had one of his rare brainstorms. He suddenly knew what his problem was, and decided to blurt it out:

"I don't have no future," he said.

The Captain's mouth fell open in surprise, then mild amusement set in, and the next second he was throwing back his head and guffawing. "Why, no one does!" he exclaimed. "Where did you get the idea that anyone did? My my," he said, now strolling along, chuckling to himself, "—this day and age, imagine that!"

Ar-Salar-Saloam scrambled to catch up with him. It seemed to him beyond reason that anyone professing to run a problem shop would fail to understand. He felt angry and betrayed.

"*Nothing!*" insisted Ar-Salar-Saloam with raised voice: *"I don't have nothing! I might as well be dead!"*

The Captain gave a sympathetic shrug: "In quicksand up to your shoulder blades, is that the way it is, my boy?"

Ar-Salar-Saloam was adamant; he wanted to throttle this grinning man. *"I am without hope! Don't you understand? I don't have nothing and I am plain without hope!"* His fists knotted up as he glared at this man. *"Are you too stupid to understand that? Can't you see I'm in pain?"*

The Captain nodded, unimpressed: "It's a tough life then, you'd say? You find the space a bit tight in your jam jar?" He seemed actually to be enjoying Ar-Salar-Saloam's wretchedness, a gap showing between his teeth as he smiled and once again strolled on.

Ar-Salar-Saloam wanted to put another gap in that man's face. He was outraged by this shoddy treatment, yet at the same time accustomed to it. He groaned. His heart was squeezing up like a small hurt thing, like a tiny bird being slowly crushed, and for a moment black spots floated in front of him as his head swam. He stomped his feet down, summoning up strength for one final appeal: *"I mean it!"* he screeched. *"I'm desperate! I'd rather change places with that Antichrist woman, that's how bad off I am!"*

The Captain did not so much as slow down: "Beyond redemption, would you say?"

Ar-Salar-Saloam felt rooted to the spot. He could feel all his juices deserting him. He was all flagged out; could think of nothing, feel nothing, except for a black recognition of the abiding unfairness of this world. Through dim eyes he watched the Captain stroll jauntily on ahead in his bright blue jacket and his yachtsman's hat, not even glancing back. He thought: *Go on, it's good riddance I say. Prance off all high and mighty, thinking only of yourself. Rue the day I ever met you, go to hell you and your problem shop, I could care less what you do. Yeah, go on, just another big cheese: what do you care, forget Ar-Salar-Saloam, his life is over, when did anyone ever care one whit about me...*

Morbid, dropping down to sit on the curb, slouching over, head down between his legs, groaning to himself *That's it, that's it, I'm down in the gutter now, down here where I belong, where they've always wanted me, where I've been coming to all these years. My trouble was ever thinking I could drag myself up, ever thinking I had a chance. Well it's over now, it's over, I've shot my last wad. I can say it now, I can admit the worst: Ar-Salar-Saloam, you do not have a single redeeming human trait. You'd be better wiped off the face of this earth.*

It penetrated through to him after a time that someone was calling his name. Slowly his head came up, he wiped the wetness from his cheeks; slowly he came back to the life of the street, to the sight of cars whooshing by, of dusty junk windows and tatty curtains behind the glass of upstairs rooms, of smoke spilling up from chimneys and the odd pedestrian coming or going in a slow drift, coming or going as if to or from some far-off dream. Over at Sally Ann's blue building a stringy-haired girl and a fat boy no older than him had their suitcases out and their guitars and were playing some kind of low-down twangy song. Across the street directly in front of him an old man in a droopy coat that wiped the pavement was leaning on two rag-wrapped crutches silently watching him. Further along, outside Man Tung Yi's Foot Parlour, the Antichrist woman was up on a box rattling a tambourine and intoning *I am the Antichrist I am the Antichrist I am the Antichrist* while her boy stood by with pained face, tugging at her dress, saying *Mama come home, Mama come home, Oh Mama come home now.* The sky had turned an unwrinkled blue, shafts of sunlight slanting through drifting clouds like tall perfect skyscrapers belonging to some future day.

The Captain was down near the Johnson Street bridge, waving an arm.

"Come on, boy! Don't lolligag! Hurry up now!"

Ar-Salar-Saloam's black mood vanished; he spun off to catch up with him.

The Captain steered them down to the water. He wore a bemused, lazy expression, now lifting an arm to point out this, now to point out that, approving of one thing, disapproving of another, saying how the breakfast at Smitty's Pancake House was made of chopped-up rubber with a little ratmeat thrown in to sweeten the taste; how the new pedestrian walkway along the Inner Harbour was a step in the right direction, though the city had skimped on it a bit; how the Undersea Gardens was not a bad idea, far as it went, while the Wax Museum was a rip-off and, to his mind, frankly an aberration; how the double-decker busses were a joy to his eyes, while he didn't care a smidgen for the Tally Ho mule-wagon tour; how the black water here surely with a little foresight or old-fashioned ingenuity could have been cleaned up a bit; how, overall, looking at it without bias and with consideration for all the mean problems of this world, the old city hadn't done too badly with its growth; complaining, however, that the government was an abomination naturally—"What else can you expect?"—and how everything cost too much. Reminding Ar-Salar-Saloam how even in a relatively decent city such as this one a body still had to bitch and complain to get a thing done; how you had to watch out for yourself and not let the little stops in life up and knock you flat.

"Your troubles now," he said, "what do they amount to, you still got your youth, you got your health. Now hope, that's another matter, I admit it helps to have that. Certainly it is the A-Number-One problem I've come up against in my shop, it seems half the people I see have either got too much or not enough." He sighed, shaking his head, guiding Ar-Salar-Saloam on to wherever it was he had in mind going. "Making no bones about it, though, I'd say hopelessness is our speciality, I'd say we've built up a good record on that very issue." He smiled, throwing an arm over Ar-Salar-Saloam's bony shoulder, pushing the visored cap high on his head. "Live and learn," he murmured, "learn and live. So all right, you've got a self-image problem, nothing unique there. But tell me, if you've a mind to, what else has been troubling you. Spit it out, my boy, let the cat fur fly!"

Ar-Salar-Saloam, as if in a trance, gazed out over the Inner Harbour's black water. The big schooner which he had seen earlier in the day passing under the Johnson Street bridge, rocked not more than twenty paces from where he now stood, its three masts shooting up like endless telephone poles above the shining deck.

"There's Auriole," he softly said. "I worry about Auriole, I worried about her the whole time I was in jail. I worried about whether she was being faithful to me, but mostly I worried about her on general accounts."

"Oh, she'll get along," laughed the Captain. "No, a hot ticket like little Auriole, you don't have to be bothered about her. Make a good wife, a good worker, once she gets over loving her dope, over wanting her fun and good times." He paused, then added: "If not for you, then for someone else."

Ar-Salar-Saloam nodded, solemn. "There's that woman who dropped dead," he went on. "That weighs on my mind, what I did to her."

The Captain lightly patted his back. "I should hope so," he said. "A business like that could ruin any poor boy's life. Yet, look at it this way: the lady was old and sick, you couldn't have known. Even her doctor said she was at the edge, could go anytime. Her heart failed, as I recall. No, she was a nice old lady and we can grieve for her, but her illness I think mitigates your guilt." He hesitated, fixing a stern eye on Ar-Salar-Saloam. "Don't get me wrong. Her heart wouldn't have quit if you hadn't come along to snatch her purse. I'm not saying you got any cause to feel scot-free."

Ar-Salar-Saloam turned to the Captain with a sad smile. He wanted to say to this odd man that his life had been hell, that he and little Auriole and a thousand people like them—all that strungout gang down at The King's Tattoo, for instance—had never had a chance, that everything they had ever done and every which way they had ever turned had been wrong and not their choice at the start. But he remained silent, not certain that wasn't fudging the cake. He felt better now, did not have that sunk-down feeling any more. He felt—as maybe Auriole would put it— real strange. Real weird, like his head had zoomed off to some high place. Just walking with the Captain, having this little talk man-to-man, had done it, he guessed. It was like a father and son walk, like the old times he had dreamed about as a kid but never had known. It was wonderful, that's what it was—the Captain's warm hand on his shoulder, the day turned so scrubbed-down and fresh. So beautiful. He didn't even have that cramped feeling in the knees any longer; that iron feeling in the head.

It dawned on Ar-Salar-Saloam that in fact he felt pretty good. That he felt some hope stirring around inside.

There was activity now on the schooner. Someone in a white suit had come out and thrown a gangplank down. Others were scooting over the deck, unlashing the riggings, tying goods down, giving a last buff to gleaming brass rails.

"What's that?" Ar-Salar-Saloam asked, pointing at a small bucket way up high on the centre mast.

"That's the crow's-nest," replied the Captain—and as this did not appear to enlighten Ar-Salar-Saloam, he explained further: "In the old days, say on your arctic or whaling vessel, the lookout man would sit up there and watch for fish. Or pirates. Or land. Whatever needed watching for."

Ar-Salar-Saloam's face brightened. He looked up at the small bucket in amazement. "Now that's a job I could have gone for," he said. "I could have whet my teeth on a job like that."

"Maybe it isn't too late," the Captain answered.

"What you mean?"

The Captain pulled back a sleeve and tapped on a wrist watch: "In about two minutes," he said, "I'm setting sail. You can sign on if you've a mind to."

"*All ready, Captain!*" someone shouted from the ship.

Ar-Salar-Saloam's heart gave a sudden lurch. Striding down the boarding plank, his long black gown whipping up about his ankles, his face frozen into an expression of permanent intolerance and hatred, was none other than the judge who that morning had lectured to Ar-Salar-Saloam so severely.

"Is he a part of this crew!" asked Ar-Salar-Saloam, fearfully.

"Don't bet on it," said the Captain. "No, he's a passenger, I'm afraid. That old toad has got a lot of shaping up to do before I'd trust him with my sails. He has had a thousand chances and ruined everyone, while you . . . well you, my boy, you've had nothing, but at least you've wound up no worse than you were at the start. Shall we go aboard?"

Some minutes later the Johnson Street bridge went up for the second time that day, and the ancient schooner with its three tall masts passed through, rocking ever so slightly in the gentle water. From his crow's-nest on the highest mast, Ar-Salar-Saloam looked over his old haunts, over the full width and length of the city, and already he knew he was going to like this job. Until now it had never crossed his mind that the geography of this or any other place could be remarkable, that this city possessed any noteworthy beauty. Now the water shimmered, all but blinding him, but with his eyes slit so narrowly and his hands up to shade them, he acknowledged that in this respect, as in so many others, he had made a profound mistake. Life was indeed beautiful. Land and water were magic, a dancing pair. It was breathtaking, to tell the truth, and he sensed that from this day he would forever go on thinking so. The sea shimmered, snowcapped mountains all round touched the sky in blissful dignity, clouds hovered within easy reach; the very rooftops of the city seemed to throb and swell and extend to him a personal *bon voyage*. He could see up there on the street beyond The King's Tattoo the Antichrist woman marching at the head of a motley band of fifteen or twenty, and the cars waiting for the bridge to come back down strung back for a block or two and honking their horns—and down there on the corner by the lamppost the rapt face of the Antichrist woman's son waving wildly up at him, now leaving that off to jump up and down and flap out his arms even more wildly and to shout out some excited secret message at him. . .

The schooner sluiced at good speed through the water, sending out waves to lick at the shore, and even up so high Ar-Salar-Saloam could feel the good spray, the fine slap of untainted air. It was cool and wonderful, better than any possible dream. It was the future, that's what it was—the fearless future splashing him beautifully in the face. It was hope and love and sweet mercy; it was all of these things.

Then at once the schooner turned out of the black ribbon of water that had been its path, and the city fell away and vanished as neatly as if it had never existed, so that only the great sea awaited. Ar-Salar-Saloam at that moment cried out with joy, with an excitement so feverish he would have fallen from his nest had he not been strapped in: *"Fish!"* he screeched in rapture—*"FISH! FISH! FISH!"*

And he went on so screeching, piloted by his own ecstasy as he spotted fish or land or other boats—as he watched for whatever needed watching for—through the entire length of his voyage, which, for that matter, has not yet ended.

"Fish! ...

Land! ...

Heaven, my Captain! It is all here! ..."

Voices

Many, many years ago—whether twenty years or ten or *last night* it is all part and parcel of that fabled once-upon-a-time—I went to the public library in New Orleans, La. in search of *The Man Who Was There* by the American writer Wright Morris, an early novel I had been searching for without success over a long period. And there it was on the shelf. I pulled it out and the pages fell open to a scrap of lined school paper on which was scrawled, "she have to check up on her hygiene." The handwriting was close to illiterate, but it seemed to me there was something high-born and noble about the text, something that struck to the heart of the identity of that anonymous "she," while at the same time conveying something quite remarkable about the speaker. There was *appeal* here, stress and urgency. Moreover, the writer, so it seemed to me, was speaking with undeniable truth. *She,* whoever *she* was, would indeed be better off—lead a happier, more stable life—if only she would, and with some haste, check up on her hygiene.

I could easily enough imagine the situation: three school girls (for I had already added a third member to this party) located at one of the long library tables, preparing homework or class report, suppressing giggles, having been several times shooshed quiet by a grim librarian (keeper of Clock and Titles)—each of these three in a dither now because what they really want to do is get across the street to the drugstore before it closes, and there wreak havoc with assembled boys. And one of them, the brightest, scribbling this note to her mate about the third: We can't go yet, this albatross with us has to first check up on her hygiene assignment; *then* we can have a Coke and eat our chips and monkey with the guys. But having neither need nor inclination to spell all this out, theirs being a closed world, reduced in firmament in which all matters of importance and significance are understood through lifted eyebrow, hand-fluttering, through shrieks and moaned syllables, through giggles and signs, coded behaviour that has no more to do with language than the grunt and throat-jerk of prehistoric man or the zoo's enfeebled baboon in his cage. Language (its study), this trio would tell us, is useless paraphernalia, a heavy burden, something *else* the addled world would heap upon their feline shoulders. Subject *this* and predicate *that*, and God protect us from a thumping modifier.

Thus this note passed with surreptitious gravity to her friend: *she have to check up on her hygiene.* And here the magic. For with its writing her wit has momentarily become unshackled from the dead world of denial, from that one which preaches *language sucks, language stinks, language is The Curse.* She has scribbled it out of mind and sky, without fear of the teacher's brutal punishment (teacher as blunt instrument); liberated in that instant from the gruesome bondage of grammatical instruction, she has got it exactly right, has said precisely what she means. *"This stump beside us has not finished yet. Bear with us, Mercy, yet a while."* Has produced, that is, a sentence perfect in all its parts, every word working to her purpose, no frills, no beating around the bush—first and last time, in all probability, in her entire life that she has ever—will ever—use language with such exactness.

And it pleased me enormously that I'd discovered the note in *The Man Who Was There* (novel, I soon learned, of a man who *is,* and *isn't*) for it added that extra dollop (donation *from* charity, flower from the cupped hands of Mistress Good Fortune), reminding me again that libraries are public in more ways than one.

Another country heard from, I thought.

The Girls Who Were Here ... are here.

My cup runneth over.

It only remained for me to hijack the line and put a story to it, with narrative speech or voice, with style and content and form that retained some fidelity to the original. Say, in a story entitled "Winter Is Lovely, Isn't Summer Hell," in which the changing seasons exist as unreliable backdrop to the characters' ups and downs—their quick shifts of loyalty and passion against the weather's quick reversals; all as narrated by an anonymous figure struck up herself from that same neighbourhood, holding vested interest in those whose story she relates, but with an eye that wants at the same time to be objective; narrator who feels no necessity to condone or accuse, one who seeks through *tone* (language's solace) to find a satisfactory dignity in the embrangled diction—search through her world for what can be found that will usefully suggest its essential qualities. *Her,* yes, this peculiarly female (as the sea is female, as the wind is) voice that proclaims the story of Ruby Tucker and Thomas Jones is in effect the story of an entire neighbourhood (any neighbourhood is foreign country, a nation, a world) caught between impermanence and transition, between tradition and new ground, between poverty on the one hand, pleasure and purpose on the other. Utilizing dream (Ruby's dream) as solid rock ("I want and will have!") to alter experience, and all circling (thus the insistent employment of time in the story, time as a pepper pot's sprinkle) forward towards some dimly glimpsed destination, with *reckoning postponed* (there the rub). Leading towards that future hour when the children churned up within this neighbourhood

> ... So it is that each night now the boys can drop off to sleep snug and warm and no doubt wondering whose side of the story they going to hear tomorrow. Wondering what going to happen next. Feeling how the story of one is the story of them all and wondering why if this is so they remain so fearful of how their fortune going to fall.

will inherit what is theirs by unresolved law of blood and lair—pointing towards that time when they will find themselves living out their own variations on and extensions of ... *the story.*

Maze, as in the Sunday comics, it being each new generation's labour to trace down the undiscovered exits.

This being not so much what the story is about as what it comes to.

So the teller's voice is the face over the back fence: voice addressing (not us the reader so much as) another woman (sea and wind are female, is the audience, too?) standing shoeless at her own back door, there waiting the story out, but a little irritated (in all probability) that she can't get in her two-cents, tell the story herself, for she surely has her own version of the story and her own preference for the way it should be told, wanting at every instant to highlight or drive home this or that difference, thinking always, "That's not the way I heard it, no, you've got it all wrong, what really happened is this!" The narrative voice moulded, then, (First Person in Third Person Disguise) to be fabric and part of what is being revealed, one intentionally crafted out of the region's soft clay to affirm that message the distant author holds most vital: voice that says, "This is *their* story (Ruby and Thomas), but it is *mine* as well, and that of friends I have here, and *your* story too if you live (or ever find yourself living) in this neighbourhood." And saying furthermore that "your neighbourhood, whatever you may *think* it is, may not be so different from ours, since this I *know to be true: We are not so different from you. Don't let my idiom mislead. We are not the odd—and stupid— people you may take us to be."

A sentimental view?

Well, no. All a matter of good clean hygiene, mental this time.

The people in "The Problem Shop" are not blood relatives of those in "Winter Is Lovely, Isn't Summer Hell," although a kind of "kissing cousins" odour clings to many of them ... the black sheep misfits who live across town and keep, mercifully, to their own neighbourhood: that area where the winos hang out and one sees signs in windows saying ROOMS and those above dingy cafés saying EATS, together with graffiti on the walls informing us that GOD IS ON THE OPERATING TABLE WILL HE LIVE OR DIE? The part of town the street cleaners, and anyone else with any choice, ignores. Last stomping ground for Ar-Salar-Saloam and his child-bride Auriole, driven there by the twin evils of necessity and circumstance and, yes, because nowhere else do they feel so much at home. Pigeon instinct at work, the instinct that survives after all others have been killed off (how otherwise could the winos, brains rattling around in their heads, soul remnants bartered hourly for a quarter, sniff out these places in city after city, nation after nation, the whole world over?).

So here Ar-Salar-Saloam is, confirmed degenerate "with no redeeming human traits," emerging there today with a very special problem. The problem being that he now recognizes the truth if not the justice of every word the judge has told him ("I'd hang you by the neck myself, given the chance") and has in fact spent the past six months sitting on his hands in a dark corner, thinking of nothing else: "Yes, I'm a bum and no good. I am a menace to society. I am without hope." Not recognizing for the moment that such perception is his salvation or that, having achieved this vision of inner disgust, the Problem Shop's relief is just around the corner. Thus, at story's end, Ar-Salar-Saloam's spirit is reborn (reconnection with that one present all along, to put it another way): he sails off into the sunset screeching *"Fish! Fish!"* (now himself a fisher of men), in the crow's-nest watching, as the Captain has told him, "for whatever needed watching for"—as the ship steers forward into a better world, leaving all grimy sins behind.

Appropriate, deserved reward, one that wants (for Ar-Salar-Saloam, for all of us) weeping applause.

The author having planted one small wrench—cruel irony—into these ordered events: is Ar-Salar-Saloam alive or dead? Has this scheme of things been hatched out of that twilight state (of grace) preceding death (the white sift of dust, his knees "buckling," Ar-Salar-Saloam "sagging down")? Has his self-recognition, repentance, come too late? The ship has gone, some might say, but was it ever truly there? The writer's tease, tid-bit for those readers for whom *texture* is the place where the heels dig in. The author might argue that he has wanted, and has shaped the story, to take the reader both ways: dramatic, uplifting conclusion for those who require reaffirmation of life's essential qualities—essential possibilities, hope, affection's penny's worth—while providing for others sobering suspicion that life—*the story!*—may not be quite what it seems.

Can the writer work such a double street? Can he have it both ways? Why not?

Yield, the song goes, to the sun's power.

About the Photographer

SAM TATA was born in Shanghai in 1911. He lived and photographed in that city—documenting the end of the Kuomintang regime and the coming of the Communists in an acclaimed series of images. After several years in Hong Kong, he moved to Montreal in 1956 where he continued his work in photo reportage and began the extended series of portraits of artists and writers for which he is best known.